HEARTBEATS & HIGHWAYS

Tarnished Angels Motorcycle Club Book 8

EMMA SLATE

©2025 by Tabula Rasa Publishing LLC

All rights reserved.

No part of this publication may be reproduced, distributed or transmitted in any form or by any means, including photocopying, recording, or other electronic or mechanical methods, without the prior written permission of the publisher, except in the case of brief quotations embodied in critical reviews and certain other noncommercial uses permitted by copyright law.

This book is a work of fiction. Names, characters, places, and incidents are the product of the author's imagination or are used fictitiously. Any resemblance to actual events, locales, or persons, living or dead, is coincidental.

Heartbeats & Highways
(TARNISHED ANGELS MOTORCYCLE CLUB BOOK 8)

I've tried so hard to stay invisible, but somehow I've captured his attention.

The tall, blond biker named Savage destroys his opponent in an illegal fighting ring, and now he's claiming *me* as his prize . . .

But there's darkness in my past, and I can't allow myself to get close to anyone.

So, I run—never expecting to see him again.

But fate has other plans.

Somehow, he battles through my walls and steals my heart.

His touch is possessive; his love ruthless and beautiful.

In the throes of passion, I fall.

But what happens when he finds out the truth?

What happens when he finds out I'm pregnant with another man's baby?

Chapter 1

"Another dark beer for me, sugar tits."

My smile tightened at the drunken lout whose eyes were glazed with booze and excitement.

"Sure thing," I gritted out.

He dropped a few sweaty dollar bills onto my tray, his gaze skating down my body. "Appreciate it, honey."

Yeah, I bet you do.

With a deep breath, I stuffed the bills into the satchel around my waist and wove my way through the crowd. Sweat and blood lingered in the air of the illegal fighting arena. Two men were currently hosing down the ring to get it ready for the last fight of the night.

Someone's hand grazed my behind. It took everything inside me not to turn and use the tray as a weapon. But assaulting a customer—a paying customer—wouldn't help my bottom line. And at the moment, that was all I cared about.

I made it to the bar in the corner. Daisy and Roxy were slinging drinks as fast as people ordered them. One of the red, glittery swatches that barely concealed Daisy's fake breasts slipped to the side, revealing a nipple.

The crowd hooted in appreciation. She looked down and grinned, fluttered her long lashes and quickly readjusted her top. "Oops."

I knew if I wore something more revealing, I'd make better money. Working in a place like this—I could barely contain the vomit that threatened to surge up my throat. But cash was king. And under the table cash was emperor.

"God, I'd *kill* for your red hair," Roxy said in way of greeting. "Please tell me those are extensions. Then I won't feel so bad."

My mouth curved. "Sorry. My hair is real."

"Damn it," Roxy muttered. "You never see waist-length natural red hair in the wild. It's gorgeous."

"Seriously," Daisy added. "You've got the Jessica Rabbit thing going on. Men are obsessed with red heads."

"Jessica Rabbit?" I asked in confusion.

"Yeah, you know, Roger Rabbit's wife?" Roxy clarified. "Ring any bells?"

"Oh, right." I shook my head.

Daisy sighed. "What can I get for you, hun?"

"Three light and three dark," I said.

"You just had a full tray five minutes ago," Roxy said. "Your beers are gone already? Impressive."

"I'm telling you, it's the red hair." Daisy grabbed a stack of plastic cups and began pouring pints.

"Twenty bucks says he nods at her," Roxy said to Daisy.

"You're on," Daisy replied.

I frowned. "What are you two talking about?"

"Savage is fighting tonight," Roxy explained. "He hasn't been in the ring in a while. But he's undefeated; a maniac."

"A sexy-as-hell blond maniac," Daisy added. "And after he wins a fight, he singles out a girl in the crowd and gives her a nod."

"He never nods at the same woman twice," Roxy went on.

"What does the nod mean?" I asked.

"It means, you're his for the night," Daisy explained.

I raised my brows at Daisy. "You're not serious."

"She's serious," Roxy said. "He's never nodded at either of us though."

Daisy crossed her fingers. "Here's hoping . . ."

"Women turn him down, though, right?" I asked.

"Never." Roxy shook her head. "You'll understand why when you see him fight."

I didn't reply. How could I? I was the new girl and I'd only been working the last two weeks. There was a fight every few nights. The job paid well and it gave me my days free. But it made my skin crawl every time I got into my uniform—a pair of tight jeans and a black pleather vest I'd found at a secondhand store. It wasn't stripping, but it felt close enough.

I told myself I'd quit. When I had enough cash to move on. But I wasn't sure that was true. When I held a wad of bills in my hand, a surge of power washed over me. The money was *mine*. I'd earned it. And so long as I had money, no one could control me.

I put the pints of beer on my tray and walked through the crowd. One by one, the beers disappeared, and tips went into my satchel.

Drinks were free. The cover at the door more than made up for the loss. The customers—mostly men—were loose with their money when they were happy and drunk.

I made it to the customer who'd asked me for a dark beer. He swept the cup off my tray. Before I could leave, he reached out and grasped my wrist. His fingers were clammy, and it took everything in me not to shake him off, but I didn't want to alert security. I didn't want to draw attention to myself.

"Stay with me," he commanded.

"Sorry." I flashed him an insincere smile. "I have to work the floor."

"Go home with me tonight."

I swallowed down my fright.

The crowd suddenly began to cheer.

Two men entered the ring. One was huge with dark hair and bulging muscles. He looked like he could break someone's arm in half like a turkey wishbone.

The other was blond, rippling with muscles, ink, and scars.

Danger and confidence poured off him, causing me to shiver.

It didn't matter if he was a few inches shorter than his opponent. If I was a betting woman, I would've put all my money on him.

"Fight's about to start," I said to the man currently holding my wrist. "You don't want to miss it."

I pulled my arm from his grasp, fear still coasting down my spine, and disappeared into the crowd.

Oscar's voice came over the microphone. "We have a special treat for you folks tonight! Get ready to witness the absolute devastation from Toro Masivo, the seven-time undefeated bare-knuckle boxing champion from Tepito in Mexico City! He's traveled here tonight to crush his opponent like a worm!" The crowd went wild, and Oscar continued. "But who is his opponent? Who will stand up to the might of the massive bull? Who has the courage to fight such a man? Tonight, a crowd favorite, the undefeated bare-knuckle champion of Waco known simply as

Savage! What more do you need to know? He's never lost, and with a name like that you'd better get ready—this fight is going to be insane!"

The throng roared with unbridled excitement. Adrenaline was in the air and people began stomping and cheering at the top of their lungs. A beer went flying across the room accompanied by a hoot from a screaming group of red-faced men.

Daisy and Roxy had warned me not to be in the middle of the crowd during a fight. Bloodlust would leak from the ring onto the floor, coating drunken men in exhilaration and determination.

I made it to the far wall and ducked behind the makeshift wooden barrier. I climbed up onto a keg so I could see the ring.

"Tonight, our fighters will have their hands taped to make sure you get to see one of them beaten to a pulp!" Oscar stated. "The only three rules in this fight are as follows; one, there will be no eye gouging. Two, there will be no blows to the top or the back of the head, or the back of the neck. And three, there will be no winner until one fighter is utterly defeated! This fight is one round only, with no time limit—just pure blood sport. The round will begin at the sound of the bell and ends when one fighter is unable to defend himself any longer. May God be with you both."

Anxiety spiked along my spine.

The bell rang.

The two fighters came together, their taped hands curled into fists, ready to trade blows. Savage's fist connected with Toro's jaw. Shock spread across the bigger man's face and then anger quickly replaced his daze. He lunged at Savage, but Savage moved out of the way and countered with a jab.

That only enraged Toro further; he punched Savage in the nose so hard blood spattered in a fine red mist onto the floor. But Savage didn't seem bothered, and only wiped his nose with his hand, staining the white tape around his knuckles blood red. He grinned like a lunatic before pouncing.

As the men beat on one other, the crowd boiled over with excitement at each successive blow. With each spray of blood, with each smack of skin, the throng roared. Toro and Savage fought the way only grown men could—they were strong enough to kill.

Toro began to slow, his movements sluggish as he tried to catch his breath. It was the invitation Savage needed. He kicked Toro's legs out from under him. After Toro fell to the ground, Savage jumped on top of him and began to pound his face like a blacksmith working a piece of iron with a hammer. After a minute Toro stopped moving, and when Savage stood over his massive, sweaty form, the huge man didn't get up.

Oscar ran into the ring and then lifted Savage's arm and declared him the winner.

The crowd roared its approval.

I shivered at the energy and adrenaline in the warehouse.

Savage's head swiveled with magnetic force; his eyes locked on mine.

My gaze widened and I gasped.

Danger poured off him. Danger and . . . something else.

Ever so slightly, he inclined his head at me.

Desire swirled in my belly.

His claim was obvious, but I had no intention of being summoned or commanded.

I'm not a whore.

I scrambled off the keg and shoved my way to the bar.

There was a lull—patrons that had placed bets on Savage were busy seeking out their winnings, and those who'd lost were pouring out of the establishment as fast as they could.

Daisy and Roxy were standing next to one another having a conversation I couldn't hear over the rumble of the crowd.

Roxy saw me first. "Hey gal. Amazing fight, wasn't it?"

"Yeah, it was something else," I said, my voice breathless as though I'd run a great distance.

"Did you see who he nodded at?" Daisy asked, looking around as if she could find the bearer of Savage's attention.

"Me," I exclaimed.

Both of them looked in my direction. Roxy let out a laugh and Daisy grinned. "Well, what are you waiting for?" Roxy demanded. "Go to him. Immediately!"

I shook my head. "No. I can't. I don't want—I need to get out of here."

Daisy studied me, all traces of humor leaving her face. "All right. Leave out the back. We'll cover for you."

"Thanks," I murmured.

I escaped out the back door, refusing to look behind me; refusing to look and see if Savage was watching me flee.

Chapter 2

I LEFT the warehouse and grabbed a cab instead of waiting for the bus in the chilly air. In my haste to get away from the fight and bloodlust, I left my jacket behind.

I closed the door to the cheap motel room I'd been living in for the past several weeks. The noisy heater under the window blasted hot air and I shivered despite the warmth.

I'd hit up a diner close to the motel and ordered a burger and fries, along with a small soda to go. I set both containers on the nightstand and then went to the heater and turned down the knob.

It was a mild winter so far, which was a relief. But the air in Texas was humid, adding a layer of dampness to everything.

I debated taking a shower before eating, but the food was still hot and cold fries wouldn't taste nearly as good. I sat down on the edge of the double bed and opened the to-go container.

Sounds of the highway filtered through the single-paned windows. Nothing out of the ordinary—just big semis and every now and again a truck without a muffler.

I polished off the burger in record time and then leisurely ate the shoestring fries.

Roxy and Daisy hadn't said it, but their disbelief that I hadn't gone with Savage had been written on their faces.

At least they weren't jealous. If anything, they'd been ecstatic for me.

The thought of Savage made fear swirl in my belly and climb up my throat. The violence he'd unleashed against Toro should've been the reason I was afraid of him. But it wasn't.

His gaze had been steady; and even across a warehouse room, I saw the intensity behind his eyes.

I understood now why violence and lust went hand in hand. I should've been appalled. His fists inflicting injury. His muscles coiling in offense.

But something had surged through my veins when I watched him move. A brutal dance that ended with his victory.

And he wanted *me* as his war prize.

I shivered and closed my eyes, reveling in the memory.

With a sigh of frustration, I wrenched my eyes open. Ignoring the rest of my food, I kicked off my worn tennis shoes and stripped out of my clothes, wanting to rid myself of the night.

I double-checked that I'd locked and chained the door and ensured the curtains were shut so no sunlight would wake me in the morning.

It was just past one a.m., and my steps were heavy as I trudged into the tiny bathroom.

As far as highway motels went, this one was decent. It might've been outdated and faded, but it was clean, and the water pressure was strong and it got scalding hot.

I stood under the spray and washed the night from my hair and body.

My mind kept wandering back to Savage. I hated that I wondered how his lips would feel against mine.

Possessive and sinful.

Before I knew what I was doing, my hand slid down my belly and then between my thighs. I touched myself and then immediately felt embarrassed. But I couldn't stop. I closed my eyes and pretended it was Savage.

His big, rough fingers spread me and slid inside.

I bit my lip to strangle my cry as he pumped them in and out of me, his thumb gently pressing against my clit.

My own fingers worked faster and faster until I had no choice but to come. I threw my head back as the water beat down on me.

When my orgasm faded and my body no longer trembled, I removed my fingers. I let the water wash away my release, but it didn't wash away my shame.

I shut off the water and wrapped a scratchy, faded white towel around myself and then did the same for my hair.

Satiated, my mind started working and I began to process my situation. There was nothing to do, I rationalized. Savage had fought; he would not be in any shape to fight again soon, so there was no chance of running into him again.

Hopefully he was already fixated on someone else. Perhaps Roxy or Daisy, who were both eager and willing.

Envy poured through me at the idea he was with one, or both of them right now.

I had no right to feel the way I did.

He owed me nothing.

"Four carne asada tacos, a side of queso, and an orange soda, please," I said, looking into my bag for my wallet.

"That sounds good. I'll have the same."

I looked behind me at the man who'd mirrored my order. My eyes widened in shock.

Savage stood behind me, wearing a pair of dark jeans, a long sleeved white thermal shirt and a leather cut. His blond hair was mussed, his nose was bruised, and one of his eyes was swollen shut.

He flashed me a smile and winced immediately when his split lip tore open. I was still standing there, frozen in terror like a fawn, when Savage handed over a couple of twenties to the guy in the taco truck.

"Excuse me, some of us would like to order," a middle-aged man said from behind Savage.

Savage looked at the man. "Manners, dude. What's the magic word?"

The stranger blinked, clearly not used to having another adult calling him out. "Uh, please."

"Happy to move, brother," Savage said. He gently grasped my elbow and moved us out of the way of foot traffic.

"What are you doing here?" I demanded, shaking off his touch—and hating that I could feel the imprint of his fingers through my jacket.

"Best tacos in the city," he said with a shrug. "And I like to celebrate my wins with tacos. Seems kind of like fate that we're meeting again like this."

"We've never met," I protested.

"No, you're right. I was hoping to meet you last night, but you left."

I took a deep breath. "I left. Yep." I huddled down in the jacket I'd borrowed from Agnes—the woman who owned the motel I was staying at. She was the one who'd told me about the taco truck.

"Why?" he asked in curiosity.

"Why? Seriously?" I raised my brows and stared at him. "You're surprised that I left last night instead of . . ."

"Going home with me. Yeah. I'm surprised." He rubbed the back of his neck. "I would've thought Daisy or Roxy had told you what the nod meant."

"They did." I crossed my arms over my chest. "Which is *exactly* why I bailed."

"Ah."

"Who did you take home in my stead?" I asked.

"I'd grin at your jealousy, but I don't want to split my lip again," he drawled.

"I'm not jealous. I don't even know you. Why would I be jealous?"

"What's that saying? Thou doth protest too much?"

"You don't even know my name," I pointed out.

"But you know mine, don't you, darlin'?"

The guy at the window of the taco truck waved at Savage. "Tacos are ready!" he called.

Savage went to the window. The guy handed him a tray with our meals and Savage brought it back toward me.

"Pick a table," he said.

The taco truck was in the middle of a parking lot and there were several picnic tables that were currently empty. I gestured to the one farthest away from the truck and sat.

Savage set the tray down in the middle of the table and hoisted his body onto the seat. He handed me a couple of napkins and I noticed his swollen knuckles.

"You still haven't told me your name," he said easily.

I paused. "Evie."

"Evie." He rolled my name over on his tongue.

I liked how he said it; rough and guttural.

"You didn't have to pay for my lunch." I reached into my bag once again for my wallet but stopped when he shook his head.

"Not a big deal," he said.

I unzipped my jacket, and his gaze immediately dropped to my chest. This time, he couldn't stop the smile—and then the laugh.

"What?" I demanded. "What's so funny?"

"Where did you get that shirt?"

"A thrift store, why?"

I liked the vintage picture of a motorcycle the moment I saw it, which was why I'd bought it.

"Charlie's Motorcycle Repair," Savage said as he read the text across my breasts. "My club owns Charlie's."

"Oh?"

"Yeah. So, after running into you this morning at my favorite taco truck and now seeing that you're wearing something that's part of my club, it *definitely* feels like fate."

"Fate." I snorted. "It's called a coincidence."

"Maybe. But fate is in control of those too." He gestured with his chin to the tacos in front of me. "Try it."

I lifted one of the hard-shell tacos to my lips and took a bite. I closed my eyes and savored the flavors.

After I swallowed, I opened my eyes to find Savage watching me.

"Good?" he asked gruffly.

"The best," I admitted.

He grinned.

We both chowed down, and it wasn't until I was in the middle of my second taco that I asked, "So you're in a motorcycle club?"

"Yep. The Tarnished Angels." He gestured to the motorcycle in a parking spot. "That's my ride."

"I know nothing about motorcycles, so I'll just say it's shiny and pretty."

He laughed. "You ever been on one?"

"No."

"We'll have to change that."

I raised my brows. "You're very assumptive."

"Come on, tell me you're not curious. A woman like you?"

"What does that mean?"

"You work in an illegal fighting ring, so that must mean you like excitement. Once I get you on the back of my bike with your arms wrapped around me, it'll be the ride of your life."

Something told me he wasn't just talking about his motorcycle.

"I work at the ring because the money is good," I said. "Why do you fight?"

"Same reason." He shrugged. "It pays well, and I like it."

"Probably doesn't hurt that all you have to do is nod and women come running to you like little sex pots," I added.

"Not all women, clearly. You kind of bruised my ego."

"I think you'll get over it."

"Nope. I won't. I'll never have the confidence to ask out another woman as long as I live."

"So dramatic," I teased, smiling despite my better judgement. "Just tell me the truth. Did you find a runner up to take home last night?"

"Nope."

"Realllly . . ."

"You don't believe me?"

"I felt the energy in the warehouse. There's no way you went home alone just because I didn't bow at your feet."

"Bow at my feet," he murmured. "I kind of like that visual."

I arched a brow. "Never gonna happen."

"Never say never."

"I'm not looking for trouble."

"What are you looking for?" he asked, pivoting the conversation. "A nice guy? White picket fence and a couple of kids?"

"Not looking for that either," I proclaimed.

I wasn't sure why I was indulging him. Savage was a stranger. And yet . . . it was easy to talk to him. He'd disarmed me—quickly. It had only been a few minutes, and I was already starting to converse with him like I'd known him for years.

And now I was on guard because getting close to anyone would be a terrible idea.

I polished off my final taco. Savage gathered our trash and dumped it into a garbage bin next to the taco truck and returned the tray.

"Ready?" he asked.

I frowned. "Ready for what?"

He gestured to his bike. "The ride of your life."

"Thanks for the offer, but I've got to get home."

"Can I see you again?" Savage asked.

"No."

He placed his hand on his chest like he'd been stabbed. "You wound me."

"Something tells me you'll recover."

He peered at me for a moment, his blue eyes suddenly brighter in the winter sun. "No. I don't think I will."

Chapter 3

"I bought some new laundry detergent," Agnes said. "And some dryer sheets."

The middle-aged woman who owned the motel handed me the key to the laundry room.

"Thanks."

When I'd shown up at the motel in the middle of the night scared and alone, Agnes hadn't asked questions, and more importantly she hadn't demanded to see my ID. She'd just looked me over, paused for a moment to take me in, and then given me a key to a room.

She was the closest thing I had to a friend.

"Are you sleeping okay?" she asked as her prematurely wrinkled brow furrowed. "You look tired."

"I *am* tired."

I hadn't been sleeping well. Every sound jarred me awake. And in those hazy moments where I was neither asleep nor awake, my mind drifted to Savage.

It had been three days since the taco truck incident, and I'd spent more time than I wanted thinking about him.

"How's the fighting ring working out for you?" she asked.

"It's working out well," I admitted. "Thanks for vouching for me."

Agnes had been my contact for getting me a job at the fighting ring. Because fighters stayed at her motel, she had a direct line of communication to the owner.

"I think I need something else, part time and during the day," I stated. "There are only a few fights a week. I have way too much time on my hands not to have a second job."

Way too much time on my hands to think.

"You'll have to commute into the city," she said. "I'd hire you here, but I'm not busy enough to warrant another employee."

"I get it." I lifted the laundry basket off the floor. "You've done more than enough for me already and I appreciate it."

"I'll keep my ears to the ground and let you know if I hear about any jobs you might want."

"Thanks."

Agnes surveyed me. "I didn't say anything . . . but I saw you that night. You came home from the fight a lot earlier than I expected."

"Oh, yeah, they let me go early."

Her brow furrowed. "You sure that's all there is to the story?"

I chewed on my lip. I was dying to talk to someone about Savage. "One of the fighters, the one who won . . . he wanted me to go home with him."

"I see," Agnes murmured.

"So I skipped out of there as fast as I could before the night was over, only . . ."

"Go on."

"I ran into him a few days ago at the taco truck you suggested."

"That seems . . . I don't know what that seems. Was he mad that you ditched him?"

I shook my head. "No. He wanted to take me out. I said no."

"Smart. You don't want to get involved with someone who fights in an illegal fighting ring."

"Or who's in a motorcycle club," I blurted out.

Her eyes widened. "Definitely not. Steer clear of bikers like the plague."

"I plan to."

The crowd was unusually rowdy. The first fight of the night started late, giving people more time to drink. Beer and annoyance flowed in equal measure.

I'd already made three trips back to the bar with an empty tray. Unfortunately, I had to wait because Roxy and Daisy were four people deep.

Frustration poured through me.

I'd been part time job hunting all day before I'd even shown up. Baristas and boutique associates were paid next to nothing and then managers had the audacity to sneer at me when I told them I didn't have any experience. Not to mention, they wanted to see my ID. Working under the table afforded me anonymity. No one asked questions.

"Sorry, sugar," Daisy said, glancing at me out of the corner of her eye. "Let me pour you some pints."

"Thanks," I said, forcing a smile.

She quickly filled the plastic cups and set them on my tray. I swept away from the bar and dove into the swarm of people.

Sweaty bodies brushed against me; there was no hope of dodging them. My tray of beers went quickly. I had one drink left when someone bumped into me, careening me into a tall, meaty man. The last pint of beer on the tray tipped over awkwardly, dousing both of us in ice cold liquid.

"What the fuck!" He spun toward me, his cheeks flushed with anger and booze. "You stupid bitch!"

"I'm sorry," I babbled. "It's tight in here and someone—"

"I don't fucking care!" He reached out and grabbed my wrist, squeezing it in his strong grip.

A cry of pain spilled from my lips.

"I know how you can make it up to me." He tugged me closer. "Fuck the fight. I'd rather party with you. Let's get out of here."

Bile swirled in my stomach, and I was in danger of throwing up. I covered my mouth just as I saw a fist collide with the man's jaw.

He instantly released me and put up his hands to defend himself.

I tried to step back to get away from the violence, but there was nowhere to turn. A throng of on-lookers were watching the makeshift fight while they waited for the real one to commence.

"You don't treat women like they're whores, and you *never* fucking touch them!"

I froze in my spot; I recognized that voice.

Savage punched the man again, knocking several teeth out this time, but that didn't stop Savage. In fact, it seemed to invigorate him. He pummeled the man until he fell to the ground, and when he put his hands in front of his face to block Savage's blows, Savage just punched right through his hands, battering him until he went limp.

The scent of blood filled the air, which only made my nausea worse.

Savage put a heavy leather boot to the man's throat and pressed.

"Savage!" I yelled.

It seemed to take all of Savage's force to turn and look at me, but he finally did. His blue eyes were bright, almost maniacal.

"Savage," I said again, this time a little softer.

The man on the ground gurgled as Savage refused to move his boot. I was sure Savage was about to crush his windpipe, but suddenly he lifted his foot.

"Get the fuck out of here, and don't ever come back. If I see you again, you'll be begging for treatment like this. This wasn't even a goddamned warm-up for me."

The man's friends helped him off the ground.

"What the fuck is going on?" Stu, the floor manager for the evening, elbowed his way through the crowd until he was at the center of the commotion.

"The bitch spilled beer on him and then that guy beat his ass," the meaty man's friend said, flinging his hand in the direction of Savage. "We were just trying to have a good time. What the fuck?"

Stu looked at Savage and then at me. "You're fired, Evie."

"It wasn't my fault!" I cried.

"We save the drama for the ring," Stu said. He looked at Savage. "If you didn't bring such a crowd with you, I'd make sure you never came back either. Evie, get out."

"Come on," Savage said, reaching his hand out for me.

"Leave me alone," I snapped, whirling and darting through the crowd. It was thick and soupy, and Savage's impromptu fight agitated the already excited throng. They were hungry for more blood.

"Evie, wait!" Savage called out.

I got to the back exit and flung the door open, stepping into the dark night.

His heavy boots clomped behind me. "Let me take you home."

I turned to face him. "You got me fired! You're not even supposed to be here tonight!"

"I came to watch the fights." His expression darkened. "I saw him grab you. I saw the fear in your eyes. What the fuck was I supposed to do? Not protect you?"

"I'm not yours to protect! And I was handling it."

"Handling it?" He took a step closer to me, his hands clenched into fists at his sides.

I instinctively stepped back.

My movement penetrated his anger, and he immediately halted. His fists slowly uncurled. "You weren't *handling* it. That guy was manhandling you. Not to mention he's over a hundred pounds heavier than you. He was drunk, and he didn't look like the type to take no for an answer."

Everything he said was true—but still. He'd cost me my job. A cash job that paid well.

"Where else am I going to get a job that pays under the table?" I asked brokenly.

"I can get you another job," he said, taking a tentative step toward me again. "At one of the bars my club owns. You'd be under our protection. No one would think to touch you, or they'd answer to me."

When I didn't move, he took a step toward me, and then another, until he was close enough to put his hands on my shoulders.

"I can't work at a bar," I stated. "I'm only twenty years old, Savage. Don't you get it? This was—this was my chance!"

His expression was steady at the mention of my age.

"Your chance for what?" he asked finally.

"My chance to make some cash so I could leave town."

"Where are you going?"

"I don't know. I don't have a destination in mind, I just—"

He squeezed my shoulders gently and then pulled me toward him. I was pressed against his warm chest, and I shivered in the winter night.

My jacket was still inside, but I wasn't going to go back for it.

"You're cold," he murmured against my hair. He dropped his arms from around me and stepped back.

"What are you doing?" I asked when he took off his leather cut and handed it to me.

He didn't reply as he unbuttoned his flannel shirt with the sleeves rolled up. He shrugged out of it and handed it to me. Savage was wearing a black tee underneath—a black tee that showed off his defined chest.

I returned his leather cut and put on his shirt, buttoning it up all the way. I fixed the collar, and turned my head, my nose grazing the fabric. It smelled of him. Warm. Earthy.

"Where's your car?"

"Don't have one," I mumbled. "I took the bus."

"Then let me take you home."

He held out his hand to me. I bit my lip in a moment of indecision, and then reluctantly took it.

Savage laced his fingers through mine, as if he was worried I'd bolt.

"Where's home?" he asked.

"The Sunset Motel. Just off the highway."

He clenched his jaw. "You're living in a motel?"

"Yes." I straightened my spine, ready to defend my life choices, but he didn't reply.

We walked around the warehouse to the front. His bike was parked on the street. He reached for the helmet resting on the seat. I thought he was going to hand it to me, but instead he gently placed it on my head and clipped the buckle. He adjusted the strap to tighten it.

"That okay?" he asked.

I nodded.

He straddled the bike and inched forward, gesturing with his chin to the spot behind him. "Get on."

I placed my hand on his leather-clad shoulder and awkwardly settled myself behind him.

"Move closer," he commanded. "Wrap your arms around me. When I lean, you lean. There's no seat back. Just hang on to me and don't let go."

I wiggled closer to him, the V of my thighs pressing against him. I blushed at the intimate position.

"You good?" he asked.

"I'm good."

"Okay. Hang on."

He started the engine. The motorcycle rumbled beneath us, and then we were off. I gripped him tight, my nails digging into his stomach as fear engulfed me. I quickly closed my eyes.

Savage's hand came around to touch my thigh, giving it a little squeeze.

I loosened my death grip on him and slowly opened my eyes. Though my hair was tied back into a loose ponytail, strands at my temples escaped, blowing across my cheeks as we rode.

With a deep breath, I forced myself to look around. The roar of the bike and the air rushing over me had my heart pounding the entire ride.

My heartbeat thundered in my ears, and even after Savage pulled into a parking lot and cut the engine, I still felt the tremors of fear and adrenaline pulsing through my veins.

"You can let me go now," Savage said. When I didn't move, he pressed, "Evie?"

I came out of my trance and hastily released him. "Sorry." I scrambled off the bike, nearly falling onto the asphalt.

"Hey, easy," he said, catching my elbow and steadying me.

My hands shook as I unlatched the helmet. "Thanks." I handed it back to him.

"You hated it," he guessed.

"No," I said. "I just . . . I was scared. But it was—"

He raised his brows.

I sighed. "Unlike anything I've ever experienced."

He climbed off his bike and set the helmet down on the seat.

"I'm this way," I said, gesturing to the side of the motel. I was covered in sweat and beer and all I wanted was a hot shower. Exhaustion pulled at my limbs.

When we arrived at my door, I turned. "Thanks for the ride."

"You can't stay here," he stated.

I raised my brows. "I can't?"

"This is the kind of place that you rent by the hour. No one actually lives here."

I frowned, not understanding what he was saying. "Savage, this is my home for the time being. It's fine. I know the owner. She's my friend."

"And as your friend, I bet she would tell you this isn't a long-term living situation."

"I don't need a long-term living situation."

"Oh, right, because you're leaving town." He cocked

his head to the side. "You don't have enough money for a bus ticket?"

When I didn't reply, he grinned. His busted lip was healing, and it didn't split this time. "Gotcha."

"Fine, you got me. I've made enough to leave, but if I do, I'll just wind up in the same situation somewhere else. So, I'll take you up on the job offer. I'll let you find me one. It's the least you can do for getting me fired."

I showed him my back as I went to unlock the door.

Pop! Pop! Pop!

Suddenly, I was pushed against the door, Savage's hard muscular body covering mine.

The squeal of tires in the parking lot had me shivering in distress.

"Was that—" I panted, "—what I think it was?"

Savage's mouth was close to my ear, his breath warm against my skin when he said, "Yeah, babe. Those were gun shots."

He'd covered me with his body. He'd protected me. Just like he'd protected me at the warehouse.

His hand settled on my hip and I closed my eyes when I felt the heat of his fingers searing through my jeans.

"What were you saying about staying here?" he rasped.

At least he didn't sound smug.

"Okay, maybe staying here isn't a good idea," I admitted.

He lifted himself off me and stepped back. I instantly missed his warmth.

I turned to face him. "Where am I going to stay?"

His head dipped down. "Tonight, you're staying with me."

Chapter 4

SAVAGE WASTED NO TIME—HE didn't even let me into the motel room to grab a spare change of clothes.

"I've got shit you can sleep in. Get on."

I wrapped my arms around him, pressed close, and soon we were zooming off into the night. As he maneuvered through the streets, my mind buzzed.

He was still a stranger, and yet when I was with him, I felt safe.

Yeah, he was a biker, and he fought in an illegal fighting ring . . . but I knew bad men.

I'd been married to one.

And Savage, for all his choices about how he lived his life, was a good man. Sure, he may have had his own moral code, but he'd literally placed his body over mine to protect me from rogue gun shots.

My arms tightened around him.

Apprehension curled through me when we arrived at a closed metal gate. Two men in jeans and leather cuts opened the gate and waved at Savage as he drove us through.

Heartbeats & Highways

He parked in a gravel lot next to several other motorcycles and cut the engine.

I slid off the bike and unclasped my helmet. "Where are we?"

He took the helmet from me. "The clubhouse."

"The clubhouse?" I frowned. "You don't have an apartment?"

"Nah. Single guy like me doesn't need one." He lifted his leg and climbed off, setting the helmet on the seat.

I heard the faintest traces of music, but I couldn't depict where it was coming from.

"There's a party going on," he said as if answering my silent question. "Doubt it's rowdy yet since it's only just past midnight, but by two a.m. it's gonna be a rager."

He clasped my hand in his and led me toward the porch.

"I don't want to go to a party," I protested.

He looked at me over his shoulder and grinned. "We're not going to the party."

I relaxed.

"Sorry about the mess," Savage said as we stepped into the clubhouse. The kitchen and living room were an open floor plan and there were dozens of beer bottles, empty red cups, and bottles of liquor.

Toward the back of the clubhouse, I heard the screen door open and then close, followed by the clacking of high heels on wooden planks.

Two women with heavy makeup, teased hair, and short skirts entered the room. The brunette smiled in surprise, parting red lips. "You're here!"

"Yeah," Savage said easily. He tightened his hold on my hand and gently tugged me into his side.

"I've missed you, baby," she purred.

My spine snapped straight, and I attempted to put

distance between me and Savage, but he wouldn't let me go.

"I've missed you too," the blonde added. She linked her arm with her friend's, her greedy gaze sliding down Savage's body.

They didn't even see me.

"Want to have a private party? With just the three of us?" the brunette asked, reaching over and gently cradling her friend's breast.

I let out a squeak and my cheeks flamed in embarrassment.

"I'm good," Savage said, his tone bland. "I'm sure some of my brothers can help you with the party you're wanting."

Without another word, Savage tugged me past them and all but dragged me up the stairs.

"God damn, she's lucky," one of the women said as we retreated.

Bile crept up my throat as their voices faded from existence.

We made it to the second floor and Savage pushed open a door. I stood at the threshold, refusing to go in.

"This is a bad idea," I muttered, declining to look at him.

"Why?"

"Why?" My gaze snapped to his, my brows furrowing. "Because you clearly had other . . . plans. Plans that didn't involve me. I'm ruining your night."

He sighed. "If I wanted to be at the party with those women, I would be. But I'm not. I'm here, with you."

I continued to examine him. His expression was relaxed, but his body was coiled tight, like he was ready to spring.

Finally, I nodded and went into his room. He came in behind me and closed the door.

The room was small, but tidy. A double bed was pushed up against one wall and there was a nightstand, a three-drawer dresser and a meager closet.

"The bathroom on this floor is communal. Don't worry," he smiled, "it's cleaned every day, so you don't have to worry about it looking like a frat house."

He went to his dresser and pulled out a pair of boxers and a T-shirt and handed them to me.

"Uhm. Thanks," I said, taking them. "But can I take a quick shower? I'm covered in beer."

"Sure." He went to his closet and reached up onto the top shelf and grabbed a clean towel. "Come on, I'll show you where it is."

He led me out of his room and traveled down the hallway to the bathroom. "The lock works," he assured me. "Take as much time as you need. I'll be in my room."

I nodded.

"You hungry?"

I shook my head.

"All right." He rubbed the back of his neck, appearing agitated. "Look, Evie, I—fuck, I don't know what to say. I didn't think. I just brought you to a place where I knew you'd be safe. Those women—"

"You don't owe me an explanation," I stated. "It's done."

He looked at me for a long moment and then he nodded. "Enjoy your shower."

∽

When I got back to Savage's room, my eyes widened in surprise.

"What are you doing?" I asked.

He gestured to the pallet on the floor. "I'm sleeping down here. You can have the bed. I changed the sheets for you."

"I can take the floor."

"You're shitting me, right?" he asked. "What kind of gentleman would I be if I made you sleep on the floor and took the bed?"

"You're a gentleman?" I teased.

"My version of a gentleman, anyway." He'd removed his leather cut and motorcycle boots, but he was still in his jeans. "How was your shower?"

"Good. Hot. I hope you don't mind, but I borrowed some toothpaste and finger brushed with it."

"That's what it's there for. Get in bed," he stated. "I'll tuck you in."

I sniggered. "Tuck me in?"

His grin was wolfish. "Yeah." His gaze dropped down my body, as if he suddenly wanted me naked.

I hastily climbed into bed and yanked the covers up to my chin.

Savage's lips twitched.

He turned on the lamp before hitting the main light, bathing his angular face in a soft golden glow. Savage leaned over me and pressed his lips to my forehead, and before I could utter a squeak of surprise, he turned off the lamp.

"Good night, Evie," he said.

"Good night," I mumbled.

I heard him moving around in the room—it wasn't completely dark because the window curtains were halfway open, letting in the moonlight.

His belt buckle jangled, and I held my breath when I

realized he was stripping off his jeans. I closed my eyes and turned my face up to the ceiling.

When he settled down and things were quiet for a few moments, I asked, "Savage?"

"Hmm?"

"Those two women . . ."

"Yeah?"

"Have you—slept with them before?"

He paused for a moment and then replied, "Yeah."

"I don't understand then . . . why did you tell them to go to one of your club brothers. Doesn't that make you jealous?"

"No, it doesn't—ah hell . . ."

"What?"

"It's just how the club operates. They're club groupies, Evie. They're not Old Ladies."

"What are Old Ladies?"

"A biker's woman. A wife or girlfriend. An Old Lady is a claim. It means she's off limits and she won't fuck around with anyone else. But Jessie and Anna aren't Old Ladies, so they can spend the night with whoever they want. And no one gets jealous."

I swallowed. "Are there . . . a lot of those types of women? Who hang around the club, I mean?"

"A fair amount, yeah."

My heart dropped into my stomach. "Oh. And have you—I mean—never mind."

"I have a past, Evie."

"Yeah."

So do I.

"You don't like the idea of me being with other women, do you?"

I worked my bottom lip through my teeth as I thought about how to reply, but he spoke before I could.

"I don't like the idea of you being with other men," he admitted.

"This is a ridiculous conversation. Your love life is your business. Mine is mine. We don't even know each other."

He didn't answer.

As I drifted off to sleep, I realized I wanted his love life to be my business.

Chapter 5

Something woke me from a sound sleep, and my heart thrashed against my rib cage in fear.

The sounds were coming from the floor—Savage was in the throes of a nightmare. Without thought, I flung off the covers and climbed out of bed.

Guided by moonlight, I saw the outline of him. He was laying on his back, his head turned away from me. I got down on my knees and placed my hand on his chest.

He wasn't wearing a shirt.

His skin was warm, and my fingers itched to explore.

Savage instantly quieted.

Whatever nightmare plagued him seemed to leave at my touch.

Savage had protected me from actual threats in real life, and I wanted to protect him from whatever demons haunted him in his nightmares.

I scooted down next to him on the pallet, kept my hand on his chest and fell back asleep to the sound of his rhythmic breathing.

The next time I awoke, early morning rays were

peeking through the blinds. My cheek was pressed to a warm chest and a muscular arm was curled around me. I blinked a few times and then tilted my head back to see if Savage was still asleep.

Blue eyes met mine.

His free hand came up to cradle the back of my head and his fingers sifted through my hair.

Savage kissed me.

I gasped in shock and Savage took full opportunity. His tongue swept into my mouth to mate with mine and a soft whimper escaped my throat.

My insides fluttered and my body melted into his.

Savage pulled back and I opened my eyes to stare at him.

I licked my lips which dragged his gaze to my mouth.

He looked like he wanted to kiss me again.

I *wanted* him to kiss me again.

"Why are you on the floor with me?" he rasped.

I debated on what to say and then settled for the truth. "You were having a nightmare. You calmed down when I touched you."

His eyes shuttered, all emotion locking down, far away from me.

But his fingers gripped my snarled hair, and he dipped his head close to mine.

I put a hand to his chest to stop him. "Savage."

"Yeah?"

I took a deep breath. "I refuse to be one of many."

His brow furrowed and he nodded slowly. "All right."

"All right," I repeated.

He gently untangled himself from me and I mourned the loss of his heat.

"Let's get breakfast. You hungry?" he asked as he sat

up. He scratched his chest, drawing my attention once again to his rippling muscles and ink. "Evie?"

"Hm?"

"Breakfast," he repeated. "You like pancakes?"

"I like waffles better."

He grinned. "Get dressed. I'll take you to breakfast."

"I don't have clean clothes," I said, pointing to my soiled pleather vest. "And it's cold on the back of your bike without a jacket."

"I'll find you a jacket. You can wear my shirt." His eyes dipped. "I like you in my shirt."

Before I could reply, he was up off the floor and reaching for his jeans.

He was beautiful, like a sleek predator. Wild and untamed. His name was Savage, and his body reflected it.

"Is that—what is that?" I asked with a gasp, pointing at a scar on his abdomen.

He looked down. "Oh. Bullet wound."

"Bullet—wound?"

"I was shot. Had to get my spleen out."

He said it so casually.

"And you're tempting fate again by fighting the way you do?"

"We all tempt fate all the time, whether we realize it or not." He shrugged. "Might as well enjoy life while we're at it. Get dressed, Evie. I'm hungry."

∼

I didn't ask where the woman's jacket came from, but Savage assured me it didn't belong to a random club groupie. The clubhouse was quiet, and I had no doubt that people were sleeping off last night's party. Savage grasped my hand and led me through the kitchen and living room which were a complete and utter mess.

The morning was bright and cool, and Savage turned up the collar of my jacket and then placed the helmet on my head. He clipped it and made sure it was tight enough.

I loved being on the back of his bike. A few days ago, I'd never even been on a motorcycle, but now I couldn't fathom life without the exhilaration. It was exciting and fun, and even though it was dangerous, I trusted Savage to keep me safe.

I trusted a man I hardly knew and yet . . .

His lips had been soft against mine. Gentle, and then hungry.

He was going to consume me.

I shivered.

"You cold?" Savage asked, looking at me over his shoulder at my movement.

"Just a little," I lied. "I'll be fine, let's go."

"Hang on, babe."

Fifteen minutes later, Savage came to a stop outside of a diner called Boots. It wasn't much to look at and my expression must've said as much.

"Trust me." He winked and then took my hand. He held open the door for me and I stepped inside. The aroma of bacon and fried things hit me instantly and my mouth watered.

A waitress told us to sit anywhere, and Savage let me have my pick.

I headed toward the back where there was a free booth.

Savage groaned.

I looked at him over my shoulder. "What?"

"I'm sorry, Evie."

"Sorry for what?"

"Well, well, well," a young woman said as she sauntered toward us with a tall, dark-haired young man right behind her. He looped his arm over her shoulder and grinned.

"Hey, Little Punk," Savage greeted. "You've got paint on your cheek."

The young woman with bright red hair scrubbed her face.

"Gotcha," Savage teased.

"You think I would've let you leave the house with paint on your cheek?" the young man asked her, looking at her fondly.

"You let me leave the house with paint on my cheek just last week," she stated.

"It was cute." He leaned down and kissed her forehead.

She turned her attention back to Savage. "Nice shiner. Did she give it to you?"

Savage reached out a tweaked her nose. "Fighting at The Ring."

"Ah, that makes more sense." The young woman glanced at me. "I've been looking for that jacket."

"Oh." I blushed. "Savage said I could—"

She reached out and unzipped the breast pocket and extracted something. "My favorite lip gloss. Thanks."

I blinked stupidly.

"Now's the time to introduce us, you heathen," the young woman drawled.

"Evie, this is Waverly and her boyfriend Dylan."

"Willa's sister," Waverly added.

I frowned. "Willa?"

Waverly's gaze darted back to Savage. "She hasn't met Willa yet?"

"No. Not yet." His gaze was pointed.

"Reallllllly." Waverly beamed. "Evie, it was nice to meet you. I'd love to stay and chat, but—"

"But you've got somewhere else to be, right?" Savage drawled. "Instead of up in my shit?"

Waverly laughed. "I'll see you guys later."

"Later, man," Dylan said to Savage. To me, he said with a smile, "Hang on tight, Evie. It's going to be a wild ride."

Waverly clasped Dylan's hand and the two of them left the diner.

Savage placed his palm on my lower back and urged me to the table. My head was spinning.

"What's The Ring?" I asked.

"The club owns a gym. It's a good cover for that thing I'm not supposed to be doing," he explained. "That thing you aren't going to tell anyone about . . ."

I bit my lip and nodded. It wasn't my business, but Waverly inspired my curiosity.

"How do you know Waverly?" I slid into the booth.

Savage took the other side. He reached out for the laminated menus and handed me one. "I've known her since she was born. She's like my younger sister. Almost sixteen, and a terror."

"I see." My brow furrowed. "And Willa is . . ."

"Waverly's older sister. More like a mother to her though. Willa and I have been friends since we were kids. She's married to my other childhood best friend, Duke. And Duke is also my club brother."

"Ah," I said, putting the puzzle pieces together. "Now her teasing you makes sense."

"She's going to run back to Willa and tell her she saw me with you." He glanced at the menu. "I don't know why I'm even looking; I know what I'm getting."

"You don't seem concerned about Waverly gossiping about your business."

"I'm not." He set the menu aside. "What are you having?"

"I don't know yet." I frowned.

"Hey," he said, reaching across the table and setting his hand on mine. "What's really going on here?"

I bit my lip. "How many of your women have you brought here?"

"Truthfully?"

I nodded.

"Zero."

I blinked. "Zero. Really?"

"Zero," he repeated. "I haven't brought anyone here. Just you."

"Just me." I sighed. "I want a waffle. A whole stack of them, with strawberries."

He grinned. "You got it. And after breakfast, I'll drive you back to the motel and we'll grab your shit."

"Why would we do that?"

"Because you can't stay there. The club owns a halfway house. There's a vacant apartment. You'll be safe there."

Chapter 6

"You sure this is a good idea?" Agnes asked as she looked out the lobby window to see Savage waiting for me.

"No. Not even a little bit," I said. "But I heard gunshots last night . . . so I stayed at his clubhouse with him."

"I heard the gunshots too, but I thought you were out working a fight."

"I was. But then . . ." I quickly explained what happened with Savage and me getting fired.

"That's . . . a lot to take in."

"Yeah." I looked at Savage again. "I don't think he'll hurt me."

"Oh, he won't hurt you. Not the way you think he will."

I frowned when I looked at her. "What does that mean?"

"It means—he's a biker. And a fighter. He lives by different rules than normal people."

"Yeah. I'm gathering that."

She hugged me to her. "I hope you find peace, Evie. From whatever it is you're running from."

I moved away from the woman who'd given me a brief respite from a cruel world. "If it turns out to be a bad decision . . ."

"You'll always have a room here."

I smiled at her in gratitude.

As I stepped outside into the cool air, I lifted the collar of my jacket. Savage was leaning against his motorcycle, sunglasses shielding his eyes. "Ready?"

"I think so."

My bag full of meager belongings was already strapped to his motorcycle behind a very tiny seat over the rear wheel well.

We climbed onto his bike and drove away from the motel. When Savage pulled into a parking lot and cut the engine, I released my hold on him and removed the helmet. I swung my leg over the bike and Savage followed suit.

He then unstrapped my bag from the rear fender. When I made a move to take it from him, he held it out of my reach. "Let me carry it for you."

I shoved my hands into my jacket pockets and nodded.

"You want to see the apartment?"

I nodded again and followed him toward the red brick structure. "The building is newly renovated. Gave us a bitch of a time. Turned out it had mold and water damage. But with Logan's help and a good chunk of cash, we got it sorted."

He punched in a code and the door to the building unlocked. He opened the front door and gestured for me to go inside first. I looked around the foyer. "Who's Logan?"

"Smoke's Old Lady," he explained. "She has her own

interior design business. The club asked for her help designing and decorating the apartments. Even though this place is for short-term stays, we didn't want the apartments to feel that way. They still need to feel like homes, you know?"

We climbed the stairs to the top floor, passed three apartments, and arrived at the end of the hallway.

"This is the only unoccupied apartment right now. I hope it's okay."

"More than okay," I assured him. "Wait, if these apartments are only for short-term stays, who lives in the building?"

"Women that Doc has offered help to."

I frowned. "Doc?"

"Boxer's Old Lady," he said with a grin. "She runs the Waco Health & Wellness Clinic."

"Oh." I paused.

"So, this is the place."

I stepped into the apartment and my mouth dropped open. I hastily covered it as I took in the beautiful space. Large windows, an open floor plan with an electric fireplace in the living room.

"Well?" Savage asked.

Tears clouded my vision. "It's perfect."

"Yeah?"

"It's . . ." I could breathe here, but I didn't want to tell him that. "Logan is talented."

"Yeah, she is." He was staring at me, and I pretended not to notice.

"The bathroom?"

"Back there." He gestured to the area behind a half-wall divide. "Along with the bedroom."

I took a few tentative steps deeper into the apartment. I wanted to glide my fingertips across the counter. I wanted to open every cabinet and cupboard and revel in the fact that I had a furnished, clean and safe place to live.

"How long can I stay?" I asked.

"As long as you need."

I turned my head so he wouldn't see me getting emotional.

"The fridge is stocked."

"It is?"

He nodded. "Had a prospect get you the basics already."

"But how? When?"

"Last night."

"Last night?"

"You were in the shower." He shrugged. "I wanted to get it sorted for you."

"You've thought of everything, haven't you?"

"Just say *thank you, Savage*."

I glared at him. "Don't bulldoze me."

"Not trying to," he insisted. "It wasn't any trouble. I could help, so I helped. Don't make this a thing, okay?"

I took a deep breath and reluctantly nodded.

"I'm waiting."

I rolled my eyes. "Thank you."

He grinned. "What was that?"

"Thank you, Savage," I said, boldly meeting his gaze.

He stalked toward me. "Phone."

I blinked. "Huh?"

"Give me your phone. I'm putting my number in it."

I reached into my jacket pocket and unlocked it before handing it to him. He punched in a number and then called himself.

"There. If there's something missing or if you need anything, just text me."

"Okay."

"Bus stop is down the street. Grocery store is two stops away," he explained. "I know you like your independence. Laundry facilities are in the basement."

I took off the jacket and tried to hand it to him. "Can you give this back to Waverly?"

"No. You keep it."

"But it's not mine."

With a sigh, he opened his phone and shot off a text. A moment later it buzzed. Grinning, he showed me the screen.

> **WAVERLY**
>
> Tell her to keep it. It looks better on her than me anyway.

"She insists," Savage said with a laugh.

"Clearly." I grinned. "Okay, well, that's sweet. Tell her thank you, please."

"I will. So, I got you somewhere safe, now how about I help you get a job?"

"What kind of job?" I asked.

"Receptionist at Three Kings—a tattoo parlor. Hours are better than your last gig anyway. The owners are good guys. You can meet Roman tomorrow if you want."

"Tomorrow is great. If you give me the address, I can figure out the bus route."

"I'll take you," he offered.

"You don't have to," I protested.

"I know I don't *have* to. I want to."

"You've done more than enough. And you've told me where the bus is. I can do it on my own."

"I know you're capable of doing it on your own. But Evie?"

"Yeah?"

"I want to see you in the morning, okay? Let me take you."

We stared at one another and then he was moving toward me. His hand swept underneath my ponytail and rested on my neck.

It was a bad idea giving in. My brain knew that.

But my body . . .

I was no match for his touch, his intensity.

My hand settled on his chest. "Okay. You can take me."

"I've got to go," he said.

"All right."

I licked my lips, my gaze dropping to his mouth.

"Kiss me goodbye," he rasped.

A half smile pulled at my lips, and I angled my head back.

His mouth covered mine. Warm, sensual, unhurried.

Long dormant desire fluttered through my belly.

Savage pulled back too soon. Far too soon.

"Open your eyes, Evie," he commanded.

I opened my eyes.

His smile was slow. "Lock up after I'm gone."

∽

My eyes flew open, and I quickly clamped my mouth shut to silence the scream threatening to burst from me. As my heart thudded in my chest, I waited for my terror to mellow. I wondered what had startled me awake. Then I heard them . . .

Soft footsteps in the hallway.

I waited.

There was the sound of a closing door and then there

was nothing. I realized I was safe, and there was no danger as my heartbeat began to return to normal.

I swung my legs off the couch, my brain still full of cobwebs from my nap. I looked at the clock on the microwave. After Savage had left, I'd immediately curled up on the couch and conked out. I'd slept a few hours, and it was now the middle of the afternoon.

Swallowing past the dryness in my throat, I got up and padded my way to the kitchen. I opened the stainless-steel door of the refrigerator and peered inside. The shelves were full of necessities. I opened the drawers, delighting at their fullness, too.

The bottle of orange juice called my name, and I felt my mouth pool with saliva.

I searched for a glass and poured juice nearly to the brim.

It was the most delicious thing I'd ever tasted. As I stood in the kitchen drinking orange juice to satiate my thirst, my stomach rumbled.

There was a carton of eggs in the fridge.

As I scrambled a few into a mixing bowl, I heard the distant opening of a door, followed by hesitant footsteps. They seemed to be pacing.

Frowning, my curiosity overrode my trepidation. I quietly trekked to the front door and looked through the peephole. A young woman who looked to be about my age with jet black hair stood in front of my door, holding a plate covered in tinfoil. She raised her fist to knock but decided against it. She set the plate down onto the mat outside my door and quickly scurried into the apartment across the hall from me.

Seems I'm not the only one who wants to keep to themselves.

I waited a moment to see if she came back out, but when she didn't, I opened my door. I crouched down to pick up the plate and peered underneath the tinfoil and smiled.

The woman had made me chocolate-chip cookies.

I wanted to call out my thanks, but something stopped me. I took the cookies and retreated.

I wasn't ready to introduce myself either.

Chapter 7

My interview at Three Kings was in two hours, and for the life of me I couldn't decide what to wear. I didn't have a lot of clothes; just some underwear, undershirts, a nightgown, a pair of jeans, and three oversized, faded flannel shirts.

My clothes didn't even take up one drawer of the dresser.

Pathetic. You're pathetic.

But the voice in my head didn't belong to me. It belonged to *him*.

"Shut up," I muttered out loud.

A knock on the front door made me freeze. Was it my neighbor from across the hall? Had she finally decided to be braver than me and introduce herself?

"Evie?" Savage called out.

My stomach flipped in excitement as I went into the living room.

I unlocked the chain and opened the door and took in his appearance. Black thermal shirt and his leather cut, along with jeans, boots and mussed blond hair. There were shadows beneath his eyes, like he hadn't had a good night's sleep. I wondered if it would've been different if I'd been next to him.

I shut that thought down.

Savage's blue eyes raked over me.

I glanced down at my attire. I was still dressed in my nightgown. And were those—yep. My nipples. Standing at attention.

Hastily crossing my arms over my chest, I stepped aside and let him in.

He cleared his throat. "I brought you a breakfast sandwich."

"I was just about to change." I blushed.

"Not on my account, I hope."

"I'm ignoring that comment." I waved him toward the kitchen. "Make yourself comfortable."

His jaw tightened and he nodded, his knuckles turning white as he gripped the paper bag.

I rushed into the bedroom. I stripped out of my nightgown and flung it onto the bed.

He moved around the kitchen, opening cabinets and drawers.

I slid into my jeans and the blue and black flannel shirt. I looked in the floor-length mirror that hung on the back of the closet door. After my shower last night, I'd brushed out my hair and let it air-dry. It had a slight wave to it, but I didn't want to put it up despite it falling all the way to my waist.

"What's that?" Savage asked as I came into the kitchen.

"What's what?"

He pointed to the mason jar covered with a dish towel that rested on the counter.

"Oh. That's my sourdough starter," I explained.

On a plate was an unwrapped breakfast sandwich. He

pushed it toward me. "How was your first night? And what's a sourdough starter?"

I blinked as he pivoted the conversation. "My first night was fine. A sourdough starter is flour and water, and it naturally grows yeast. So, I can bake my own sourdough bread. I had to go to the store and get the flour, but—"

"You went to the store?"

"Yes."

"Last night?"

"Yes."

"You took the bus? At night?"

"Of course I took the bus." I frowned. "You told me where the bus stop was. What else was I supposed to do? I wasn't going to walk."

"You didn't call me."

"Why would I call you?" I demanded.

"So I could've gotten the flour for you."

"That's ridiculous," I stated.

"I don't like you riding the bus at night," he said gruffly. He took a bite of his sandwich.

"Is this okay?" I gestured to my outfit. "What I'm wearing?"

"Not as nice as the nightgown, but it'll do."

"Savage!" My face flamed with heat.

He chuckled. "You look fine. Why are you worried?"

"I don't know what to wear to an interview at a tattoo parlor," I murmured.

"Exactly what you're wearing. You're a shoo-in."

I reached for the sandwich on my plate. We ate in silence until he polished off the last bite of his food.

"So, you bake bread?" he asked.

"Yes." I plucked a piece of bacon from the plate that had fallen from my sandwich and popped it into my mouth.

"Why?"

I paused and looked at him. "What do you mean, *why?*"

"I mean, baking your own bread. That's so . . . life on the prairie."

"I grew up on a farm. Baking bread was part of that life."

"No kidding? Like with chickens and stuff?"

"Yeah." I nodded. "Have you ever had freshly baked sourdough?"

"Don't think so."

"You'd know. And I make it because I like to. Don't you have things in your life you do just for the sheer enjoyment of it?"

"I guess."

"Like what?"

He thought for a moment and then replied, "Long rides on my motorcycle."

I finished the sandwich and then picked up Savage's plate and set it in the sink.

"I missed you last night," he said.

"Missed me?" I asked, trying for nonchalant even though my insides swirled with pleasure. "Oh?"

"I didn't sleep well."

I turned to face him and gestured to my eyes. "Yeah. I noticed." I cocked my head to the side. "Is that usual for you?"

"Yes. I never sleep well." He rubbed his jaw, scratching the stubble on his chin. His brow was furrowed. "Except . . ."

"Except what?"

"The night you crawled up next to me." His blue gaze pinned me to the floor. "That was the best night's sleep of my life."

We stared at one another, something surging between us. Something I didn't understand. Something that made me want to run and hide under the bed until it disappeared.

That night would forever be imprinted on my mind. As was the kiss we'd shared when I'd woken up in his arms.

He raked a hand through his hair in agitation. "Fuck, Evie. Waking up with you in my arms was like—"

"Don't swear," I blurted out.

"Does swearing bother you?"

I nodded.

"I'll try and stop."

"No, you won't." I snorted.

"No, I won't," he admitted with a boyish grin.

I went to the cabinet and pulled out an empty quart-sized mason jar and set it down in front of him.

"What's this? You gonna make me my own sourdough starter?"

"No. This is your new swear jar. Every time you swear, you put a dollar in the jar."

He stood up from his seat and reached into his jeans pocket for his wallet. He fished out a twenty-dollar bill and dropped it into the jar.

"Preemptive," he explained with a wry grin. "We both know how the fuck this is gonna go."

I let out a laugh that came from deep within my belly.

"You're beautiful. But you're fucking stunning when you laugh."

My expression softened. "Really? You really think that?"

"God, yes." He growled. "I can't stop thinking about you."

"You can't?" I whispered.

He came toward me and cradled the back of my head

in his large hands, tilting my chin up so I was forced to look at him.

"I fantasize about your lips."

I blinked. "You do?"

"Yeah, I do."

And then his mouth covered mine. I sighed and he captured the sound.

"Open for me," he murmured against my lips.

I opened and his tongue swept inside. I clung to him as our tongues met. I lost myself in the feel of him. I grazed his chest—reveling in the hardness of his muscles beneath my fingertips.

He held me with his strong hands like I was delicate, like I was something to be cherished and protected.

I ripped my lips from his and pressed my forehead to his chest so I could catch my breath and get my bearings.

Savage's arms tightened around me. "Fuck."

I looked up at him again and couldn't stop my grin. "Good thing you pre-paid on the tip jar."

Chapter 8

"We should get going," he said, but he didn't release me.

"Oh. Right."

When I didn't move, he tightened his arms, and his head descended again.

I met his mouth, hungry for something I couldn't name. When Savage's lips covered mine and his tongue was in my mouth, I ceased to think at all. All I could do was *feel*.

He makes me want to feel everything.

"Evie," he growled against my mouth.

My hands slid up his back, underneath his leather cut. "Hmm?"

"Evie, we have to stop."

His hands grasped my shoulders, and he gently pushed me away, keeping his hands on me.

My eyes fluttered open. "Why do we have to stop?"

Savage grinned down at me. "Because you have a job interview. And if I keep kissing you, it's gonna lead to other things . . ."

"Oh," I sighed dreamily.

He kissed my forehead, and let his lips linger. Eventually, he pulled back. "Get your jacket."

I gathered my belongings and shrugged into my jacket. Savage went out into the hallway and waited as I locked up the apartment.

"Do you know who lives there?" I asked, pointing to the door across the hall.

"I do," Savage said, allowing me to go ahead of him.

"What's her name?" I asked as we headed down the stairs toward the lobby. "She left cookies on my doorstep yesterday, but she didn't knock and introduce herself."

"Cookies? I didn't see any cookies on your counter."

I blushed. "I ate them all."

Savage let out a laugh, amusement coating his expression. "Love a woman with a healthy appetite."

His innuendo was unmistakable, and it sent shivers of pleasure down my spine.

"Why didn't you knock on *her* door and thank her for the cookies?"

"I don't think she's ready for social interaction. Otherwise, she'd have knocked first. So, I'm respecting her privacy."

We made it to the lobby and Savage opened the front door of the apartment complex and I stepped outside. I followed him to his motorcycle.

"Her name is Cozy," he said, handing me a bike helmet. "You know, shit's not adding up for me."

"About what?" I placed the helmet on my head and clipped it.

"You."

"What about me?"

"All of it. You working at an illegal fighting ring, living at a motel by the highway, and now you won't even introduce yourself to your neighbor. Something's got you spooked. But I'm patient. You'll tell me when you're ready."

My heart drummed in trepidation. Savage saw way more than I gave him credit for. "You? Patient? Oh, please. I don't believe that for a second."

"I can be patient," he stated. "For you."

He got onto his motorcycle, and I climbed on behind him. I pressed against him and wrapped my arms around his muscular body. Savage squeezed my thigh, and we were off.

My brain was buzzing from our kisses and conversation. I wished Savage was exactly as he appeared to be; nothing more than a rough and tough biker who wasn't capable of seeing beneath the surface.

But he was so much more than that.

He couldn't know about my past. He could *never* know about it.

He zagged down a street and eventually pulled into a parking lot and cut the engine. I looked at the sign on the building.

"Thanks for the ride. And for breakfast."

And for the bone-melting kisses.

I swung my leg over his motorcycle and climbed off and then handed him the helmet.

He slid off his bike.

"What are you doing?" I demanded.

"Going inside with you."

"But why?"

"So I can introduce you to Roman," he said easily.

"But you already told him about me, didn't you? You don't need to tag along. I don't need an emotional support human."

"Chill. I have an appointment with Homer—Roman's

brother," Savage said with a wry grin. "Two birds, one stone. Come on. You don't want to be late for your interview."

I hustled after him. He opened the door to the tattoo parlor and allowed me to enter first. I liked the space immediately. There were leather couches and chairs for customers, a coffee table with magazines to flip through, and the walls were decorated with photographs of finished custom artwork.

I began to relax.

But then two hulking giants appeared from the back hallway and terror filled my throat.

"Savage," the dark-haired man greeted, holding his hand out to Savage.

Savage clasped his palm and gave it a shake. "Hey, Roman."

Roman dropped Savage's hand. He looked at me and flashed a grin. "You must be Evie."

My voice was trapped in my throat, so I settled for a head nod.

"This is my brother, Homer," Roman said, gesturing to the blond giant next to him. The man's face was covered in a scowl, and I instantly took a step back, accidentally bumping into Savage.

"Don't mind his expression," Roman stated. "He's a gentle giant."

Homer turned his gaze toward his brother and gave him a glare.

Roman chuckled.

"You ready?" Homer asked, focusing his attention on Savage.

"Yeah, I'm ready." Savage stepped away from me, leaving me cold and unsure. "I'll be in the back."

"Okay," I whispered.

I watched Savage disappear down the hallway with Homer, leaving me alone with Roman.

"So, the job's pretty easy," he began. He waved me toward the reception counter. "My sister, Brielle, has been filling in for us. She'll be in when we open to show you the appointment scheduling system. There's a mini fridge behind the counter with sodas and we keep snacks in the back."

Roman looked at me and frowned. "You okay?"

"Don't you want—I mean, isn't this an interview?" I asked.

"Yeah, it's an interview."

"But you're talking like I have the job already."

"You're friends with Savage, yeah?"

I wouldn't call us friends. Friends didn't share steamy kisses in kitchens. Friends didn't fall asleep in each other's arms. I wasn't sure *what* to call us, but Roman was waiting on an answer.

"Yeah, we're friends," I said finally.

"He vouched for you. You need a job, and we need a receptionist."

"But your sister . . ."

"Has a job decorating wedding cakes. Her business partner is still on maternity leave, but Brielle is itching to get back to the bakery. So, we need a new receptionist as soon as possible. Job's yours if you want it."

"I want it," I blurted out. "I'll be a good receptionist, I promise."

Roman smiled and the terror I'd felt melted away as I smiled back at him.

"Is there a dress code?" I asked, glancing down at what I was wearing.

"You're dressed fine," Roman assured me. "We're a family run business; we don't do anything formal. We're open Wednesday to Sunday, noon to six. Sometimes we'll book an appointment during off-business hours, but Brielle will give you the rundown on that. Sound okay?"

"It sounds great."

Roman's cell rang and he fished it out of his back pocket. He looked at the screen. "Sorry, I gotta take this."

I nodded.

He pressed a button and put the phone to his ear. "Hey." He wandered toward the hallway and disappeared. I heard a door shut and then the muted sound of his voice.

I went to the leather couch and took a seat. I was flipping through a motorcycle magazine when the front door opened.

A redhead carrying a bakery box blew into the tattoo parlor. She hoisted her bag onto the counter and set the box down. Her keys and phone followed, hitting the glass counter with a *thunk*.

She let out a labored sigh, her head swiveling to take in the room. She paused when she saw me.

"Hey," she said with a wide smile as she approached me. "You must be Evie."

I nodded.

"I'm Brielle," she introduced.

"Nice to meet you," I murmured.

"Have you met Roman yet? Did he give you the lay of the land?"

"Oh, he was starting to, but then he got a phone call."

"Do you like donuts?"

"Donuts?"

She nodded. "Yeah, donuts. I brought a dozen from Pie in the Sky—the bakery where I'm a cake decorator. I had a meeting there this morning with Brooklyn and I almost never leave empty handed."

Her exuberance and energy had my head spinning.

She didn't wait for me to reply. She all but skipped back over to the counter to grab the box of donuts. She cut the string holding it closed, propped the lid open, and brought it over.

The scent of sugar and flour hit my nose and made my mouth water.

"I'm partial to the blueberry buttermilk," she said, reaching in the box. "But you can't go wrong with any of them."

I was overwhelmed with choices. I decided on the glazed chocolate.

"Wait," Brielle said. She set the box down on the coffee table and shoved the donut into her mouth as she walked behind the counter. She crouched down where I couldn't see her, but then she called out, "We've got milk. You want some?"

"Sure," I said, unable to stop the smile from blooming across my face. "You keep milk in the mini fridge?"

"Only since I started filling in," she said as she returned with a sleeve of plastic cups and the carton of milk. "It's become routine for me to bring some sort of baked good. It keeps them happy."

"Noted."

She poured a cup of milk and handed it to me.

"I'm not going to lie, I'm glad as hell you're taking over. I'm getting squirrelly. I need to get back to my love of decorating wedding cakes."

"Why haven't you been doing that?" I inquired as I dunked my donut into the milk.

"Brooklyn's been on maternity leave. So she scaled way back on the catering side of things. But she's ready to get back to work." She gestured to the donut. "Good, right?"

"Very good."

"So, how did you meet Savage?" she asked.

"Excuse me?"

"How did you meet Savage?" she repeated. "Roman didn't tell me. He just said a new girl Savage met was starting and that I'd need to train her."

"Oh." I frowned. Other than Savage telling me the illegal fighting ring was a secret; Savage and I had never actually discussed what to tell people about how we met. I also didn't want anyone knowing that I'd been working there either.

Brielle's blue eyes were stuck on me, avid with curiosity.

I settled for some version of the truth. "I met him at a taco truck."

"A taco truck?"

I nodded.

"And you just casually mentioned you needed a job?" she asked in confusion.

"It came up in conversation." I shrugged.

She looked like she was about to ask another question, but then a door opened and Roman entered the main room.

"Ah, fuck yeah," Roman said, walking over to us and reaching into the box of donuts and pulling one out.

Brielle poured another cup of milk and handed it to Roman.

"Carton's almost empty," she said.

"Evie can run out and grab another," Roman said.

I stood up. "I can do that. Just point me in the direction of the nearest grocery store and the bus stop."

Brielle looked at me. "Bus stop? Is your car broken down or something?"

"I don't have a car," I explained.

Roman pulled a set of car keys from his pocket. "You can take mine."

I stared at his outstretched hand but didn't make a

move to take the keys. I bit my lip before finally admitting, "I also don't know how to drive."

Roman and Brielle quickly exchanged a look.

"So, you're taking the bus every day to work?" Brielle asked.

"I plan to. I mean, I didn't this morning. Savage gave me a ride."

"What did I do?" Savage asked, startling me as he swaggered back into the main room, eyebrows raised. "Ooo, is that a bear claw?"

"Yep." Brielle lifted the box of donuts toward him.

"You gave me a ride," I explained.

"Is he going to drive you here every morning?" Brielle asked.

"*No*," I said at exactly the same time as Savage said, "*Yes*."

I glared at him.

Savage took a bite of the bear claw. After he swallowed, he said, "I don't like you riding the bus."

"That's not your choice," I stated.

Roman reached back into the box of donuts that were quickly disappearing.

"Save some for Homer and Virgil," Brielle stated. "They're going to want some."

"But they're not here," Savage announced. "Homer left out the back. It's just us."

"See, I can eat their donuts if I want," Roman stated and then took a comically large bite.

"Where did he go?" Brielle asked.

"And is he—is he coming back?" I questioned.

Roman patted me on the shoulder. "Don't let Homer's surly nature worry you. He's a good guy, but—"

"But he's very much a crotchety old man," Brielle said

with a grin. "And it's really fun to annoy him. I'll teach you how to get under his skin. It's easy."

"I don't want to get under his skin," I protested. "I just want him not to hate me."

"He won't hate you," Brielle promised.

"And if he gives you shit, you come to me. I'll have a word with him." Roman finished the rest of the donut.

I didn't want Homer to give me attitude, and I didn't want Roman to have to intercede on my behalf. I just wanted to do my job, make sure everyone was happy, and then go home at the end of my shift.

"Are you legally blind or something?" Brielle asked, her gaze turning to me.

"Excuse me?" I asked.

"Are you legally blind? Is that why you don't drive?"

"*Brielle*," Roman warned.

"What?" Brielle looked at her brother and frowned. "If she works here, she has to know how we are."

"How *you* are," Roman stated. "Which is nosey and annoying. You don't have to answer Brielle's question, Evie."

An awkward pall fell over the room.

"I need to get going," Savage said. He looked at me. "Walk me out?"

With a frown, I nodded and followed him. The door to Three Kings closed behind us and we stood on the pavement in front of the parlor.

"So, I'm leaving," Savage said unnecessarily.

I nodded.

"And you can call me if you need anything. I know you won't, but if you change your mind and want a ride home, just give me a buzz about half an hour before the end of your shift and I'll come and get you."

"Why is it so important to you that I not take the bus?" I asked.

"Because I like looking out for you." He shrugged. "And it's no trouble. Really."

A car pulled into the parking lot, momentarily distracting me from our conversation—a conversation that seemed to be about something neither of us wanted to actually talk about.

The driver's side door to a vintage restored car opened and a dark-haired man climbed out. He swaggered to Savage and slapped him on the back in greeting.

"I didn't know you were here," the dark-haired man said.

"I had a meeting with Homer about a new tattoo. I'm leaving now. Meet Evie, your new receptionist."

The man turned his attention to me and smiled, a wide, easy-going grin that immediately put me at ease. I smiled back.

"I'm Virgil. Nice to meet you, Evie."

"You too," I stated.

Virgil let out a laugh. "Man, I haven't seen someone with hair that long in years. And it's red. It's like having a back-up Brielle."

Virgil and I laughed, but Savage's expression remained passive, except for the clenching of his jaw.

"Brielle brought donuts," I said. "If you hurry, you might be able to get one. Roman might've eaten yours by now, though."

"Shit, I better get in there." He saluted Savage and then looked at me. "See you in a bit."

The front door to the tattoo parlor opened and then closed, leaving Savage and I alone.

I was still smiling when I met Savage's gaze. He didn't look happy.

"Virgil's a huge flirt," he announced. "Don't fall for his charm."

Before I could reply, he turned and stalked toward his motorcycle.

The front door to Three Kings opened again behind me and Brielle popped her head out. "You ready for me to show you the lay of the land?"

Chapter 9

SAVAGE
I can't sleep.

SMILING, I typed out a reply.

ME
Try warm milk.

SAVAGE
Fucking vile.

Three dots appeared on the screen and a moment later another text appeared.

SAVAGE
Did I wake you up?

ME
No. I've been awake.

SAVAGE
> Are you wearing that cute little nightgown you were wearing this morning?

ME
> Yes

SAVAGE
> Are you going to invite me over?

I stared at my screen, biting my lip. I hadn't been able to stop thinking about Savage all day. Brielle probably wanted to hit me for my inattention at various times.

SAVAGE
> Evie, are you going to make me beg?

I loved the idea of him begging. Savage didn't have to plead for a woman's attention, ever.

But he was begging for me.

He's impossible to ignore.

If I invited him over, that implied he would sleep here. Next to me.

My heart stumbled with nerves, but a delicious coiling of desire swirled through me, too. Savage was irresistible.

ME
> Come over.

A moment later, I heard a knock. I climbed out of bed and went to the front door. I peered through the peephole to see Savage standing at the threshold. I undid the chain and lock.

"Were you—were you standing outside my door this entire time?"

"Yup."

"How did you know I was going to let you in?" I demanded.

He lifted a paper bag. "I didn't want to take any chances, so I brought you a bribe."

My smile softened. "I don't need a bribe. You're enough."

His expression froze for a moment and then his grin deepened. "Wait 'til you see what I brought."

I stepped away from the door frame and stood back to let him inside. His gaze skated down my body in appreciation.

"Fuzzy socks," he commented.

"My feet get cold."

"Adorable."

He set the bag onto the counter and reached into it. "I brought you tacos."

"Tacos? At ten o'clock at night?"

"Why not? I got them from our spot."

"Our spot, huh?" I asked, unable to hold back my grin. Bubbles of happiness ballooned in my chest, making me feel light and carefree for the first time in years. "So, that reminds me, Brielle asked me how we met today. I sort of lied and told her it was at the taco truck. I remembered what you said about people not knowing about the fighting."

He pushed a wrapped taco toward me. "You're right about that. I told Roman the truth, though. That we met at the illegal ring."

"*What?*" I gasped. "You did? Why?"

"Relax," he said. "Roman won't tell anyone. And that includes his brothers."

"Why wouldn't he tell them?"

"Because I asked him not to."

"But won't Homer and Virgil be curious?"

"Well, sure. You're basically a stray. But the club helps a lot of strays."

"Stray?" I repeated. "You pity me."

"What?"

"This is charity work for you, isn't it? What am I to you?" I asked, a wave of anger rushing through my veins. "Am I just part of a motorcycle club charity outreach program or something?"

His eyes widened. "Evie, no, I didn't mean—"

"You kissed me because you feel sorry for me, don't you?"

"*Hang the fuck on*," he growled. "I wanted to kiss you the first night we met, but you ran."

"Yeah, because you nodded at me like a—like a—king summoning one of his mistresses!" I began to pace across the kitchen. "Don't do me any favors, Savage. I won't be a conquest. And I won't be your stray. Thanks for the tacos. You can go now."

He raised his brows. His black eye was slowly fading; it was turning purple. It only reminded me that he was a fighter, a biker; a man I had no business getting involved with. I'd let my guard down and Savage had wasted no time at all worming his way into my life.

I hadn't been careful. I hadn't kept the promise I'd made to myself—stay unattached. Stay uninvolved.

"You're not a conquest," he said, jarring me out of my thoughts. "And if anyone feels like a stray, it's me. Showing up on your doorstep with a taco bribe so you'll let me sleep next to you because I—I don't sleep, Evie. Not for more than a few hours at a time, and never deeply. But that night you were next to me . . . waking up with you . . . no bullshit. It was—my mind was quiet. Do you know what that's like?"

I pondered his words, felt them deep inside all the way

down to my marrow. "Yes. Because I don't have a quiet mind either."

We both fell silent.

I reached for the taco and unwrapped it. I squeezed a lime wedge over the top of it and then took a huge bite. I moaned in delight.

"For the love of Christ," Savage muttered.

"What?"

"What? What do you mean *what*? The noises you make when you enjoy food are downright pornographic."

My eyes widened.

His gaze was steady, bright, and fixated on me. "You're peace and chaos wrapped in a gorgeous package and I don't know what to do with you."

It seemed Savage was just as confused about our connection as I was.

I picked up the tin foil covered plate that rested on the counter and placed it near him. "I made brownies."

"Yeah?"

I nodded. "I left a plate for Cozy earlier. But I made extra."

He unwrapped the plate. He picked up a brownie and took a bite, his eyes closing in enjoyment.

"Good?" I asked with a knowing smile.

His eyes flipped open. "Better than good. You're hot *and* you bake. I'm in so much fucking trouble."

I bit my lip. "Savage, I'm not ready to—if you sleep in my bed, it's just to sleep. Okay?"

"Okay," he said easily.

My exhale was shaky.

"The idea of having sex with me terrifies you," he murmured.

"I've—I've heard some things about you . . . in the bedroom."

"My reputation precedes me?" He grimaced. "What did you hear?"

"Let's see; in the short time I've known you, I've already heard you're an *animal* and *maniac*."

"I'd never hurt you," he said softly.

I swallowed; my throat suddenly parched. "It's not *that*. It's—I don't have a lot of experience, Savage. And from the sound of it, you do."

"I do," he admitted. "I won't shy away from that. Tell me about your past."

"What?"

"How many men have you been with?"

I nibbled my lip which drew his attention. "One."

"One," he repeated.

I nodded, feeling the heat rise to my cheeks.

"Is your hesitation because of your lack of experience or because the experience was terrible?"

My eyes widened in shock.

"It all makes sense," he said slowly. "The motel, the cash job under the table, your skittishness at getting too close to me—or anyone, really. You're on the run from your ex, aren't you?"

I shook my head in negation.

"You can be honest with me," he urged.

"He's not my ex."

His brows slashed together in confusion. "You mean you're still with him?"

"No, I mean—" I took a deep breath, "—he died, Savage. It was a bad marriage, and I was left with nothing. I'm not running from anyone. I'm just trying to start over."

Savage took a step toward me tentatively, like he was afraid I'd bolt if he approached too quickly. "Fuck, Evie. I'm sorry."

Tears, unwelcome and unbidden came to my eyes. I

hastily turned away from him so he wouldn't see, but it was too late. He set a hand on my shoulder and gently turned me toward him, pushing me into the wall of his chest. I pressed my cheek against his shirt and breathed him in, my breaths rickety, the tears falling even though I didn't want them to.

"I'll help you start over," he whispered gruffly. "Whatever you need. You need time? I can give you time."

But my worry was that I didn't want time. That I was suddenly hurling myself toward him like a comet toward the Earth. And I worried that I wasn't making a good decision, and I was afraid of the fallout.

But there was this man—this strong, beautiful man—who protected me, found me a safe place to live and a job where my heart didn't beat in fear every time a large man stepped toward me.

"Maybe I am a stray," I admitted softly.

His fingers drove through my hair, and he gently tugged my head back so he could stare into my eyes.

I got lost in his gaze. Pools of brightness banished the darkness of my past.

"Maybe we can be strays together."

Chapter 10

Savage continued to hold me long after I'd recovered. When I finally made a move to leave the security of his embrace, his arms tightened.

"Another minute," he murmured, resting his chin on my head.

I smiled against him.

"Waverly told me once that a twenty second hug triggers the release of oxytocin which helps reduce stress, improves your mood, and deepens emotional connection."

"We've hugged longer than twenty seconds," I pointed out.

"Hmm. True. But I like you here." He squeezed me and then let me go.

Savage grabbed the plate of brownies and headed toward the bedroom.

"What are you doing?" I asked, turning off the light and following him.

"When I wake up in the middle of the night, I'm going to need a snack. Don't want to risk waking you, ergo, the plate of brownies is going next to the bed."

"Ergo, huh?" I asked with a smile.

The bed was already mussed, and I made a move to straighten it up. Savage placed the plate on the nightstand and then sat down to take off his boots. After he did, he stood again and then hung up his leather cut and stripped out of his jeans and shirt.

That left him in nothing but a pair of boxers with his bare chest exposed.

My eyes widened. "*Oh my.*"

He smirked. "Oh my? Is that your version of a swear word? If so you gotta put a dollar in the jar."

I bit my lip to stifle my grin. "Not even close. You will be the only one contributing to the swear jar."

"What are you going to do with all the money I end up shelling out?"

"Not sure. Maybe I'll buy myself a present." My gaze wandered back over his body. I stared at his thigh.

His muscular thigh. The thigh I wanted to bite.

Good lord.

"Eyes up here, babe. I'm not a piece of meat."

My head shot up and he grinned.

I gestured to the bathroom, flustered at being caught staring at him. "I don't have a spare toothbrush, but feel free to finger brush with toothpaste."

"A woman concerned about oral hygiene. I like that." He winked and then sauntered to the bathroom.

Yeah, I'm in so much trouble.

The admission about my past hadn't tripped him up. And my show of emotion hadn't terrified him either.

Savage returned to the bedroom, and I went to brush my teeth. I looked in the mirror. My cheeks were flushed and the shadows beneath my eyes were disappearing.

Maybe I was slowly coming back to the land of the

living. Maybe my husband hadn't beaten the spirit out of me.

I rinsed my mouth and dried my face with the hand towel. After shutting off the light, I went back to the bedroom.

Savage had already climbed into bed and made himself comfortable. The lamp next to the bed was turned on so I hit the main light, and the room went mostly dark. I crawled into bed and flipped over onto my back, pulling the covers up to my chin.

"That's not really going to work for me," Savage said.

I looked at him. "What do you mean?"

Without a word, he lifted his arm and patted his chest. "Let me turn off the lamp."

The room was suddenly bathed in total darkness as I scooted closer to him and settled in the crook of his body. My hand went to his pec, and he covered it with his own.

"Thank you," he murmured.

"For what?"

"For letting me stay the night . . ."

"Thanks for wanting to be here," I replied.

He brushed his lips against my forehead. "Night, Evie."

⁓

The next morning, I found myself sprawled on top of Savage. My hip was hiked over his waist, and I felt his erection pressing against my leg. My nightgown was bunched around my waist. I felt his hot skin . . . everywhere.

Embarrassment coasted through my belly, but delicious desire pooled between my legs.

I hesitantly looked up to see if Savage was still sleeping. He wasn't.

His blue eyes were open and clear.

I swallowed. "I should move."

Savage's arm tightened around me. "Don't you dare."

"But I'm—"

"Exactly where I want you to be," he interrupted.

I bit my lip in worry, his gaze dropping to my mouth. And before I could over think the moment his lips covered mine and his hands delved into my tousled hair.

He held me to him as he rolled me over onto the bed so that I was on my back. Savage hovered over me. Our bare legs tangled, and he deepened the kiss.

I closed my eyes and sank into the mattress, and I wrapped one leg around him to keep him pressed against me.

His hand skated up my leg to grip my outer thigh. He kissed me as he stroked my skin.

I tumbled deeper into the cavern of desire where there was no light, only the sensations of Savage's warm breath, his tender touch, and the leisurely, easy movements he made to tantalize me.

I wrenched my mouth from his and sucked in a breath of air. "Savage," I moaned.

"I know," he said, pressing his forehead to mine. "God, I know."

With a groan he forced himself away from me.

My fingers went to my lips. They were swollen and tingly.

With just a few kisses, my body was begging for him. It was greedy and demanding, and it took over every part of my being.

My mind had no say in the matter.

He looked at me, his eyes liquid with need.

I licked my lips. "Please."

"Please what?"

"I want you, Savage."

"I know, baby. I can feel the heat of you."

Savage moved toward me, sliding his leg between my thighs and gently pressing against my cleft.

I moaned as sparks of pleasure shot through my core.

"You want me?" he rasped.

I nodded eagerly.

"Not right now," he murmured, dotting my skin with his lips. "Not this morning."

"Why not?" I panted as his hands skated across my body.

"Because I want time with you. Nice and slow. Not a quick fuck."

"Savage—"

"Yes, I am a savage. An animal. But you deserve to be fucking worshipped. You don't deserve a quick roll in the hay."

"Rolling in hay can be fun," I purred.

"You're a vixen." He laughed softly. "Plenty of time for *rolls in the hay*. We'll get there. Trust me."

I sighed in remorse, my ardor cooling despite the heat of his body near mine.

He kissed me on the lips, quickly, and then pulled back. "So, let's drink some coffee and in a few hours, I'll drive you to work. And tonight, I'm taking you out to dinner."

"Dinner?"

"Yeah, babe. It's called a date. And I promise it won't be at a taco truck."

Chapter 11

"Evie? Earth to Evie." Virgil waved his hand in front of my face.

I snapped to attention. "Sorry, what did you say?"

"I asked if you could move my three o'clock to four, and you didn't even reply because you look all comatose. What were you thinking about?"

Savage—naked and inside me.

"Uh, groceries," I lied. "Sure, I can change that for you. No problem. Sorry."

"Great. Hey, me and the guys are going out tonight for darts and beer. You wanna come?"

Joy fizzed through me at his invitation. Despite my resolve to remain aloof, his smile was so affable, so open, that I found myself nodding. "Yeah, that sounds great. Except I can't drink."

"What do you mean?" His brow furrowed.

"I mean, I'm only twenty."

"Holy shit, you're only twenty?"

"Well, yeah." I frowned. "Why? Is that a problem?"

"Nope. My crush is cured," he stated.

Heartbeats & Highways

"Crush? What crush?"

"My crush on you," he explained with a grin. "Don't worry, I won't let it get in the way of our working relationship."

I snorted. "I'm glad to hear that."

"Plus, I'm pretty sure Savage would've punched my lights out if I made a move on you considering he's already claimed you. So this is good, actually. We'll be friends. Yeah, friends . . . I can have female friends."

Claimed me?

I wanted to ask Virgil to expand on his comment, but his cell rang, and he answered it, effectively ending our conversation as he left the room.

Why did the idea of Savage claiming me make my insides flutter and desire pulse between my thighs?

While there was a lull, I texted Savage about the invite to hang out with the Jackson brothers.

SAVAGE

> Yeah, let's go with them. We'll have our date another night.

I hadn't meant to invite him along, but I wasn't going to try and explain that through a text.

"I hear you're going out with us tonight," Roman said as he entered the front room.

"Yeah, is that okay?" I asked quietly.

"More than okay," he assured me.

"Is it okay if Savage comes?"

"Sure thing." He paused, looking like he wanted to say something. "Do you like peanut butter crackers?"

I blinked. "Yes."

"Hang on, let me get some and then we're going to have a talk."

I looked in the direction Virgil had gone.

"He's on the phone with our mom. Trust me, it'll be a while." Roman left the room to grab the snacks and then returned.

"What do you know about the Tarnished Angels?" Roman asked, opening a package of crackers and handing them to me.

I smiled at his fraternal instincts and took the package. "Uh, not much. Just that Savage is part of the club."

"Look, I don't normally get involved in other people's business, but you work here. And I know *how* you came to work here. And as the oldest, my big brother instinct is strong."

I shifted on my feet, waiting for him to continue.

"They don't operate within the normal bounds of society. They're *bikers*."

"Who live a certain kind of life that most people wouldn't resonate with?"

"Something like that, yeah." He frowned. "Not too long ago, they were involved in some really bad shit. And bad shit doesn't just go away because you decide it does."

I swallowed, thinking of my own past. "You're warning me to stay away, aren't you?"

"No. I'm too late for that already. I see how Savage looks at you. I'm just saying be careful. Tread lightly."

I pondered his words. "Thanks for looking out for me."

His smile was easy. "Sure."

"I'll think about what you said."

"No, you won't." He shook his head.

"I won't?"

"Nope. You're already involved with Savage. They say when you stop looking for a relationship, that's when it happens."

"I wasn't looking for a relationship," I murmured.

"My point exactly," he drawled.

"Are you single, Roman?"

"Yes. I'm afraid of love," he replied dramatically.

"Oh please." I laughed.

"I'm not sure. Why do *you* think I'm still single at thirty-six?"

I rolled my eyes. "You're not single because you're afraid, that's for sure."

"No? Then why am I single?"

"Commitment shy, maybe?"

"No."

"You just haven't found the right woman yet," I suggested.

"I guess."

He suddenly looked tired, like exhaustion was weighing him down.

"What's your type?" I asked.

"Why?"

"Just curious."

"Tattoos and attitude."

"That's kind of vague."

He grinned and shrugged. "There's plenty of women who'll keep me company until I find the right one."

I laughed. "And there it is."

"And there it is," Roman agreed.

～

Savage was waiting for me when I walked out of Three Kings. If the Jackson brothers weren't behind me, watching, I would've run to him and demanded he kiss me.

But I forced myself to remain steady as I approached him.

He was leaning against his bike. "Is that any way to greet me?"

I paused for a moment and then launched myself against him. He caught me and gave me a kiss that had my head spinning.

Hoots and hollers sounded behind us.

"When you two stop groping each other," Virgil called, "meet us at Spurs!"

Savage saluted but kept one arm around me. He looked down at me. "I missed you."

"Yeah?"

"Yeah. Did you miss me?"

"We were only a part for a few hours," I said with a laugh.

"Yeah, and I couldn't stop fantasizing about your mouth and your legs." He leaned down and whispered in my ear, "Specifically your legs wrapped around me, and you pressing yourself against me."

My heart thundered in my chest.

I pulled back and smiled at him. "We should go."

He nodded and handed me a helmet.

We climbed onto his motorcycle and zoomed out of the parking lot.

Spurs was a cowboy bar and restaurant. It wasn't overly crowded, and the Jackson brothers had already grabbed a table near one of the pool tables.

"We already put an order in for wings and nachos," Roman said as we joined them.

Homer glanced at me, an annoyed expression on his face.

Did he not want me here?

A waitress came by to take our drink order. Savage grabbed my chair and scooted it closer to him and then placed his arm around my shoulder.

Virgil smirked at Savage's demonstrative show of physical attention.

"So," Virgil said. "What kind of tattoo are you getting, Evie?"

I frowned. "A tattoo?"

Roman nodded. "You work at a tattoo parlor. Your tattoos are on the house."

"Oh." I nibbled my lip. "That's nice of you. But I don't want a tattoo."

"How can you not want a tattoo?" Virgil demanded. "Everyone wants a tattoo."

I grinned at his astonishment. "Not me."

Our waitress returned with our drinks and passed them out around the table. "Food should be up shortly."

She left and Roman continued the conversation. "Well, if you ever change your mind, let us know."

"Yeah, and hypothetically, who would you choose to ink you?" Virgil asked.

"Not you," Savage piped up, taking a pint. "I've seen the way you look at her ass."

"Easy, man," Virgil stated. "She's got hearts in her eyes, but only for you."

Savage looked at me. "Is that true?"

I smiled at him but said nothing.

"You wanna throw some darts before the food comes?" he asked.

I nodded.

He stood back and took my hand, helping me up from my chair. The dart board we walked to was on the other side of the bar, far enough away from our table that the Jackson brothers couldn't hear our conversation.

"He's hit on you already, hasn't he?" Savage asked.

"Who? Virgil?"

"Yeah."

"You don't have anything to worry about with Virgil."

"That means I'm right," Savage said. "Did he ask you out?"

I placed my hand on Savage's chest. "No. Let it go, Savage."

He covered my hand with his and nodded. "You throw first."

"I don't think Homer likes me," I said as I came back from the dartboard with the darts in hand.

"He doesn't really like anyone," Savage said. "Don't take it personally."

I faced the dart board and let it rip. My first dart landed near the edge of the board. "I do take it personally. I work for him. I'd like our interactions not to be so . . . tense."

"Has he said anything to you?"

I shook my head. "On the contrary, he doesn't talk to me at all."

"So wait, you *want* him to talk to you?"

I threw another dart; this one landed closer to the bullseye. "I want him not to look at me like I'm an inconvenience or like I'm in his way."

"Ah, gotcha. You want me to talk to him for you?"

"*No!*" I shouted. The bartender looked at me in curiosity. I shot him a smile and then focused on Savage. "No," I repeated again, much softer this time. "I want to handle it myself. I'll just give it some time."

My last dart hit the bullseye, giving me a great feeling of satisfaction. Savage went to the board and gathered the darts. He was a much better dart thrower than I was and stacked his darts on the triple twenty and the outer bullseye ring.

"Don't feel bad," he teased. "I've spent far too many hours throwing darts with Duke and Willa."

"Practice makes perfect," I joked. "I'm going to use the bathroom before the food comes out."

"Right through there." Savage pointed to the doorway that was tucked toward the back of the bar.

I turned to leave him when he grasped my hand. "You're forgetting something."

"What?" I frowned.

He tapped his mouth and grinned.

Laughing, I stepped forward and placed my lips on his for a quick peck.

"That's better."

I used the restroom and came back out onto the floor, a smile on my face in anticipation of seeing Savage again.

A huge body stepped in front of me.

I ground to a halt and looked up at the man wearing a black cowboy hat and a button-down shirt with pearl snap buttons. "Excuse me," I said, trying to step around him.

"Where you goin', darlin'?" His brown eyes flickered with interest as he raised his beer pint to his lips and took a sip. "Can I buy you a drink?"

"No, thank you." My tone was polite but firm, even though my heart thundered in fear.

When I tried to step around him, he mirrored my movement and effectively blocked me from leaving.

"Please move." My voice trembled.

He snaked a free hand out and grasped my waist to haul me to him. My nose collided with his chest, and I got a whiff of his pungent aroma.

Bile churned in my belly.

"Let me go!" I shouted.

He leered down at me, appearing like he hadn't heard me. Or if he did, he didn't care.

I placed my hands on his chest and attempted to shove him away, but he felt like a wall of bricks.

Suddenly, Savage appeared behind the big man, like an apparition clad in leather and danger.

"You heard the lady," Savage stated, his voice low.

"Buzz off," the man growled, gazing over his shoulder at Savage. "This is between me and the pretty little redhead."

"Dude, you do not want to make me tell you again," Savage stated.

My gaze was trained on Savage, but he didn't look away from the threat to glance at me.

"You got a problem, Ox?" Another man approached and stood next to Ox.

Savage's eyebrows raised. "Ox? Your name is Ox?"

Ox puffed out his chest which only made him seem bigger. "Of course, dumb ass. I'm as big as an ox. You *do not* want to fuck around and find out tonight, boy."

Something flashed over Savage's face. "What if I do?"

"What's going on?" Roman demanded, appearing with Homer and Virgil and flanking Savage. The three of them were coiled, ready to spring into action.

"Ox was just letting me go." I looked up at Ox. "Weren't you?"

He glanced down at me and blinked sluggishly. He'd had one too many beers. I could see the sheen in his eyes.

A bell rang from the kitchen, signaling food was up, but it reminded me of the illegal fighting ring and the start of a round.

Only now we were in public and the last thing I wanted was for Savage to go all . . . *Savage*.

I wanted to do everything in my power to diffuse the situation, so I once again pushed away from Ox, gently this time.

He let me go.

I immediately side-stepped Ox and slid in between him

and Savage, placing myself in front of Savage who hadn't taken his eyes off Ox.

"Savage," I murmured. "Savage, *look* at me."

My hands came up to cradle his face.

Finally, whatever spell was cast on him broke and his gaze slid to mine.

We stared at each other for a few heart beats.

"Take me home," I commanded.

Chapter 12

Savage closed the apartment door behind me and leaned against it for a moment.

"You shouldn't have done that," Savage said.

"Done what?" I demanded, whirling.

"Gotten in front of me. I wasn't . . ."

"In your right mind?" I asked gently.

His blue eyes burned with intensity as he looked at me and inclined his head in affirmation. "How did you know you'd get through to me?"

"I didn't." I bit my lip. "But I couldn't stand there and let you get into a fight. I couldn't let the Jackson brothers get dragged into it either."

"We could've held our own, no problem. We could've taken the dumb oaf and any of his friends."

I nodded. "Yes, I know you could have. That's why I had to stop it."

"I don't get it."

"I've seen you fight, Savage," I said. "I know what you're capable of. In the ring, you're lethal. But out here, in the real world . . . what would've happened if you'd really hurt him? The police could've gotten involved. I didn't want you in that kind of trouble."

He absently rubbed the back of his neck. "Didn't think about any of that shit. I never do. I just saw the fear in your eyes when he wouldn't let you go."

I took a step closer to him. And then another.

"I know." I placed my hand on his heart, loving the solid steady rhythm of it. "I've never had anyone want to protect me like you do."

"I'll always protect you, Evie. I'd kill for you."

My eyes widened in shock.

"You don't know my world," he said gruffly. "But we protect our women. By any means necessary."

I might not know the biker world, but I knew Savage. And to me that was a declaration.

Despite my better judgement, despite my desire not to get attached, I was tired of running, tired of fighting. I wanted him. Every piece of him. His good, his bad, his ugly. Because even his ugly was beautiful to me.

I was falling for a man named Savage.

"Savage," I whispered, tears glistening in my eyes. "I want—I need you. Take me to bed."

"You sure, babe?" his tone was soft, but intense. "Because there's no going back after this. You'll be mine."

I exhaled a trembling breath but boldly met his gaze. "Make me yours."

We stared at one another for a moment and then he leaned close, pausing just before he got to my mouth. And then his lips took mine. He slid his tongue between them, and I welcomed him. I opened my mouth and let him in.

Let him all the way in.

My hands pressed to his chest and worked their way across his shoulders. My fingers tangled in the hair at his nape.

He gently urged me toward the couch and laid me down, so I was flat on my back. Savage loomed over me, his mouth weaving an erotic spell.

His hand slid underneath my flannel to rest on the swell of my breast. His thumb grazed my nipple over my camisole, and when it pebbled, he groaned into my mouth.

"I need to see you, babe," he whispered.

"Yes," I gasped.

"Let me see you."

I opened my eyes and stared into his. They were glimmering jewels of need, raking me over and causing me to shiver.

He sat back and lifted himself off me. But only so he could hold out his hand to me. I placed my palm in his and he hoisted me up. And then he led me to the bedroom.

Savage stared down at me.

He slowly unbuttoned my shirt and removed it. Then he peeled off my camisole and tossed it aside. His hands reverently cupped my breasts.

"God, you're beautiful," he croaked.

"I need to see you too," I demanded.

He reluctantly took a step back so he could take off his leather cut. He placed it on the back of the chair and then tugged his shirt over his wide shoulders.

And then he came to me.

My fingers traced the ink along his pec.

He bent his head and pressed his warm lips to my sternum. His hands slid to my rib cage and held me as his mouth continued its descent.

When his lips met the band of my pants, he looked up at me.

I nodded.

His fingers went to the snap of my pants and then he was rolling them down my legs.

Heartbeats & Highways

I was suddenly embarrassed that I was wearing cotton briefs. They were white and cheap. I wanted to wear lace and beautiful things and have Savage take them off like he was unwrapping a present.

His nose nudged the elastic of my underwear, and he inched it lower with his teeth.

"You tease." I chuckled.

"I'm savoring the moment," he said quietly, looking up at me again. "Haven't you ever wanted to savor something?"

I ran my thumb across his expressive mouth. "Not like this. But there's a first time for everything."

He smiled and then he slowly tugged down my underwear, letting it pool around my ankles. I stepped out of it and stood completely bare before him.

And then he did something I never expected; he grasped my butt cheeks and squeezed the right one.

"Lift," he commanded.

I lifted my leg which he settled over his shoulder, baring me to him.

He buried his nose in the thatch of red curls between my legs. He inhaled deeply. "God all-fucking-mighty."

Heat bloomed in my cheeks, both in embarrassment and desire.

His tongue darted out to taste me and I thought I was going to combust.

Savage's grip on me tightened as his tongue became determined. It sought my pleasure; it chased my need.

"Mhmm," he rumbled.

My fingers slid through his hair and cradled his head, letting him devour me. He sucked me into his mouth, and I bucked against him.

"Like that, do you?" he murmured. "You're going to

come on my tongue, Evie. You're going to come so hard and you're gonna demand more."

"Yes." I gasped as his words pushed me closer to the edge.

He flattened his tongue and played with the tender place between my thighs. He swirled and lapped, and I shook with the need to come.

"Savage," I whispered.

"Let go, babe. Let it all go."

He licked harder and harder until I had no choice but to scream and come. Savage clamped my thigh, keeping me open and in place, but he still didn't stop stroking me with his tongue.

My breaths came in pants and my eyes opened.

Savage looked up at me, his eyes wicked, his mouth glinting with my release. He gently lowered my thigh and stood. He leaned down and kissed me with tongue. I tasted myself on him and it only made me ravenous.

"More," I begged.

He grinned and gently placed his hand on my sternum before giving me a slight push. I fell back against the bed and opened my legs.

Savage stripped out of his jeans and boxers and my eyes widened at his massive erection.

He took himself in hand and began to stroke his length. "I want to do filthy things to you, Evie."

"Like what?" I panted.

"I want to touch myself while I watch you do the same and when I come, I want to come all over your belly. And then I want to flip you over and fuck you from behind, nice and slow. And after I've recovered, I want to fuck your mouth. I want to feel myself at the back of your throat. I've got plans, babe. So many plans."

"I think you're all talk and no action." My head dipped and I looked at his shaft and licked my lips.

He suddenly stopped stroking himself, but only so he could reach into his jeans pocket and retrieve a condom.

I arched a brow. "How long have you been carrying that around?"

"Long enough. I wanted to be prepared so that when you were ready, nothing could stop us. I told you I'd protect you. In all ways . . ."

My heart melted in my chest. I held out my hand to him.

He climbed onto the bed and ripped the wrapper with his teeth.

The tip of him glistened with pre-cum and my mouth watered. I wanted to taste him.

"Later," he growled. "You can taste me later."

"Did I say that out loud?"

"Yes."

"I had no idea," I murmured. "I feel like I'm under a spell."

"Me too."

He rolled the condom down his large shaft. He leaned over me and propped himself up on an elbow. With his other hand, he guided his erection toward my opening.

I was slick from my release, but I wasn't satisfied.

He teased his crown at the seam of my body, and I felt the head of him glide in.

"Oh God," he moaned as he slid inside me, filling me.

I gasped at the feeling of him. He was large and I wiggled, trying to adjust to him. Every movement sent sparks of pleasure shooting down my spine.

"You're gorgeous. Flushed everywhere." He lifted my leg and wrapped it around his waist. "Hang on, babe. I'm gonna make you come again."

He slid his hands beneath my bottom and angled his pelvis. I cried out in joy and my eyes rolled into the back of my head.

"Eyes on me," he commanded.

My eyes flipped open, and I stared into Savage's soul. His thrusts became ruthless, dominating. I was so primed, so eager, my body a slave to his.

I arched up, meeting him demand for demand.

"Come with me, Evie," he growled.

I clenched around him as my second orgasm tore through me. Wave after wave of rapture pulsed through my body and then Savage gripped my hip and slammed into me.

Savage roared like an animal, clasping me to him before stilling. He collapsed on top of me, burying his face in the crook of my neck.

I could barely breathe, but I didn't care. I never wanted him to leave.

"Evie?"

"Hmm?"

"My leg is cramping."

I giggled.

He lifted himself up and stared down at me, an unburdened smile spreading across his face. He kissed my forehead, the tip of my nose, and then my lips.

"Give me a moment to recover," he whispered against my mouth. "And then we're doing that again."

Chapter 13

My night was filled with passion.

Savage had only the one condom, but I found there were so many other ways to share pleasure.

He opened my eyes to a world I knew nothing about. He cared more about my satisfaction than his and he spent hours discovering what I liked.

In between bouts of love making, we showered, we cooked, we built intimacy with tender touches and lingering looks.

It was three o'clock in the morning and we were in bed, the bedside lamp casting a warm glow. I studied his tattoos and ran my fingers along his ink.

"How did you get the name Savage? Is it a nickname?"

He shook his head. "It's a road name. A name my brothers gave me. My real name is Cooper. Cooper Boddington."

"You do *not* look like a Cooper," I said with a smile. "Savage suits you."

"Thanks, I think." He looked thoughtful. Savage raised

his hand and flipped it over; he pointed to a tattoo at the base of his thumb.

"I've known Duke and Willa since we were kids," he began. "Duke and I were in the foster system, and Willa may as well have been. Her mother wasn't around a lot . . . Anyway, the three of us have been thick as thieves since we were children. We all have the same tattoo, a three-leaf clover. Two leaves tattered and torn, and one perfect one. The perfect one is Willa."

I took his hand and brought it closer so I could see his tattoo better. I traced a finger across it. "It's not faded. Don't these things fade with age?"

"I recently got it touched up." His hand curled around mine. "My childhood was bad, Evie. Really bad. And the club . . . they gave me a place to channel the rage that I'd been carrying around inside of me since I was young. I'll tell you more in time. But I gotta give it to you in pieces."

"There's a lot to it, isn't there?"

"Yeah."

"So the three of you grew up here?"

"Yeah." He looked down at me. "What about you? You said you grew up on a farm."

"Yeah, I did."

"In Texas?"

"In Oklahoma. Near Broken Bow." I snuggled against him.

"And your husband . . . how did you meet him?"

"I really don't want to talk about him," I stated.

"Okay." He shrugged like it didn't bother him. "Tell me more about the farm. What was it like?"

"Smelly," I joked.

"Do you know how to milk goats?"

I sighed. "Yes. And cows."

He smiled. "What about chickens?"

"You don't milk chickens."

"No . . . did you collect eggs?"

"Yes. And I killed roosters too. Anything else you want to know?"

He scratched his ear. "Did you like it?"

"Parts of it," I admitted.

"Like what?"

"The self-sufficiency. We had a garden, some fruit trees, our own meat." I shrugged. "It's hard, I guess. Busy. There was always something to do. Some project that needed to be done."

"Do you miss it?"

"I don't miss being bound to it."

"What do you mean?"

"I mean, when you live on a farm there are animals that rely on you. Rain or shine. They'll take care of you and provide, but you have to take care them too. It's a lot of work."

"Sounds like it."

"I'm not sure how I feel about the city just yet."

"No?"

"Everything is both easy and hard. Does that make sense?"

"Not really."

I smiled. "It's loud, too. Very loud. I'm still not used to the noise."

"So, you prefer farm life, even with all its cons?"

"I understand farm life. I'm not sure I understand city life. It all feels so . . . I don't know. Working hard feels different in the city. It feels insurmountable, actually."

"Explain that to me."

I sighed. "Well, for example, my job."

"You don't like your job at Three Kings?"

"It's not that. It's just . . . it doesn't feel like it matters?

I'm doing this thing that occupies my time. I take home a paycheck. But it doesn't feel like I'm actually *doing* anything. I don't know how to explain it."

"It's the hamster on the wheel." Savage pressed a kiss to my head. "Every day looks the same. You run and run, but no matter what you do you don't feel like you're getting anywhere."

"Yes, exactly. On the farm you feed your chickens, then the next day you gather eggs. You plant a garden and then you harvest it and eat what you grew. You keep bees and they give you honey. It's *real*."

"You had bees?"

I nodded. "We had this garden that wasn't for planting. It was full of wildflowers for butterflies and bees to feed from and pollinate. It was my favorite spot, actually." I looked at him and gave him a wry smile. "Like I said, I'm not sure how I feel about city life just yet."

We fell into companionable silence until he spoke again.

"You really don't want a tattoo?" he asked, his gaze languid.

"I really don't."

"You'd look good with a tattoo here." He traced the knobs of my spine.

"But I'd never be able to see it," I remarked.

His grin was devilish. "But I would."

"How would—*oh.*"

Savage laughed and wrapped me in his arms, pulling me on top of him. "Think about it."

"Oh, I am."

He shifted his thigh so that it pressed between my legs. "I'm dying to be inside you again."

"Next time, bring more condoms."

"Tonight. I'll bring a mega-box, and we'll see how

many we can get through." He tucked a strand of hair behind my ear.

"Those girls were right. You *are* an animal in bed." My teasing smile dimmed when he didn't smile back. "Savage?"

"I'm sorry about them," he said softly. "I'm sorry you had to hear that."

"It's fine, Savage. I won in the end, didn't I?" I touched his furrowed brow with my fingers. "I got you in my bed and I'm keeping you."

"You're keeping me?" he asked, a slow smile sliding across his lips.

"Yep. You're mine." I leaned down and gently bit his nipple.

He sucked in a breath. "I think I'm going to like being kept."

～

"You got laid," Virgil said as I set my purse on the counter of the tattoo parlor.

"Excuse me?" I squawked.

"Yeah, you totally got laid," he said again. "Your eyes are bloodshot, your cheeks are flushed, and you've got whisker burn on your neck. I'm totally right. Right?"

"Even if I did get laid—which I'm not saying I did— do you really think I'd talk about my private life with you?"

"I've never been more convinced that I'm right," he said.

"What are you right about?" Roman asked as he appeared from the back.

"Evie got laid."

I groaned. "Shut *up*, Virgil."

"Yeah, shut up, Virgil," Roman reiterated. "Evie's private life is private."

"Thank you, Roman." I beamed at him.

"So, it doesn't matter if she looks happier than we've ever seen her or that we caught the goodbye kiss between her and Savage before she came inside and that we all know the truth. It's not our concern."

I glared at him.

He winked.

"Why are you guys spying on me?" I demanded.

"Spying? Who's spying?" Virgil asked. "You were right there. Out in public. For everyone to see."

"Oh," I said slowly. "I get it now."

"Get what?" Virgil asked.

"You're not getting *any*, so you've got nothing to occupy you. Got it."

"Hey, I'm getting plenty," Virgil boasted.

"Sure, uh-huh."

"You okay?" Roman asked, his eyes filled with concern. "I mean about last night at Spurs and that shit going down."

"Nothing went down," I protested.

"Yeah, because you stopped it." Virgil shook his head. "I can't believe you got Savage to walk away from a fight."

"Thanks for talking him down." Roman clenched his fist. "We would've gotten involved, but I'm glad it didn't come to that."

I frowned. "What if there had been a fight?"

"We would've backed up Savage," Virgil said easily.

Roman stared at me. "I saw your face, Evie. You were scared. And that's not okay. Not at all."

"Yeah." Virgil nodded and placed his hand on my shoulder. "We were ready to protect you. Sorry, Evie. You're stuck with us."

His words made tears fill my eyes.

"Oh, no. Don't do it," Virgil warned. "Don't cry."

"Can't help it," I mumbled, reaching for the tissues.

"All you do is make women cry," Roman quipped.

"One of my many talents," Virgil drawled. "One of my many talents."

Chapter 14

"Okay, we'll see you then. Bye." I hung up the phone, made sure the appointment was logged in the computer system, and then focused on the customer patiently waiting at the reception counter.

I shot her a bright smile. "Hi, thanks for your patience. What can I do for you?"

She smiled back. "Hi, my name's Brittany. I have an appointment with Homer at 12:45."

I looked at the computer and clicked the mouse. "Great, you're all checked in. He'll be out in just a few minutes. Can I get you something to drink? Water? A soda?"

"No thanks, I'm good." She tossed glossy brown hair over her shoulder. "Can I ask you something?"

"Sure."

She leaned closer and lowered her voice. "Is Homer seeing anyone?"

"Seeing anyone?" I repeated.

"Dating," she clarified.

"Oh." I frowned. "I—uh—don't know, actually."

"This is my second visit," she whispered conspiratorially. "And I'm dying to ask him out. But he's kind of aloof, so I don't know if he'll say yes."

I'd worked at Three Kings for a week, and Homer had yet to warm to me. Whenever I had a question, I asked Virgil or Roman, steering clear of the grumpy Jackson brother entirely.

"Yeah, sorry." I shot her a smile of commiseration. "I don't have any insight for you."

"I'm gonna go for it," she announced. She took a seat on the leather couch and picked up a magazine.

My stomach rumbled and I was dying for a hardy meal. But the guys hadn't come out and requested lunch orders yet. I grabbed the banana from my bag and wolfed it down.

Homer appeared from the back hallway. He glanced at me finishing off the last of my snack and frowned. I hastily tossed the peel into the trash. He turned his attention to his pretty client, who not so subtly straightened her spine which thrust her breasts forward.

"Brittany," he greeted. "You ready?"

"Sure thing." She stood and picked up her purse and sauntered toward him. His expression didn't change as he guided her toward his tattoo chair.

The front door opened. I looked to the entrance, a smile of greeting waiting on my lips. Brielle strode through, a brunette ambling in behind her.

"Hey, girl," Brielle greeted.

"Hi," I said.

"I brought you and the boys lunch," Brielle announced, setting the brown paper bags onto the counter.

"How did you know I was famished?" I asked with a laugh.

"Just luck," Brielle said. "Evie, this is my best friend,

Jazz. Jazz and I own part of Pie in the Sky, but also, we've been friends since high school."

"Nice to meet you," I said, looking at Jazz.

"Nice to finally meet you, too, new girl. I wanted to meet you sooner, but Brielle said not to startle you with my exuberance. How are the guys treating you?" Jazz asked.

A long, fat braid slid off her shoulder as she leaned forward and began to unpack the brown bags.

"They've been great," I said honestly.

"Even Homer?" Brielle inquired with a knowing smile.

"Even Homer."

Jazz looked at Brielle and rolled her eyes. "She's loyal."

"Yeah, since we all know Homer is a grump," Brielle added. "How's Savage?"

"Perfect," I said with a sigh. He gave me a ride to and from work every day. And he'd spent every night the past week in my bed.

"Aww," Jazz said with a smile. "I love the beginning stages of a relationship. All sex and talking."

There was more sex than talking with Savage, but I was definitely not complaining.

"I heard about what happened at Spurs," Brielle said. "That must've been intense."

"I kinda wish I'd been there," Jazz said.

"You didn't miss anything," I stated.

"Yeah, because you got Savage to walk away, right?" Brielle asked. "That's what Roman told me."

"Savage walked away from a fight? Interesting," Jazz murmured, peering at me.

With the Jackson siblings, it was apparent that my private life wasn't going to remain so private.

Duly noted.

Virgil appeared from the back. "Aw, you guys brought us lunch? Awesome. I'm starving."

Heartbeats & Highways

Brielle handed him a container. "Your favorite."

"What's your favorite?" I inquired.

"Grilled cheese with tomato and sweet potato fries, and a side of chipotle aioli for dipping."

I looked at Brielle. "I thought Pie in the Sky was a bakery."

"It is," Brielle said. "But Brooklyn expanded it into a café."

"Ah," I said in understanding.

"We didn't know what you liked, so we brought a few sandwiches," Jazz said.

"Oh, thanks," I said, feeling grateful and at ease. "That's nice."

"Roman gets the BLT." Brielle looked at the containers that all had shorthand writing on them, found the BLT and set it aside.

"Homer gets the turkey avocado with sprouts." Jazz rolled her eyes and moved it to the other side of the counter.

"You can have your pick," Brielle said. "Ham and cheese, chicken pesto, or the caprese."

"Chicken pesto, please," I said.

"Awesome," Jazz said. "That means I get the caprese."

"And I get the ham and cheese," Brielle said. "Yay."

"I'll wait to eat," I announced.

"Why?" Brielle asked. "Dig in now while it's still warm."

I glanced at Virgil who had already opened his sandwich and was chowing down. "Eat," he insisted.

The banana had done nothing to satiate me. I was still hungry. My appetite lately had been insane. No doubt all the calories I was burning because of Savage.

"Okay, if you insist," I said, opening the box with the chicken pesto sandwich.

"So, how do you like working here?" Jazz asked as she stole one of Virgil's fries. He lightly smacked her hand, but then offered her the chipotle sauce.

"I love it," I said as I took a bite of the chicken pesto.

"You don't have to lie just because Virgil is here," Brielle teased.

I grinned as I swallowed. "Oh, wow, this sandwich is so good. And I'm not lying—I am enjoying it. The hours are great, and only one of my bosses is annoying."

"Which boss would that be?" Roman asked as he appeared. "I knew I smelled hot food."

Jazz handed him the box with the BLT.

"Virgil," I teased.

"Hey, I'm not annoying," Virgil said as he literally flicked my ear.

Brielle snorted. "You guys gave me so much shit when I filled in as your receptionist."

"Yeah, because you're our sister," Roman said. "We actually *like* Evie."

Brielle threw a fry at her brother which pegged him in the chest and then fell onto the counter.

"No food fights," Jazz stated.

I took another bite of my sandwich as the four of them teased and joked with each other. It was clear that Jazz was considered a part of the family and Roman and Virgil treated her as such.

Each day, I grew more and more comfortable here. I hadn't even thought of picking up and moving on. Not now.

"I guess you're still taking the bus?" Brielle inquired.

"She takes the bus?" Jazz asked.

"Yeah, she can't drive," Brielle explained.

"Savage has been giving me rides on his bike," I explained. "He's not a fan of me taking the bus."

The chicken suddenly turned sour in my mouth which filled with saliva. I set my sandwich down.

"Evie?" Roman asked. "You don't look so good."

"Her face is pale," Virgil announced.

"I think I ate too fast." I hastily placed a hand in front of my mouth and scrambled off the stool. In my desire to get to the bathroom, I slammed into Roman who hadn't moved out of the way quickly enough.

"Easy there, linebacker," Roman muttered as he rubbed his chest.

I pushed the door open and made it to the toilet just in the nick of time. My body shook and the back of my neck broke out in sweat. Once I was sure the contents of my stomach were empty, I flushed the toilet and then washed my hands. I cupped my palms underneath the water and drank a mouthful, swishing to rid my mouth of the acrid taste of bile.

I wet a paper towel and bathed my brow and then lifted my hair to cool down the back of my neck. My stomach no longer felt jittery.

As I opened the door to the bathroom, the only noise I heard was the faint sound of Homer's tattoo gun. There was no conversation coming from the front room.

Four pairs of eyes watched me retake the stool.

"You okay?" Roman asked gently.

"I think I'm getting sick."

Without pause, Roman placed his hand against my forehead. "You don't feel warm. Just kind of . . . clammy."

"Gross," Virgil muttered.

I glared at Roman. "I'm not clammy. I put a wet paper towel to my forehead. I think I'll get some air."

"Take a ginger ale," Roman said to me.

Nodding, I crouched down to the mini fridge and took the last one.

Homer and Brittany appeared in the front room.

"We brought lunch," Jazz said to Homer. "We made your usual."

"Thanks," he said gruffly.

"I'm ready to pay," Brittany said to me.

"Why don't I get you squared up," Brielle said to Brittany. "Evie's getting some air."

"Thanks," Brittany chirped.

Homer took the box of food.

"See you tonight, Homer," she called.

He didn't reply to her statement, disappearing into the back once again.

I sidled around Roman and trekked toward the front door. Cool air hit my cheeks and immediately made me feel better. I sipped on the ginger ale, letting my stomach settle.

The front door opened, and Brittany stepped outside. She put her sunglasses on and had her keys in her hand. "You okay? I heard you throwing up."

"Yeah, I'm fine. Just an upset belly."

"Whew. Anytime I throw up, I start to worry that I'm pregnant." She shook her head. "So I invited Homer to this place with live music my friend's playing at. I don't know if he'll show, but I hope he will."

She didn't even realize I hadn't replied to her, so lost in her own excitement about a potential date with Homer.

My skin buzzed with terror.

Pregnant. I can't be pregnant.

There was no way . . .

Was there?

"Anyway, see ya," Brittany said. With a wave, she headed toward her car.

My phone buzzed with a text.

SAVAGE

hey babe can't pick you up today. Club shit. I can send a prospect to drive you.

I took a deep breath and replied.

ME

Don't worry about it. I'll take the bus.

SAVAGE

Evie, no

ME

let it go. Will I see you tonight?

SAVAGE

not til late. You'll probably be asleep, so I'll crash at the clubhouse. I'll bring you breakfast tomorrow.

I stuck my phone into my pocket and then went inside.

Brielle and Jazz were cleaning up the remains of lunch. Roman and Virgil had disappeared. No doubt they'd headed into the back.

There was a weird, tense energy in the room, but I couldn't figure out why. Jazz's expression was pinched.

"I'm gonna use the restroom," Brielle said. "Then we can get out of here."

Jazz nodded as she put the last box into the paper bag. The door to the bathroom closed and I was about to ask Jazz what was wrong when the phone rang. I answered it and booked a session with Virgil. As I hung up, the bathroom door opened, and Brielle returned to the main room.

"Ready?" Brielle asked Jazz.

Jazz glanced up from her phone and nodded. "Yeah. Bye, Evie."

"Bye," I called after them.

The door slammed shut and I spent the rest of my shift watching the clock tick by.

Chapter 15

The timer on my phone dinged. I pressed the screen to silence it.

I picked up the home pregnancy test.

Big fat positive plus sign.

The second one had two lines.

The third read PREGNANT.

"Oh, God," I murmured.

The news had me sinking to the floor of the bathroom. I pulled my legs to my chest and rested my forehead on my knees.

I thought I'd escaped my husband. I thought I'd be able to leave the past where it belonged.

But a part of him lived on.

My life had taken a turn for the better. I'd met Savage and he'd opened up something inside of me that I didn't even know existed.

I smiled, I laughed, I loved.

It would all go away—Savage would go away—when I told him I was pregnant.

A sob broke my lips.

I wasn't sure how long I sat on the cold, tiled floor of the bathroom. Long enough for my tailbone to go numb.

Finally, I hoisted myself up. I gripped the counter and looked in the mirror. My skin was pale, and I looked . . . scared.

I didn't want to be scared.

There was a pair of scissors in the kitchen, and I went to retrieve them before returning to the bathroom.

I looked in the mirror again as I combed out my long, waist-length hair. It hadn't been cut in years.

With a deep breath, I started snipping.

I didn't stop until strands of red covered the porcelain sink.

I'd cut off my past.

And I'd look to the future.

~

Savage's mouth dropped open when I answered the door the next morning.

"Your hair . . ."

I touched my head, nervous about his reaction. My hair now fell to the middle of my breasts. "Is it okay? Do you hate it?"

"Hate it? I fucking love it. It was gorgeous before, but the cut suits you." He stepped into the apartment and shut the door behind him. And then he cradled my cheeks in his palms. "You're beautiful."

Savage kissed my lips, clearly wanting to deepen it, but I placed my hand on his chest and gently pushed him back.

He frowned, his hands dropping. "What's wrong?" He cocked his head to the side. "You've got shadows beneath your eyes."

"So do you," I pointed out.

Heartbeats & Highways

"I didn't sleep well without you next to me."

"I didn't sleep at all," I murmured.

"What's wrong, Evie?"

I took a deep breath. "Sit down, Savage."

"I'll stand," he said tightly as he clenched his fists. "Tell me what's going on."

"I'm pregnant," I blurted out.

He blinked. "Pregnant?"

"Pregnant," I confirmed with a nod.

"I don't understand . . . We used protection. Are you sure you can tell you're pregnant so soon?"

"Savage," I whispered, my gaze filled with worry as I looked at him.

"Oh . . . it's his," he stated in realization. "Your husband's?"

I closed my eyes and nodded. "We'd been trying for a while, and I didn't think . . . and then he died and I was so relieved. Only now, it's . . ."

When he didn't say anything, I forced myself to open my eyes and look at him.

"This is the worst possible timing," I said, defeat coating my voice. "I just got happy. I just fell in love with life and with . . ."

I couldn't finish the statement.

"Do you remember what I said to you? The first night we slept together?"

I nodded.

"Tell me then," he said, his voice low. "Tell me what I said to you."

"You said there was no going back. That I was yours."

"And I meant it."

"Savage, you can't—this is too much, too soon. You don't have to do this. I can do it on my own."

"Why do it on your own when you have me?"

I buried my face in my hands and started to cry. He wrapped me in his arms and hugged me, resting his chin on my head.

When I quieted, he held me with one arm and used the other to pry my hands away from my face and forced me to look at him.

"I'm in love with you, Evie. I'm so damn in love with you I can't see straight. When I'm not with you, I physically hurt. I'm in. I'm all in."

"But it's so early in our relationship," I whispered.

"Doesn't matter." He notched his thumb and forefinger underneath my chin. "Say it, babe. Give me the words."

My tongue snaked out to wet my dry lips. "I love you, Savage."

"You trust me?"

I nodded.

"Then don't be scared. I've got you."

～

Savage took me to bed and held me while I slept. But when I woke, he was gone.

Frowning, I picked up my phone. I had one text from him.

SAVAGE

had to run an errand. took your apartment keys. back soon.

I had a few hours before I had to be at work.

Worry cascaded down my spine.

Savage and I had declared our love for one another, but now I was waking up alone. My emotions—and hormones—were all over the place.

I dragged myself to the bathroom and into the shower.

I'd forgotten I'd chopped my hair and was momentarily shocked when I shampooed it and it was more than a foot shorter.

When I got out of the shower, I was disappointed that Savage still hadn't returned. I got dressed and combed out my hair to let it air dry.

I was in the middle of whisking eggs when I heard the key in the lock and Savage came in.

The knot of terror loosened immediately when I saw him and his smile.

"Hey, babe," he greeted as he tossed my apartment keys onto the counter.

"Hi."

He peered at me. "You were worried that I ran out on you."

I shrugged and then nodded.

"Fuck, I'm sorry. I'd never—but I needed to do something."

"What did you have to do?"

"I had to buy you a present," he explained with a self-satisfied grin. "Can I show it to you?"

"Sure. Where is it?" I asked. "I don't see any bags."

"It's too big for a bag. Come on."

He went to get my jacket for me that hung in the closet, and I slipped into a pair of shoes. I grabbed the apartment keys, and he took my hand, closing the door behind us.

When we got out to the parking lot and stopped, I frowned. "I don't understand."

He gestured to the black SUV. "That's your gift."

"What?"

"I bought you—us—a car."

My mouth dropped open in shock. "You bought a car? For us?"

"Yeah." He grinned. "And I'm gonna teach you how to drive it."

I burst into tears and pressed my forehead to his chest. He embraced me tightly. "Hey, it's okay."

"I know it's okay," I blubbered. "It's just that no one's ever done something so sweet for me before."

"Can't having you riding on a motorcycle while you're pregnant. Gotta keep you and our baby safe."

A fresh set of tears poured from my eyes. His words, so simple, so casual, told me everything I needed to know.

He pulled back ever so slightly. "My next order of business—feeding you."

"I was making breakfast," I murmured.

"I've been up for hours. I'm in the mood for a burger."

"I don't have any ground beef."

He laughed and his arms squeezed me. "I meant, let me take you out. And then I'll drive you to work."

Savage released me and then hit the clicker to unlock the car. He opened the passenger side for me. I climbed in, loving the rich smell of new leather.

He closed the door and then went around to the driver's side.

"We gotta get you to a doctor," Savage said. "Just to check you out and make sure everything's good."

I wasn't a fan of doctors.

"I can take you to see Doc." Savage pulled out of the parking lot. "She runs the clinic, remember?"

"Oh. Right."

"You'll like her. She's got a good bedside manner. Want me to call her?"

I nodded absently.

He reached over and took my hand in his. "I'll take care of you, babe. I promise."

Chapter 16

Virgil stalked across the Three Kings parking lot as Savage helped me out of the SUV. "Nice set of wheels."

"Thanks," Savage said. "It's Evie's."

Virgil raised his brows. "Evie's? But Evie doesn't know how to drive."

"She will." Savage turned me to face him and cradled my cheek. "I'll see you later."

Because Virgil was standing right there, my farewell kiss was short. Far too short.

I walked with Virgil to the front door. "Are Roman and Homer here yet?"

"No. Not yet." He looked at me. "Why?"

"Because I need to talk to you guys."

"I think I know what this is about," Virgil said as he remotely disarmed the alarm before letting me in.

"You do?" I shucked my coat as I walked into Three Kings.

"Yeah. You want to tell us you're Savage's Old Lady. Which, duh. He bought you a car. That's like an engagement ring on steroids."

There were a lot of things Virgil said that I had to process.

Savage had told me he loved me, but he'd never said anything about me being his Old Lady.

Homer and Roman finally arrived and after they got settled, I took a deep breath and said, "Can I talk to you guys for a minute?"

"Sure," Roman said. "Everything okay?"

"Better than okay," Virgil piped in. "Savage bought her a car."

"He did what now?" Roman asked in surprise.

"Virgil," I muttered.

Virgil nodded. "And he's teaching her to drive."

Homer rubbed his jaw. "Can we get on with this?"

I swallowed my nerves and decided that being quick was the best course of action. "So, uhm. I'm pregnant."

"Sit down," Homer groused.

I blinked. "You're firing me, aren't you?"

"No," he all but snapped. "But you look like you're going to pass out and you might hit your head."

I raised my brows in surprise but then sank down onto the stool behind the counter.

"So, you're pregnant," Roman repeated.

"I've got a lot of questions," Virgil stated.

"I'll draw you a diagram," I said.

Virgil's brow furrowed at my remark. "Did you just imply that I don't know how babies are made?"

I couldn't hold in my giggle.

"She's teasing me," Virgil said to his brothers with a grin.

"Yeah, I see that," Roman added with a laugh.

Homer remained steadfastly stoic.

My smile slipped and I sobered.

"How far along are you?" Roman asked.

"I'm not sure. I think about five weeks. Savage is going to take me to the doctor to find out."

"Five weeks," Homer repeated.

I saw them put the puzzle pieces together, their expressions clearing in understanding when they realized the baby wasn't Savage's.

"Who's the father?" Virgil asked.

Homer smacked his head. "Tact."

"*You're* telling *me* to have tact? That's rich." Virgil rubbed the back of his head.

"You don't owe us an explanation," Roman said.

"I kind of do. I mean, I work for you and you guys have been good to me." I took a deep breath. "I was married to—to not a nice man. He passed away and I got a chance at a fresh start, so I came to Waco. I met Savage. He got me this job. And now I . . ."

The three of them stared at me, shock permeating their faces.

Even Homer. But he was the first one to recover. "You can't take the bus anymore."

"I can't?" I asked.

"No." He shook his head. "If Savage can't drive you to and from work while you're studying to get your license, then you call one of us. We'll pick you up or drop you off. Whatever."

"But that's ridiculous," I said in exasperation.

"It's my condition," Homer growled. "If you want to keep working here, you accept the rides. No exceptions."

I looked at Homer and bit my lip to stop myself from smiling.

His frown deepened which unfortunately made me break. A laugh escaped my mouth, and I hastily covered my lips with my hand.

"Are you laughing at me?" Homer demanded.

"I'm laughing because I just realized you're not so scary after all," I said, laughing again. "You're a secret softie."

Roman and Virgil joined in, their laughter ringing throughout the tattoo parlor.

"I agree with Homer. About you not taking the bus," Roman said after he collected himself.

Virgil nodded in agreement.

"I'll accept the rides," I said when my giggles had run their course. "And thank you."

The handle of the front door turned and then there was a knock after the door failed to open. "Hello? Are you guys open?"

Virgil went to the door and unlocked it. A man well over six foot five instinctively ducked underneath the doorframe and stepped inside. He was thick in the neck and shoulders, his arms covered in tattoos, and a bushy beard concealed most of his face.

My head tilted back so I could meet his gaze. "You must be Moose."

Moose grinned. "That's me."

I looked at Roman. "Your first appointment is here."

"I see that." Roman laughed and stalked forward, holding out his hand. "How're you doing, Moose?"

"Can't complain." Moose clasped Roman's hand in his large paw and gave it a vigorous shake.

"You're new," Moose said to me.

"Yes. I'm Evie."

"Let's get you in the chair. I'm excited to finish your back," Roman said.

"You and me both." Moose followed Roman down the hallway, but he wasn't at all quiet when he said, "What happened to Brielle?"

"She went back to her regular job."

"Cool. Pie in the Sky, right?"

"Don't even think about it," Roman warned.

"Don't even think about what?"

"Asking my sister out. She's off-limits."

∽

"You were right. Homemade sourdough bread is the best," Savage said.

He brushed his lips across my bare belly and my fingers sank into his hair.

"How are you doing? Are you okay?" he asked.

I painted his mouth with my pointer finger. "Better than okay."

"It's been an intense few days. I was just checking."

"I'm the one who should be checking on you," I stated. "I clobbered you with a lot."

"It's okay," he murmured dreamily. "I like this."

"Savage?"

"Hmm?"

"Am I your Old Lady?"

He froze and then he lifted his head to stare at me. "Are you my Old Lady?"

I bit my lip in fear, but I forced myself to plow forward. "Virgil said something earlier today . . . it just got me thinking. You bought me a car and you said you loved me. But you never said anything about wanting me to be your Old Lady."

Savage stared at me intently. "An Old Lady is more serious to a biker than a wife. A wife is just . . . it's paperwork that can be re-written and dissolved if things don't work out. An Old Lady . . . that's a claim on *life* with someone—a promise that you're willing to die for them. A promise you're willing to ink on your own skin. Babe," he smiled, "what do you think I meant when I said there was no going back? That you were *mine*."

A slow smile stretched across my face.

He kissed my stomach. And then he kissed lower.

"I should punish you," he whispered against my skin.

"For what?"

"For doubting my feelings for you."

He slid my thighs open and stared at the naked heat of me. He gave me one slow lick.

"Hmm. Yes. Definitely gonna punish you. I won't let you come for hours. And when you finally beg me, maybe then I'll allow it."

I shivered in desire.

"I guess I'll just have to suffer," I murmured.

He licked me again. "I guess you will."

Chapter 17

"Savage, I'm going to be sick!"

I ran from the bed and dashed into the bathroom just in the nick of time. My head was over the toilet as Savage came into the doorway, bare-chested, and well-rested.

When I was sure I wouldn't throw up again, I flushed the toilet and rose. Glaring at him, I went to the sink and brushed my teeth.

"You weren't supposed to see that," I said.

"I'm going to see it all," he said quietly. "Every moment. I'm not missing anything."

Tears gathered in my eyes, but I turned away from him to hide. But darn the man, he saw anyway and pulled me to him.

"Better?" he asked when the storm of my emotions had passed.

"Yeah." I sniffed.

He took my hand and led me out of the bathroom and into the kitchen. "Sit." He pointed to a stool.

I sat.

Savage went to the front door and opened it. He

turned back to me and closed the door, a paper bag in one hand and a pastry box in the other.

"What's that?" I asked in confusion.

"I texted a prospect to pick you up some things."

"You've mentioned prospects before, but you never explained what they are."

"Prospects are club bitches. They gotta prove themselves before they patch in. They're at our beck and call. I texted Roads this morning before you were even awake to bring me what I wanted. Wasn't gonna wake you when you were wrapped around me, humping my leg."

"Humping your—are you kidding?"

He grinned. "No. Let me show you what I got you. Or what Roads got you." He opened the pastry box and held it out to me. "Home-made croissants from Pie in the Sky which will be easy on your belly. And pickles."

"I've heard of weird pregnancy cravings, but pickles first thing in the morning is a little too much for me."

"The croissants are for you. The pickle juice is for the baby. It's good for hydration."

I shook my head.

He nodded. "You get a croissant and then you're taking a shot of pickle juice. Willa swears by it."

"Willa?" I asked in confusion. "Waverly's sister?"

"Yes."

"She's got a baby?"

"She's still pregnant. Third trimester. She's making Duke's life hell. Come on, babe. Eat the croissant, you'll feel better."

I took a croissant and tore a piece off. It melted in my mouth. I hummed with pleasure.

Savage's gaze heated. "If you keep making those kinds of noises, I'm not going to be able to keep my hands off you. And we've got an appointment to get to."

"Appointment?" I asked after I swallowed.

"Doctor's appointment," he clarified. "Doc was able to squeeze you in this morning before work."

"Oh."

Savage unscrewed the pickle jar. I could smell the vinegar immediately and my nose wrinkled. He got me a glass and poured a shot's worth into it.

"Plug your nose," he suggested as he inched it toward me.

With a sigh, I picked it up. I lifted it in a silent cheer. "Bottom's up."

∼

We sat in the waiting room of the clinic. I bounced my knee in nervous agitation. Savage placed a hand on my thigh and gave it a squeeze.

"You've got nothing to be worried about," Savage stated. "Doc's great. You'll like her."

"I don't have much experience with doctors," I admitted.

"What about when you were a kid and got sick?" he asked.

"My family prayed over my bedside if I got sick. If I broke a bone . . . well, let's just say you didn't want to break a bone."

Savage looked at me like he wanted to ask more questions—but thankfully, a woman in a white lab coat and cropped blonde hair strode into the waiting room.

"Savage," she greeted with a wide smile.

"Doc." Savage stood up, and I followed suit. "This is Evie."

"Evie." Doc smiled and turned a shrewd blue gaze to me. "Nice to meet you."

"You too," I murmured.

"Shall we?" Doc gestured to the hallway. "Savage, we'll see you after—"

"No," I interrupted. "He's coming with me."

"Oh. Okay. That's your choice. Let's get you and the baby checked out," Doc said, once again gesturing to the hallway.

Nodding, I walked a pace behind her with my hand clasped in Savage's. We arrived at the end of the hallway, and she pushed open the door, gesturing for us to go in first. She closed the door behind her.

"Sit," Doc said, patting the exam table.

Savage let go of my hand and I scrambled up onto the padded table, the crisp white paper crinkling under my bottom.

"Savage said this is your first prenatal visit." Doc picked up the tablet.

"Yeah."

"I'm gonna ask you some questions and then I'll do an ultrasound, but you might not be far enough along to see anything yet. Okay?"

I nodded.

"What was the date of your last period?" she asked.

I thought for a moment. "I don't remember exactly."

"Best guess?"

I gave her an answer, glancing at Savage. He shot me a smile and I relaxed.

She had me step on a scale, take a urine test, asked about my medical history, and if I was allergic to any medications. I was ashamed that I didn't have a lot of information, but Doc wasn't judgmental, and Savage had been correct about her bedside manner.

"Now for the not-so-fun part," Doc said. "I'd like to do a pelvic exam. Perhaps Savage should wait in the—"

"He's staying," I interrupted.

Doc nodded, her expression blank.

I shucked out of my jeans and tank before putting on the dressing gown. Then I took off my underwear and shoved them into the leg of my jeans.

After I climbed back up onto the exam table and placed my legs in the stirrups, I looked at Savage.

He came to stand beside me and took my hand and gave it a squeeze. He immediately calmed the nerves in my belly.

Thankfully, Doc's touch was gentle, and it was over quickly.

She stripped off her gloves and set them on the silver tray. The tablet device on the counter beeped. Doc picked it up and pressed the screen, her expression not changing.

Doc looked at me and smiled. "Now for the sonogram. Because you're so early, I have to do a transvaginal ultrasound to get the best results. Hopefully we'll get lucky and be able to see your little peanut."

"Okay."

Doc glanced at Savage. "I'm guessing you're staying for this part, too?"

"Yep," he replied, his hand still clutching mine.

She maneuvered the sonogram machine close to the exam table. She fiddled with a few knobs, put on another pair of gloves, and then gently inserted the wand.

A moment later, I heard a *whoosh, whoosh, whoosh,* like a galloping horse.

Doc smiled. "Well, look at that. We got lucky. That's your—"

She suddenly stopped talking and her brow furrowed.

"What?" I asked, panic rising in my throat. "What is it? Is everything okay?"

Doc peered at the screen and moved the wand. Then

she looked back at me with a wide smile. "Everything is perfect. But actually, I think you're further along than we thought. The gestational sacs are bigger than they'd be at five weeks."

"Wait, did you say *sacs*?" Savage asked. "As in more than one?"

"I did indeed," Doc said. "Your urine test came back with high hCG levels. I wanted to wait to confirm with a sonogram before I said anything, but I was right."

"Right? Right about what?" I asked.

"Congratulations, Evie. You're having twins."

Chapter 18

I blinked. "*Twins?*"

"Yes."

"Twins?" Savage echoed.

"I can't be having twins," I protested.

"But you are." Doc pointed to the screen. "See these two little peanut-looking shapes here? Those are your babies."

Babies. As in more than one.

"*Doc,*" hysteria rose in my voice, "I was just starting to wrap my head around the idea of having one baby. But two?"

"Twins?" Savage asked again.

"Yes," Doc said patiently, her gaze bouncing from me to Savage and back to me as she gently removed the sonogram wand. "Look, I know this is scary. It's scary even when you think you're ready for it."

"How would you know?" I snapped, sitting up.

"Because even though I'm married with a stable career, a supportive husband, and a large friend group, I'm still fucking terrified," she said easily.

She set the probe down and then removed her gloves.

My eyes widened in surprise. "You're pregnant?"

"Yes. I'm pregnant," she admitted with a laugh. "Doctor's coat hides a lot. I'm not even sure I have the maternal gene, but I'm hoping it kicks in at some point. Look, you're never really going to be ready for this. But you're not alone."

She glanced at Savage, and I followed her gaze. He looked completely shell-shocked.

"Savage?" Doc asked.

"Hmm?"

"Sit," she commanded. "Before you faint."

"I'm not going to faint," he said, even though he looked like he was in danger of doing exactly that. He dropped my hand and went to the chair by the wall and collapsed into it.

"You have a support system," Doc said, addressing me again. "I know we just met, but this clinic is here for you now from this day forward. We just opened up a mother and child wellness center, so the timing is perfect for you. We offer free childbirth classes. One is starting soon and runs eight weeks long. Boxer and I are actually going to take it. So, if you decide to attend there will be at least one familiar face when you show up."

"Why are you being so nice?" I asked with a sniff, feeling tears cloud my eyes.

"Because I want to help. That's all I've ever wanted to do." Doc smiled. "It's okay to be scared, but you're going to be fine. I have faith in you."

"How can you have faith in me? You don't even know me."

"Savage cares for you," Doc said slowly. "That's all I need to know."

"Babies," I repeated. "Gadzooks."

She nodded and laughed. "Gadzooks, indeed." Doc patted my shoulder. "You two take a moment. Get dressed. I'll be outside when you're ready."

"Okay."

I sat on the exam table, my mind a swirling mess of disbelief. Time ceased to exist.

Savage started to laugh.

I whipped my head around, my gaze widening in shock. He was bent over in half, his shoulders shaking with mirth. When he finally sat up, he wiped the tears from his eyes.

"You're a jerk," I snapped. "I can't believe I fell in love with such a *jerk.*"

That only seemed to make him laugh harder.

I hopped off the exam table and stalked toward him.

"You're a *heathen!*"

He placed his hands on my shoulders and tugged me to him.

I wasn't sure what to do, so I wrapped my arms around him and hugged him tight.

Savage finally calmed down and rested his chin on my head. "You know what this means, don't you?"

"That I'm never going to see you again?"

"Such dark humor in one so young," he joked. He pulled back so he could stare down at me. "No, it just means we'll have two kids we can teach to be menaces instead of one."

My smile was watery. "I don't think they'll need help with that. I think they'll be able to do it all on their own."

He leaned down and kissed my lips. "It'll be okay. Trust me, it's all going to be okay."

I sighed.

Savage released me and I dressed quickly. He opened

the exam room door, and we walked down the hallway. Doc was talking to the receptionist at the desk.

She shot me a smile, her gaze darting between me and Savage. "Everything okay?"

I nodded. "Yeah. Everything's good."

Doc nodded. She slid a red folder across the counter to me. "Some reading material, my recommended brands of prenatal vitamins, and the baby class schedule. Oh, and of course your first sonogram photo is in there from today."

I opened the folder and sticking out of a pocket was a black and white picture. I slid it out and looked at it. The shock of the news still hadn't worn off. I quickly tucked it away and closed the folder and put it in my large shoulder bag.

"Thank you," I said. "For everything."

"Absolutely." Doc smiled. "Sandy can get you scheduled for your next appointment. I'll see you at class, yeah?"

"You will, yeah," Savage said.

Doc studied Savage for a moment and then she pushed away from the counter and disappeared down the hallway.

Sandy booked our next appointment, and Savage added it to his phone calendar. Smiling, I took his hand as we headed outside.

"So, this baby class . . ." Savage said as he opened the passenger door for me.

I hoisted myself up and set my purse onto my lap. "Yeah?"

He closed the door and headed to the driver's side. Once he got in and settled, he picked up the thread of conversation. "Willa and Duke took one."

"Yeah? What are they exactly?"

"To get new parents familiar with newborns, changing diapers, how to bathe a baby properly. Should be fun," he said.

"Oh yeah?" I asked with a smile.

He glanced at me and grinned. "Everything's fun with you."

I bit my lip as I pondered.

"What are you thinking about?"

"Can I ask you something?" I asked.

"Sure."

"Why was Doc so surprised that I wanted you at the appointment? It was like she didn't know we were together."

He sighed. "She didn't know we were together. She does now, though."

"Wait, are you *hiding* me?" I demanded. "I'm not really your Old Lady, am I?"

"Yes, you are," he stated emphatically. "But you've got to understand . . . I haven't talked to the club about it yet."

"Talk to the club, what does that mean?"

"It means when a brother wants to make a woman his Old Lady, they discuss it in Church. That's what we call our meetings."

"But why?" I asked in confusion. "Our relationship is about you and me. No one else."

"You know how I told you being an Old Lady is more than just being a wife? If something were to happen to me . . . the club would take care of you. You and the baby—fuck, *babies*. You get a family when you become an Old Lady. So that's why brothers talk about it in Church. It's a commitment from dozens of people to care for you for the rest of your life, so it's very much their business."

"Oh." I nibbled my lip. "And you haven't talked about it in Church yet. Why not? You sure you're not waiting for—"

"Willa and Duke are my best friends. We've been friends since we were kids, long before the club was ever in the picture. I want you to meet them first before I take it to Church."

"I see."

"That'll happen soon. But I . . ."

"What?" I demanded.

He grinned at me. "Want you to myself for just a little while longer."

Chapter 19

Three Kings was still closed by the time Savage dropped me off. Roman had given me a set of keys, so once I had the key into the lock and the door partially open, I turned toward the parking lot and waved to Savage.

I slipped inside and closed the door, locking it behind me, and then I went to disarm the alarm. I dug the folder out of my bag and set it on the counter.

I took a seat on the stool and opened the folder. I pulled out the sonogram and stared at it again before setting it aside. I read through the information that Doc had provided.

It was suddenly all too overwhelming, and the first sob broke past my lips, shattering the silence in the room. I was in the middle of a sob fest when the sound of a key in the lock startled me. The door opened and Homer stepped inside.

I paused mid cry as his eyes met mine and then a fresh set of tears fell. He quickly closed the door.

"Why are you crying?" he grumbled.

I cried harder.

Homer approached the counter, his gaze riveted on the sonogram. He picked it up and I lunged for it, but he took a step back and I couldn't reach it.

He looked at it and frowned. "Did you get bad news at the doctor?"

"No."

"Then why are you crying?" Homer glanced down at the sonogram again.

"Because I'm having twins and I'm terrified, you moron!" I yelled.

Homer set the sonogram down onto the counter. "Grab your shit."

I gasped. "You're firing me? For calling you a moron?"

He rolled his eyes. "No. Now grab your shit. Let's go."

"Where are we going?" I sniffed, hastily wiping underneath my eyes.

"To a place that's gonna make you feel better."

I frowned in confusion.

"I'm trying to be human here," he muttered in exasperation.

I stuffed the papers back into the folder and picked up my purse. Homer already had the door open, and he waited for me. He locked up the parlor and remotely set the alarm.

Without a sound, I followed him to a bright red muscle car with black racing stripes on the hood, wondering where he was taking me.

⁓

Homer pulled into a parking spot on the street and cut the massive engine of the car.

"Where are we?" I asked.

Heartbeats & Highways

"Pie in the Sky," he announced.

I frowned. "And *why* are we here?"

"So you'll stop crying."

"I've already stopped crying," I pointed out.

"There's baked goods in there," he muttered.

I stared at him.

"What?" he demanded.

"You're a teddy bear," I said in realization, my jaw dropping open.

"I'm *not* a teddy bear."

"You *so are*. Why else would you bring me to a bakery if you weren't a big 'ol teddy bear?"

"I don't like crying women."

"You could've kicked me out of the tattoo parlor," I said. "Or left me there by myself. You didn't have to drive me to a place full of delicious treats to make me feel better."

He paused. "Are you? Feeling better?"

I smiled.

Homer glared.

It only made me smile wider.

With a sigh, he reached into his jeans pocket and pulled out his wallet. "Here's a twenty. Get whatever you want. Stay as long as you want. Take the day off."

"Take the day off?"

"Yep. The last thing I need is for you to break down into tears again. Tears are bad for business."

"I'm giving you exactly three seconds to prepare yourself," I said.

"Prepare myself? For what?"

"For my incoming hug."

"What? No, I don't want—"

I reached across the car and wrapped my arms around his shoulders. "I won't tell anyone, I promise," I whispered.

"Can this be over now?" he pleaded.

I dropped my arms and moved away. "Thanks, Homer."

"Take the twenty."

I shook my head. "You've done enough. Keep your money. I'll see you tomorrow."

"Tomorrow," he agreed with a glower. "Send Jazz out here, will you?"

"Jazz is working?"

He nodded.

"Okay," I said with a sigh. "I'll send her out."

A cheery bell rang when I opened the bakery door and immediately my spirits lifted at the smell of sugar and lemon in the air.

A few of the tables were occupied, but there was no line at the counter. Jazz closed the register drawer and looked up. She smiled in surprise.

"Hi, Evie! Oh my God, your hair looks amazing!"

"Thanks." I gave her a shy smile.

"Are you on your way to Three Kings?" she asked, looking behind me. "Is Savage with you?"

I shook my head. "Actually, Homer just gave me a ride here. And I have the day off."

She raised her brows. "Oh?"

I nodded. "He—ah—asked for you. He's out front."

Jazz tossed her long, dark braid over her shoulder. "Then he can wait out there all he wants."

"What am I missing?" I asked. "What's with you two?"

Brielle came out of the back kitchen, carting a tray of freshly baked bear claws. "What's with who?" She set the tray down on the counter. "Hey, Evie. That hair cut looks great on you."

"Thanks," I replied, suddenly realizing why Homer

had brought me here of all places. It hadn't just been the promise of baked goods, but the company, too.

Teddy bear, through and through.

"Homer's out front," Jazz said to Brielle. "And he's asking for me."

"And you're not going out there," Brielle said with an unhurried smile.

"Nope."

Brielle laughed and turned to me. "Jazz has been in love with Homer for as long as any of us can remember. My brother is also in love with Jazz, but he refuses to stake his claim."

"Why?" I asked.

"Million-dollar question." Brielle shrugged. "He drove you here? Before work?"

I shook my head. "It's a long story, but he ended up giving me the day off."

A cell phone rang, and Brielle fished it out of her apron pocket. She looked at it and smirked. She tapped the screen and put the phone to her ear. "She's not coming out."

"Homer?" Jazz mouthed at Brielle, who nodded.

"She's done, Homer," Brielle said. "She's done waiting for you to make your move. When I caught you two yelling your feelings for each other during Mom and Dad's Christmas party, I gave you both my blessing. There's no reason for you to—" She paused. "All right. Hang on."

She held out the phone to Jazz, who shook her head. "I'm not talking to him."

Brielle put the cell to her ear. "Did you hear that? She's not—fine, I'll tell her." She hung up the phone. "He said that if you don't go out there and talk to him then he's going to come in here and carry you out over his shoulder."

Jazz's eyes glazed over.

"Ew, that should be hot, but it's my brother . . ." Brielle wrinkled her nose.

"It's very caveman-esque, but he'd never actually do it. He's all bluster." Jazz looked at me. "So, what are you having?"

"I'll have—"

The door to the bakery opened and Homer loomed in the doorway.

"Uh-oh," Jazz muttered.

"Yeah, big *uh-oh*," Brielle agreed. "Hey, Homer."

Homer didn't say anything—he just stalked across the room with his eyes on Jazz. He came around the counter.

"This is a health code violation," Jazz taunted. "You don't work here."

Without a word, Homer bent down, cradled the back of her head, and kissed her. Only when she was melting in his arms did he pull back.

"You—you . . ." Jazz couldn't seem to form a word as she stared up at him.

Homer said nothing. Instead, he grasped her hand and all but dragged her to the exit. She didn't utter a protest.

The bell on the door jangled before closing behind them.

"Huh," Brielle said, chewing on her lip.

"Huh, what?" I asked.

"I guess telling Homer that Jazz was going on a date tonight finally got his ass in gear." She grinned.

I smiled back. "I guess so."

"They better name their first kid after me. Now, seriously, what are you ordering?"

Chapter 20

I sat at a corner table, nursing my hot chocolate and nibbling on a fresh bear claw when Jazz finally returned. Even from the slight distance, I could tell her cheeks were flushed and there was a sparkle in her eyes.

She saw me and waved before getting back behind the counter. Brielle said something to her that caused Jazz to nod. Jazz made two drinks at the espresso machine while Brielle ducked into the back, returning a few moments later with a young woman who took up residence at the register.

Jazz handed Brielle a cup and then the two of them walked toward me.

"Mind if we join you?" Brielle asked.

"Not at all. I'm dying to know what happened between you and Homer," I said with a laugh.

"And I'm dying to know why Homer brought you here and gave you the day off," Brielle said.

I sighed. "Jazz first. Then I'll spill."

"He told me I wasn't going on a date tonight and that I needed to cancel," Jazz said with an arrogant grin.

"And you punched him in his face, right?" Brielle asked.

"Nope. I said I'd cancel." Jazz took a small sip of her drink. "But I'm not going to." She looked at Brielle. "By the way, I know you were the one who told him I was going on a date in the first place."

"Just trying to move this relationship along. You've been really tightly wound, you know. So the sooner you and Homer get together, the happier we'll all be. Plus, my parents are dying for grandbabies."

"I'm not ready for babies," Jazz said, but then she immediately contradicted what she said because her eyes went glassy with longing. "Mhmm. Homer babies . . ."

I lifted my hot chocolate to my lips to hide my smile.

"Your turn," Brielle said to me.

"I'm guessing your brothers didn't tell you. . ."

"Tell me what?" she asked.

"I'm pregnant," I said.

They sat in stunned silence.

"And before you ask, no it's not Savage's. The father is my deceased husband. Savage is my . . . boyfriend, and he's made it clear that he's sticking around. Oh, and I found out today at the clinic that I'm actually having twins."

"That's a lot of information all at once." Brielle cleared her throat. "So you had a husband . . ."

"Yeah."

When it was clear I wasn't going to elaborate, Brielle raised her brows and said, "So, er—congratulations?"

Jazz scratched her cheek. "Yeah, should we be happy for you or . . ."

I paused. "Happy. Mostly happy. There's a lot of terrified in there too, but definitely happy."

"I don't know what's crazier. The twin thing or the Savage being your boyfriend thing," Jazz murmured.

I knew how important it was for Savage to tell Willa and Duke first that I was his Old Lady, so I didn't divulge that now. But it would've explained why Savage was willing to raise the babies as his own.

"Yeah, this week has kind of been a whirlwind." I shook my head. "That's why Homer drove me here and gave me the day off. He came into work, and I was crying behind the counter. He saw the sonogram and—"

"You have a sonogram?" Jazz asked.

I nodded.

"Can I see it?"

"Sure." I opened the folder on the table and handed it to her.

She stared at it. "Oh, wow. Yeah. Twins."

"Twins," I repeated. "I was freaked out and crying and he drove me here and gave me the day off. He did it while growling and grumbling, but he's just a big teddy bear. He did not like being called that, FYI. And I wasn't supposed to tell anyone, but it's true."

"I know it's true," Jazz said forlornly. "That's why I've been in love with him since high school. Something about him just calls to me. I can't help it."

Brielle chimed in, "I felt like such an idiot when I realized you guys had feelings for each other. Guess I can't put detective skills on my resume."

"I hid it from you for years," Jazz said. "Though in the last few months, I don't know . . . I just couldn't hide it anymore. I decided to rip the Band-Aid off. Either he wants to be with me, or I'm moving on. Enough unrequited pining."

"It's requited," Brielle said. "But I still don't know why he won't date you."

"Because it won't just be dating," I said. I looked at Jazz. "Right? This is a mate-for-life situation, isn't it?"

Her shoulders slumped and she nodded. "I've imprinted on the grumpy bastard. But I really don't want to talk about it anymore. Let's talk about you. When did you find out that you were pregnant?"

"I took a home pregnancy test a few days ago. Actually, the day that you guys brought us lunch, Homer's client said something about how every time she throws up, her first worry is that she's pregnant. It got me thinking . . . and yeah, here we are."

"Homer's client?" Jazz repeated. "The hussy who threw herself at him?"

"That would be the one. Don't worry, he didn't throw himself back." I patted her hand. "Savage took me to the wellness clinic this morning for my appointment."

"You met Doc, didn't you?" Brielle asked.

I raised my brows. "You know Doc?"

"We know Doc." Jazz smiled. "The Tarnished Angels back the clinic."

"I didn't know that about the club," I murmured. "I knew they did the halfway house for women, but didn't know that about the clinic. But Savage told me about Doc."

Jazz looked at Brielle and then back to me.

"Don't do that," I muttered.

"Do what?" Jazz demanded.

"Have a conversation without me. What aren't you telling me?" I asked.

"You tell her," Brielle said.

Jazz sighed. "You know that whole mate-for-life thing? Well, the Tarnished Angels are like that."

"What do you mean?" I inquired.

Brielle replied, "The guys in the club know instantly if they want to be with someone forever."

"Old Ladies, you mean, right?" I asked.

"Yeah, Old Ladies." Jazz nodded.

I nibbled my lip. I needed to talk about it with someone; I just hoped they could keep a secret.

"Savage asked me to be his Old Lady," I said slowly. "He—ah—hasn't talked about it with the club yet because he wants me to meet Willa and Duke first."

"My head is spinning with all of your news," Jazz said.

"Tell me about it," I said with a laugh.

"You'll love Willa," Jazz said.

"She's one of our best friends," Brielle added.

"So how are you feeling about all this?" Jazz asked.

"I'm happy about Savage. I'm even happy about the baby . . . babies. I didn't think I'd be able—anyway. I'm happy, but I'm overwhelmed too."

"What are you doing the rest of the day?" Jazz asked, changing the subject.

I shook my head. "Nothing. I could text Savage and ask him to come pick me up, but I'm not ready to go home."

"I've got to get back to work and start the bread for tomorrow," Jazz said. "You want to help?"

I smiled. "I'd love to."

I was in the middle of shaping bread dough when the back door of the kitchen opened and a brunette with a baby strapped to her chest strode inside.

She blinked. "Hi."

"Hello," I greeted.

"Uh, no offense, but who are you?"

"No offense taken," I said with a laugh. "I'm Evie. I—"

"Oh, *you're* Evie." A smile stretched across the woman's face.

"You've heard of me?"

"Brielle and Jazz might have said something about you."

I pointed at her. "You're Brooklyn."

"Yes." She smacked her forehead. "Sorry. I forgot to introduce myself, didn't I? New mom brain and everything. I thought the pregnancy brain was bad. Mom brain is like a million times worse."

Something to look forward to.

"Well, it's nice to meet you," I said. "Jazz left to get ready for her date and Brielle ran out to deliver the Reynolds wedding cake."

"I see," Brooklyn said, running a hand down the sleeping baby's back. "That still doesn't explain why you're back here baking. Aren't you the new receptionist at Three Kings?"

"Yeah, I am. Homer gave me the day off," I explained. "He dropped me here. And I wasn't ready to go home, so Brielle and Jazz kinda . . ."

"Took you under their wings." Brooklyn smiled.

"Something like that."

"You hungry?"

I shook my head. "No, I ate already."

Brooklyn nodded toward the cooling bread on the wire racks. "You made these?"

I nodded.

"Jazz never makes loaves with such ornate scoring."

I paused. "I have some experience baking bread. I kind of like bread as an art form."

She smiled. "Well, they're gorgeous."

"Thank you." My gaze dipped to the baby at her chest. "How old?"

"Few months. This is Palmer."

My heart swam in mush. "She's beautiful."

Brooklyn beamed. "She is. But I'm biased."

The young woman who was watching the register popped into the back. "Oh, hey, Brooklyn. I didn't hear you come in."

"Hey, Kendall. I just got here," Brooklyn replied.

"Evie, Savage is up front," Kendall said.

I frowned. "He's here?"

Kendall nodded.

"But I didn't text him. How did he know I was here?" I asked.

"No idea," Kendall said.

"Oh, well, I'm not done yet. I have to get this loaf into the oven—"

"I'll take care of it," Brooklyn said. "I just need to make myself a coffee first."

"I'll make it for you," Kendall offered.

"Thanks," Brooklyn said with a smirk, "but I want to see Evie and Savage in action."

I raised my brows at her.

"Oh, yeah. In case you didn't know, you're kind of famous around here." She winked.

"What exactly did Brielle and Jazz say about us?" I demanded.

She mimed locking her lips closed, but then grinned. Brooklyn strode out of the kitchen to the front and greeted Savage. With a deep exhale, I followed.

Savage was smiling and nodding, his gaze straying to the baby at Brooklyn's chest every now and again.

But the moment he saw me, he focused his attention completely on me.

"Hey," he greeted.

"Hi. How did you know I was here?"

"Homer."

I bit my lip. "Oh."

"She's been in the back baking bread for the last several hours," Brooklyn explained. "Jazz showed her the ropes."

"You ready?" Savage asked.

I nodded. "Bye, Brooklyn. Kendall."

"See ya later," Brooklyn said with a smile.

I grabbed my purse and folder from the small office and then followed Savage out of the bakery.

"Why didn't you text me that Homer had given you the day off? I would've come and picked you up."

"I assumed you had stuff to do," I said. "Plus, I wasn't ready to go home."

"Homer said you were crying."

"Yes."

Savage unlocked the SUV and pulled open the passenger door for me. "Why?"

"Why do you think?"

He closed the door and went around to the driver's side and climbed in. "Overwhelmed, huh?"

"Yep."

"You didn't want to go home and be alone."

"No, I didn't," I admitted. "I just needed to zone out for a bit, you know?"

"I know."

"How do you quiet your mind when it starts to run wild?" I asked.

He rubbed his jaw, the raspy sound of his scruff loud in the otherwise silent car. "Ride my motorcycle for long stretches of time. That's what I was doing for the last several hours actually."

I swallowed the lump in my throat. "You regret your decision, don't you?"

"Evie," he said quietly. "You gotta stop thinking I'm going to bail. I'm not bailing. I just had—it was a lot to digest. That's all."

"I told Jazz and Brielle I was your Old Lady. I hope they don't blab."

He grinned. "They probably will."

I groaned. "Sorry. I need to confide in people and talk about everything from this past week. I get what you mean by it being a lot. Life is happening so fast and I'm reeling."

"So, let's take control back," he said.

I frowned. "Control. Okay. But how?"

Chapter 21

I GRIPPED the steering wheel of the car. "Are you sure about this?"

"I'm positive. You just drove around the parking lot for an hour. You can definitely handle the side streets."

"Oh, I'm not worried about driving on the road. I can drive a tractor—I know I can drive a car. I just meant—"

"You can drive a tractor?"

"Yes."

"Ah, the farm life. You learned how to drive a tractor but never learned to drive a car?" He frowned.

"Never got around to it," I evaded. "But I'm not worried about driving in traffic. I'm worried because I don't have a license."

"It's fine."

"It's not fine. It's illegal. What if I get pulled over?"

"I'm friends with a lot of cops."

"You are?" I asked in disbelief.

"The club is," he amended. "So don't worry about it. You ready?"

"I'm ready."

I put the car into gear and then crept out of the parking lot. We were driving for a few minutes when Savage said, "You can give it a little gas there, Grannie."

"*Hey.*"

"You're going under the speed limit. Don't be afraid of the pedal."

"Fine."

I pressed the accelerator and let out a laugh of excitement when the car zoomed forward.

"Easy, Tom Slick."

"Tom Slick?" I asked, immediately letting off the gas. "What's that?"

"A cartoon."

"Huh. Never seen it."

"What about *George of the Jungle*? Or *Rocky and Bullwinkle*?"

"Are you sure you're not just making stuff up?"

The GPS chimed a direction. I put on my turn signal and changed lanes.

"You seriously haven't seen *George of the Jungle*?"

"I really haven't."

"You didn't watch cartoons growing up?"

"I didn't watch TV at all," I replied.

"Why not?"

"We didn't have a TV in the house." I pulled into the lot of the apartment building and parked. "Am I in the lines?"

Savage opened his door to check. "Right on the edge, but technically, yeah. You did good."

"Thanks." I smiled.

We got out and headed for the apartment building.

"I can only come up for a little while," Savage said. "I have some club shit to take care of."

"Oh." My happiness dimmed. "Will you be back tonight?"

He smiled softly. "Yeah, babe. I'll be back late tonight, but I'll crawl in bed next to you."

"And how will you do that?" I asked. "You don't have keys."

"I took your apartment keys when I went to buy the car. Made a copy."

"That was very presumptuous of you," I said with a laugh.

"Woman, you're my Old Lady now. Better get used to it."

He punched in the code to the apartment complex and then we stepped inside. We didn't talk again until we were in the apartment.

I turned to him, wondering if I was brave enough to ask for what I wanted.

"Today was intense, Savage. And I need—I need to feel connected to you," I said, meeting his gaze. "Will you take me to bed?"

He froze for a moment, and I was afraid he'd say no because of our time limit, but then he was charging toward me. He lifted me in his arms, his mouth fusing to mine as he walked to the bedroom.

Savage placed me in the middle of the bed and then began to undress like a fiend. In his haste to get naked, he almost fell over, causing me to laugh.

He mock glared at me. "Woman, you do not laugh when I get naked. That's not good for my ego."

I reached out to grasp his erection. "Your ego is just fine."

"Why do you still have clothes on?"

"I didn't want to miss the show."

I lifted my shirt over my head and tossed it aside. My pants and underwear were quick to follow.

"Spread your legs, babe. I want to see you," he growled.

I laid back and did as he commanded. Savage had rid me of my shyness. Nothing was off limits to him. Whatever I asked for, I'd get.

Every time we were in bed, he proved that his one and only goal was to please me.

Tears suddenly came to my eyes.

"Why are you crying?" he asked as he looked at me with concern.

"I was just thinking . . . This is true intimacy. And you make me feel so safe. I feel safe with you Savage, and I never thought I'd have that. Ever."

His expression was solemn as he got on the bed and crawled up my body so that he could stare into my eyes as he loomed over me.

His name was Savage and yet he was so gentle with me. Caring. Tender. When I needed it.

"I love you, Evie," he whispered.

"I love you too."

His mouth held mine captive. His tongue robbed me of breath. But I didn't need to breathe. I just needed to feel.

He slid his fingers through my wetness and then painted my thighs with my desire.

I wanted nothing between us.

"I want to feel you," I murmured against his mouth. "I want to feel you come inside me. Please, Savage."

He groaned against my lips. "You sure?"

"I'm sure."

"I've never been with a woman without a condom," he said, pulling back so he could meet my eyes. "It'll be my first time."

I smiled up at him. "I promise I'll be gentle."

Laughing softly, he took himself in hand and slid into me.

He gasped and I silently crowed in triumph. I was giving him something he'd never experienced.

Our eyes remained locked on one another as he began to move. Slow, deep; I felt every ridge of him.

His back slickened with sweat and my nails raked across his shoulder blades. He grasped my thigh and urged me to lift my leg.

I took him deeper. I took everything he wanted to give me.

Our breaths mingled and our skin flushed with heat. The fever of desire spread through both of us; we moved in an intimate dance where we touched and kissed. Heat built between us.

"I'm close, babe," he gritted. "Feels so fucking good."

"Me too, Savage."

"Come with me, Evie." His hand snaked between our bodies to touch me.

I came with a surprised cry and Savage tumbled into his release a few seconds later. He dropped his head to the crook of my shoulder and stayed inside me.

I clenched around him, causing him to shudder in pleasure.

"Ah, sensitive," he mumbled, brushing a kiss along my collar bone. He lifted himself up and he gently slid out.

"I'm gushing out of you."

"Mhhm." I stretched my arms over my head. "Hand me my shirt."

He leaned over the bed and grabbed the garment from the floor to give to me.

I put it between my legs and yawned. "I need a shower. And a nap."

Savage cradled my cheek, stopping me from rolling over and getting up.

His blue gaze was bright with emotion. "Love you, babe."

I turned my head and kissed his palm. "Love you too."

∽

After a hot shower, we curled up in bed. We kissed, we touched, we communicated without words. A chiming phone momentarily roused me from my doze.

"Your cell," I murmured against Savage's bare chest.

"Yeah. I gotta get going."

I coiled around him tighter. "No. Stay with me."

He groaned. "I wish I could, but I have to go."

I reluctantly released him.

Savage got up and began to move around the room.

"So, what do you mean you have *club stuff?*" I asked in curiosity. "That's sort of vague."

"It's vague on purpose," he said.

"Are you not allowed to tell me?"

He shrugged. "I can tell you some things. Other things I can't—and I'll never be able to. Just the way of it."

I nibbled my lip. "You're not—are you fighting tonight?"

Savage looked at me and sat down on the bed next to me. He gripped my thigh when he stared into my eyes. "No, babe. I'm not fighting tonight. I'm done with all that shit."

I swallowed. "You are?"

He nodded. "Don't need it anymore."

A knot I didn't know I had loosened inside of me. "You sure?"

Savage leaned closer and kissed my lips. "I'm sure, babe." His hand settled on my belly. "You're all I need."

Chapter 22

Savage slid into bed beside me sometime in the middle of the night.

"Need you, babe," he whispered.

And then he slipped into me from behind. Half asleep and dreaming of him already, I was more than ready for him. His hand cradled my breast, and this thumb grazed my nipple.

I moaned and turned my head over my shoulder, searching for his mouth. He met my lips, and our tongues dueled for dominance.

He let go of my breast and grazed his fingers over my belly between my thighs. I wrenched my mouth from his and cried out my release.

Savage thrust deeply, plunging into my wet heat before finally coming with an animalistic growl.

He stayed inside me for a moment, kissing my shoulder before slowly pulling out. His release coated the back of my thighs.

I fell back asleep with him wrapped around me.

The next day, I attempted to button my jeans, only to find that they didn't want to close. Savage came into the bedroom, bare-chested with a cup of coffee. He watched me struggle until I finally flopped onto my back on the bed, sucked in, and got them closed.

"And so it begins," I grumbled.

"And so it does," he said, setting his coffee cup down on the nightstand. He took me into his arms, and I let him. "Guess we need to go shopping, huh?"

"Shopping, gross."

"Hang tight." He released me.

"What are you doing?"

"Texting Brooklyn and asking if she has any of her old maternity clothes that you can borrow."

"That would be amazing," I said with a wide smile. "Then I wouldn't have to go shopping! But wait, that means you're telling her I'm pregnant."

"Your body is gonna do that in a few weeks anyway, babe. Might as well tell her now."

"But that means other people will know too." I nibbled my lip.

"The club you mean."

I nodded.

He shrugged.

"Don't you want to be the one to tell your club all this? Not let them find out from Brooklyn?"

"I'm asking Brooklyn to be discreet, okay? She won't say anything. Well, she'll probably tell Slash."

"Slash?"

"Her husband." He paused. "Yeah, you're right. There's a good chance the club is gonna find out."

I groaned.

"Don't worry about it. It'll be fine. The sooner they know, the better."

"I thought you wanted to tell Willa and Duke before anyone else."

"They know about you already."

"They do?"

He nodded. "Yep. But they don't know I made you my Old Lady."

"Why not?"

"Because I can't just spring that on them. It's a big deal and I want them to meet you first, so they get why I asked you to be my Old Lady as fast as I did."

A few moments later, his phone buzzed. "Brooklyn's gonna go through her closet and grab all her old stuff."

"Yay."

He kissed the end of my nose. "We have time for a driving lesson."

"I'd rather go to the DMV so I can get my permit."

"You sure you're ready for that? You have to take a written exam, you know."

"I know, I've been studying the manual at work. Please take me?"

"The DMV makes me homicidal," he groused.

"I'll make it worth your while . . ."

"Yeah? How?"

"I'll cook you dinner and then perform sexual favors for you."

"Let's go," he said, ushering me toward the door.

I raised my brows. "You might want to put a shirt on first."

He grinned. "I got excited and forgot I wasn't wearing one."

My gaze dropped to his jeans. "Yeah, I bet you did."

I walked into work with a radiant grin spread across my face.

Virgil and Roman had already unlocked the shop and were enjoying a cup of coffee by the counter.

"Hey," Roman greeted, a quizzical smile on his lips.

"Hi," I chirped.

"I don't mean to be a dick," Virgil began, "but like, you are happy as fuck right now."

I mock-glared at him and pointed to the glass swear jar I'd installed. The Jackson brothers had dirty mouths, and the jar was already halfway full.

With a sigh, he fished out a dollar and put it into the jar.

"Am I not allowed to be happy this early in the morning?" I asked.

They exchanged a look. "No, you are," Roman said. "But you took the day off yesterday."

"I did."

"Because you were crying," Virgil added. "Homer told us."

"I *was* crying, yes. But I'm better now," I assured him. "Did Homer tell you *why* I was crying?"

"Yep. I guess double congratulations are in order." Roman said as he began to smile.

"Yeah, it would seem so."

"You should've seen Homer when he got here and told us." Virgil laughed. "The man hates emotion. He looked like he was going to puke."

"Then he'd have been in good company," I joked. "That's all I seem to do nowadays. Where is Homer anyway?"

Roman rubbed the back of his neck. Virgil smirked.

"What? Did I scare him off with my hormonal tears?"

"No. His absence has nothing to do with you actually," Roman said. "He—ah might've . . ."

"Might've what?"

"Found out that Jazz didn't cancel her date last night," Virgil said. "So, he showed up and crashed the party."

"That's wild, but it still doesn't explain why Homer's not here now."

"He's . . . *occupied* at the moment," Roman said.

I frowned. "Okay?"

"He's screwing Jazz's brains out," Virgil said baldly. "They've been dancing around each other for years and last night it all finally came together."

My cheeks heated with embarrassment. "Oh. Well. As long as they're happy."

"Happy is not a word I'd associate with Homer. But if anyone has a chance of making him a few notches above surly, it's Jazz," Virgil explained.

"Do we expect him in today at all?" I asked.

"Doubtful," Roman said.

"So I should cancel and reschedule his appointments," I stated.

"Yep," Virgil said. "Good luck with that."

"Why do I need luck?"

"Because he's got himself a fan club . . ." Roman looked at Virgil.

"Yeah, there's a beautiful woman who aggressively flirts with Homer every time she's in his chair. She's not going to be happy that she has to reschedule."

"Well, I'm not scared of her," I said, marching around them to get behind the counter. "Now if you'll excuse me, I better get to work."

The door to Three Kings opened and a tall, very pregnant blonde strode in carrying a few canvas totes full of clothes. She looked at me.

"Hi. How can I help you today?" I asked pleasantly.

"You're Evie."

I looked at her in confusion, but I nodded.

She beamed. "I'm Willa. Savage's—"

"Best friend. Right. Hi."

"Hi." She laughed. "I brought you Brooklyn's maternity clothes. She would have brought them to you herself, but Palmer had a pediatrician's appointment, so I volunteered."

"Oh, that's so nice of you." I smiled. "Thanks. I can take those and put them behind the counter."

"Don't think for one moment this visit is altruistic," she beamed as she handed me the bags. "I wanted to meet you in person and invite you to dinner sometime this week. Ever since Waverly told us about you, I've been bugging him to bring you around. Savage has been keeping you all to himself and giving me excuse after excuse."

"After excuse," I said with a nod. "Well, we can't have that. I'd love to come to dinner."

"Great. Let me give you my number. You can text me when you talk to Savage and figure out your schedule."

I unlocked my phone and handed it to her. She punched in her number. "I'm texting myself, so I have your number, too."

Heavy footsteps tromped down the hallway and Roman appeared with a burly, bearded client. "See you in a few weeks, Rudy."

Rudy clapped Roman's hand.

"Hey, Willa," Roman greeted.

"Hi." She waved. "I just popped in to say hello to Evie and now I'm going."

Heartbeats & Highways

The door jangled shut as she left. Rudy quickly squared up with me and then headed out, leaving me alone with Roman.

"Stop looking at me that way," I said.

"What way?"

"Like you're curious about why Willa was here."

"I *am* curious." He shrugged. "You don't have to tell me though."

"She invited me to dinner at her house," I said. "Thoughts?"

"Bring a loaf of your homemade sourdough."

∼

After smoothing over the ruffled feathers of Homer's customers and booking a few more appointments for Virgil and Roman, it was the end of the workday.

Savage waited for me in the parking lot and when I went out to meet him, my heart lifted. I carted out the canvas totes.

He cocked his head to the side, asking a silent question.

"Willa brought me Brooklyn's clothes."

"Did she." He pressed a button and the hatchback opened, and I set the clothes inside the car.

"She also invited me to dinner."

He groaned. "Damn it."

"She knew what you were doing—giving her the runaround and keeping me all to yourself. Give it up, Savage. I have to meet them."

"Yeah, I know." He rubbed the back of his neck. "I just wanted . . ."

"What? You've made me your Old Lady. I'm pregnant. They're your best friends. The sooner I integrate into your life, the better." I reached out and touched his chin. "Trust me."

He stepped closer and cradled the back of my neck as he peered into my gaze. "You didn't kiss me hello."

And then his lips crashed into mine.

He assaulted my senses.

I drowned in the passion of his kiss.

But Savage was my life raft.

I placed my hand on his chest and moved even closer, wanting more of what he was offering.

His tongue invaded my mouth, and I whimpered against him.

He growled low in his throat, clasped my waist, and hauled me toward him.

While he continued to kiss me, he maneuvered me until my back was against the side of the car. Savage slid his thigh between my legs and gently pressed the heat of me.

Sparks of lightning ricocheted through my body.

I reached for him. Eager. Needy.

More.

He cradled my cheeks and then pulled back to stare at my mouth.

"Fuck," he murmured.

I swallowed and nodded.

He cracked a grin.

"Let's go," he said, opening the driver's side door. "You're driving home."

"Yeah right," I quipped. "I'm liable to crash after all that."

Chapter 23

"How's Sunday?" I asked as I put the dishes into the dishwasher.

"For what?" He snapped the container of leftovers closed and stuck it into the fridge.

"For dinner at Willa and Duke's?"

He let out a sigh. "You won't let it go, will you?"

"No. They're important to you. Therefore, they're going to be important to me. So, let's just go and have fun and not make such a big deal about it."

"But it is a big deal. You're a big deal."

I grinned.

He took my left hand and brought my knuckles to his lips. His thumb skated over my pinky. Once . . . then twice. Savage paused and then gently forced my fingers to straighten. Except the pinky finger was slightly bent and raised in one spot.

"What happened to your finger?"

My heart skidded through my chest. "I broke it."

He frowned. "How? I know broken fingers. This looks . . . the scar . . ."

He met my gaze. Steady. Waiting. Unrelenting.

"It was a meat tenderizer," I said quietly. "For burning his dinner, the first year we were married."

He hauled me close and caged me within his embrace. I coiled myself around him and buried my nose in his shirt.

"That wasn't the only time he was physical. Was it?"

"No."

"Fuck, Evie. Did your family know?"

"My parents died when I was eighteen. I was already married to him. There was no one I could . . . anyway it doesn't matter anymore. He's dead and I'm with you."

"God, I had no idea."

"Why would you? I didn't say anything about it."

"Yeah, but—it makes sense now. Why you didn't want to go home with me that first night."

I smiled against his chest. "That had more to do with not wanting to be another notch on your bedpost."

He gently ran his fingers through my hair, his grip tightening ever so slightly and gently easing my neck back, so I had to look at him. "I'm a fighter. You saw me in the ring and then you saw me beat the shit out of that guy who grabbed your wrist. I can't believe that didn't turn you off."

I licked my lips. "You covered my body with yours when we heard the gunshots. It was instantaneous—like you didn't even have to think about protecting me. You just did. I know violence at the hand of a man. And I know you'd never raise your hands against me."

"Have I ever scared you?"

I thought about his question for a moment, searching my memory for a time that I was afraid of Savage. "When you ran out of the warehouse after me. You came toward me and your hands were clenched. I remember taking a step back, and when I did you immediately stopped in your tracks. Afraid isn't the right word . . . but my past . . ."

"What about when we were at Spurs, and I almost got into a fight, and you stepped between me and Ox?"

"No, I wasn't afraid."

"You shouldn't have done that," he murmured. "I was in the red zone."

"And yet, I was able to call you back. You're intense, Savage. But even so, I know you'd never hurt me."

His eyes glittered with emotion. "I'm so fucking sorry, Evie. I'm so sorry your husband hurt you."

"I came here to start over because when he died, I was finally free. Free to meet you. Free to fall in love. The past can only hurt you if you let it. I don't want to look behind me anymore. I want to look forward."

He settled his hand on my belly. "Then let's look forward together."

An hour later, I was on the couch reading a baby book I'd found tucked into the bag of clothes Willa had brought me. Savage was pacing nonstop.

"What's with you?" I asked.

"Sorry, babe," he apologized even as he continued to pace. "I've got all this energy inside me. I've got to get it out."

I flung the book aside and stood. "I can help with that."

"No."

I halted in my steps toward him. "No?"

He rubbed the back of his neck. "I mean, I need to fucking hit something. I'm angry, babe. I'm so damn angry and if I take you to bed, you'll get that anger. And I won't do that to you."

My gaze softened and I nodded.

"I can't stop thinking about what you told me about your husband," he admitted, his voice low. "And the only thing I can think to do, is get in the ring and beat the shit out of someone."

"But you said you quit."

He shook his head. "I meant get in The Ring—at the gym the club owns and spar with another boxer."

I took a deep breath. "I see."

Savage came to me and dropped to his knees and wrapped his arms around my waist. He placed his cheek against my shirt.

My hands sifted through his hair. "Do what you have to do, Savage."

He looked up at me, his expression slashed with awe. "You really understand me, don't you?"

I ran my thumb across his mouth. "You are who you are. And I love you. If you need to box to quiet your mind, then who am I to tell you no?"

He pressed a kiss to my stomach.

My phone chimed from the counter.

"Who could be texting me?" I asked in confusion. "No one texts me."

"Look and see," he suggested.

I stood and walked to the counter and peered at my screen. "It's Brielle. She's asking if I want to come over and hang out with her and Jazz."

"Nice."

"Tonight," I clarified.

"You should go," he said. "Don't just sit here stewing while I'm at The Ring."

"Good idea," I said, shooting off a reply text.

"I'll drive you over there. And pick you up when I'm done. I shouldn't be more than an hour or two. Acid'll go hard."

"Acid? That's who you'll be boxing with?"

"Yeah. He's skilled. He keeps pace with me. I'll be

fucking wrecked when I'm done. And I'll be able to sleep." He kissed my forehead. "Get your purse. Let's go."

⁓

Two dogs greeted me the moment Brielle opened the door.

"Oops, sorry. I forgot to warn you." Brielle scooped up the white scraggle-muffin of a dog and then shooed the other, bigger one, back from the door.

"Don't worry about it. I love dogs." I came into the open floor plan loft and held out my hand to the dog in Brielle's arms. "Not as much as lambs, but I love dogs."

"Lambs?" Jazz asked from the kitchen as she opened a bottle of wine.

I blinked, not realizing what just slipped out of me. "I grew up on a farm."

"Ah," Brielle said as she moved deeper into the living room. "No lambs here. You'll have to settle for Fluffernutter and Cuddle Bug." She set the small dog down. "That's Fluffernutter. The big, sweet girl is Cuddle Bug."

"And before you say anything, yes, we know how ridiculous the names are. You should hear us calling for them at the dog park," Jazz said with a laugh.

"Oh, I can only imagine," I said, chuckling. "Savage is going to The Ring to box with Acid. He'll pick me up when he's done. We've got about two hours for you to tell me everything that happened between you and Homer."

Jazz poured two glasses of wine. "What can I get you to drink?"

"Water's good."

She nodded and went to the cabinet to get a glass.

Brielle grimaced as she walked to the counter to pick up a glass of wine and said, "I want to know too. But, like, a PG version. I don't want to know about your aerobic activities with my brother. I'm happy for you and all, but there are some details I just do *not* need."

"I had to reschedule all his appointments today," I said. "So . . . you must've kept him occupied."

Jazz filled a glass of water and then grabbed the other wine goblet and strode toward me. "Evie, take the couch. I'll sit on the rug."

I walked to the couch and plopped down on one end and the large dog immediately jumped up and crawled halfway into my lap and then laid down.

"She has no sense of personal space," Brielle said with a grin as she took the other end of the couch.

"Clearly." I rubbed her ears and she let out a big breath and burrowed deeper against my side.

"Okay." Brielle took a drink of her wine. "Tell us all the things."

"Well," Jazz began. "I didn't cancel my date." She looked at Brielle. "Thanks for telling him that."

Brielle raised her glass.

"Anyway, Homer was pissed. Like, *livid*. I've never seen him so mad." Jazz grinned. "The date was the spark that pushed him over the edge. *Finally*. So, like the grumpy caveman he is, he dragged me back to his apartment and . . . well, ya know. We spent the night together." She glanced at Brielle and then to me. "We, ah, didn't do much talking, if you catch my drift."

"I think we catch your drift," I said with a laugh.

"We woke up and he cooked me breakfast. And then he asked me to move in with him."

The room was silent.

"You said yes, didn't you?" Brielle guessed.

"Actually, I punched him," Jazz said.

I raised my brows. "You *punched* him?"

"Okay, maybe not *punched*. But I slapped him."

"Why?" I asked in confusion.

"Because he's made me wait for years for him and he had the audacity to skip all the steps in a relationship. He doesn't get off that easy. Well, actually, he did get off—"

"Focus," Brielle interrupted.

"I told him I wanted to be wined and dined. Wooed. He doesn't get to jump ahead just because he's finally ready to be with me."

"And that talk took all day?" I asked in confusion. "That's why he had to cancel his appointments?"

She shook her head. "No. I left his apartment this morning. He lives in this building, by the way. I have no idea why he'd cancel his appointments. Do you know where he is?" Jazz looked at Brielle, who shook her head.

"I didn't see his car in the lot when Savage dropped me off here," I said. "He might be back by now, though."

"I should go knock on his door," Brielle said.

"No, don't do that," Jazz said. "Let him stew. Let him figure his shit out. I've got him right where I want him."

"And where's that?" I asked.

"Addicted to me." Jazz grinned. "I gave him some Jazz-nip. He'll be back for more."

Chapter 24

I ATTEMPTED TO ROLL OVER, but I encountered fur in my nose. I cracked my eyes open and saw a dog nestled up against me. I'd been spooning Cuddle Bug.

The clock on the microwave read five-thirty. My groggy brain finally put the pieces together; I'd fallen asleep last night on Jazz and Brielle's couch.

I wondered what had woken me up, but then I heard it: the sound of the shower.

After gently nudging Cuddle Bug off the couch, I was able to sit up. They'd left the stove light on which gave me just enough illumination to see the coffee table and not bash my knee.

There was a snick of a key sliding into the lock and then the door opened. Jazz was carrying her shoes and trying to be stealthy, but Cuddle Bug went to investigate which only startled Jazz. She knocked into the entryway table and let out a low curse.

"I'm awake," I announced.

"Oh, thank God," Jazz said. She quickly closed the door and set her shoes down.

"I didn't mean to fall asleep on your couch. You should've woken me."

"Don't worry about it. You looked far too peaceful to wake up. I sent Savage a text to let him know you were crashing with us."

"Oh. Thanks for that," I said. "Uh, not to be dramatic, but I've got about five minutes before my body realizes it's awake and decides to upchuck."

"There's a second bathroom." Jazz pointed to a door I hadn't noticed before. "Do what you need."

"Thanks. So you were with Homer?"

"I was," she admitted. "He came up here after you fell asleep. And I let him convince me to spend the night with him. The man does not know how to share a bed, though. I didn't get any sleep."

"Uh-huh," I drawled.

She giggled. "Seriously. Anyway, I'm gonna feed the dogs, then take them out for a bathroom break. Then I'm napping for a few hours before I have to be at the bakery."

My stomach swirled and I jumped up off the couch. "Oh no."

Jazz stepped out of the way as I barreled past her to the second bathroom. A few minutes later, I was back on the couch.

I heard a door open and a moment later Brielle strode out in a robe, a towel wrapped around her head. "Thought I heard you guys moving around," Brielle said. "You mind if I hit the light and get the coffee going?"

"Have at it," I said. "And what you really heard was me throwing up."

The kitchen light came on. "I did hear that, yes." Brielle smiled. "But I was trying to be nice first thing in the morning. Jazz came back?"

"Yep. She took the dogs out." I cocked my head to the side. "You're up early."

"I gotta get to work and decorate a hundred cupcakes." She grimaced. "I can drop you off at home if you want."

"That would be great, thanks."

"Can I get you anything? Toast? Orange juice?"

"Both of those, actually." I laughed. "So, when exactly did I conk out? I don't even remember falling asleep."

"Jazz was in the middle of picking her wedding colors. I would've passed out too, but she *is* my best friend. And I'm going to be maid of honor."

"She's talking about a wedding already? I thought she was making Homer work for it."

"She is," Brielle said. "But she's also Jazz, and she's wanted him for years. So the moment she believes he's truly committed, she's gonna want a wedding."

"Wild."

Brielle shrugged. "My parents will be overjoyed. They've started demanding grandbabies. Roman gets it the worst because he's the oldest. But when Homer and Jazz tie the knot, the focus will be off the rest of us. Which is why I say the sooner the better."

"So you want kids?"

"Eventually." Brielle pulled out the orange juice carton and poured a glass. "Kinda hard to give them grandchildren because my brothers scare off any man trying to get close to me. So I'm kind of in a lose-lose situation. I might have to move just so I can date in peace."

"You wouldn't really move, would you?" I asked, taking the glass she brought me.

"Nah. I can't imagine living away from my family, but man, they make it hard sometimes."

The front door opened and the dogs still on leashes

Heartbeats & Highways

bounded into the living room. Cuddle Bug jumped up next to me and I removed her leash and gave her ears a scratch.

Fluffernutter ran in circles around Brielle's legs and then sat so Brielle could take off his leash.

"Homer says he'll give them a longer walk later before he goes to work," Jazz announced. She looked at me. "Another perk of her brother living in the building? We time-share the dogs."

"What happens when you and Homer live together? Who gets the dogs?" I asked.

"We haven't really talked about it," Brielle admitted. "Because up until a few days ago, the idea of me and Homer together was just a fantasy."

"What about you, though?" Brielle asked as she put two slices of whole grain toast into the toaster and pressed the lever.

"What about me?" I frowned.

"I mean, what are you going to do about the apartment you're living in?" Brielle asked.

"Still not following."

"Well, you can't stay there forever," Brielle said. "It's sort of a transition place, for women in need, right?"

"Yeah." I nodded. "I haven't thought too far ahead, actually. It's not like I have the money to get a real place yet."

"What about Savage?" Jazz inquired, taking a seat on the couch.

"What about him?" I asked.

"Has he said anything to you about moving to a place more permanent?"

"No."

Her question made my mind swirl. He lived at the clubhouse which wasn't a viable solution for the future. But we hadn't discussed it yet.

The toaster popped.

"Butter?" Brielle asked.

I shook my head.

"Dry toast?" Jazz wrinkled her nose. "Yuck."

"When you're puking your guts up because you're pregnant with Homer's baby, then maybe you'll understand the need for bland," I said.

"Homer's baby . . ." She sighed.

"Oh crap," Brielle muttered. "Full steam ahead, huh, Jazz?"

"Hmm. Fuck this slow crap. I've waited too long already."

~

There was a box of Moonglow pears and a note waiting for me on my doorstep. I looked at the door across the hall, wondering if my neighbor was on the other side, staring at me through the peephole. In case she was, I smiled and waved before going into my own apartment.

My apartment that had no personal touches and no dog to greet me.

My apartment that had no men's boots by the door, and no leather cut hanging in a closet.

Savage wasn't here.

I liked waking up next to him. I liked our morning routine of pickle juice and croissants. I liked his toothbrush resting next to mine.

I liked the permanence of him, but this apartment was just the opposite.

It was six-thirty in the morning when I texted Savage, so I didn't expect a reply. I set my phone aside.

Then I got to work peeling the pears.

I was halfway through the box when Savage walked through the front door holding a crate of canning jars.

"Good morning," I greeted with a smile, my eyes raking over him as I set down the peeler. "Your face doesn't look too worse for wear."

He set the crate down on the counter and then wrapped his arms around me to kiss me hello. When he pulled back, he said, "I asked Acid to spare my pretty face."

"You sleep okay?" I asked.

"As well as I can when you're not next to me," he admitted. "My clubhouse bed is comfortable, but I don't like it there without you, babe. I need to be able to feel you next to me."

"Hmm." I kissed him again. "I think I have to be honest with you. I slept with a very furry companion last night. She doesn't kiss as well as you, though."

He grinned. "Yeah, Brielle sent a photo of you spooning her dog. Fucking cute as hell. That's the only way I'll ever share you, babe."

"I was just going to make some breakfast. Have you eaten?"

"No," he croaked, his gaze sliding down my body. "I haven't eaten."

I pointed at him. "Behave."

"But it's my favorite thing to eat."

My insides quivered and desire swirled through my belly. "You can have that for dessert. If you're a good boy and eat your entire breakfast."

He sat on a stool at the counter. I moved the pears to one side to give myself some room. I grabbed the carton of eggs and cracked several into a mixing bowl.

"Now I get why you needed the canning jars," Savage said. "Where did you get the pears?"

"My neighbor across the hall," I said, whisking the eggs and turning on a stove burner. "They were on my doorstep when I got home this morning."

"And you still haven't met each other, huh?"

"Not yet. I'll leave a jar of pear jam on her doorstep to thank her."

"Why don't you just knock on the door and introduce yourself?"

"I'm waiting for her to make the first move. She's skittish. You gotta be patient with this sort of thing." I dumped the eggs into a pan and they sizzled.

"Hmm. So, tell me about last night. Give me the deets."

"You're such a gossip," I said with a laugh.

"Damn right. What happened between Jazz and Homer?"

"They're together. But like, not *together*, together."

"I don't have any idea what that means."

"It means Jazz wants to be wined and dined, but Homer wants to rush through all the steps of dating and just be in a committed relationship. But Jazz also doesn't seem like she's going to make him wait long either."

The eggs were cooked, and I used the spatula to spoon them onto two plates and set the bigger pile in front of Savage. "Juice?"

"Sure."

I opened the fridge. "So can I talk to you about something?"

"Shoot."

I poured him a glass and then another for myself. "What are we going to do about my living situation?"

"What do you mean?"

I gestured to the apartment. "This is a transition place,

Heartbeats & Highways

for women in need. I should move out and find something else. Something more permanent."

"Ah."

"There's one issue with that, though," I said.

"Which is?"

"Money. As in, I don't have any. I mean, I have *a little* from the few fights I worked before you got me fired. And as much as I love working at Three Kings it's not gonna cut it. Not for rent, a car, and all the baby stuff I'm going to need for twins."

Savage picked up his fork and took a bite of his eggs. "These are good."

"Thanks."

He continued to eat, looking completely nonplussed.

"Are you going to say anything?"

"Eat your eggs. Protein is good for you and the babies."

"Savage . . ."

"I already bought a car for us, so you don't have to worry about that."

"Yeah." I nodded slowly. "Technically I guess you did, but I don't drive it and it's not really—"

"You're on the title," he interrupted. "It's your car."

"Seriously?"

"Yup."

"Well, that's news to me." I took a sip of my juice.

"Don't worry about rent, either. I'll cover it. We'll start looking for a place that's big enough for the four of us when you're ready, okay?"

I shook my head. "Not okay."

"Why not? Are you worried about us living together?" He smirked. "Hate to break it to you, but we already live together. I moved in without you even noticing."

"I noticed—and it's not that. It's . . ."

"Tell me."

"You promise you won't get mad?"

"No. Now tell me what's on your mind. I'm listening."

"You've been so generous, Savage. The car and the doctor's appointment. Wanting to go to the birthing classes . . . God, it's been wonderful."

"Then what's the issue?"

"I don't want you to think that I—that because my past was hard and I came to this city with nothing . . . I don't want you to think all I want from you is your money."

"Babe," he said gently. "I could never think that. Ever. But I can take care of you, and I'm already in love with you."

I swallowed. "Randall controlled our money. And in the end, I had nothing to my name."

"Ah, I see what this is really about." He nodded. "Okay."

"Okay what?"

"I'll never use money to control you. We'll set up a bank account that I have no access to and I'll put money in there and you spend it however you want."

"Which again, that's so generous of you, Savage. But that's the whole point. It's still *your* money. It's still *you* giving it to me. I want to make my own way in this world, even though we're together."

"Tell you what." He got up off his stool and came to me. "I'll cover the big things, okay? You keep your money and spend it however you want, and if you wanna start saving and buying cars and houses I'm good with that too."

"But how are you okay with that?" I asked in shock.

"Because money is one of those things that's only able to control you when you don't have it. But I've already got money. What am I supposed to spend it on if not you and the babies?"

I sighed. "You're wonderful."

"I know." He kissed my nose. "Eat, babe. And don't worry."

He let me go and I picked up my fork. After I swallowed a bite, I asked, "What kind of place do you want? Something open, like a loft or . . ."

"You know, I've never really thought about it," he said.

"No?"

He shook his head. "As long as the place is comfortable, what do I care what it looks like?"

"But what does comfort look like for you?" I asked.

"What does it look like for *you*?" he countered. "Do you like this apartment? The layout? The size? The colors?"

"I'd prefer a place with no stairs."

"Why no stairs?"

I took a deep breath and then said, "If there are no stairs, no one can push you down them."

My admittance weighed in the air between us. I kept my gaze trained on him. His body tightened and he looked ready to spring from his stool. He clenched his fists instead.

"I shouldn't have said that," I said with a worried frown. "Now you'll have to go back to The Ring."

He shook his head. "Don't ever feel like you can't share something like that. Even if it makes me want to punch a wall."

"Just when I think I'm moving past it, I—things come up."

"Damn it," Savage muttered. "I'd kill him myself if he were still alive. The idea of him hurting you . . ."

He got up off his stool and came around the counter to me. Savage reached out and pulled me to him.

I buried my nose in his chest and breathed him in.

"You never flinch," he murmured against my hair.

"Hmm?"

"When I approach you or touch you. You don't jump or pull back."

"I feel safe around you. Protected." I tilted my head back so I could meet his eyes. "I'm not afraid of you."

His hand cradled my face, and he skimmed a thumb across my cheek. "And I'll never give you a reason to be."

Chapter 25

When I pulled into the parking lot of Three Kings, Virgil and Roman were already there. Roman climbed out of his car and reached into the passenger side to grab a brown paper bag.

I unlatched my seat belt and reached for the door.

"Wait," Savage commanded. "Let me get it for you."

"I'm perfectly capable—"

"It's a manners thing, woman. Let me be a gentleman. All right?"

My lips quivered in amusement. "All right."

I waited for Savage to come around and open the door for me. He took my hand and helped me out of the driver's side of the car and then he pulled me to him.

"Have a good day today," he said.

"You too."

Savage didn't seem to care that Roman and Virgil were taking their sweet time going into Three Kings. He leaned down and brushed his lips over mine. I clung to him, silently demanding more. He obliged and slid his tongue into my mouth.

We didn't pull apart until Virgil's howling and whistling became too much.

I couldn't help but laugh at Savage's annoyed expression. He looked at me and raised a brow. "You think this is funny?"

"Yes, I do." I pecked the end of his nose. "Virgil is just trying to get a rise out of you. I think it's working."

"Something's working." Savage shifted positions, his thigh brushing against my leg. "You get a rise out of me . . ."

I blushed.

"I never did get my dessert," he whispered in my ear before biting my lobe.

"Good things come to those who wait," I teased. "See you later."

I reluctantly stepped away and headed toward Three Kings.

"Morning," Virgil drawled, waggling his eyebrows.

"Behave," I reprimanded.

"Yes, ma'am."

"Where's Homer?" I asked.

"On his way," Roman explained. "I got you something."

"You did?" I asked.

Roman handed me the paper bag. I opened the top and looked inside. "You didn't."

"I did," Roman said with a smile.

"That was so nice of you," I said. Without thought, I reached out to him and gave him a one-armed hug.

"What did he do?" Virgil asked as he unlocked the front door.

"He got me chocolate milk." I beamed. "I had a craving for it yesterday."

"My big brother. Thoughtful guy," Virgil stated. "I have a bag of gummy bears I'm willing to share."

"You're thoughtful too," I said with a laugh. "You guys are like the brothers I never had."

"We try," Roman said.

"If you want, later I can give you a wet willie. Really drive home the fraternal feeling." Virgil opened the front door and gestured for me to go in first.

I went through the doorway, immediately heading for the alarm system. "What's a wet willie?"

"You're kidding, right?" Virgil asked.

"No, I'm not kidding. I have no idea what that is." I grabbed the paper bag from Roman and took it to the reception counter.

"Spare her the demonstration," Roman said to his brother.

Virgil looked offended. "I wasn't going to give her a demonstration."

"Liar." Roman laughed and then addressed me. "A wet willie is when someone sucks on their finger and then shoves it in your ear."

I wrinkled my nose. "Ew."

"You've never had one of those? Really? It was a staple in our household growing up," Virgil said. "Along with wedgies. You've heard of wedgies, right?"

"Nope. I think I can forgo a demonstration on that too, whatever it is."

"It's when you grab someone's underwear band and yank up hard on the backside," Virgil explained. "Ask Brielle about the time I did it when she was talking to the captain of the football team in high school."

"I'm sure she'd love to tell me that story." I rolled my eyes and put the chocolate milk away.

The front door opened, and Homer strode inside.

"Huh," Virgil remarked.

"Huh what?" Homer glared.

Virgil rubbed his lip. "I thought for sure getting some ass would've changed your attitude. Clearly, I was wrong."

"It's not *ass*," Homer snapped. "It's Jazz. Be respectful."

The three of us fell into silence.

Homer looked at me. "Can I talk to you?"

"Me?" My brow furrowed. "Sure."

"You two," Homer said to Roman and Virgil. "Beat it."

"Fine, but you know we'll listen from the hallway," Virgil said.

"Not this time." Roman clapped his younger brother on the shoulder. "Let's go."

Virgil shook his head in disappointment but trailed after Roman.

After the sound of two doors closing, Homer turned to me.

"Yes?" I asked.

"What do women like?" he blurted out.

I frowned. "That's way too general. I'm not following."

He sighed. "You were with Jazz and Brielle last night, right?"

"Yes."

"So I'm sure Jazz said some things about relationships . . ."

"Still not following you."

"God damn it, I want to convince her to be with me after years of dancing around each other, but I don't have a fucking clue how to do that." His dark expression cleared, and he suddenly looked forlorn.

"Oh," I said quietly. "You want to show her you actually care about her, don't you?"

"Yes," he gritted out.

"And you don't know how to do that."

"No, I don't."

"You've known Jazz a long time," I said. "You really have no idea how to woo her?"

"Would I be baring my soul and asking you for help if I had any idea on how to woo her?"

I wasn't going to tell him that by admitting his feelings for her, he'd done half the work already. Jazz was my friend; she deserved a happily-ever-after, but she also deserved Homer putting forth some effort.

"Well?" he prodded.

"I'm thinking."

When I was silent for a few moments he demanded, "Can you think faster?"

"Do you want my help or not?"

"Yes."

"Then give me some time. I'll think about it today and come up with a list. And before we go any further, why aren't you asking Brielle what Jazz wants? Why me?"

"She's my sister and it feels . . . weird. I want to leave Brielle out of this."

"Have you texted her today?" I asked.

"My sister? No."

"No, not your sister. Jazz," I said with a roll of my eyes.

"No. I haven't." He paused. "I should text her."

"Yes," I said gently. "You should text her something sweet."

"I'm not sweet."

"Be sweet for her. Trust me, she'll love it."

"Or she'll think I've had a lobotomy," he muttered. He pulled out his cell and stared at it.

"This is the part where you unlock your phone and send her a text," I teased.

"I don't know what to say."

"How about something like, '*I didn't like waking up without you.*'"

Homer nodded quickly. "Yeah, that sounds good. Wait . . ."

"What?"

"Does that sound like something I'd say?"

I held in a smile.

"It doesn't sound like me," he rasped.

"You're going to have to show her a different side of yourself," I said. "That's the only way it's going to work."

"Yeah."

"Just press send, Homer."

He sighed. "Here goes nothing."

~

"She still hasn't texted me," Homer said as he leaned on the counter after his last client of the day left.

"She's playing hard to get," I said.

"Why?"

"What do you mean, *why?* She doesn't want to make it too easy for you."

He raked a hand through his disheveled hair. "I'm going insane."

"Okay, here's what you're going to do." I slid him the list I'd made. "Read this over and implement these items one by one. But for now, you're going to go buy some flowers and you're going to show up at her apartment with them. Then you're going to ask if you guys can take the dogs for a walk. *Together.*"

"Together."

"*Together,*" I repeated.

"That might just work," he said, looking relieved. "Thanks."

I smiled. "Good luck."

Homer rushed out the door.

"Were his pants on fire?" Virgil asked as he strode out into the reception area.

"He had somewhere to be," I said vaguely. I looked at Virgil's customer; a cute, curvy woman sporting a shoulder bandage and a new tattoo. "Ready to square up?"

"Yes, please," she said, holding her credit card to the screen. She looked at Virgil. "Thanks."

"I'll see you in two weeks," he said.

"Sounds good."

She signed her name on the tablet. With a smile and a wave, she left.

"Okay, now that Sarah's gone, tell me the truth. Where did Homer go?"

"None of your business," I said. "I'm not giving you more fodder to make fun of him."

"Aw, you're protective. I like that."

My phone buzzed with a text from Savage, telling me he was on his way.

I couldn't stop the smile from spreading across my face.

"Someone's happy," Virgil teased.

"I am happy," I admitted.

"It's because you get to spend your working hours with me, isn't it?" Virgil asked.

"That's part of it," I said with a laugh.

"Just so you know, you can always come back to work after your maternity leave," Virgil said. "I mean, you'll always have a job with us if you want one."

I blinked furiously. "Oh."

"What's wrong?" Virgil asked. "You look like you're about to cry."

"I *am* about to cry."

Virgil reached for the tissue box next to the computer and shoved it at me.

I grabbed a few tissues and quickly blotted my eyes.

Roman and his client appeared from the back. "What did you do to her?" Roman demanded, glaring at his brother.

"Nothing," Virgil defended.

"You did *something* to her," Roman's customer added.

"Shut up, Milton," Virgil snapped.

"He said something sweet," I said. "And that made me cry."

Roman raised his brows. "You were being sweet? I don't buy it."

"Maybe she has low blood sugar," Milton said.

"Give her your gummy bears," Roman stated.

"I already ate them," I muttered, drying my eyes.

"This looks like a family matter. I better get out of here," Milton said. "Later."

When Milton was gone, Roman said to Virgil, "Okay, what did you say to her?"

"Nothing. I just said that she had a job here as long as she wanted, even after she was done with maternity leave."

Roman grunted. "That *is* sweet."

Virgil puffed out his chest. "Told ya. I can be sweet."

"You're nicer to me than you are to your own sister," I stated.

"Brielle has a thick skin from many years of verbal torture," Virgil explained. "You, do not."

"Plus, you're pregnant," Roman added. "And no one wants to be the reason a pregnant woman is crying."

"I'm crying now," I pointed out.

"Yeah, but not because we were insensitive tool bags," Virgil said. "I was just being sweet. And make sure you tell

Savage that. He's already annoyed that I witnessed the tonsil hockey."

"I'll tell him," I assured Virgil. "Also, my baby classes are starting soon, and I'll need to leave early."

"How early?" Roman asked.

"Five-thirty," I said. "It runs for eight weeks. Is that okay?"

"That's no problem," Roman said. "We can make that happen. We'll work around your schedule. Whatever you and the babies need."

I burst into tears again.

Virgil glared at Roman. "Look what you did!"

Chapter 26

"Hey," I greeted with a smile as I strode across the parking lot toward Savage.

He was leaning against the SUV, looking casually bored. "Hey."

I stopped walking. "What's wrong?"

"Nothing."

"Not nothing. What is it?"

"Get in the car."

"No."

He sighed. "Get in the car and we'll talk."

"I'd rather talk out here," I said, taking a step back.

"I'm scaring you. Fuck. I said I wouldn't scare you." He unclenched his hands. "Can we talk in the car? I want privacy. I promise we won't drive anywhere until you're ready. Please?"

"All right," I said finally.

He went around to the passenger side door and opened it for me. I trailed behind him slowly, with heavy steps, but I was determined to override my trepidation.

After I got in, Savage closed the door and then went

around to the driver's side. He climbed in, shut the door, and sat in silence for a moment.

"Savage?" I prodded.

"I've been in a mood all damn day," he said softly. "All because you hugged Roman."

I frowned. "You're upset because I hugged someone else?"

"I'm upset because I'm jealous," he stated, looking at me, a wry smile finally crossing his face. "And I've *never* been jealous over anyone."

"You have no reason to be jealous," I stated. "Yesterday I wanted chocolate milk, and we didn't have any. Roman bought a carton for me today. That's why I hugged him. That's all."

He let out a groan.

"What?" I demanded. "What did I say?"

"I'm a complete ass. I know it. But now I'm jealous that he brought you something just because you wanted it. I wish it had been me."

"You didn't know," I said. "And you can't be responsible for seeing to every one of my needs."

"I can sure as hell try," he growled.

"Savage," I began, reaching out and cradling his cheek in my hand. I ran a finger across his stubble. The feel of it against my skin caused me to shiver in pleasure. "Roman views me as a little sister. Like he sees Brielle. And I see him, Virgil, and Homer in a fraternal light. Okay?"

He turned his head and kissed my palm. "Okay."

"I only want you."

"You want me?"

I met his bold gaze and nodded.

He sighed and kissed my palm again before taking it in his own hand. "This is new territory for me."

"What is?"

"Feeling possessive."

Nerves skated through my belly. "Randall was a possessive man. I'm not sure how I feel about you being possessive, too."

He squeezed my hand and let it go. "This is my own shit. You don't need to worry about me being like your husband."

I nodded and finally buckled myself in.

"I have an idea," he said.

"What's that?"

"Tonight, we'll order in. And after dinner, I'll get on my knees and beg your forgiveness."

"On your knees, huh?"

"With my tongue between your legs." He grinned wickedly.

I pressed the start button for him. "What are you waiting for?"

~

"Tell me about your childhood," Savage commanded as he dug his thumb into the arch of my left foot.

I flipped the page of the baby book I was reading and pretended I hadn't heard him.

When I didn't reply, he pressed his finger between the book and forced it lower.

I looked at him. "Sorry, did you ask me something?"

"I asked about your childhood."

I frowned. "What about it? I told you I lived on a farm."

"Yeah. But you never talk about your parents. All you told me about them was they died when you were eighteen."

"They did." My gaze dropped back to the book.

Savage wrenched it from my hands and tossed it to the floor.

"Hey!" I made a move to get up, but he tightened his hand around my foot. "You're holding my foot hostage."

"Why won't you talk about your childhood?"

"Why won't you?"

"What do you mean? I told you about my history with Willa and Duke and how I grew up."

"Hmm. Not really. You glossed over everything else." I cocked my head to the side. "Do *you* talk about the losses you've suffered? Or do you bury them deep and try to forget?"

"Is that what you do?"

"Why do you answer a question with a question?"

"Why do you?"

We stared at one another. We were at an impasse.

A vibrating buzz of a cell phone broke the moment.

Savage reached into his jeans pocket for it and looked at the screen. "Damn, I gotta take this." He answered the phone with a brusque, "Yeah? Fuck. Yeah, okay. I'll take care of it." He ended the call and set his phone on the arm of the couch. "I've got to go."

"Oh. Okay." I breathed a sigh of relief.

"Hey," Savage commanded. "Don't think for a second that we're done with this conversation." He stood up and leaned down to kiss me. "I won't forget about this. I want answers, Evie."

~

For the next few days, our schedules didn't align. Savage was gone before I woke up, and I was in bed before he got home. He crawled into bed and made love to me before pulling me close and falling asleep.

I had a prospect take me to work in the mornings and one of the Jackson siblings drive me home. Savage regularly checked in via text, but they were quick as though he was too busy to put much thought into them.

Because he'd been busy with the club, it meant he didn't have the ability to ask me more about my childhood and upbringing. I hoped enough time had passed that he'd forgotten about it entirely and that we could continue sailing along in a blissful state of desire and growing intimacy.

"Stop fidgeting, you look beautiful," Savage said as he closed the passenger door.

"I can't help it. I'm nervous," I admitted.

"There's no reason to be nervous," Savage said.

He opened the back door of the SUV and pulled out my gifts.

"They're your family," I said. "I want to make a good impression."

"Then just be yourself." He hugged me to him, and I immediately collapsed against his side, seeking his reassurance.

He took my hand and led me toward the door.

"You didn't tell me they lived in the country," I said with a smile.

"I wanted it to be a surprise. After dinner, I'll take you to meet the neighbor's horse."

"I'd like that."

I thought we'd get to the front porch and Savage would knock, but he surprised me when he walked into the house without invitation. I was immediately assaulted by the scent of garlic and tomato.

"We're here!" he called.

A man with dark hair strode out of the kitchen, holding a bottle of beer. He clapped Savage on the back in greeting and then turned to me. "Hi, I'm Duke. Nice to finally meet you."

"Nice to meet you too," I said shyly.

"Willa's in the kitchen and she just put the meatballs in the oven," Duke said. "Come on, let's get you guys some drinks."

Duke turned and we followed him down the hallway. Willa stood at the oven; a dishrag slung over her shoulder.

"Hi!" Willa chirped, a huge smile on her face as she turned to us. She embraced Savage quickly and before I knew it, she was hugging me too.

"What can I get you guys to drink?" Duke asked.

"Beer for me," Savage said. "Evie?"

"Water's fine," I said. "I brought you some things."

Savage handed Willa the tote bag. She reached into it and pulled out the loaf of bread. "Is this homemade?"

"Yeah, it's sourdough," I said. "I hope you like it."

"I'm sure I'll love it, thank you." She beamed. "I heard about your breadmaking skills from Brooklyn, actually."

"Oh." I felt my cheeks heat. "You did?"

"There's also homemade pear jam in there," Savage commented.

"Willa, what can I do to help?" I asked.

"Nothing," she announced. "The meatballs just went in, I'll put the noodles on in a bit, and I'm going to have Sailor and Waverly make the salad."

"Where are the co-conspirators?" Savage took a drink of his beer.

"Out in the shop. They found a dresser on the side of the road, and they were giving it a good cleaning," Willa said. To me she explained, "Waverly and Sailor are big into furniture flipping. Duke, will you get them?"

"Sure thing." Duke headed for the back door and disappeared.

"Oh, damn it," Willa said. "I forgot to get a baguette for garlic bread."

"Just use the sourdough," Savage said.

"Good idea." Willa smiled at me. "Evie, would you slice it?"

"Sure." I detached from Savage's side and went to the sink to wash my hands.

"Savage, grab her a cutting board."

"Yes, Commander," Savage quipped.

"Did you explain about Sailor?" Willa asked.

"Yes, he told me on the way over," I said. "I love your house."

"Thanks. I can give you a tour later if you want."

"That sounds great."

The back door opened, and two teenagers tromped in. Duke came in behind them and shut the door.

"Evie!" Waverly greeted me with exuberance. She looked me up and down. "Why does that outfit look familiar?"

I smiled. "Because it once belonged to Brooklyn."

"Ah," Waverly said. "Well, it looks great on you."

"Thanks."

"As does my jacket," she quipped.

"Are you going to continue ignoring me?" Savage asked her.

"You're way less interesting than your girlfriend," Waverly said.

He wrapped an arm around her and ruffled her hair before releasing her. "Hey, Sailor."

"Hi, Savage," she said with a smile. "I'll forgo the hair ruffling if you don't mind."

"Your loss." Savage shrugged.

"She's right, her jacket does look good on you," Sailor said to me. "But I'm kind of jealous because she promised that jacket to me."

"In a few months I'll be too big for it. And then I'll give it to you," I stated.

"Will you guys make the salad?" Willa asked.

"But I want to ply Evie with questions," Waverly said. "Like is Savage a total simp? He's a total simp, isn't he?"

"Don't answer that," Savage said to me. "I've got a reputation to uphold."

"Yeah, he's a total simp," Sailor said with a nod.

"I need help lighting the patio lamps," Duke said to Savage.

"Let's do it."

"Are you okay if we eat outside?" Willa asked me. "The heat lamps will take away the chill in the air. And the sky is clear so there's no chance of rain."

"Sounds good to me."

"So, you've worked at Three Kings for a couple of weeks now," Waverly said as she opened the fridge. "Have you gotten Homer to smile yet?"

Chapter 27

Dinner was not only delicious, but it was filled with laughter and flowing conversation. I watched Savage interact, noting the easy charm that emanated from him. But there was a relaxation in his body that was impossible to miss.

These were his people, his family.

He teased Sailor and Waverly like they were his own sisters. He watched Duke and Willa with an absent-minded smile and every time one of them did something sweet for the other, Savage patted my leg under the table.

"You guys clean up," Willa said. "I want to show Evie the house. Then we'll have dessert. Sound good?"

"Sounds good." Duke kissed his wife. "Dinner was incredible, babe. Thanks for cooking."

She clasped his face and ran a thumb across his cheek. "My pleasure. Evie?"

I wiped my mouth with a cloth napkin and then got up. Savage lifted his hand and placed it on the back of my thigh, giving it a squeeze. I touched his shoulder and then followed Willa.

"You guys load the dishwasher," Duke said to Waverly and Sailor. "Savage and I will bring you the plates."

Willa and I went inside.

"Savage didn't tell me you guys lived out in the country," I said as we trekked down the hallway.

"We needed the space," Willa explained. "And we really do love it out here."

"I'd love it too," I admitted. "I grew up on a farm. The smells and sounds are familiar to me."

Willa nodded. "It took a little getting used to. The wind would change and suddenly all I'd smell were the neighbor's sheep. But the house is big, and Waverly and Sailor bunk together in the apartment attached to the shop."

We climbed the stairs, and I placed my hand on the wood railing.

"This is the nursery," Willa said, opening the door next to the master bedroom.

The room was painted sage green. A mural of baby animals and a circus took up one entire wall.

"This is beautiful," I remarked.

"Brielle," Willa said with a smile. "It was all Brielle."

"No way," I said with a laugh. "She has incredible skill."

"Don't I know it." She took a seat in the rocking chair in the corner and placed her hand on her belly. "I'm ready for her to be out of me."

I laughed. "Little quirk of nature, huh? Otherwise, we'd just get bigger and bigger . . ."

I went around the room, examining the furniture, running my hand across the smooth railing of the crib.

It was expensive, and sturdy.

"Savage said you're having twins," Willa said softly, her gaze trained on me. "That must've been a shock."

"Yes. It was. Almost as much of a shock as finding out I was pregnant."

Willa began to rock in the chair. "Savage also mentioned you were married . . ."

She trailed off, obviously waiting for me to expound and explain my situation.

"Yes, I was married. He passed away not too long ago. I know how it looks," I said softly. "It's been a whirlwind, believe me. I didn't expect—I fell in love with Savage *fast*. Before I even knew I was pregnant."

"Of course you fell in love with him quickly," she said. "It's Savage. He's impossible not to love. But Evie . . . you're *pregnant*. I understand the hormones, believe me. But are you sure you're not just latching on to the first person that's offered you security and stability?"

"That was blunt."

"I know. But I can't really tip-toe around it."

"Yeah," I murmured. "I guess you can't."

Willa didn't really know me. All she saw was that I was a young, pregnant woman, in love with her best friend who was willing to raise my babies as his own. I could see how from the outside, it looked like this wouldn't last.

Only Savage and I knew what we had and what we were made of. It might've been early in our relationship, but I knew it was special and no one could convince me otherwise.

"I need to use the restroom," I said, wanting a moment to escape the heaviness of our conversation.

"Sure thing. There's a bathroom down the hall," she replied.

I walked out of the nursery and found the bathroom. I closed the door and leaned against it, breathing heavily for a moment. The room was hot. Old houses had a ton of quirks, and this one was no different.

I opened the window to let in some cool, fresh air and then I sat on the toilet lid to gather my thoughts.

"What are you doing, Savage?" Duke's voice drifted through the open window.

"What do you mean *what am I doing?*"

"Don't play dumb."

"Why don't you tell me what *you* think I'm doing," Savage taunted.

"You were jealous of me, weren't you?" Duke asked.

"You're out of your God damn mind," Savage growled.

"What other explanation is there? Willa's about to have the baby, you finally noticed shit can't stay the way it's always been, so what do you do? Run out and find a woman—*a pregnant woman*—and what? You claim her? You wanted an instant family, huh?"

"You better watch your fucking mouth," Savage snapped.

"What do you actually know about her? You met her one random morning at a taco truck and you get her a job and put her in the halfway house . . . You're takin' her to doctors' appointments like you've been with her for years, man. What the fuck, brother?"

"Is there a point to all this?" Savage asked.

"Is this because of Tracy?"

"No. It has nothing to do with her."

Duke sighed. "You and Evie just met. And you're already acting like she's your Old Lady."

"Duke," Savage said sternly. "Evie *is* my Old Lady."

"What?"

"I brought her to dinner to meet you first before I called Church to tell the brothers."

"What the fuck? You've lost it. Utterly fucking lost it."

"*That's enough*," Savage snapped. "Best friend or not, I

won't stand here and let you fling this shit at me. You dated Willa in secret, so don't stand there all high and mighty and tell me what to do."

"That was different, and you know it."

"Why? Because you've loved Willa since we were kids? You loved Willa longer than I've loved Evie so you win?"

"It's not about *winning*. It's about making sure you're not gonna . . ."

"Gonna what?" Savage asked.

"What if the other shoe drops? All I'm saying is, you don't have to rush this thing with Evie. You can take your time getting to know her."

"Take my time. I don't *want* to take my time. I don't need to. She's the one for me. I thought you'd be happy for me. Clearly, I was wrong."

"I do want you to be happy. But I also want you to be careful."

"Thanks for your concern." Savage's tone was bitter.

"Savage—"

"No, fuck this."

There was a knock on the bathroom door, followed by Willa calling out, "Are you okay?"

Grimacing, I rushed to the window and quickly shut it, wishing the sound of the wooden frame hitting the sill wasn't so loud.

"I'm good. Be out in a sec!" I called back.

"Okay. I'll be downstairs."

I used the bathroom and was washing my hands when there was another knock on the door.

"Evie, it's me," Savage said.

I quickly dried my hands and went to open the door. Savage's expression was tight with emotion.

"We're leaving," he decreed.

"All right," I said softly.

He raised his brows but said nothing at my quick agreement. He took my hand and we went downstairs to the kitchen. Willa was cutting up a banana bread loaf and placing slices onto dessert plates while Duke was wiping down the counters. Waverly and Sailor had disappeared.

"Ah, good. Just in time for dessert." Willa glanced at Savage and then at me.

"We're leaving," Savage announced.

"Why?" Willa asked.

"Ask your husband," Savage stated. "Come on, Evie."

"Thanks for dinner," I said.

Savage and I left their house and got into the car. He sat in the driver's seat, staring out the window.

"I heard your talk with Duke," I said.

He didn't look at me. "Yeah?"

"Yeah, I was in the upstairs bathroom, and I heard through the open window." I nibbled my lip. "He doesn't like me."

"He doesn't know you." He clenched the steering wheel.

"You should tell him how we really met, Savage."

"That would just invite more questions."

"Doesn't he have a right to ask them?" I asked. "He's your best friend. They're your family. They just want what's best for you."

"You're what's best for me."

"I agree." I placed my hand on his arm. "Don't be mad at him. Think about how this looks from his perspective. He's not wrong for being concerned."

"You're being way too understanding about this."

"What should I do?" I asked. "Demand you stop being friends with them? Choose me over your best friend? That would prove his point. I know how you feel about me. I also know how crazy fast this has been for us. Both of those things can be true."

When he didn't reply, I asked, "Savage? Who's Tracy?"

I thought he wouldn't reply because he was silent for so long, but he surprised me when he said, "She's a girl from my childhood. She was someone I failed to protect. And I carry that guilt with me every day."

I didn't press him to tell me more.

It seemed we both had pasts we were trying to keep in the past.

Chapter 28

"I need to go for a ride," Savage said the moment we got to the apartment building parking lot.

I took a deep breath and nodded. "I understand."

He leaned over and kissed my cheek. "That's one of the many reasons I love you."

"Oh yeah?" I asked, a slight smile on my face.

"Yeah. You just—let me be who I need to be."

I swallowed. "Are you coming back tonight?"

"I don't know," he said. He tapped his head. "It's really fucked up in there right now. And I don't wanna saddle you with all of it."

"You can saddle me with it," I insisted. "We're in a relationship. That's what you're supposed to do."

"Yeah." He nodded slowly. "This is new for me, you know? I don't always know how to do this."

"I don't know how to do this either. My marriage was hardly a shining example of success." I reached over and linked his hand with mine. "I want you to always be able to go for rides, do what you need to do to clear your head. But I also want you to sleep next to me every night."

He lifted our hands to his mouth and kissed my knuckles. "From now on, no matter what goes down, as long as I'm not on a run, I'll sleep next to you."

I frowned. "What's a run?"

"A run for the club," he explained. "I'm actually leaving tomorrow morning to go on a run up to Idaho."

"Tomorrow morning? Way to give me a head's up."

"Sorry, babe. It came together last minute."

"What's in Idaho?"

"Another club chapter," he explained. "We can't ride our motorcycles up there this time of year. The pass is mostly ice. So we'll caravan in cars."

"Are you going to take the SUV?"

"No. I'm leaving it here for you in case you want to get some driving practice in. I'm sure Roman or Virgil wouldn't mind riding shot gun."

"How long will you be gone?"

"A week? Ten days? Not sure."

"Ten days?" I squeaked. "You're going to miss our first baby class. And probably our second one, too."

He rubbed his jaw. "Fuck. Yeah, I didn't think about that. Sorry, babe."

"It is what it is, I guess," I murmured. "How are you going to sleep without me?"

"Few shots of whiskey," he said dryly.

"Savage," I murmured.

He ran a hand through his disheveled hair. "It is what it is, babe. I'll figure it out."

"But what will *I* do without you?"

"You start looking at places. When I get back, we'll see a few that you've chosen and decide which one is best for us. Okay?"

"Okay."

He unclasped his seat belt. "Let me get you to the door

Heartbeats & Highways

and then I'm going for a long ride. Don't worry, babe. I'll be back before bedtime."

He returned from his ride when I was dozing on the couch. He carried me to bed and worshipped me with his body, as if apologizing the only way he knew how.

I fell asleep in his arms, my naked body wrapped around his.

The first night he was gone on his run to Idaho, I forced myself to lay in the middle of the bed, at a diagonal.

His scent was on the sheets, but it wasn't enough to lull me to sleep.

I was still awake at three a.m.

I rolled over to reach for my phone, wanting to text him, but not wanting to wake him up if he'd somehow managed to fall asleep.

With a sigh, I got up. I went to the refrigerator and pulled out the leftover dessert Savage had picked up a few days ago from a hole-in-the-wall Italian restaurant.

I was just sticking a fork into the cheesecake when I heard sounds outside my door.

Frowning, I tiptoed to the peephole and looked through it and saw my neighbor across the hall setting something down onto my doormat.

I quickly unlocked the door and yanked it open, causing the young woman to squeak and pull back. "Gah!"

"Sorry," I said. "I heard someone moving around out here and I thought I'd finally introduce myself."

"Maybe don't startle the neighbor who leaves you gifts, or the gifts might stop. Did I wake you?"

"No. I was already awake." I looked down at the mat. "What are you leaving me this time?"

A smile touched her lips. "Loose leaf herbal tea."

"Nice."

"Yeah."

I cocked my head to the side. "You don't sleep much, do you?"

"I sleep." She defended.

"Hmm. The purple shadows underneath your eyes say otherwise." I gestured to my apartment. "I'm awake and working my way through a plethora of Italian desserts. You want to join me?"

She bit her lip. "You sure?"

"I'm sure."

"What about your boyfriend? The biker one."

"Ah, you've been watching me through the peephole, have you?"

She had the grace to blush.

I laughed. "He's gone for the next week or so. Come on. We got Italian a few days ago and I need to finish the desserts." I waved her across the threshold and then picked up the gift she'd left me. "It's past time we got acquainted; don't you think?"

"Probably, yeah. I'm not good at small talk though. It's why I haven't introduced myself."

"I'm Evie."

"Cozy. Short for Cozette, but please don't call me that."

I smiled. "Okay. Pick your poison. I've got a chocolate torte, a panna cotta, a crème brûlée, a—"

"Whatever you're not having," she said. "I'll eat anything."

"The cheesecake is mine."

"The chocolate torte, please."

I handed her the box and got her a fork. Then I took my dessert and headed to the couch.

"So, you don't sleep much, huh?" I asked, shoveling in a bite of cheesecake.

"Few hours here and there," she said. "Every little noise makes me . . ."

"Jump. I get it." I looked at her. "You still sleeping with your shoes on?"

"What?"

"Your shoes. You sleep with them on, don't you? So if you have to run, you're ready."

She paled.

"I wish I didn't understand, but I do," I said quietly.

"Is that why you're here?"

I shook my head. "I'm here because—well, because of luck. I guess."

She took a small bite of the chocolate torte. "It's good."

"Yeah, I bet it is."

"So Savage left?"

I raised my brows. "How do you know his name?"

"I heard him," she said. "Sorry, it's not like I meant to stalk. But I—yeah."

"Forget it. And yeah, he's out of town on club business."

"Club? What club?"

"The Tarnished Angels Motorcycle Club."

We were silent as we ate a few bites of our dessert.

"You got a plan?" I asked suddenly.

"A plan? For what?"

"For what comes after this. This place, I mean. We can't stay here forever. Even if we want to."

"No, not really," she admitted. "Do you have a plan?"

"Kinda." My hand went to my belly that now had a little pooch. "Savage and I are getting a place together. I can't raise my babies here."

"You're pregnant?"

"Twins."

"Wow."

"Yeah."

"Is he the father?"

"Aren't we getting bold with our questions," I drawled.

"Sorry, I've been kind of lonely in my apartment. And now that I have a human to talk to, I'm taking full advantage."

I let out a chuckle. "I appreciate the honesty. No, he's not the father."

"Ah. I get it now. You were running from a bad relationship. That's how you wound up in this halfway house, huh?"

I shook my head. "No. My bad relationship ended when my husband died."

"Oh wow," she murmured, biting her lip as her brow furrowed.

"You want to ask another question, don't you?" I said with a laugh.

"Kinda."

"Go ahead," I urged.

"When did he die? I mean, did you know you were pregnant?"

"He passed before I knew." I shook my head. "Boy, that was a shock."

"I'll bet." She paused. "I was in a bad relationship too."

"I'm glad you got out."

"I'm glad you got out too."

～

Cozy fell asleep on my couch sometime around four o'clock in the morning and I didn't have the heart to wake her. After covering her with a blanket, I tromped back to the bedroom. I dozed off for a while but then woke up when I heard Cozy moving around.

My morning sickness wasted no time in asserting its control of the situation. When I'd composed myself, I went into the kitchen. Cozy had made herself a pot of coffee and was eating a piece of homemade sourdough bread.

I smiled.

"Hope you don't mind," she said.

"I don't mind at all. I thought for sure you'd have gone back to your apartment, though."

"Nah, I didn't want to sneak out like a one-night stand." She giggled. "So I thought I'd stay and see if you needed help."

"Help. With what?"

"With . . . I don't know."

She didn't want to be alone, and neither did I.

"You ever been to Pie in the Sky?" I asked suddenly.

She shook her head.

"I'm about to change your life," I stated. "I'm gonna shower, and then I'm taking you to the best bakery in the world."

Her face brightened. "Really?"

"Really."

"Okay." She bit her lip. "I have a car. I can drive us. It smells like worm jerky, but it gets me from point A to B."

"Why does it smell?"

"Uh, well, it belonged to this guy who was cheating on his girlfriend. She found out and she put a thing of fishing worms in his trunk, but like way up there where he couldn't find them under the carpet. It was summer and it was in the garage for a while and . . . yeah it was bad."

"Wow."

"Yeah, I got the car for a *steal* of a deal. The smell is almost completely gone."

"Really?"

She shrugged. "Well, maybe breathe through your mouth. And we'll bring a bag in case you need to puke."

"Why don't we just take my car?" I asked. "I have my permit, and you can be my adult in the passenger side."

"You don't have a license?"

I sighed. "No. I plan on getting it while Savage is away. I want to accomplish something while he's gone."

"Noble."

Unfortunately, I discovered my car had a dead battery when it failed to start.

"It's *brand new*," I groaned in frustration. "That's annoying."

"Worm-jerky mobile it is," Cozy said, twirling her key ring.

"In that case, you're driving."

We got into her car. The smell wasn't that bad—not until she turned on the heat.

I hastily put a hand over my mouth to keep the bile in my stomach.

Cozy looked at me. "You're being dramatic."

"You lied *big time* about the worm jerky smell."

"You must have a sensitive nose. I can hardly smell it."

"Must be the pregnancy thing," I muttered. "Adding heat just made it worse. And now it's on my clothes and on my skin. I'm going to need three showers just to get the stench out."

"How about, *thanks, Cozy, for driving us?*"

"Thanks, Cozy, for driving us. I'm sorry if I—no, pull over *right now*."

We'd barely rolled to a stop before I had the door open, and I was throwing up.

I hastily wiped my mouth and closed the door. "Okay, carry on."

"Such theatrics," Cozy teased.

"Remember when we weren't on a first-name basis or even friends? That was fun, right?" I quipped in return.

"No, but seriously. You okay?"

"Yeah, thanks. I'm good." I leaned my head back against the seat and closed my eyes.

"I know it's not ideal, but you're welcome to practice driving my car," she said.

"Really?"

"Well, sure. You want to get your license, and your car battery is dead."

"Yeah. That's true. You really wouldn't mind?"

"Not at all. What are friends for, right?"

I smiled. "Friends. Yeah."

Cozy pulled into a parking spot outside of Pie in the Sky and cut the engine. I grabbed my purse and climbed out of the car.

"Oh, sweet merciful Lord," I moaned after taking a deep breath. "Fresh air."

"You missed your calling." She slammed the driver's side door shut. "You should've been a comedian."

We walked to the front door of the bakery, and I opened it, the bell jingling a cheery hello.

I waved for Cozy to go in first and we both got in line. It was several people deep but moving swiftly.

"This place is cute," Cozy said. "I love the pink washed brick behind the espresso machine."

"Their savory food is good, too."

It was finally our turn to step up to the counter. Jazz was putting a few dollars into the tip jar, but when she lifted her head to greet us, her smile went from customer service professional to friend.

"Evie! I didn't know you were coming this morning,"

Jazz said. She turned toward the back and called out, "Brielle, Evie's here!"

"Last minute decision," I explained.

Brielle came out of the back, her red hair piled up on her head as she wiped her hands on a dish towel.

"Hey," she said, blue eyes bouncing from me to Cozy.

"Brielle, Jazz, this is my friend and neighbor, Cozy," I introduced.

"Oh, you're the neighbor. The one that leaves cute little gifts on Evie's doorstep," Jazz said with a smile.

"Like a faerie," I joked.

"You're not supposed to take gifts from faeries," Brielle said.

"Says who?" I demanded.

"The Irish," Brielle explained. "And I'm Irish so I'd know."

"This conversation is devolving," Jazz said. "What can I get you?"

I looked at Cozy. "You order first. My treat."

We took our pastries to a corner table and sat down.

"So where do you work?" I asked Cozy.

She bit her lip. "I'm kind of in between things right now."

"I see."

"And you?"

"I'm a receptionist at Three Kings." When she looked confused, I clarified, "A tattoo parlor. It's closed Mondays and Tuesdays. Hence the reason we can linger here this fine Tuesday morning. Brielle's brothers own the place."

"Ah."

"And Jazz is her best friend."

Jazz approached with our drinks. A latte for Cozy, hot chocolate for me.

"You haven't touched your scones," she admonished.

"Too busy gabbing," I explained.

Jazz pulled out the chair next to me. "The first rush is over. I have a few minutes to hang out."

"Good," I said. "Get Brielle. I need to pick your brains."

Jazz turned her head over her shoulder, preparing to yell. I hastily put a hand over her mouth. "I've had a bad night's sleep, and I smell like worm jerky—I can't do loud."

I lowered my hand.

"Worm jerky?" Jazz asked.

"Never mind," I muttered.

"Fine. I'll go get her. Be right back." Jazz hopped up.

I broke open my scone and took a bite. Jazz returned with Brielle a minute later and the four of us crowded around the tiny marble café table.

"I was summoned," Brielle said.

"I need help," I blurted out.

"Help? With what?" Jazz asked.

"I need to find a new place to live. Savage and I are officially moving in together." I waited for their shock, but it never came. "Seriously? You're not surprised?"

"Uh, he bought you a car," Brielle said.

"And you're his Old Lady," Jazz added. "Moving in together seemed kind of inevitable."

"Wait, he bought you the SUV?" Cozy gaped.

"Yeah. He did."

"Whoa. Wait, what's an Old Lady?" Cozy asked.

I quickly explained and then got back on track. "Savage said he'd take care of the rent and everything. But it feels . . . I want to contribute, you know? But I can't pay a lot. He's out of town on a run up to Idaho, but he said to start looking and we'd find a place when he got back. But I'd love to find something on my own and just sort of . . .

surprise him. And I want to get my license while he's gone. I want to show him that I . . ."

When I trailed off Brielle gently prodded, "That you what?"

"That she doesn't need to be taken care of," Cozy said, her eyes sliding to mine. "Right?"

I nodded. "So do you guys have an idea of where I can find a clean, safe place to live with Savage that I can afford?"

"Hmm." Jazz's brow furrowed in thought.

I looked at Brielle. "You said you were Irish. Know any leprechauns who want to give me their pot of gold?"

Chapter 29

One scone and half a cup of hot chocolate later, Brooklyn showed up.

"Can I talk to you?" Brooklyn asked, looking at me specifically in the group of ladies.

I frowned in confusion but got up from my chair. I glanced at Jazz, who was grinning.

"What? What do you know that I don't?" I demanded.

"You'll find out," she said.

"It's nothing bad," Brooklyn said with a smile. "But it's my thing, not Jazz's." She ran a hand down the back of the baby slung across her chest.

I wondered how the heck I was going to take care of two babies at the same time. Even with Savage by my side, I would still feel overwhelmed.

"Follow me," Brooklyn said to me. "How are the clothes working out for you?"

"They're perfect. Thanks so much."

"No thanks needed. Your loaf of sourdough that Savage brought me was thanks enough."

Her praise warmed my heart.

I trailed after her to the back of the kitchen. She went to a flight of stairs and slowly began to climb it. I followed her without a word.

"This building used to belong to my father," she explained as we continued to ascend the stairs. "I inherited it when he passed. It used to be his leather workshop, and upstairs was a storage room. When I decided to open a bakery, I had the storage room converted into an apartment."

She pulled out a set of keys from her pocket and unlocked the door.

"It's not big," she explained. "But it's yours if you want it. For you, Savage and the babies."

I looked around the apartment. It had a small kitchen and a bedroom, with a door to a bathroom cracked open so I could see inside.

It was quaint and cozy, and I couldn't explain it, but it immediately felt like home.

"You'd rent the apartment to me? Really?" I asked, turning to her.

"Well, that's the rub . . . I won't rent it to you," she replied.

"But you just said—"

"Hang on, let me explain. I want something more from you than rent," she said. "I want your homemade sourdough."

"Huh?"

"I want it baked fresh on the premises," she said.

"But you make homemade bread on site already."

"Yeah, and it's good. But yours is better. And I want the best."

"So wait, let me get this straight; you're offering me a rent-free apartment in exchange for making sourdough?"

"Yeah." She beamed. "It'll be a lot of sourdough, at

some point. I don't just plan on using it for the café. I plan on selling it by the loaf."

"You really think people will buy my bread?" I asked in surprise.

"I do. I'd buy it myself," she said. "I have to warn you though, deliveries come really early. If you agree to stay here, you'll hear the trucks. And you'll probably hear the sounds of the café too. It might be a big change after the quiet of your current place, but there you have it."

Tears constricted my throat. "Jazz texted you, didn't she?"

She nodded.

"Why are you offering this place to me?" I asked quietly. "You don't even know me."

"I know enough," she said. "I know what it's like to want to do it on your own. I know what it's like to think you have to. But you don't. I know you have Savage, and that's wonderful, but you have me and Willa, and the club, too."

I hadn't spoken to Willa since having dinner at her house. And I had no idea the state of Savage and Duke's relationship because of me.

Brooklyn looked around. "So, the apartment?"

I sighed. "I'll take it."

~

"I'll drive you to work tomorrow," Cozy said as she shut the passenger door. "Or rather, you can drive us to Three Kings in my car and then I'll pick you up when you're done. Then you can drive us home."

"Who needs a boyfriend when I've got you?" I teased.

She smiled. "Well, I won't have sex with you, so there's that."

I groaned.

"What? What's wrong?"

"Nothing. Just another way to miss him. Ten days is a long time for him to be gone."

"He's good then?" She waggled her brows.

"Can you lower your voice?" I demanded. "Or at least wait until we're inside before we have this conversation?"

She shrugged and then punched in the door code. "Let's go to your apartment. I'd invite you to mine, but all I've got is diet soda and some crackers."

"You don't cook?" I asked.

"Not really. I bake. But cooking is different."

"Well, now I know how to repay you for letting me drive your worm-jerky-mobile. I'll cook you dinners."

"No, stop, don't," she said drolly. "It's too much."

I giggled. "That was convincing."

We tromped up the stairs and I whipped out my keys but came to a halt when I saw a bouquet of orange and yellow marigolds on my doorstep.

"Someone sent you flowers," Cozy said.

"Yes, I see that," I said.

"Savage?"

I leaned down and picked up the bouquet and handed my keys to Cozy. She opened the door for us, and I walked into the apartment and set the bouquet onto the counter and then reached for the card.

Miss you, babe. ~Savage

My heart flipped over in my chest.

"Ugh, you've got a dopey grin on your face," Cozy groaned and then spoiled it with a grin.

She went to the tea kettle and filled it with water before sticking it on the stove and turning on a burner.

Heartbeats & Highways

"These are gorgeous," I said, burying my nose in the fragrant bouquet.

"Are you going to tell him you're moving into Brooklyn's place?" she asked. "Or let it be a surprise?"

"I'll tell him. I mean, I'll be moving all his things to the new place."

"I can't believe you're moving out just when we became friends."

The tea kettle started whistling so I went to the cabinet and pulled out two mugs. "Wanna try the tea you gave me?"

"Sure."

I fixed us two cups of tea and we took our mugs over to the couch. I sat down and a wave of exhaustion poured over me. "We'll still see each other all the time."

"No, we won't," she said, her tone sad. "You'll start nesting and get all wrapped up in Savage and then when the babies come—"

"Hey, you can't shake me now," I said with a tender smile. "I'm not used to having friends. I didn't have any growing up and now I'm sort of collecting them. Sorry, but you're stuck with me."

"You didn't have friends growing up? Really? Were you a loner?"

I nibbled my lip when I said, "My parents were very strict and religious growing up. And when I was fourteen, they moved our family to a farm."

"Where are they now?" she asked. "Or are you not close to them?"

"They died a week after my eighteenth birthday," I said, looking away from her.

"Oh, Evie. I'm sorry. I'm sorry I asked."

A tear leaked out of the corner of my eye. "It's okay. It

was a . . . strained relationship but they were my parents, you know?"

"Yeah."

Thankfully she dropped the subject.

We sipped our tea in silence, and I wondered if I'd said too much.

She eventually went back to her place, giving me some time to myself. I tidied up the apartment, every now and again sniffing the bouquet.

My phone buzzed and I leapt at it with excitement.

"Well, hello," I greeted with a wide smile.

"Hey, babe," Savage said. "How are you doing?"

"Terrible." My tone was light. "You haven't even been gone that long and I can't handle it."

"I feel the same way. You get the flowers?"

"Yeah, they're beautiful."

"Just like you."

My heart melted in a puddle, and I nearly cried because of my hormones, but I somehow reined it in.

"So you should be proud of me—"

"I'm proud of you."

"You don't even know what I'm going to tell you," I said with a laugh.

"Tell me."

"Well, I finally met Cozy and we're friends now. She's even giving me driving lessons in her car."

"I'm glad you guys are friends, but why are you driving her car? What's wrong with yours?"

"The battery is dead."

"What the fuck? It's brand new."

"I'm saying."

"I'll text a prospect to get it taken care of, but the minute it's fixed, I want you practicing in that car. It's a fucking tank and I know you'll be safe on the road."

"Okay. But there's more."

"More? What else is there?"

"We're moving into Brooklyn's apartment over the bakery. It's perfect for us, Savage. It's homey and quaint, and Jazz and Brielle will be right downstairs most mornings, which I love. And Brooklyn said she won't charge us rent, if I bake sourdough on site so she can sell it."

"I told you not to worry about rent," he said.

"Please, Savage. I need this." My tone was soft, pleading. "I need to know I can take care of myself. I need you to know that too."

He sighed. "If I gain twenty pounds because we live above a bakery and we've got a steady supply of baked goods, you can't get mad at me."

I giggled. "We can call it sympathy weight. Because I'm going to gain twenty pounds easy. Probably fifty."

"You'll be beautiful," he assured me.

"You say the perfect things," I sighed. "I wish you weren't missing our baby class. I don't want to go without you. Maybe I'll take Cozy."

"I got the class postponed."

"You what?"

"Yeah, I called and asked if she could push it back."

"How did you make that happen?" I demanded.

"Magic," he joked. "I threw myself on her mercy and said I was a first-time dad and that I didn't want to miss anything. I must've said the right thing, because she delayed the class."

"Savage . . ."

"Evie, I gotta get back on the road. I'll call you tonight from the motel, and babe . . ."

"Yeah?"

"Be naked. We're going to have some fun together."

Chapter 30

"Shouldn't you be leaving?" Virgil asked.

"Leaving?" I looked up from the computer. "Leaving where?"

"Your baby class. I know Savage is out of town, but I'll go with you if you want."

My lip wobbled.

"Oh no, don't. Please God, don't cry!"

"Okay." I bit my lip and took a few deep breaths. When I was under control, I said, "Savage got the baby class postponed because he didn't want to miss it."

"The powers of persuasion," Virgil said with a grin. "I wish I had that. You want to go to dinner with us after work?"

"I was going to have dinner with my friend—my neighbor from across the hall," I said. "But I'll ask her if she wants to join."

"Oh, she's the one who drove you to work this morning?"

"Yep."

Heartbeats & Highways

A prospect had showed up on my doorstep, courtesy of Savage, but I'd rejected his offer.

The front door jangled as it opened, and Cozy walked in.

"Speak of the devil," I remarked.

"You were talking about me?" Cozy asked.

"Yeah." After introductions were made, I said, "Virgil is inviting us out for dinner."

Cozy nibbled on her lip. "Oh. Yeah, I guess we could go out."

"You don't want to," Virgil said. "That's okay. I won't be hurt if you guys bow out."

"No, it's just . . ." She looked at me. "You promised me a home-cooked meal and I was really looking forward to it."

"What were you gonna make?" Virgil asked.

"Country fried steak, mashed potatoes, green beans, and homemade sourdough biscuits."

Virgil blinked. "That sounds better than going out."

"Hey, why don't we just do dinner at my place?" I suggested. "You and Roman can come over. I'll call Jazz and Brielle. Let's make it a party."

"That means Homer too," Virgil said.

"The more the merrier." I smiled and looked at Cozy. "You good with that?"

She beamed. "Very good with that."

"Who's good with what?" Roman asked, appearing from the back.

"Evie offered to cook dinner instead of going out tonight. Her baby class was postponed so we're going to her place," Virgil explained.

Roman didn't reply to Virgil's statement. When the room went silent, I looked over at Roman and saw that he was watching Cozy.

Then I glanced at Cozy; she was staring at Roman.

I eyed Virgil, who raised his brows.

"Uh, Roman, this is my neighbor, Cozy. She lives across the hall from me."

When Roman didn't reply, I said to Cozy, "Cozy, this is my boss, Roman."

She didn't reply either.

"What's going on?" Virgil stage-whispered to me.

"I think they're performing a mating ritual," I stage-whispered back.

"What can we bring?" Roman asked suddenly, not taking his eyes off Cozy.

I opened my mouth to reply when Cozy said, "Beer. Bring beer."

"Dessert?" Roman asked, his voice raspy.

Cozy licked her lips. "Chocolate . . . anything."

Virgil looked at me and grinned. "My parents are going to be so happy."

~

"We're terrible friends," Virgil said.

"The worst," Cozy agreed.

"We literally just let a pregnant woman cook us dinner while we sat around and talked," Roman added.

"She told me I was doing it wrong," Virgil said. "I tried to help."

I was supine on the couch, my lids drooping in exhaustion, but a smile spread across my face. "I derive a great deal of joy from cooking for people I care about."

It turned out dinner was a smaller party than anticipated. Jazz and Homer were too busy seducing each other to want to spend time with anyone else and Brielle's excuse had been cryptic and mysterious. My antenna was up that she'd met a man and didn't want her brothers to know, and being a loyal friend, I didn't tell them my thoughts.

Roman and Cozy hadn't been able to take their eyes off each other all night. At some point, the staring at one another had turned into talking, then into teasing, and finally into open flirting.

"You guys cleaned up the kitchen," I said. "For that I'm grateful. Nothing worse than cooking and then also having to do the dishes."

"When does Savage get back in town?" Virgil asked.

"A week to ten days," I said. "I want to get my license before he gets back and settle into my new apartment."

"New apartment?" Roman asked. "Where are you moving to?"

"Brooklyn offered us the apartment over the bakery," I said with a smile. "She's having it deep cleaned and then she said I could move in."

"Shouldn't take a lot of time," Virgil said. "You don't own very much."

I glared at him.

"What?" he demanded. "You don't. This place came furnished."

"And Brooklyn's place comes furnished too." I shrugged. "It'll definitely make moving easy."

"Savage sent her flowers," Cozy stated. "The marigolds."

"No way," Roman said.

"Way," I said with a laugh. "Aren't they gorgeous?"

"Gorgeous," Roman repeated. "I never thought I'd see the day."

"Right? Savage was so unlikely to take a wife," Virgil quipped. "But I like you guys together."

"I'm not his wife," I stated. "But I am his Old Lady."

"What?" Roman asked in shock. "When the hell did that happen?"

"Several days ago. A week, maybe. I don't know. Time is a blur right now," I said.

My phone pinged with a text. It was Savage—and it was dirty.

I made a noise. Cozy was looking at me with a raise of her brows.

"So, dessert?" I asked.

My phone pinged again. And again, and then again.

"Someone doesn't want to be ignored," Virgil said.

"Ten bucks it's Savage and he's missing her," Roman said.

Virgil scratched his jaw. "In that case, I think I'll take off."

"Hmm. Yeah, me too." Roman looked at Cozy.

Cozy nodded. "Yeah, I'm too full for dessert."

I frowned. "You were the one who told Roman you wanted dessert in the first place."

"You eat it," she said.

"It's an entire cake," I said. "I can't eat it all."

"It's only six inches. You can definitely eat it," Cozy said.

"Don't make a joke," Virgil muttered. "Don't make a joke."

"Joke?" I asked in confusion. "What do you mean?"

"Stay sheltered, kid." Cozy rose from her seat and hugged me, whispering, "I'll have my phone on. Call if you need a late-night buddy because you can't sleep."

"Thanks." I pulled back.

"Thanks for dinner." Virgil gave me a one-armed hug. "We need to do it again soon."

"Yeah." Roman shoved his brother playfully. "So you don't have to cook." He embraced me. "It was great."

Heartbeats & Highways

I saw them to the door and locked up behind them, but not before I saw Roman and Cozy step closer to each other.

I pressed a few buttons on my cell and a moment later, Savage answered.

"Babe," he greeted.

Delicious pleasure curled through me.

"You have my attention," I purred.

"Are you in the bedroom?"

"No."

"Well, go in there and then get on the bed. I'm calling you back because I need to see your face."

The line went dead.

A thrill shot through me as I nearly ran to the bedroom and then settled myself on the bed.

My phone rang again, and I answered it. Savage's face filled the screen. He was lazing against the headboard and his chest was bare.

"Not fair, babe. You're seeing me, but I'm not seeing you."

I angled my phone and propped it against the lamp. Then I whipped off my shirt.

"Fuck, I miss you."

"I miss you, too," I croaked.

"Touch yourself. Let me see."

I cradled my breast in my hand and grazed my thumb across my nipple. It puckered quickly.

Savage's eyes heated. "That's it."

"What are you doing?" I asked.

"I'm wrapping my hand around my hard dick."

A pulse throbbed between my thighs.

"I'm leaking. At the thought of your warm, wet mouth. Of my fingers plowing through your hair while you're on your knees. How do I taste?"

"Perfect." I licked my lips as my fingers went to the button on my jeans. I quickly shucked them off. "Salty and delicious."

"Are you touching yourself? Are you wet?"

"I—I don't know."

"Slide your fingers into your panties, Evie. And tell me."

Biting my lip, I did as he commanded.

I wasn't wet. I was gushing. Only I couldn't bring myself to tell him. I moaned instead, my eyes closing.

"Show me your fingers, Evie."

My eyes popped open, and I removed my fingers from my panties to hold them up to the screen.

"Taste yourself."

With but a moment of hesitation, I then stuck my fingers in my mouth.

"How do you taste?"

"Not as good as you."

His grin was wicked. "When I come in your mouth, are you gonna swallow me down all the way."

"*Yes.*"

I stuck my hands back into my panties, playing with myself while Savage's filthy, erotic words spun a spell between us. Our eyes remained locked on each other; our breaths hitched. And when we came, we came together.

My heart thundered in my chest and despite the distance between us, I felt close to him.

"You're fucking gorgeous," he growled. "All flushed and pink. Can't wait to come home to you and taste you myself. Sleep well, babe. I know I will."

Chapter 31

After a bout of morning sickness, I made coffee for Cozy and tea for me and then I marched across the hallway.

I knocked on the door and waited.

When no one came, I knocked louder.

The door suddenly opened, and my jaw dropped in surprise.

Roman stood in the doorway, wearing last night's clothes, looking completely disheveled and half asleep.

"Evie," he greeted. "Good morning."

"Uh, hi, Roman," I said awkwardly. "I didn't know—"

"Nothing happened." He stood taller.

I raised my brows.

"Cozy invited me in for a nightcap and we kept talking and then it was suddenly three in the morning, and I didn't want to drive, so I slept on the couch."

"You don't owe me an explanation," I said with a smile.

"I don't, do I?" He scratched his chin which was in need a of a shave. "You're right, I guess I don't."

"You're both adults. You can do what you want. Or not." I peered around him. "Where's Cozy?"

"Still sleeping," he said, his cheeks flushing.

"You didn't sleep on the couch," I stated with a grin. "You little liar."

"Nothing happened," he insisted again. "We slept. That's all."

"Hmm. Well, okay." I handed him a cup of coffee. "This was for Cozy. But if she's not awake yet . . ."

Roman took the mug. "I'll tell her. Ah, see you at work later."

I grinned. "Yeah, see ya."

He closed the door, and I went back to my apartment. I sipped on my tea and was nearly done with the cup when there was a knock on my door.

"Come in," I called.

Cozy opened the door and entered. She was still in her pajamas and fuzzy socks, but she was also holding the mug of coffee I'd given Roman.

"Hi ya," I greeted with a smile.

"Hi," she said, raising the mug. "Can I get a refill? Roman drank mine."

"Have at it." I waved her toward the pot.

She shuffled over to the coffee pot and filled her cup. "Say it."

"I'm saying nothing."

"Nothing happened," she stated.

"That's what he said."

"Okay, *something* happened," she admitted. She went to my fridge and pulled out a carton of cream. "We talked. A lot."

"Okay."

"About everything."

"Everything, like, what does that entail? Did you tell him about your past?"

"What? No!" Cream splashed into her coffee mug.

"Then you didn't really talk about everything," I said.

"Does Savage know about your past?" she countered.

"We're not talking about me."

"Ah, so he doesn't."

"He knows I was married. And he knows it wasn't a happy marriage."

"But there's more, right?" Cozy asked. "With women like you and me, there's always more."

"No," I lied. "There's no more. He died. I started over."

"Uh-huh . . . right." She looked at me. "Does he know about your parents?"

I squirmed. "I don't like talking about my past."

"Obviously. I don't either. What if we . . ."

"Yes?"

"Make a pact," she said. "A ghost-sister pact or whatever. You can tell me things, and I can tell you things, and we keep each other's secrets."

I couldn't tell her the truth about my marriage or my parents. It would open up a can of worms that could never be contained.

"Okay." I nodded. "But you can't judge me."

"As long as you promise not to judge me."

"Deal," I promised.

"You go first," she said.

I took a deep breath and told her how I'd met Savage and the illegal fighting ring.

Her mouth dropped open. "Wow."

"Yeah."

"And you believe him? That he walked away."

I nodded. "Yeah, I do believe him."

"Why?"

"What do you mean?"

"I mean, he just said he walked away and that was that?"

"Well, sure. Why would he lie to me? It's not like he can hide the truth. He tells other people he bare-knuckle boxes at the club's gym. But he told me the truth. I have no reason not to trust him."

"Even after your bad marriage? You trust Savage to tell you the truth?"

"I do," I said quietly. "He's nothing like my husband. He might enjoy fighting, but with me, he's been nothing but gentle. Tender."

"You haven't been together very long," she murmured.

"The other shoe could drop, you mean?"

She nodded.

I shrugged. "I don't know, Cozy. Randall—my husband—was not a good man. He wasn't able to hide his temper for long."

"How old were you when you got married?"

"Seventeen."

"*Seventeen!*"

I mentally smacked myself. I'd gotten so comfortable with Cozy I hadn't been guarding everything I'd said. "I meant eighteen," I said stiffly, trying to course correct.

"No." She shook her head and met my eyes. "You slipped. You got married at seventeen? How is that even possible?"

I took a deep breath. "I told you my parents were really religious, right?"

She nodded.

"Well, my husband was religious too. And so they gave their parental consent for me to get married at seventeen."

"Seventeen," she murmured. "When I was seventeen, I

was sneaking out of my bedroom window and running with the bad boys."

"And your ex was a bad boy, wasn't he?" I asked, desperately wanting to get the spotlight off me.

"A bad boy who was actually a really bad man. He was into drugs. I stayed when it was just pills and coke." She swallowed. "I left when I found out it had turned into needles and unprotected sex with hookers."

"Oh, Cozy." I reached across the couch and grabbed her hand.

She gave mine a squeeze. "I was lucky. I could've gotten HIV or Hep. But thank God the tests came back clean. I made a promise to myself. That I wouldn't play fast and loose ever again."

"And you didn't tell Roman because it's a heavy topic."

"I didn't tell Roman because I'd have to tell him that I haven't finished piecing my life back together yet. And even when I do, I'm not going to put myself in that kind of situation ever again."

I frowned. "And that means, what exactly?"

"Marriage," she blurted out. "I'm not having sex again until it's with my husband. And I know how he'll react when he finds that out."

"You think he'll bail," I said.

"Why *wouldn't* he bail?" she asked. "What man would wait?"

"A ring is no guarantee that a man will treat you right either," I said gently.

"So that's it then? I'm fucked? And not in a good way?" She looked desolate.

"No." I shook my head. "But we do have to judge each man individually. On their own merit. On their own actions. Don't make the choice for Roman. Tell him the truth and let him decide if he can live with it."

She arched a brow. "So you're pushing me to be honest with Roman and let him choose how he deals with the truth, but you won't tell Savage about your past? Why not? I mean, you're certainly not telling *me* everything. I know you're only giving me little pieces of your story. Are you scared that Savage won't love you anymore if he knows the truth?"

"My past is ugly."

"So is mine. But you're Savage's Old Lady. Your situation is different."

"Maybe." I shrugged. "But you want something real with Roman, right? So he deserves the truth."

"So does Savage."

Maybe she was right. Maybe I needed to come clean and tell him everything. The idea of doing that made bile stew in my belly.

But if I wanted to build a life with Savage, something that lasted, he deserved to know every part of me. Every wretched dark part of me.

Chapter 32

Days later, Brooklyn texted that the apartment was finally ready for me to move into. During the deep clean, they'd found a leaky sink pipe, and it needed fixing, so there had been a delay. With the help of Cozy, Roman, and Virgil, I moved into the apartment above the bakery. Not that Savage and I had a lot of belongings, but Roman and Virgil refused to let me lift anything.

"They're just clothes," I protested as the two of them unloaded the back of my SUV that had gotten a new battery, courtesy of a club prospect.

"Doesn't matter," Virgil said. "We're gentlemen."

"Yeah, even if you had a couch, Virgil and I would take care of it."

"We need to have a party for you," Virgil said.

"A housewarming party?"

"That and we need to celebrate you getting your license," Roman said.

"I don't need a party," I insisted.

"You're getting a party. Roman, Homer, Jazz, Brielle, and I all got a party when we passed," Virgil explained.

"Yeah, but I'm not part of your family."

"Yes, you are," Roman said. "Cozy, get the door, will ya?"

"Sure," she said.

I stopped walking and stared after the three of them.

"What?" Virgil asked. "Are you okay?"

I promptly burst into tears.

"Oh man," Virgil muttered. "Not again."

"Come on, you little hormone stew," Cozy said, marching over and wrapping an arm around me. "Let's get you settled."

Two hours later, my fridge was stocked, the clothes were put away, and the four of us were chowing down on pizza.

Jazz and Brielle came up to see the apartment on their breaks.

"Brooklyn asked me to give you a rundown of the security system," Jazz said, grabbing a second slice of pizza. "So I'll come up after work. Sound good?"

I nodded.

"You sure you don't want me to stay the night with you?" Cozy asked. "First night in a new place, you know?"

She looked at me, her face wreathed with concern. I knew her offer wasn't completely altruistic—she wanted to stay with me, so she didn't cave and invite Roman to spend the night with her. Cozy still hadn't told Roman about her past and how she wanted to shape her future.

But I wasn't going to be her scapegoat.

"No, I think it'll be good to be here by myself." I looked around. "Bond with the place, you know?"

"Your sourdough starters are liking their new home," Brielle said. "They've doubled in the last hour."

"Fantastic," I said. "I'll come down and tend to them. The dough should rise overnight."

Heartbeats & Highways

"I worship at your sourdough alter," Brielle said. "I'm hopeless when it comes to making bread. I'm not allowed. Every loaf comes out like a doorstop."

"You have other talents," Jazz teased.

"I do, indeed," Brielle quipped with a waggle of her brows.

"Brothers, standing right here," Roman drawled.

"Oh yes, hello." Jazz waved. "Okay, one more piece for the road and then I really do need to get downstairs. Kendall is handling the register all alone."

"Let's go," Brielle said. The two of them tromped toward the door. "I'm glad you'll be close by, Evie."

"Yeah, we can always come up here on breaks and hang out for a bit," Jazz added around a mouthful.

"Sounds fun," I said.

"It does sound fun." Virgil frowned.

"You're invited too," I said with a smile. "Whenever you want."

"Not whenever," Roman said. "What happens when Savage gets back in town? They're gonna be playing house and shit."

I cleared my throat and raised my brows.

With a sigh, Roman pulled out his wallet from his jeans pocket and grabbed a dollar bill. "This is the last of my change." He handed it to me.

"Then stop by an ATM," I warned.

"The swear jar is really working, isn't it?" Virgil asked. "I don't say *fuck* half as much as I used to."

I held my hand out toward him.

"What?" he demanded. "I wasn't swearing, I was using the word to demonstrate a point."

"Yeah, what's up with the swear jar?" Cozy asked.

"Evie doesn't like a dirty mouth," Virgil explained. "Well, maybe Savage's, but you know."

"Go away," I groaned, my cheeks heating. "Swearing is a hard habit to break."

"So?" Cozy asked.

"So my husband used to swear. And I don't want to be reminded of him."

The room fell silent.

"Makes sense," Virgil said finally. "Besides, we don't want to be swearing up a storm by the time the babies arrive on the scene. We gotta set good examples."

"Then they shouldn't be around you at all," Roman said with a laugh, shoving his brother.

"I'm gonna be the fun uncle," Virgil said.

Somehow, in the short time I'd been in Waco, I'd found myself a patchwork family.

And no matter what, I wouldn't let go of it for anything.

∽

I was on the couch, reading about some of the less than stellar pregnancy consequences, when the buzzer sounded.

Frowning in confusion, I got up and went to answer it. I pressed the intercom button.

"Hello?"

"Hi, it's Willa. I brought you a pie as a housewarming gift. Can I come up?"

"Sure." I buzzed her in and then unlocked the apartment door.

"I'm coming," she called from downstairs. "But I'm big and have to take it slow."

I giggled. A smile was still on my face when she appeared.

"Okay, I kind of lied," she said as she ambled into the

apartment. "The pie is a housewarming gift, but also a peace offering."

"Oh yeah?" I crossed my arms over my chest. "What kind of pie?"

"Cherry."

"Rats. That's my favorite kind." My gaze narrowed. "You asked Savage, didn't you?"

"I might have."

I took the pie and set it on the counter. "Can I get you a glass of milk?"

"Yes." She shrugged out of her coat and placed it on the couch. "I've been trying to figure out a way to apologize for what happened at dinner. I didn't mean to be so blunt with you."

"You have nothing to apologize for. You're protective of Savage. I understand that."

She sighed. "Duke told me about his conversation with Savage."

"Oh?" I opened the fridge.

"I wish you hadn't overheard the conversation."

"How did you know I overheard? Did Savage tell you?"

"Yeah, he told me." She paused. "Sometimes he can talk to me the way he can't talk to Duke."

"I'm glad he has you." I went to the cupboard and opened it to pull out two glasses. "For what it's worth, I don't want him at odds with Duke. I never want to get between them. Or between you and Savage."

"I know that."

"But . . ."

"But—oh hell, I'm just going to be honest, okay?"

I poured us two glasses of milk and nodded for her to continue.

"Savage has never had a serious relationship."

"Yeah, I gathered that much."

"You did?"

"Yes. We were talking about his possessive tendencies, and he explained that he'd never felt that way before. So, I just assumed if he was feeling that way about me, it means he really cares."

"The reason I bring it up is because going from having no serious relationships at all—ever—to suddenly having an Old Lady . . . It just made Duke—and me—our antennae went up, you know?"

"I get it, Willa, I really do. Considering who Savage is, it would've been a hard pill to swallow if I'd been normal and this wasn't so fast. But I'm pregnant with twins and it's all so recent. So, not only is he in a relationship with me, but he's also suddenly deciding to be a father to babies that aren't even his."

I set the glasses of milk on the counter and then pulled out two forks and handed her one.

"You're taking this all too well," Willa said, removing the foil on top of the pie.

"You, Savage, Duke and Waverly . . . you're a family. You have your own ecosystem. And now you're about to add your own baby to the mix. I came along and *boom*. The entire dynamic has changed."

"There's room for you in our family, Evie. You and the babies."

Tears gathered in my eyes.

"I mean it. Just don't judge Duke by a conversation you were never supposed to hear."

"I may never have been supposed to hear it, but it was said all the same. Anyway, I told Savage not to hold it against Duke. It comes from a place of love, that's all."

She smiled. "I get it now."

"Get what?"

"Why he fell in love with you so fast. You understand people. You understand Savage, too, don't you?"

"Yes." I sighed. "I fell in love with him before I knew what was good for me."

She laughed. "Yeah, he has that effect."

"The Savage effect."

She held up her fork and I clinked mine against hers. "To the Savage effect."

Chapter 33

"Evie. Evie, wake up."

"No." I snuggled deeper into the pillows. "Dreaming. Nice dream."

"I know, you're dreaming of me."

My eyes flipped open, and my heart soared in happiness. And then I leapt at Savage who was sitting on the edge of the bed. I could only see the faintest outline of him because he'd left the bedroom light off, but the nightlight in the hallway was lit.

His mouth sought mine.

"Missed you so fucking much," he said against my lips.

"Not as much as I missed you," I whispered.

"Not possible."

His hands skated up and down my body. Shivers of desire erupted along my skin. He'd already taken off his cut and shirt and my hands traced his shoulders and then my finger sank into his hair.

Savage laid me back against the pillows, refusing to remove his mouth from mine.

He undressed me slowly, peeling my clothes from me like he had all the time in the world.

"Savage," I whispered.

His mouth moved from my lips to my cheek down my neck to my collar bone. He paid homage to my breasts and nipples, taking them into his mouth. He lavished them with focused attention until they strained into peaks. But eventually, he drifted lower and his tongue slipped between my thighs.

"Missed this, too, babe."

Savage ate like a man having his last meal. He ate like he'd never tasted anything so sweet in his life. And he didn't stop, not even when he wrung a cry from my lips and tears filled my eyes.

He didn't even stop as I came on his tongue, shaking with the tremors of my release.

And while I was in the throes, he slid up my body and into me.

He groaned and dropped his head. "I don't care about anything else. I just want to live inside you."

"Yes." I arched against him and my nails clawed his back.

"Mark me, babe. Gouge me. Draw blood."

I was mindless with pleasure. It was like I'd been plugged in to an electrical socket. I felt everything. Maybe it was the hormones. Maybe it was our reunion.

Maybe it's just Savage.

He ground his pelvis against me, rubbing his massive shaft on that perfect spot inside me and white spots of lightning appeared behind my eyes.

"Squeeze me," he commanded.

I clenched around him.

He thrust and thrust until I was coming and then he

was coming too, and the sounds of us mixed together in a joyous symphony of pleasure and release.

Savage stilled inside me. He framed my face with his hands and placed kisses all over my forehead, cheeks, nose and lips.

"Don't move," he said as he slid out of me.

I clenched again as he went, causing him to shiver. He got up and felt around for something and then he turned on the lamp.

He had a week's worth of stubble and I knew I'd have whisker burn on my skin.

"This is for you."

He held out a long thin box wrapped in black paper with silver ribbons. I took it from him and lifted the lid. It was a velvet jewelry box. I flipped it open and saw a dainty gold chain with two pearls inside a golden pea pod.

"Two peas in a pod," I said quietly.

His hand settled low on my belly. "When I saw it, I thought of you immediately."

"Savage," I whispered. "I love it." I leaned over and brushed my lips across his. "Put it on me?"

"After."

"After what?"

"After we shower." He took the box from me and set it on the nightstand.

We showered, lingering and touching, soaping each other. We kissed and stayed in long after we were pruny and steam filled the room.

"How did you get into the building?" I asked, sliding into bed, my wet hair sticking to my neck.

"I've had a key to the bakery for ages. And Brooklyn texted me the new security code."

Savage climbed in bed next to me and then hit the lamp.

I groaned. "My alarm is going off in two hours. That's going to mess with my sleep schedule."

"Because middle of the night homecoming sex didn't." He opened his arm, and I snuggled into his side. And because Savage was finally in bed next to me, I fell into unconsciousness quickly.

It felt like I'd been asleep for five minutes when my alarm went off. I silenced it, hoping it didn't wake Savage.

He slept right through it.

I got dressed and quietly crept from the bedroom and went down to the bakery to make sourdough.

A few hours later, with the sourdough loaves cooling, I went back upstairs to the apartment. The strong coffee the barista had brewed smelled earthy and bold, so I brought Savage a cup, along with a breakfast sandwich.

But he was still asleep.

Grinning, I decided to wake him up.

I gently pulled back the covers and grasped his morning erection.

He wasn't fully cognizant when I wrapped my lips around him, but I knew he was enjoying himself when he sank his fingers in my hair and used me and then came in my mouth.

I swallowed him down, loving that I didn't leave a drop.

When I removed my mouth and I looked up at him, his eyes were glittery with desire.

"You might want to text Roman," he rasped.

"Why?"

He grinned. "You're gonna be late for work."

"I can't be late for work," I protested. "I'm leaving early tonight for the baby class. I don't want to take advantage of them."

"Babe, I just got back in town, and I need to be inside

you again. Now are you gonna text Roman and tell him you're running late or what?"

~

"What a gorgeous necklace!"

I looked up from the piece of scrap paper I was doodling on and stared at the blonde. My hand instantly went to the chain around my neck, and I remembered the gift Savage had given me just that morning.

"Thank you." I smiled and then booked her another appointment with Virgil.

Once she left, the parlor was quiet except for the faintest sounds of tattoo guns buzzing in the background. I got lost in the sketch I was creating as I sipped on a carton of chocolate milk.

The door opened and I looked up with a smile to greet the new customer. My smile died on my lips when Duke walked in.

He didn't have an appointment, so I assumed that meant he wanted to speak to me.

"Evie," he greeted, his tone soft.

"Hi, Duke." When he stood there, clearly unsure of what to say, I ventured out, "You and your wife have a habit of accosting me at my place of work."

He smiled slightly. "Corner you, you mean, so you have no chance of escape."

I laughed softly. "Can I get you something to drink? I've got soda, chocolate milk or—"

"I'm fine. Thanks."

When he fell silent once again, I prodded, "So, are you going to talk, or are you going to make me pull it out of you?"

Heartbeats & Highways

"I wanted to have a word with you. In private, if we can."

I looked at the computer. There was only one more client due that afternoon.

"Oh." My brow furrowed. "Let me ask Roman if I can bail earlier than expected."

"Sure."

I headed into the back and quietly rapped on Roman's door. The sound of the tattoo gun fell silent and then he opened the door a crack.

"Hey, what's up?" he asked.

"Can I cut out early?"

"Savage is here already?"

I shook my head. "Duke. He . . . needs to talk to me. Homer only has one more client the rest of the afternoon. You might get some foot traffic, but—"

"No sweat. Virgil can cover the front after he cleans up his station."

"Thanks."

He pitched his voice lower. "You good?"

I nodded.

"Okay. See you tomorrow."

I went back to the front and grabbed my purse and keys.

"I'm ready," I said.

"Great. There's a diner a few blocks from here. You want to follow me?"

"Yeah."

I was in the twilight zone. Duke had barely spoken to me the night I'd gone over to his house for dinner. I'd heard what he's said to Savage about me. And soon I'd be sitting across a table from him. Just the two of us.

Twenty minutes later, we were in a booth, our menus

handed to the waitress and Duke's attention was completely focused on me.

"Savage won't talk to me, and he won't return my calls," Duke said finally.

I frowned. "You didn't speak at all while you were both on the road?"

"The road? Oh, you mean Idaho?" Duke shook his head. "I didn't go. Not with Willa close to her due date."

"Ah."

"I don't blame him, but . . ."

"I never meant to come between you," I voiced. "You have to know that."

"I do." Duke nodded. "Willa told me I was being a bonehead, and she's right. The fact of the matter is that it doesn't matter how I feel about your relationship. You and Savage are together now. He and I have been friends—*family*—for years. I won't lose him over this."

"I understand," I said gently. "But that doesn't change how you feel about me."

"I don't *know* you." His eyes searched my face. "Savage has a protective streak. A reckless streak too. I just don't want it misplaced, you know?"

"I know. Believe me, I know how this looks."

"Is that why you haven't ripped into me?"

"You're protective of him. I understand that. But I love him, Duke. I'm not going anywhere."

The door to the diner opened and Duke's face went slack. I frowned in confusion at his reaction and then looked over my shoulder.

Savage strode up to our table, looking from me to Duke.

"What are you doing here?" I asked in surprise.

"Wanted to know why you were at a diner a few blocks

from Three Kings when we're supposed to have an early dinner before our baby class."

"But how did you know I was here?"

"I'm tracking your phone."

"You're *what?*" I squeaked.

"Scoot over, babe."

I was still reeling from his announcement when I scooched over. He slid in next to me and placed his hand on my thigh. "Gotta know you're safe."

"You could've told me," I muttered.

He squeezed my leg. "We'll talk about that later."

"Brother," Duke greeted.

"What are you doing, talking to my woman without me?" Savage's tone was angry, harsh.

It was my turn to put my hand on his leg.

"How long are you gonna do this?" Duke demanded.

"As long as I feel like it."

"Don't be a dick," Duke grumbled.

"You started it," Savage shot back.

"I apologized to you. What the fuck more do you want?"

"Apologize to Evie," Savage stated. "Apologize for what you said about our relationship."

"What did I say?"

"You insinuated that this shit isn't real. So, apologize."

Duke stared at Savage and then his gaze slid to mine. "I'm sorry, Evie. I want to get to know you. And you're welcome at our home anytime."

Savage wrapped his fingers around mine.

"Thanks, Duke," I said.

"We good?" he asked, his gaze bouncing between me and Savage to finally rest on Savage.

"Yeah, we're good."

"You still want to punch my face in," Duke said.

"I do. But I'll get over it."

The scent of our food arrived just before the server appeared.

"Here ya go. One pastrami on rye. And a burger well done with a side of fries."

"Thank you," Duke said.

The voice of the server sounded familiar, and I looked up. Recognition flashed across her face when she met my gaze. "Evie?"

"Hi, Roxy," I murmured.

"It's good to see you!" she said. "Daisy and I have been wondering how you are. After you got fired, I wasn't sure what happened to you."

My heart beat in my ear and the words tangled in my throat. "Me? I didn't know you worked here."

"Just started last week." She looked at Savage and grinned. "Guess the chin nod thing actually worked in your favor, huh?"

"Yeah, I guess so," I said, feeling Duke's eyes burning into me.

"Can I get you something, Savage?" she asked.

"I'm good. Thanks," he said. His tone was light, unbothered, but his leg had tensed under my hand.

A bell dinged and she looked over her shoulder. "I gotta grab that order. But I want to catch up, Evie!"

She dashed away before I could reply.

"Huh," Duke said. "That was weird. She knows you both. And oddly enough, made it sound like there's history there."

Savage and I remained silent.

"Someone want to tell me what the hell is going on?" Duke demanded.

Chapter 34

Duke's statement hung in the air between us.

I was going to let Savage field this one.

"Evie and I didn't meet at a taco truck like I told everyone," Savage said quietly. "I met her when I was fighting in an illegal fighting ring. Roxy was a bartender at the venue, and Evie was working there serving drinks."

The diner was mostly empty, but that didn't stop Savage from pitching his voice low.

"Son of a bitch. I knew there was something going on with you." He stared at Savage. "The random black eyes and split lips. You weren't bare-knuckle boxing at the gym with Acid, were you? That was just a cover."

"It was mostly a cover," Savage agreed. "But sometimes I really was fighting with Acid."

Duke's attention turned to me. "And you got fired why?"

Savage replied before I could. "Some drunk put his hands on her and I punched him out. They fired her because of me. They weren't going to forbid me from fighting because I brought in too much money."

"So you got her a job at Three Kings to make up for it. Got it." Duke leaned back against the booth. "You tell the Jackson brothers the truth?"

Savage paused and Duke cursed.

"Just Roman," Savage insisted.

"Why the hell didn't you tell me?" Duke growled.

"I wasn't going to tell you because that would mean I'd have to tell you what I was up to. And I didn't want you to feel divided between me and the club. You know how Prez would've felt about this."

"If you'd told me, I would've understood *why* you felt like you had to take care of Evie."

"And then you would've doubled down on your feelings about our relationship. Come on, it wouldn't have helped. It would've made it worse, and you know it. It would've made you think you were right—that I had some complex about saving her and that I don't really care about her."

Duke shrugged and then sighed. "I don't want to argue about it anymore. You clearly care about her, and this is real. Are you still fighting?"

"No. I quit," Savage said. "Soon after Evie and I got together."

Duke looked at me. "Well, I guess I have you to thank for being a calming influence on him."

"He came to that conclusion all on his own," I announced. "But I'm happy he's not doing it anymore. I'd be nothing but a bag of worry each time he got in the ring."

"Don't tell Willa," Savage stated. "I know you two share everything, but I don't want her to know about this."

"Agreed," Duke said. "She doesn't need to know."

My stomach rumbled and I picked up the burger. I offered Savage a bite first, but he shook his head, choosing instead to take a fry.

"You're really done with it?" Duke pinned Savage with a stare.

"I'm really done with it," Savage promised.

"Good."

Savage reached across the table and took half of Duke's sandwich.

"What the fuck do you think you're doing?" Duke demanded. "Evie offered you her burger."

"You think I'm going to take food out of my pregnant woman's mouth? You're out of your mind."

∽

We left the diner with Savage and Duke's friendship on the mend. They bro-hugged it out and then Duke got on his motorcycle and left.

I hoped the turbulence was truly behind them.

Savage walked me to the car and said, "Thank you."

"For what?"

"For being fucking gracious. You could've held that shit against Duke."

I shook my head. "That's no way to live, Savage. And it'll make things a lot easier moving forward." I touched his cheek. "I wouldn't have let this continue. At some point, I would've enlisted Willa's help and gotten you two to talk."

He turned his head and kissed my palm.

"His reaction to you fighting was odd, though," I said softly.

"What do you mean?"

"I mean, I thought he'd give you a lot more grief. Or there would've been a lot more deliberation about telling your club president. But there wasn't, was there? To him, you come before the club."

"When we patch in, we're supposed to put the club

first and always. And for the most part we do. But Duke, Willa and I . . . Life was once a pile of shit, and only the three of us got each other through it. The club is there for us, too. But Duke and Willa are different." His eyes remained on me. "And now you. You're everything to me."

I hugged him and pressed my head to his chest. He wrapped his arms around me and kissed my hair.

"We better go or we're going to be late meeting everyone before our baby class."

I pulled back. "How am I supposed to eat again? I'm stuffed. Not to mention exhausted."

"You've had a full day already," he agreed. "Let's go to the restaurant and I'll buy you dessert. There's always room for dessert."

Savage followed me on his motorcycle to the French restaurant. We walked in, hand in hand.

"Good. Sutton and Viper already got us a table," Savage said, leading me to the couple.

"Oh my God, you're so pretty!" a petite brunette said.

I giggled and looked at Savage. "I like her."

"Sutton, Evie. Evie, Sutton."

"Sit next to me," Sutton demanded, gesturing to the empty chair next to her.

"Chill, spitfire. You're overwhelming her." The hulking giant next to her wrapped his arm around Sutton's shoulder. "I'm Viper."

"Nice to meet you," I said.

"Doc and Boxer are on their way," Sutton said. "They should be here in a few. Should we order some appetizers while we wait for them?" She placed a hand on her round belly.

"Her blood sugar is dropping. Bratty Sutton I can handle. Bratty and hungry Sutton? Forget it," Viper said, peering down at his wife with amusement stamped across his mouth.

Doc and Boxer arrived. After Boxer introduced himself, Doc pulled me to the side and said, "How are you doing? Are you feeling okay?"

I nodded and smiled. "Better than okay, actually."

Doc beamed. "Good." She squeezed my hand.

"When are you bringing her to a club barbecue?" Sutton asked Savage after we'd all taken our seats.

"When everyone is back from Idaho," Savage said easily.

I frowned. "They didn't come back when you came back?"

"No, some of the boys had to stay up there a few days longer," Savage explained.

"So you're not hiding her from us anymore?" Sutton demanded.

Savage drawled, "I tried to ease her into you crazy lot but—"

"Never gonna work," Boxer said. "We're insane, but you'll learn to love us."

The server arrived and took our order. Savage and I decided to split a meal. Savage kept his hand on my thigh, slowly inching it upward. It was difficult to pay attention to anything.

"What about you, Evie?" Doc asked.

Savage pressed a finger against the seam of my body.

"What about me?" I hoped I didn't sound breathless.

"Do you want to go to prenatal yoga with me and Sutton?" Doc repeated.

"Oh sure, yeah, that sounds great."

Savage slowly began to rub me.

"I don't want to go," Sutton whined. "I'm not really athletic."

I stared at my plate and willed the heat away from my cheeks.

"It's not like I'm asking you to play pickle ball," Doc stated.

"I just want to be a lazy veal," Sutton said. "And lounge on the couch."

"There's plenty of time for that," Doc assured her.

I reached under the table and grabbed Savage's finger, wrenching it back, which made him wince in pain.

"Do we have time to order dessert?" Sutton asked.

"Something chocolate," I voiced.

"Let's get one of everything and share!" Sutton suggested.

I looked at Savage and grinned.

He grinned back. Savage tucked a strand of hair behind my ear and leaned down to whisper, "I told you you'd like them."

~

Savage kissed my stomach as we lazed in bed that night. "You've got a little belly now."

"Yeah," I said with a laugh. "Still a few more weeks before I have the belly pop, but then it will be pretty obvious. According to the baby books I've been reading anyway."

He rested his head on me and took a deep breath. "I'm gonna read them, too."

My heart warmed. "Yeah?"

"Yeah. I want to know everything there is to know about the babies and your body changing." He traced his fingers across my hip. "Have you thought of baby names yet?"

I chuckled. "It's a little early for that, don't you think?"

"No. Don't think so."

"We won't know the sex of the babies until our twenty-week appointment."

"Doesn't hurt to get a head start," he said.

I raked my hand through his mussed hair. "Okay. We can talk baby names. But if we settle on names, we can't share them with anyone."

"Why not?"

"I'm superstitious," I said. "My parents always said not to share the baby's name before it's born because it protects the baby from evil spirits."

"I've never heard that," Savage murmured. "But if it's important to you, we won't tell anyone."

"Thank you."

"So, your parents were superstitious, huh?"

"Yeah." I shifted my body to get more comfortable.

"You never talk about them."

"They weren't just superstitious; they were *deeply* religious. And as I got older, they grew more . . . fanatical."

"You said they died when you were eighteen?"

I took a deep breath. "Yeah."

"How? Was it a car accident?"

"No," I murmured.

Savage propped his head up and rested his chin on my sternum so he could look at me. The light from the lamp bathed him in a soft hue, but the contours of his jaw looked like stone.

"I told you they were fanatical, right?" I took a deep breath. "They took their own lives—joint suicide. They believed their lives were meant to be sacrifices so their souls could ascend to a different plane of existence, and they could be with God."

Savage watched me for a moment but didn't reply.

"I know. Crazy, right?"

"They left you at eighteen. To fend for yourself against a physically abusive man."

His shoulders tensed and I waited. Would he get up and need to go for a ride to clear his head? Would he need to go spar to get out some of his anger?

Savage's arms tightened around me. "They didn't protect you. They left you vulnerable. Alone. I'm so sorry, babe."

I wasn't going to give him empty platitudes and say it was okay because it wasn't. Parents were supposed to protect their children. And mine had abandoned me, essentially feeding me to the wolves.

"Yours didn't protect you either," I murmured.

"At least I had Willa and Duke. And at least you and I found each other, too."

"We get to do it differently," I whispered. "Our babies will never know that kind of fear or loss."

"No, they won't," he agreed.

We fell silent for a while, and I let him ponder what I'd unveiled about my parents. It was a lot to take in.

He finally spoke again. "I haven't told you how I got the name Savage."

"You haven't. No."

I waited for him to gather his words.

"I grew up in foster care," he said softly. "It was my third foster home in a year. I was fourteen. Full of anger, resentment. But my foster mother, she was kind despite life beating her down. Despite her husband beating on her."

He let me go and sat up, facing me on the bed.

"She made sure I had clean clothes, lunch for school. She did her best, you know? She couldn't have kids of her own, but the way she treated me . . . she really wanted them. She would've been good at it. A good mother, I mean. She was a good mother, to me . . . for a while. But maybe it was a blessing she couldn't have kids because her husband was a dick. An angry drunk. A useless piece of shit."

He reached out and clasped my hand in his.

I linked our fingers like a lifeline.

"She got sick. Uterine cancer. She was gone in three months. That fucker moved a new woman into the house not even two weeks after she died. The woman who moved in with us had a sixteen-year-old daughter. I didn't like the way he looked at her."

I knew where Savage was going with his story, but I let him talk. I let him purge his past.

"One night, her mom was gone. She worked the graveyard shift at a gas station. I heard his heavy, drunken footsteps as he came up the stairs. I ran down the hall to Tracy's room to protect her, but when I got inside the lock on the door was broken. We dragged the dresser in front of the door to slow him down. We climbed out the window into a huge oak tree next to the house. We sat in the tree together. He shoved against the door, like he was throwing himself against it. He either gave up or passed out. But it wasn't a permanent solution, you know? Because he'd made the decision to hurt her, and it was only a matter of time before he did."

I was quiet and waited for him to go on.

"A few days later, we came home from school and as soon as I opened the front door that motherfucker clocked me so hard he knocked me out cold. He was so much bigger than I was . . . When I woke up, I panicked and ran to Tracy's room to find her. He had her cornered. Her shirt was torn, and her lip was bloody. I was too late. Her eyes were glazed, like she'd just mentally checked out, so she didn't have to process what had just happened. I lunged for him. Jumped on his back and started choking him. It was enough for her to get away. She ran to the neighbors while my foster dad beat me senseless. But because he was drunk, he got tired and passed out."

"*Savage*," I whispered, horrified.

"Somehow, I dragged myself up and limped over to the neighbors. Tracy's mom eventually showed up and said the police were on their way. She told me they were moving out, and that she was going to press charges and that he'd never get to hurt Tracy again."

His eyes drifted from my face to look over my shoulder. Like he was staring into the past, trying to find the last piece of it to divulge so he'd never have to tell his story again.

"I knew if I was still there when the cops showed up, it was going to start all over. A new foster home, some new asshole to fuck up my life. I wouldn't do it, and I couldn't protect Tracy, so I just left. Went to live on the streets. Bounced between living with Duke and Willa. Had a gym teacher who suspected what was going on and used to leave the door to the locker room unlocked so I could shower and shit."

He swallowed. "Anger fueled me. The idea of revenge kept me going. When I was prospecting for the Tarnished Angels, I finally had my chance. I was living at the clubhouse, and I'd been fighting for years. Training, you know? One night, I went to that old house. That decrepit, stinking, moldy old house. He'd been out of prison for a couple years already and was sitting in his recliner when I kicked the door in. He tried to fight, but I was young and strong as a bull. He was old. Used up by life and booze. He tried to hold his own, but he was no match for me. He finally begged me to stop. That's when I beat him to death with a fucking pipe wrench. Didn't stop until his skull had caved in."

The visual turned my stomach. I clenched his hand tighter.

"Duke was with me that night," he said. "He told the club. And then they gave me the name Savage."

"Does Willa know? How you got the name?"

"Yes. They were the only people outside of the club who knew the story of my name. Now you know, too."

"Thank you for sharing that with me." I brought our hands to my mouth and kissed his knuckles. "It explains so much about you. The fighting, the anger . . ."

"You're incredible, you know? You love me and accepted the fighting and the anger all without knowing about my past."

I tugged him toward me. "Hold me, Savage."

He turned off the lamp and then folded his body around mine and rested his hands on my belly. I fell asleep, sheltered in the protection of his embrace.

Chapter 35

I woke up and knew from the sound of his breathing that he wasn't asleep. I stirred against him and rolled over so that my cheek was pressed to his chest.

His hand immediately went to my head and his fingers combed through my hair.

I glanced at the clock. It was the middle of the night.

"Nightmare?" I asked him. "About your past? You shared a lot with me."

"No." He pressed a kiss to my head. "Just woke up and my brain turned on. But it's not because of what I told you."

I relaxed. "What are you thinking about?"

"Our baby class."

"What about it?"

"I'm annoyed."

"About what?"

"Things."

I snorted. "It's late, Savage. Stop being cryptic and tell me what's on your mind."

"When we went around the room and introduced

Heartbeats & Highways

ourselves, everyone said they were married. We're not married. We don't share the same last name. I don't like that."

"Oh."

"And then I started to think about our future and what our family was gonna look like. I want a big family, Evie. It's something I never got to experience or grow up with. I know it's crazy to even be talking about it, since the twins aren't even here yet. But I think we should talk about it."

I licked my lips. "I need some water."

"I'll get it for you."

He flipped on the lamp before padding naked to the kitchen. I listened to the cabinet opening and closing, the sound of water from the faucet. Savage returned and held out the glass to me. I took a few greedy swallows before offering it to him. He finished it off and then set it on the nightstand.

I tucked a strand of hair behind my ear, nerves shooting through my chest.

"What?" he asked, settling down on the bed next to me.

"I thought you didn't care about marriage? I thought being an Old Lady was more of a commitment than marriage."

"It is," he said. "But there are other sorts of protections that come with marriage. Fuck, and the more I think about you having my last name, the more I like the idea. I want us to be a family."

"And you want these babies, and any future ones we might produce to have the same last name."

"Yes. So, what do you think?"

"About marriage or more babies?"

"Both."

"You're kind of clobbering me with a lot right now."

"I know. Sorry about that. I just—can't hold it in."

"Yeah, I gathered as much," I murmured.

"So, what do you think?"

"I think you're getting way too ahead of yourself," I said quietly.

"Ahead of myself? Really? You're already my Old Lady, Evie. What's the difference if I add a ring to your finger and my last name to yours."

"I never want to get married again," I blurted out.

He fell silent.

"I love the idea of a big family, too," I went on. "I never had that."

"Huh."

"What?"

"The idea of having more babies with me doesn't terrify you, but marriage to me does? That makes no sense."

"Maybe not," I allowed. "But right now it's how I feel. Please, Savage. Don't talk about marriage, and don't talk about more babies. Let's just enjoy this time right now. Okay?"

He cradled my cheeks in his hands and gave me a smile. "Whatever you want, Evie. I just want you to be happy."

I swallowed, tears threatening to spill out my eyes. "Savage . . ."

"I won't talk about it anymore," he promised. "Doesn't mean I can't try and change your mind, though. In fact, I'm gonna do everything in my power to do just that."

"How are you going to change my mind?" I asked.

He grasped my legs and hauled me to the edge of the bed. "Lay back and I'll show you."

Heartbeats & Highways

With a sigh, I picked up Savage's boots and set them by the door. I tidied up the living room. In the last few days, it felt like Savage's belongings had exploded through the small apartment.

I put the dishes in the dishwasher and started the coffee maker.

Yes, I could go downstairs and get us coffee, now that we lived over a bakery, but I was still in my nightgown, and I had no interest in getting dressed.

It was just past six in the morning and Savage had come to bed a little after three. He'd been out doing something for the club—he hadn't shared anything else with me—but when he'd climbed into bed, he'd gently woken me up and then made love to me.

I hadn't complained, but it was wreaking havoc on my sleep schedule. I was exhausted from being in my first trimester, not to mention the early hours I was waking up for the bakery. And even though I went back to bed for a few hours before going to Three Kings, it felt like I was giving my life away to work.

"Morning," Savage said, yawning as he padded out into the living room.

"Sorry," I said. "Didn't mean to wake you."

"It's okay." He ran a hand across his face. He had a few days of scruff, and I'd thoroughly enjoyed the rough feel of it between my thighs when Savage made me come with his tongue.

My cheeks heated just thinking about it.

"I heard you moving around," he explained. "Not really sure what woke me exactly."

I pursed my lips. "It might've been the boots I set down. With a heavy hand."

"Ah, yeah, that would've done it."

I bit my lip and held my tongue.

He frowned. "What?"

"Nothing."

"Not, nothing. It's something."

"It's no big deal, really."

"Babe, I've had three hours of sleep. I'm barely conscious, but I'm not stupid enough to miss that you're pissed at me. So tell me what it is and I'll fix it."

My gaze softened. "You know I love living with you."

"Yeah."

"You know I love when we go to bed together. You know I love when you're out late at night, how you come home and wake me up . . ."

His grin was slow. "Yeah."

"But I absolutely hate that you don't pick up after yourself."

I held my breath, waiting for him to explode.

"Ah," he said finally. "The boots . . ."

"The random clothes strewn about. The dishes in the sink. Can you—I mean—will you try to put things in their designated spot? It's a small apartment. And when stuff doesn't get put away it makes it feel even smaller."

"How long have you been waiting to say something?"

"Two days."

He arched a brow.

"Okay, four."

"Why didn't you tell me? Why did you wait to explode?"

"I didn't explode."

"No. Not yet. But I have a feeling if you hadn't told me today, I would've come home to you throwing my boots at my head."

"I'm sorry. I don't mean to be a nag, I just—"

"Hey." He sauntered toward me. Savage placed his hands on my hips and pulled me to him. "You're not a nag.

You're asking for something that I'm not giving you. I'll do better, babe. I promise."

I leaned into him and pressed my face to his chest. "Thank you."

"But you gotta do me a favor in return."

"What's that?"

"You're not allowed to stew. If something pisses you off, you tell me. We'll talk about it and deal with it. Yeah?"

I nodded.

He grasped my hair and tilted my head back, so I was forced to meet his gaze. Savage stared down at me for a long moment and then said, "I'm not Randall. You don't need to be afraid of my reactions when you're honest with me about things that are important to you."

My shoulders instantly dropped. Sometimes I hated that he knew where my quirks came from. Other times, it made it easier because it felt like he just understood me.

He leaned down and brushed his lips across mine. "I need something else from you," he said huskily.

"What?"

"I woke up hard. Grab the counter, babe."

A delicious thrill shot through me, and I did as he commanded.

He slid behind me, his hands grazing underneath my nightgown and working it up my hips.

"Widen your legs."

I widened them.

He slithered my underwear down my thighs, and I stepped out of them. And then he was kneeling behind me, spreading my cheeks and tonguing me from behind.

I bent my head and shivered at the pleasure.

He ate me slow and thorough and didn't stop until I was coming.

Savage rose and smacked a cheek, causing a cry of pleasure to escape my lips.

I heard him shuck his boxers off and then felt the crown of him at my entrance. He slid inside me, bending his large chest over my back. As he thrust, his hand came around to play with me. His other hand went to my breast, teasing my nipple through my nightgown.

"God, I love this," he groaned as he continued to drill into me. "Say you love it too."

"I love it," I cried out, my forehead hitting the counter. The cool stone bathed my skin, a stark contrast to the fever inside me.

"I want to do this every day," he growled. "Wake up, fuck, smell you on me all damn day, come home to you and bury myself inside you again and then fall asleep there."

His words were primal, marking me as his.

"Tell me you want that too."

"I want it," I gritted out. "Please, Savage."

He knew what I was begging for. He pinched my clit, and I clenched around him.

Savage moaned, bit my shoulder through my nightgown, and came with a force.

He gathered me to him and held me close as our breathing returned to normal.

The coffee maker sputtered, and I giggled. "Done before the coffee was even brewed. That must be some kind of record."

He laughed and gently eased out of me. A gush of wetness hit my inner thighs.

I shivered at the loss of him.

"I need a shower before I go downstairs," I said, turning around to face him.

He hiked up his boxers that had been around his

ankles. "You also need a shower buddy," he said with a wicked grin. "Someone to help you clean those hard-to-reach places."

"Hmm. Tell you what. Why don't you let me jump in this one alone. While I'm baking bread, you go back to sleep for a bit. When I'm done, I'll wake you up nice and slow."

"Today's gonna be a good day."

"It already is." I patted his chest.

Chapter 36

"Babe, I'm worried about you," Savage said as he took my bare foot into his hand and began massaging it.

My head tilted back in ecstasy. "My arch. Please massage my arch."

He obliged. "Did you hear me?"

"It's hard to pay attention to anything right now. That feels so good."

"You gotta slow down," he said.

"Slow down? Slow down how?" I asked with a gasp. "Oh, yes. Right there."

"You're working too much."

"I like my jobs."

"You have jobs, plural. And one of them makes you get up super early. You need your rest."

"I'm resting," I insisted.

"No, you're not. It's the first trimester, babe. Between the morning sickness and the exhaustion, you've got to take it easy."

"I have to wake up early to make the sourdough loaves—do you know we're selling out by noon? We've had to make five new starters. But I always go back to bed for a few hours before going to Three Kings. And once I'm at Three Kings, I just sit on a stool. It's not labor intensive."

"What are you trying to prove? That you can do all the things? Forget the money for a second. Do you *like* working as much as you are?"

It was a lot, he wasn't wrong. And even though I had two days off from Three Kings because the tattoo parlor was closed, I was up every morning for the bakery.

"I'll talk to Roman," I said softly. "And see if I can go down to four days a week."

"Four days would be good." He nodded.

"I think he wants to hire Cozy anyway," I said with a smile. "Keep her close, you know?"

"Speaking of close." Savage cleared his throat and patted my ankle, signaling for me to give him my other foot. "There's a barbecue at the clubhouse this weekend. Everyone's back in town. You finally ready to meet the rest of the club and all the other Old Ladies?"

⁓

"I've gotta take off," Savage whispered, pressing a kiss to my naked shoulder.

I stretched underneath the covers and hastily covered my mouth as I yawned. "What time is it?"

"A little after seven."

I hadn't had to get up early to bake bread, so I'd thought we both would've been able to sleep in, wake up leisurely, and then go about our day.

"Are you sure you have to leave right now?" I arched my back and let the sheet slip off my body.

"Babe," he growled. He cupped my breast, immediately stroking my nipple with his thumb.

"I need you." My eyes cracked open.

"I'm already running late, and—"

I shimmied the rest of the sheet off me and spread my legs. My hand went between my thighs, and I played with myself for a few moments before showing him my desire on the tips of my fingers.

He groaned as he began to unbuckle his belt. "This'll have to be quick."

"Fine by me."

I gasped as he plunged into me. Not three violent thrusts later I was coming, hard, clenching around him. I squeezed him and lifted my legs, taking him deeper. His lips captured mine and he rolled his hips, coming with a jerk.

Savage buried his head in my neck, breathing hard.

I kissed his ear. "You don't want to be late."

He eased out of me and looked down at his half-erect shaft. "You made a mess."

"I make no apologies," I purred.

Savage grinned. He hiked up his boxers and then his pants.

"You're not going to wash it off?"

"Nah, I want the reminder of you on me all day." He kissed my lips and then my forehead. "I really do need to get out of here. But I left you a breakfast sandwich on the counter. See ya tonight."

Savage kissed me again and then he was gone.

I was asleep before I even heard the front door close.

The next time I woke, it was to my alarm. I rolled out of bed, quickly making my way to the bathroom. Nausea rolled in my belly. I couldn't wait for the morning sickness to pass.

After I showered and brushed my teeth, I dressed in a pair of jeans with an elastic waist and one of Savage's flannels. I layered it with a man's sweater I'd found at a thrift store.

I was cozy and warm, and as sweet as it was for Savage to leave me a breakfast sandwich, I put it in the fridge for later and headed down to the bakery for a hot meal.

Brielle was taking a batch of buttermilk blueberry donuts out of the oven when I entered the kitchen.

"Morning," I chirped.

"Hey, gal," she greeted with a smile.

"Are those donuts ready yet?" Jazz asked, popping into the back.

"Yes, they're ready." Brielle stuck her tongue out at Jazz, and she rolled her eyes.

"Can I get one of those?" I asked hopefully.

"Absolutely." Brielle grabbed a plastic bakery sheet and quickly grabbed a warm donut and handed it to me. "You want to hang back here with me or eat out in the café?"

"Back here is great," I said.

Jazz picked up the tray of donuts and headed to the front. "Tea this morning? Or hot chocolate?"

"Tea, please."

"I shall return," Jazz announced. "Brielle?"

"Coffee refill. Thanks."

Jazz nodded and headed back up front.

"Busy today?" I asked.

"Busy every day," Brielle said with a grin. "I'm surprised you didn't hear the commotion."

"I slept through it," I said. "Actually, I fell back asleep after Savage left and heard absolutely nothing. Thanks for making the bread this morning. How did the loaves turn out?"

"Nary a doorstop among them," Brielle quipped.

"They turned out well. Not as gorgeous as yours, but no complaints from the customers. How's the donut?"

"Perfect," I said. "But what do I have to do to get some eggs?"

While I was devouring crispy bacon and fried eggs, Jazz finally returned with the tea and coffee. "Sorry about the delay. We got hammered out there. Random rush."

She set the tea down in front of me. "So, you want to come over Saturday night? We're celebrating."

"Celebrating what?" I asked, polishing off the last of my eggs.

"I'm moving in with Homer." Jazz's cheeks flushed with happiness.

"What? Already?" I asked in surprise.

She snorted. "You're one to talk. You and Savage already live together, and you like, just met. Homer and I have known each other for years."

"No, I didn't mean it that way," I said. "I just thought it was going to take him a long time to woo you." I looked at Brielle, who was smirking. "What? What did I miss?"

Jazz rolled her eyes. "Brielle walked in on us. She's kicking me out, basically."

"I'm not kicking you out," she protested with a laugh. "You're only moving one floor down. I'll still see you all the time. Only, I won't walk in and have to see my brother's bare ass. This is for my sanity as much as it is about your happiness."

Jazz grinned. "I'm really happy about it, actually. So Brielle and I are having a packing party, and I thought you'd want to join."

"She means help packing boxes," Brielle added.

"And eat some food," Jazz stated. "But yes to the box help."

"I'd love to," I said. "I really would. But I've got plans Saturday."

"Oh?" Jazz asked.

"Club barbecue," I announced, my gaze bouncing between them. "I'm finally meeting the rest of the club and other Old Ladies."

"Well, well, well, the plot thickens," Jazz teased.

"This is serious," Brielle added.

"More serious than what?" I asked with a laugh. "Us living together? Savage raising these babies as his own? He said he wants to marry me."

"He does?" Jazz asked softly.

I nodded. "Which is weird to me, because I'm already his Old Lady which means more in his world anyway."

Brielle frowned. "Did he actually propose?"

"No, but he made his intentions clear."

"What did you say when he told you what he was thinking?" Jazz queried.

"I was honest and told him I don't want to get married again."

Silence reigned in the back kitchen, but I could hear the chattering and hum of conversation in the café.

"But you're living with him," Jazz said slowly.

"Yes."

"And raising the babies together," Brielle added.

"Correct."

"And as you said, you're his Old Lady. So marriage would be more of a commitment how? I don't understand," Jazz said.

"Have you ever been trapped in a bad marriage?" I asked.

Jazz shook her head.

"Well, I've been in a bad marriage before. And I guess

I'm gun shy. Even though I *know* Savage is nothing like my first husband, I'm still hesitant."

"Oh." Jazz's face cleared. "I understand now."

"What did Savage say when you explained your reasons for not wanting to get married again?" Brielle asked.

"He said he understood, but that he was going to do everything in his power to convince me to change my mind."

"And how is he going to—oh." Brielle laughed. "The burning cheeks say it all."

"I need to get going," I announced. "Thanks for breakfast. And congrats on moving in with Homer."

"I can't wait to tell him to pick up his socks," Jazz said dreamily.

"Ick." Brielle shuddered. "Homer's socks."

Chapter 37

"I hear congratulations are in order," I said to Homer as I walked into Three Kings.

He grunted.

"Seriously?" I demanded.

"Seriously what?"

"You don't seem at all happy that Jazz is moving in with you."

"I'm happy." He pinned me with a stare. "This is my happy face."

"You look like a prisoner on death row. Why so sullen?"

"He's not being sullen," Roman said as he came from the back. "That's just Homer. That'll be the same face he makes in his wedding photos. The same expression he wears when Jazz tells him she's pregnant. We just accept him and move on."

"Is Virgil here?"

"I'm here." Virgil appeared from the doorway. "What's up?"

"I need to talk to you guys," I said, setting the box of donuts down onto the counter. "I brought baked goods."

"You're quitting, aren't you?" Virgil said, a frown marring his face.

"What? No."

"No?" Roman asked. "Then what's with the bribery box?"

I flipped it open and held the box out. The three of them took donuts and began to chow down. "I'm not quitting, but I do need to ask if it's feasible for me to go down to four days a week."

"Sure," Roman said. The chocolate glaze was gone in three bites. "Got a sour cream in there?"

I held out the box again to him and he dug into it. "Sure? That's it? That's not going to be an issue?"

"No, it's not going to be an issue," Virgil said. "Besides, what did you think we would've said when you needed time off, to you know, have your babies?"

"Yeah, but I'm not even close to my due date. That's a long time away."

"Not that long," Homer muttered. "It'll be here before you know it."

"Cozy wanted something part time," Roman said. "And not early mornings. She's got no problem picking up the slack. You want to go down to three days? Cool? Two? No worries."

"You think hiring your girlfriend is a good idea?" Virgil asked him.

"She's not my girlfriend," Roman said.

"Not yet," Virgil said. "But she will be."

"No. She's gonna be my wife," Roman said. "She just doesn't know it yet."

"Moving slow, I see," Virgil drawled.

"I'll move as slow as she wants," Roman said. "But it won't be a Jazz and Homer situation. That's years in the making."

"Yeah, how Homer didn't die of blue balls, I'll never know," Virgil quipped.

"Stop talking about my balls." Homer glared, causing his brothers to laugh.

"Mom's gonna be so happy," Virgil said. "First Homer starts shacking up with Jazz, and now there's a woman on the horizon for the golden boy."

"I'm not the golden boy," Roman protested.

"Yeah, you are. You're Mom's favorite and we all know it," Virgil said with an easy smile. "He never got in trouble for any of our pranks," he explained to me. "And she never blamed Homer because he's Homer. So I always got punished enough for the both of them."

Roman shoved his younger brother. "Pretty sure Brielle's the favorite."

"I was just talking about us boys. Anyway, with you and Homer down for the count, that might give me a little breathing room with Mom. She's been on me for years about settling down even though she knows I'm not interested." Virgil shook his head.

The front door opened and a little girl who looked to be about six years old ran inside. She came to a halt, her brown eyes widening. "Are those donuts?"

"Yeah, kid, these are donuts," Virgil said. "But ah, where's your mom or dad?"

"I don't have a dad," the girl stated.

The door opened again, and a bombshell brunette with curves for days strode inside. She frowned. "Clementine, what did I tell you about running ahead of me?"

"But, Mom," Clementine whined. "You said we needed help, so I came inside to ask for help. They have donuts."

The bombshell raised her brows. "Donuts, huh?" She looked up from her daughter. "Sorry about that. Do you mind if I use your phone? My cell battery is crap, and it died on me. I need to call a tow truck."

"What's wrong with your car?" Virgil asked, not taking his eyes off the woman.

"The front is smoking," Clementine said, eyeing the box of donuts with wishful intent.

"Let me take a look," Virgil said.

"Oh, I don't want to be any trouble," the woman said. "Just a phone would be fine."

"I insist." Virgil flashed a mega flirty grin. "I'm Virgil."

"Riley." Her eyes went to Clementine. "Ah, can Clementine hang out here while we look at my car?"

"Sure thing." I smiled. "I'll keep her company."

"Okay, but what about a donut?" Clementine asked hopefully.

"One donut," Riley allowed.

Clementine grinned.

"Let's go take a look at your car," Virgil said, placing his hand on Riley's back and guiding her to the front door. It jangled shut behind them.

"Another one bites the dust," Roman said with a grin.

"What bites the dust?" Clementine asked.

"Never mind," Roman said. "You like chocolate milk?"

∼

"Are you on your way?" Savage asked.

I climbed into the car. "I'm leaving now."

"You sure you'll be able to find the clubhouse okay?"

"Yes. I'll plug the address into my phone. I should be there in about half an hour."

"Okay, babe. Drive safe."

Heartbeats & Highways

On my way to the clubhouse, I heard a siren behind me. I looked in the rearview mirror and saw the blue and red lights of a cop car swirling.

Swallowing my nerves, I pulled over onto the side of the road and rolled down my window. The cop got out of his car and sauntered toward me.

He came to the driver's side window. I couldn't see his eyes because he was wearing a pair of sunglasses. "License and registration."

"Sure thing, Officer," I said, my heart pattering away in my chest. I leaned over to the glove box and grabbed the registration and then opened my wallet for my ID. I handed him both documents.

While he was examining them, he asked, "Do you know why I pulled you over?"

"No, sir. I don't."

"You were speeding."

"I apologize," I said, attempting to look ashamed. "I was excited. I'm due at the clubhouse and I'm already running late."

He paused. "Clubhouse?"

"The Tarnished Angels clubhouse," I clarified.

"You run with the Tarnished Angels?"

"I'm Savage's Old Lady."

I instantly felt guilty for pulling the Old Lady card, but I really didn't want to get a ticket, and I remembered what Savage had told me about the police in Waco.

The cop handed me back my license and registration. "Look, you weren't going that fast. I'll let you off with a warning tonight, but watch your speed, okay?"

"I will. Thank you."

"Tell Colt Officer Fletcher said hello."

"I sure will."

I rolled up my window and waited for the cop to get into his car before slowly getting back on the road.

Savage hadn't been lying. Mentioning the club's name had gotten me out of a ticket.

If you can't beat 'em, join 'em.

~

I stopped at the gate of the clubhouse and waited for the two young men in jeans and leather cuts that said Prospects on them to open it for me.

They waved me through, and I turned the car toward the gravel lot. I parked next to a motorcycle and cut the engine.

I was barely out of the car before Savage was standing in front of me.

"Jesus, woman, what took you so damn long?" he demanded, wrapping his arms around me and kissing me in greeting.

When I could catch my breath, I said, "I got stopped by a cop."

"*What?*"

"Relax." I pressed a hand to his chest. "I told him I was your Old Lady. He let me go with a warning. You weren't lying about the club's influence with law enforcement."

"We know people," he agreed. He stepped back and took my hand. "You hungry? The grill's hot and there are about seven different types of salad. Bean salad, potato salad, coleslaw, fruit salad, and other salads I don't recognize."

I laughed. "Yeah, I'm starving. Feed me."

"Oh, I'll feed you," he quipped, leading me toward the clubhouse.

There were two bikers on the porch who I hadn't met yet.

"Crow," Savage introduced. "And Acid."

"Nice to meet you," I said.

"We're gonna get Evie some food. Catch you guys later." Savage ushered me into the clubhouse.

"So that was Acid, your sparring buddy?"

"Yep."

"He doesn't look very friendly," I remarked.

"He's been through shit."

"As we all have," I remarked.

"Yeah." Savage frowned. "His best friend was a prospect at the same time he was, but he died. It changed him. This life changes you."

I squeezed his hand in understanding.

"There's sodas and sparkling water in a cooler outside," he explained with a roguish smile. "For all the pregnant and non-drinking Old Ladies."

We walked down a hallway past several closed doors. I was reminded of the first and only time I'd been here. It felt like so long ago, but it really wasn't.

Savage pushed open the screen door to the backyard. Kids and dogs ran around while women sat in a circle of camp chairs, holding babies and plates of food.

The bikers congregated near the grill and there were at least three tables laden with food and desserts.

The bonfire was already lit, giving off a welcoming heat.

"Come on, let me introduce you to the brothers."

Duke hugged me immediately and there were no lingering questions in his gaze. I appreciated his demonstrative affection. I lost track by the fourth name, pressing into Savage's side as I tried to memorize who was who. "This is Colt," Savage said, gesturing to the man with dark hair. "He's our club president."

"Officer Fletcher asked me to tell you hello."

Colt frowned. "You know Fletch?"

"Not well. We were—ah—recently introduced. When he pulled me over, wanting to give me a ticket." I blushed and shot Savage a look. "Turns out I was speeding."

Savage raised his brows. "You? Speeding?"

"That's what I'm saying. I got excited on my way here."

"Did you get the ticket?" Colt demanded.

"No. I told him . . ."

"Yeah?" Colt prodded. "What did you tell him?"

"I told him I was Savage's Old Lady," I admitted. "He let me go with a warning and told me to tell you he said hi."

It felt like all the noise of the party had come to a stop and silence descended on the group.

Colt finally broke the spell. He grunted. "We work on cops' bikes for free and are friends with a few others."

"Oh?" I frowned in confusion.

"Club owns a motorcycle repair shop."

"Charlie's, right?" I asked, looking at Savage.

Savage grinned. "Right."

"Cops, firefighters, and first responders get their work done free of charge," Colt elaborated.

"Ah," I said. "That's nice of you."

Colt, Zip—the vice president—and Boxer all laughed.

"Why is that funny?" I demanded.

"Come on," Savage said, taking my hand. "Let's get you something to eat."

He ushered me toward the tables of food and handed me a paper plate.

"Are you going to explain why my comment made them laugh?"

"We don't do anything because we're *nice*. For example, Fletch gets his bike worked on for free and then he doesn't give you a ticket. See?"

"Ah, so it's bribery."

"We like to call it a mutual exchange of benefits," Savage said with a mock glare.

"Whatever you say." I looked around the party. "I'm gonna need a diagram to keep everyone straight. Who do those kids belong to?"

"The tall, gangly dark-haired one is Silas. He belongs to Mia and Colt. He's not their biological kid though, they adopted him."

"Okay." I nodded. "And the other two?"

"Cam and Lily." Savage shoveled a heaping mound of potato salad onto my plate.

"Go on . . ."

"Their parents died not too long ago," he said, pitching his voice lower and meeting my gaze. "Boxer and Doc became their legal guardians."

"Both parents?" I whispered.

Savage nodded. "Within a couple of months. I'll tell you about it later when we're alone."

Nodding, I looked back at the kids playing with two dogs and a soccer ball. My hand immediately went to my belly.

"They're lucky," I murmured. "To have the club."

Savage met my gaze. "Lucky. Yeah."

Chapter 38

Savage brought me over to the group of Old Ladies who were sitting close enough to the bonfire to stay warm, but not so close that they would overheat.

"Go away," Willa joked. "No boys allowed."

Savage sniggered and kissed my lips briefly. "Sit," he ordered.

I took a vacant chair in the circle of women and settled my heaping plate onto my lap.

"Something to drink, babe?" Savage asked me.

"Oh, water's good. Thanks." I beamed up at him. He squeezed my shoulder and then left.

"Well, I never thought I'd see the day when Savage acted like a puppy for a woman. I'm Logan," she said with a smile. "I'm with Smoke."

"Smoke, right."

"Should I do a quick round-robin of who's who?" Willa asked.

"Please," I begged.

Willa went around the circle, pointing at women and

naming off their husbands. Everyone except Rach was with a biker.

"We need name tags," Mia said.

"I've got it pretty well sorted, I think," I said, shoveling in a bite of fruit.

Savage returned with my water and then almost immediately left again to join Duke and the others.

"You guys look like smitten kittens," Joni said. "Totally unable to take your eyes off each other."

"You're one to talk," Sutton said to Joni. "You and Zip are trying to win the award for most sexual eye contact."

Joni rubbed her baby's back. "It worked, didn't it?"

"We should start a book club," Rach announced. "Which is really just an excuse to eat chocolate and gossip."

"We do that now," Mia said with a laugh.

"Yeah, but if it's a book club, we can read smutty romance novels and then our men can reap the rewards," Sutton said. "Logan knows a thing or two about smutty romance novels, don't you?"

Logan laughed. "I might know a thing or two. And Smoke definitely isn't complaining."

I ate my food, loving the banter and camaraderie from this group of women.

"How are you liking the apartment?" Brooklyn asked, patting the baby resting against her chest. "You can be honest."

"I love it," I admitted.

"And the delivery trucks don't bother you?" Logan asked. "They were hard to get used to when I lived there."

"You lived there?" I asked in surprise.

"For a time," Logan replied.

Mia's daughter, who'd been occupying herself on the blanket within the circle, crawled to Logan and then placed her hands on her legs and stood up. Logan scooped the girl up into her arms and bounced her on her lap.

"When are you adding to the baby pile?" Joni demanded.

"Soon," Logan said, smiling down at the baby.

"How soon?" Joni asked.

"Whenever one of Smoke's super-sperm decides to set up shop in one of my eggs," Logan quipped. "We're no longer using protection, so . . ."

"Oh, yay," Allison said with a soft smile.

The woman hardly said anything; but she was kind. They all were.

Tears came to my eyes, and I hastily turned away to dab them with a napkin.

"Hormones, or something else?" Mia asked with a wry smile.

"Both?" I said with a watery laugh. "This is nice. I've never had friends before and I . . . this is just nice."

"Group chat," Joni announced. "It's time to put you in the group chat."

"Group chat?" I asked in confusion.

"For the Old Ladies," Mia clarified. "It's easier to experience it than it is to explain."

"Be warned, though, a lot of the texts you're going to get are just inappropriate memes and dirty jokes," Willa said. "It's part of the charm."

"You'll get used to us." Mia smiled. "Promise."

∼

The sun set and the babies were put to bed. I'd moved

Heartbeats & Highways

the camp chair closer to the blaze and turned up the collar of my coat. Savage perched next to me on a log, resting his hand on my thigh.

My head was a whirl. I was happy and full, and I was with Savage and the family he'd carved out for himself.

I'd been welcomed and teased, and I truly felt like I belonged here.

"How you feeling, babe?" Savage asked me softly.

"Good." I turned to him with a smile. "They're wonderful."

"Yeah, they are." He rubbed his jaw. "Duke hugged you."

"Noticed that, did you?"

"Yeah. I think it's going to be okay," he said quietly. "I think I'm gonna get everything I didn't know I wanted."

He stole a hand across my belly and stared into my eyes.

"You God damn son of a bitch!" a biker yelled from across the bonfire.

The sound of a fist meeting flesh turned my stomach.

"What the hell?" Mia asked, standing from her chair but not rushing to investigate.

Savage pulled away from me and shot up. He rushed to the two men who were fighting on the other side of the bonfire. Despite the light from the blaze, I couldn't see their faces.

"Hey, break it the fuck up," Colt growled, sandwiching himself between the two men.

"What's going on?" Joni asked.

I looked around the bonfire at the Old Ladies, waiting to see if anyone knew anything. Logan's expression was tight, and her lips were clamped together.

"It's Smoke's right," Boxer said to Colt. "You beat Zip

into oblivion when you found out he was screwing your sister."

"I wasn't screwing Joni," Zip announced. "I mean, I was, but I was planning on making her my Old Lady."

"He's been fucking my daughter," Smoke roared. "I want satisfaction!"

"Fine," the other biker said. He cracked his neck. "You want to pummel me? Go right the fuck ahead. Won't change a damn thing. I'm claiming Tavy."

"Fuck, Raze," Boxer muttered.

Smoke lunged for Raze, but two other bikers held Smoke back.

"If you want to fight, we're taking this to The Ring," Colt said. "You can bash each other all you want, but not here."

"Let's fucking go," Smoke seethed. "I'll put you in the ground. Brother or not. How fucking dare you!"

Logan's breath hitched and she made a noise. A noise that seemed to break through Smoke's haze of rage.

His shoulders slumped. "Son of a bitch," he muttered. "You can let me go. I won't kill him."

The two bikers holding Smoke let go of him and Smoke marched toward the clubhouse. Logan trailed after him.

"Fuck," Colt said, looking at Raze. "Is that why Tavy isn't here tonight? You wanted to tell Smoke without her present?"

Raze nodded.

"I need a fucking drink," Colt stated. "Church tomorrow to discuss this shit."

I looked at Mia, Joni, and the others. "What was that all about?"

Brooklyn cocked her head to the side. "Well, I guess

Tavy and Raze have been dating in secret and it just came out. Did you know?" She looked at Mia.

"No, I didn't," Mia said softly. "Logan did, though. Did you see her face?"

"Who's Tavy?" I asked.

"Smoke's daughter," Joni explained. "And Logan's best friend."

"And Smoke's daughter has been . . . with his biker brother? Oh," I murmured.

"Not just a biker brother," Mia expanded. "But Smoke, Raze, and a few of the others are actually from the South Dakota chapter. They lost their president, so they joined up with us in Waco. So Smoke and Raze go way, way back."

"And you're not supposed to sleep with a brother's female family member. It's part of their code," Joni said.

"But you and Zip—"

"Yeah, and when my brother found out, he beat the shit out of Zip," Joni explained. "It was his right as my brother."

"Huh." I looked at Savage, who was speaking to Raze in a low voice.

"Logan will smooth it all over," Joni said.

The group of women fell silent and then Sutton laughed. "Tavy and Raze. I didn't see that coming."

Savage slapped Raze on the shoulder and then marched over to me. "Hey, babe."

I tilted my head back to look at him. "Hey."

"You wanna see my room?"

"You mean you want to show her your penis," Willa joked.

"If she's willing," Savage said with a wicked grin.

"I'm always willing," I blurted out. "I mean—"

The Old Ladies cackled like hens.

I grasp his outstretched hand. He hauled me up and we walked toward the clubhouse. He opened the screen door and ushered me inside and when I tried to walk to the stairs, he tugged me back.

"I've been to your room," I said. "It's up there."

He shook his head. "I got a new room on the first floor."

We walked a few paces, and he gestured to a door. After flipping on the light, he waved me inside before shutting the door behind us.

The furniture was the same, but the room itself was bigger.

"Not much different," he said. "But this one has its own bathroom."

I frowned. "That hardly seems like a reason to change rooms."

"All the brothers with Old Ladies get rooms with bathrooms. I didn't get to give you a full tour of the place—the Old Ladies were determined to have you to themselves tonight, but tomorrow I'll show you the tiny homes being built out in the field. They're for the brothers who have babies. Don't know if you noticed, but the club is breeding like bunnies. We needed more space, and the single brothers who live here don't need to be awake at all hours of the night due to screaming babies."

"That would kind of cramp their style," I said with a laugh. "I am amazed at how many babies there are."

"Those of us with Old Ladies are determined to keep the species going." He leaned down and kissed my lips. "I didn't get it before, but now I do."

"What? What didn't you get?"

"Going to bed with the same woman in my bed every night, holding your belly, watching you grow our babies. I thought Colt, Duke, all of them were crazy. How could they want such stability? And then I realized they had everything that was missing from my life. Stability. Comfort. Intimacy."

His hand snaked up the back of my shirt. "Come to bed, babe. Let me show you how much you mean to me."

Chapter 39

Savage's phone buzzed.

I kept my face buried in the pillow but opened one eye.

He reached for his cell which rested on the nightstand. He sighed. "I gotta go."

"What time is it?" I asked.

"Eight. Prez is calling Church. To discuss the Raze thing." He peered down at me. "You need to throw up before I hop in the shower?"

"Savage," I moaned.

"What? Don't you usually puke your guts up in the morning?"

"Yes," I agreed. I sat up for a moment and then I ran to the bathroom.

When I was done with the morning sickness, I went back to the bedroom. Savage had gone to the kitchen to grab me a glass of orange juice. Thankfully, he'd put on a pair of sweats first.

He handed the glass to me, and I drank three gulps.

He kissed the end of my nose. "Better?"

"Better," I agreed. "Why does the suffering of pregnancy start with morning sickness and end with painful messy childbirth?"

"Couldn't tell ya. But, at least at the end of it, we'll have two beautiful babies."

"Nature's cruel joke of how they come out," I grumbled.

He kissed my forehead and then went to the bathroom. He shut the door and then I heard the sound of the shower going.

I finished my juice and thought about a naked Savage in the shower. I knocked on the door of the bathroom and then opened it.

"If I promise to keep my hands to myself, can I get in there with you?"

"It's not your hands I'm worried about, but my own. I'm done though. You climb in and when I get out, I'll get you a fresh towel."

I got into the steaming water and glided past Savage. He was beautiful. All rippling muscles and ink. It was a wonder we ever got out of bed.

Oh, right, we barely ever do.

I slid the shower curtain closed and shampooed my hair.

"A fresh towel is on the rack for you," he said a few moments later. "Get dressed and head to the kitchen for breakfast. I'll meet you there after Church."

"Okay."

"I grabbed some clean clothes for you from the apartment. They're in the top drawer."

"When did you do that?" I asked.

"When you weren't looking. Come out here and let me kiss you goodbye."

"I've got shampoo in my hair." I poked my head out and met his lips. "You might be thoughtful packing clothes for me, but we need to do something about your shampoo, conditioner, and soap situation."

"What? You don't like drugstore generic?" he quipped.

"I can smell the chemicals. I'm going to get us something natural."

"Whatever makes you happy, babe." He kissed me one more time for final measure and then he was gone.

I finished up in the shower and after towel drying my hair as best I could, I padded naked into the bedroom. I opened the top drawer and pulled out a pair of underwear and immediately grimaced. They were so unattractive. I made a mental note to ask the Old Ladies a good place to get lingerie. I needed to spice things up.

With a sigh, I got into my jeans and sweater. Savage hadn't brought me socks, so I borrowed a pair of his.

The kitchen was a zoo, and the Old Ladies were bustling around the room trying to feed the kids and keep them satisfied, all the while making enough for the army that was currently having Church.

"Good morning," Mia chirped. "Coffee?"

"Half a cup please," I replied. "Can't have too much with the babies."

Mia poured me a half cup and offered me cream, which I took. "What can I do to help?" I asked.

"Nothing," Mia said. "Brooklyn, Sutton and I've got it."

I smiled at the baby on Mia's back that was in a carrier. "Looks like you've got a helper."

Mia turned her head and grinned over her shoulder at her daughter. "She loves it up there. I get so much done with her on my back, it's amazing. She's like a little possum."

I laughed and took my coffee to the living room. Joni

moved over on the couch, and I smiled my thanks as I sat down beside her.

I looked around the room at the Old Ladies. So many of them had babies or were pregnant. It felt like I'd walked into a tribe, a group of women who understood one another and were at the same place in life.

"First batch is ready," Brooklyn called out.

The baby Doc was holding began to cry.

"Your daughter needs a change or a breast," Doc said to Brooklyn.

Brooklyn sighed and took her daughter. "I swear I just fed her."

"I'll take over your cooking spot," Willa offered, moving to get up from the chair.

"No, you rest," Rach interjected, handing her son to Doc. "You're about ready to burst. Relax. I've got this."

I was just about to get myself a helping, when Savage appeared from the hallway.

"Hey," I said to him with a smile. "Can I make you a plate?"

He didn't reply and his jaw clenched.

My smile slipped off my face.

"I need you to come with me," he commanded.

I swallowed. "Okay."

My eyes darted around the room. Everyone was slowly stopping what they were doing and staring at us. I set my mug down and ducked my head and then followed him out into the backyard.

Bikers stood in a cluster, and I was pleased to note that Raze and Smoke didn't look hell-bent on killing each other.

But when they saw me, all conversation ceased. We passed by them, and I caught Duke's eye. His jaw clenched too, and he turned away.

My heart began to beat in fear.

Savage led me to a building that was bigger than a shed but smaller than the clubhouse. He held the door open and gestured for me to go inside. He followed and then closed the door.

Colt and Zip were sitting at the head of the table.

"Have a seat, Evie," Colt said.

His tone didn't brook for an argument. I sat, and Savage took the chair next to me. I set my hands in my lap, fisting them tight.

Colt set his linked hands on the table and stared at me. "Duke reached out to a friend of the club who runs private security and has access to police records and shit like that. He ran your name when Savage told him he made you his Old Lady. We run everyone, so don't take it personally. Except unlike everyone else, you popped up as a missing person out of Broken Arrow, Oklahoma. The missing person report was filed by Randall Carson, Sr."

Blood rushed to my head as it pumped furiously through my veins. It was a roar in my eardrums, silencing everything else around me.

"*Evie*," Savage prodded. "Why is there a missing person report filed on you?"

The coffee in my belly churned. "I'm going to be sick."

I shoved back from the table, somehow got the door open in time, and retched onto the grass. When my stomach was empty, I wiped my mouth. Trembling, I went back inside and took my chair. There was a bottle of water waiting for me, the lid already unscrewed. Savage nudged it toward me. I picked it up and took a long drink.

My insides were shaky.

"It's time to tell us the truth, Evie. We need to have all the facts," Colt commanded. "And don't leave *anything* out."

"It's ugly," I murmured. "And I haven't been honest with you. With any of you."

I looked at Savage when I made the pronouncement.

He took my hand in a show of support. Even though what I was about to tell them was horrible, it was time for honesty.

"I should start at the beginning, then. And tell you the full story." I took a deep breath and looked at Savage. "I'm originally from Texas. Northern Texas. But when I was fourteen, my parents moved us to a place called The Farm in Oklahoma. The closest city is Broken Arrow."

Savage frowned, but he remained silent, nodding at me to continue.

"It's five hundred acres of private farmland. My parents and nineteen other families lived on the land. We're called . . . the Seed Reapers."

"Seed Reapers?" Savage repeated.

I swallowed. "It's a cult. I was raised in a cult, Savage."

No one said anything, so I blazed on.

"When I was sixteen, I got engaged to the Grand Patriarch's son. When I was seventeen, I was bound to Randall, Jr. and married," I clarified.

"The Grand Patriarch . . . That's the leader?" Colt asked.

I nodded.

"You were married at seventeen?" Savage croaked. "You never told me that."

"If I told you the truth, it would've raised a red flag."

Savage clenched his jaw. "Babe, you being evasive about your past was the biggest red flag of all. I knew something was up, I just didn't know what. Go on. We have to hear it all now."

My shoulders slumped. "Randall was two years older than me. After we were married, we moved in together on the other side of The Farm. Far from everyone. He was the Grand Patriarch's son, so we had a private spot just outside the community. The beatings started a few months after we were married—because I kept getting my period..."

I took another sip of water.

"Sow, grow, harvest, rest," I murmured, almost to myself.

"What?" Savage asked.

"We had four seasons. Sow, grow, harvest, rest. Not only did they correspond with the planting of crops, but our relationships mirrored them too. The name. The Seed Reapers, that's where it came from."

"I don't understand," Colt said.

"We . . . all of us—the girls . . . we were bred for sowing. In the sowing season, we got married. The growing season, we were pregnant. The harvest season, we gave birth. The rest season was for recovery, so we could have more babies the next year. The whole purpose of the cult is to grow in size. That's how they found me and my parents. When I was fourteen, we were visiting Broken Arrow, and my dad met the Grand Patriarch . . . The cult looks for people they can convert, and the women who join become the breeders . . . it's usually their daughters. My parents were already hyper-religious. It was easy for the Grand Patriarch to convince them to move to The Farm."

Savage frowned. "But you told me—"

"Let her talk, Savage," Colt commanded.

Savage nodded and clamped his mouth shut.

"After a year together," I said quietly. "I still wasn't pregnant. He blamed me for his family not growing. A week after my eighteenth birthday, my parents committed joint suicide in a grand sacrifice to God in the hopes it would make me fertile. I didn't find that out until months later—that the Grand Patriarch had convinced them that if they sacrificed themselves that my womb would finally take seed."

My stomach turned when I thought about it. "Ironic, isn't it? Both my parents died so I could have children, and now I'm pregnant with twins."

Savage's hand tightened on mine and the room was silent.

I forced myself to keep talking. "Another year went by and still nothing had happened. I was nineteen and just coming out of the fog the loss of my parents caused. Grief is strange, you know? They were fanatics, and they abandoned me, but they were still my parents. I was completely lost without them."

I shook my head. "One night the Grand Patriarch came over for dinner. He watched me all night long—calculating. I pretended to go up to bed, but I hid in the hallway upstairs so I could listen to his conversation with my hus—Randall. The Seed Reapers don't believe in divorce. You have to understand, they're literal in their belief system. There are no exceptions, not for anyone. In our—*their* world, the only way out of a marriage is death. And that night I heard them plotting ways to get rid of me so Randall could take a new wife—a more *fruitful* wife."

It sickened me to recount my past.

"Every winter, there was a festival, I guess you could call it. To say goodbye to winter and to usher in the spring. I was supposed to have an *accident*."

I rubbed the back of my neck.

"I struggled with what to do. I didn't know how I was going to escape. It's not like I had any money. The cult had been my life since I was fourteen. But I remembered the outside world even though I was sheltered. I remembered a sense of *normalcy*. I was so scared, but I knew I had to escape."

I took a deep breath. "A few days before the festival, Randall was very high up on a ladder on the second story of our home removing a dead wasp's nest. I was holding the ladder steady on the concrete. I didn't even—there was this moment, and I just yanked it as hard as I could out from under him. He grabbed onto the rain gutter in a panic, but it wasn't strong enough to hold him. He went down and hit his head on the concrete. It knocked him unconscious. His breathing was . . . it was really loud and steady, and he was almost gurgling like he wasn't going to wake up."

"Agonal breathing," Savage explained. "It happens when someone has a traumatic brain injury . . ."

"Then what happened?" Colt prodded.

"I tried to see if I could wake him up . . . but when I couldn't, I went to get the tractor . . ."

"What did you do with the tractor? Did you bury him—alive?" Colt asked.

I fell silent and clamped my mouth shut.

"The rest of it," Colt commanded. "You can tell us, Evie."

I forced myself to look Savage in the eye. I forced myself to be brave. I forced myself to look at the man I loved when I told him something that might make him stop loving me.

"I got the tractor," I said, my voice sounding very far away in my head. "And used the loader bucket to pick him up and dump him in the pig pen behind the barn. The pigs . . . after a few days, if you don't feed them, they'll eat anything—and I mean *anything*. We'd stopped feeding them a few days before, to get them ready to sacrifice for our winter festival, and when I dropped him in . . ."

Silence reigned for several beats.

"Wow," Zip said. "You're so perfect for Savage."

"*Zip*," Colt warned.

"What?" he demanded.

"This isn't a joking matter. This is some serious shit," Colt said.

Savage hadn't reacted to anything I'd said. His expression was clear of emotion and for the first time in a long time, I couldn't get a read on him.

I bowed my head. "After that, I—went on the run. Grabbed some things of value and some money Randall had stashed away. I took my papers from before we came to The Farm, and I bought a bus ticket. I didn't think about there being a missing person's report. That doesn't make sense to me."

"Why not?" Colt asked.

"Local law enforcement doesn't have any jurisdiction on The Farm. I don't know why, but it's the way of it. We—they deal with everything internally, even punishment. The Grand Patriarch must be using the police to find me, that's all. He'd never tell the authorities what I did, even if he knew the truth—which he doesn't."

"So, he's trying to get you back," Colt said. "It's what I'd do if someone crossed the club, and we needed to deal with it on our own."

"So, what happens now that you know the truth?" I asked, fear creeping into my voice.

Colt and Savage exchanged a look and then Colt said, "I'll look into it, and the club will handle it."

"You're not going to toss me out? I'm a stranger who lied to—"

"You're not a stranger," Colt stated. "You're Savage's Old Lady, which makes you family now. Your problems become our problems. And the club will protect you."

My throat thickened. "Thank you."

He inclined his head. "You haven't told anyone else

about any of this have you? Not your new friend, what's her name? Cozy?"

I shook my head. "She doesn't know anything. I haven't . . . I'd never planned on telling anyone anything about this. I'd hoped . . . I don't know, maybe they would've let me go. Forgotten about me eventually."

"From what you've told us these aren't the type of people to ever stop looking for you," Zip said.

"I planned to keep moving, never staying in one place for long." I looked at Savage. "I didn't expect you to change everything for me."

"I've got to tell the rest of the brothers," Colt said. "Bring them in on what's going on."

I nodded.

"I'm gonna walk Evie to our room, then I'll be back," Savage said.

"Ten minutes," Colt said.

Savage tugged my hand and we both stood. He held the door open for me and I walked through the doorway, out into the winter sunshine. Knots of fear coiled through my belly. The truth was out there. Ugly, horrible. Irreversible.

We strode across the backyard to the clubhouse. I opened the screen door and went inside. I could hear conversations coming from the kitchen, but Savage took my hand again and led me to his room. We didn't say anything until the door closed behind us.

I collapsed onto the bed, exhaustion I didn't know I was carrying dropping from my shoulders.

"Are you mad at me?" I asked tentatively.

"Yes."

I looked up at Savage and frowned in confusion. His face wasn't pinched, and his eyes didn't glitter with rage.

"I'm madder at myself than I am at you, though. I

knew you were hiding things about your past. I just didn't know how deep it went. And by the time you started telling me shit, I was too damn in love with you to insist you tell me everything."

I swallowed. "I'm sorry, Savage."

"How the hell am I supposed to protect you if I don't have all the facts?"

"I never wanted you to know," I murmured. "I never wanted you to . . . to look at me differently."

He crouched down in front of me and placed his hands on my thighs. He stared into my eyes. "After I talk to the boys, I'm coming back up here and we're going to have a long talk, so you understand."

"Understand what?"

"That there's nothing you could do that would stop me from loving you."

Chapter 40

"Babe."

I pressed my face into the pillow. "Hmm."

"Babe, wake up."

My eyes flipped open. Savage was sitting on the edge of the bed and his hand was on my hip.

"What time is it?" I asked, stifling a yawn.

"A little before eleven," he said. "You conked out for a bit. You want to get out of here?"

I swallowed. "That depends."

"On?"

"Are we okay?" I asked, my voice stilted.

He paused for a moment. "No. We're not okay. We're not even close to being okay. Which is why we need to get out of here so we can have some damn privacy to discuss shit."

I nibbled my lip. "What happened in Church?"

"The brothers have been brought up to speed. That's all I'm gonna say about it."

"Are they—do they hate me? Does Duke hate me now?"

His gaze softened. "No. They don't hate you. And Duke doesn't either. Not even a little bit. If anything, they're more protective of you now than before. Knowing your history changes things. I mean, some of them guessed it was bad, but no one had any idea . . ."

Part of my tension eased, but until Savage and I had fought it out, I wouldn't be all right.

"Yeah. We should go," I said. I slowly sat up, feeling groggy.

"You hungry?"

I shook my head.

"You threw up."

"I remember."

"So you must be hungry."

"Must I?" I demanded with a hint of snark. "Or maybe I just have too much on my mind to think about food."

He sighed. "Fine. Let's get home. I'll follow you on my bike."

I was worried about seeing the Old Ladies in the living room on my way out. The last thing I wanted to do was put on a brave face and pretend like everything was fine when it wasn't. But thankfully, the living room was clear of people. The kitchen was tidy. There was no evidence whatsoever of friends and family sharing a meal together the night before.

My pulse drummed in my ears the entire drive home. I didn't even remember my journey; I was functioning on autopilot, and even though Savage claimed there was nothing I could ever do that would force him to turn away from me, I didn't believe it.

I'd lied to him. And I'd been prepared never to share the darkest part of my soul with him.

How did you come back from that?

I parked in the back of the bakery and Savage glided his bike next to me. I cut the engine of the car, grabbed my purse, and climbed out as Savage got off his motorcycle.

Savage took my hand and led me to the bakery. Thankfully, Brielle and Jazz weren't working so I didn't have to fake a smile.

I waved to the girl rolling out dough and then went up the stairs, Savage trailing behind me.

After we went into the apartment, I put my purse onto the kitchen counter and then moved to the farthest corner of the room.

"What are you doing?" Savage asked me bluntly.

"Giving you space."

He paused. "You think I'm going to hurt you."

"No."

"No? Then why are you all the way over there?"

"Habit," I admitted.

His expression softened. "Can we sit? On the couch?"

"Okay." I gingerly walked to the couch and perched on the end. Savage took the spot in the middle and just stared at me.

"I'm gonna try and put into words what's going through my mind," he began. "Normally, I'd get on my bike or go to The Ring. But if I left you now, you'd think . . . Hell, you'd think I was abandoning you but I'm not." His jaw clenched. "I'm mad at you for not trusting me. But I'm mad at myself, too. When we met, I knew you were hiding things from me, but I didn't suspect *this*."

I swallowed.

"You were working under the table and living in a motel. I thought you were fleeing a domestic abuse situation. And even after you told me he'd died . . . I didn't even consider that you'd killed your husband."

Heartbeats & Highways

I flinched at the ugliness of the truth. "Did you tell Colt? About how you really met me?"

"No. I left that out. Because that would implicate me in shit I shouldn't have been involved in." He cocked his head to the side. "You left that out too—of your story."

"I'm good at keeping secrets, I guess." I rubbed my third eye. "So, what do we do now?"

"Come here."

I scooted closer to him. He reached out and gently cupped the back of my neck and stared into my eyes. "You can't keep shit from me when it's really important, Evie. Never again."

"I promise."

"Can I ask you something?"

"Anything."

"Was it rape? Is that how you got pregnant?"

Rape. Such an ugly word.

"No," I whispered. "It wasn't rape."

"Then how did you get pregnant? If he didn't force you?"

"If I had any chance of escape, I couldn't let him know that I'd overheard him and his father talking. So I . . . played the role of his beloved wife. It was the hardest thing I've ever done, but I had to survive."

"While plotting to kill him."

I recoiled.

"No babe, I didn't mean—I told you what I did to my foster father. It wasn't a judgement. It was understanding."

"Oh."

"Fuck, I can't believe I just . . ."

"What?"

"I said I wanted a big family. You probably think I'm just like your husband."

"No!" I emphatically shook my head. "You're nothing

like him, Savage. You love me. You protect me. You'd do anything to make me happy. When you said you wanted a big family, how were you supposed to know about my past?"

"I was supposed to know because you were supposed to trust me with this." His jaw clenched. "Do you have any regrets? About what you did?"

"Regrets? No." I shook my head. "It was me or him, you know? But I don't think I've dealt with it, Savage. It feels like someone else did it."

He dropped his hand from my neck so he could pull me into his arms. "I wish I could say that's the end of it, but it won't be. It'll come for you in the moments you don't expect. A flash in the middle of happiness, a feeling of anxiety. You'll remember what you've done, and you'll have to process it each time."

I placed my hand on his heart.

"And each time, I'll tell you that you made the right choice. We're going to be okay, Evie. We're going to get through this."

My lips quivered. "You promise?"

"I promise."

~

I reached for him in the middle of the night. Savage's side of the bed was cold, and I wondered how long he'd been up and if the energy in his body had been too much and he'd had no choice but to go for a ride on his motorcycle.

But I heard the soft close of a cabinet and exhaled.

I got up and padded out into the living room. It was completely dark except for the oven hood light.

Savage stood at the counter, his back facing me. The glow illuminated his sculpted shoulders and beautiful ink.

Heartbeats & Highways

"Did I wake you?" he asked, turning around.

I shook my head. "You couldn't sleep."

"No. I couldn't sleep," he admitted. "And then I got a text."

"A text? From who?"

He didn't say anything for a moment and then he finally replied. "The owner of the illegal fighting ring."

"He's asking you to come back," I guessed.

"No. He's *telling* me to. The bookies lost a fuck load of money on the fight with Toro and they need to make it back."

"Toro," I repeated as I went to Savage. "You've already beat him once, so—"

"It's not Toro this time. They know he can't beat me. There's someone else—except they won't tell me who I'll be fighting until the night of the fight."

"Don't do it. You walked away once. Now *stay* away."

I put my hand to his heart, and he covered my fingers with his palm. "I wish I could, babe. But there's a problem. I've cost them a lot of money by quitting on short notice after I beat Toro. There's bad blood between us now, and the owner of the fighting ring is threatening to tell the club if I don't fight one last time. If I want this wrapped up for good, then I've got to get in the ring again."

Fear coasted down my spine.

I wanted to beg him not to do it. We'd just come out the other side of something so horrible . . . We were already struggling to survive the truth of my past.

But I kept my mouth shut.

"I need you there," he said softly. "Ringside. And after I win, we'll walk out of there hand in hand, and never look back."

I swallowed. "Of course I'll be there, Savage."

Chapter 41

The warehouse smelled like blood and adrenaline.

This was the modern-day version of the colosseum. Excited revelers looking for a distraction from their everyday lives were chanting and yelling and calling for men to battle each other with their fists.

My hands were clenched at my sides.

I was standing at a corner of the ring with Savage, Duke, and Acid, waiting for Oscar to introduce the fighters. We were surrounded by people.

Oscar stepped into the ring and picked up a microphone. "Ladies and gentlemen, as you know, tonight's fight features Savage, the winner of the match with Toro Masivo, and a mystery fighter that's about to enter the ring and reveal himself. All bets have been placed on hold until the announcement of our challenger, and only after revealing himself will betting for tonight's fight commence. Ladies and gentlemen, please welcome tonight's mystery fighter, Brutus, into the ring!"

Brutus appeared from the crowd and slipped through the ropes, his massive, sweaty form primed and ready to

Heartbeats & Highways

fight. The sheer size of the man caused the mob to go wild, and men rushed to the bookies in the corners of the room as fast as their feet could carry them. Money changed hands and a murmur settled over the warehouse.

Acid had come to lend his support. He was one of the few people who knew what Savage had been up to. His expression was tight and he kept stretching his jaw and neck muscles like he was nervous. He was speaking to a patron in the crowd, and the next thing I knew Acid slipped away from us and disappeared.

Savage was wearing a pair of gym shorts, and he was shirtless. Every now and again he'd glance at me and squeeze my hand.

Savage and Brutus were scheduled to be the last fight of the night and even though my brain buzzed with adrenaline, my body was exhausted at the late hour.

I wouldn't take a deep breath until Savage walked out of the fighting ring, never to return.

"Where's Acid?" Savage asked. "I need him to get the ice buckets ready for my hands."

"I saw him a few minutes ago, but he went into the crowd. I don't know where he is. I don't like this, Savage. I don't like this at all," I said.

He looked at me, a lazy smile appearing across his lips. "You've seen me fight before. It's going to be okay."

"Yeah, but that was before I loved you." I brushed my hand across his forehead.

"Ladies and gentlemen!" Oscar's booming voice came through the microphone. "Thank you for your patience. We have a change in the lineup for the final fight of the evening . . ."

I glanced at Savage whose brow furrowed in confusion.

"Brutus will not be fighting Savage tonight," Oscar continued.

The crowd booed and men began to scramble toward the bookies to undo their bets and get their money back.

Oscar raised his hand to quiet the crowd and waited for the animosity to die down before he spoke again. "Another fighter has challenged Brutus, tagging himself in to fight in Savage's place. And trust me when I say you're in for a wild fight! Savage might be a maniac in the ring, but Acid is the man who trains with him and has taught him everything he knows. If Savage is a maniac, what does that mean for Acid? Tonight, you get to find out! Please welcome to the ring, Acid!"

My eyes widened as I saw Acid, now bare-chested and in a pair of gym shorts climbing into the ring.

"What the fuck?" Savage demanded. "What's he doing?"

"No fucking idea," Duke murmured.

Savage dropped my hand and strode toward Acid and called his name through the din of the crowd. Acid came to the edge of the ring to speak to Savage. Acid murmured something and then looked at me before looking back at Savage again.

"What's happening?" I asked Duke as I glanced up at him.

Duke's expression was contained. "I'm not sure."

My attention returned to Savage and Acid. Savage looked furious and was arguing with Acid, but after a few moments, Acid simply held out his fist to Savage and nodded. Savage paused and then tapped Acid's fist before returning to my side.

"What was that about? What's going on?" I asked.

Savage took my hand and clenched his jaw before he replied. "Apparently Brutus killed the last man he fought, and Acid said I've got a family to think about. He promised the promoter five fights without pay in exchange for my last fight tonight. So their choice was simple. They'll make a lot more money with Acid than they will with me."

The bell rang, signaling the start of the fight.

Acid struck first—a sharp jab to Brutus' chin.

The crowd roared with pleasure.

Brutus slowly turned his gaze to Acid, his eyes glittering with philistine rage.

He attacked.

The two men traded blows, one after the other.

Pop. Acid got his nose broken by a roundhouse kick from Brutus.

Snap. The crack of a fist against Brutus' jaw as Acid boxed his way to bloodying Brutus' mouth.

Ribs cracked.

Sweat and blood flew through the air. The rumble of the mob drowned out the grunting of the two fighters, brawling like possessed barbarians. Minutes passed.

Acid was battered and though his nose was badly broken and gushing blood, Brutus' right eye was swelling shut from Acid's accurate jabs.

The fight had slowed; both men were running out of gas. There was only so much that adrenaline could fuel. Now grit would determine the victor.

Acid was in close, boxing like a titleholder when Brutus hooked a foot behind Acid's right ankle and pushed him down hard. When he landed, he didn't move, momentarily stunned. No doubt the air had been knocked from his lungs.

His hands slowly came up to protect his face, but it was too late. Brutus ran up on Acid and as he loomed over him, he lifted his foot and stomped on Acid's face like he was a roach.

One of Acid's teeth flew across the mat and his lip split

open and began to bleed. Acid rolled over, grunting in pain. His hands went to the mat, like he was about to push himself up. But his arms shook with weakness.

Brutus lunged and dropped an elbow on the back of Acid's neck with the weight of his entire body.

The cheers cut off mid roar—silenced horror filled the arena.

Acid went limp. Blood continued to pour from his broken nose and split lips.

His breathing sounded like a rattlesnake in his chest.

I knew that sound . . .

No, God no . . .

Chapter 42

The waiting room at the hospital was melancholy. Acid had been rushed to emergency surgery and there had been no news yet from the doctor.

Brothers of the Tarnished Angels Motorcycle Club had congregated to keep vigil. Savage had left me with Willa and Duke while he spoke to Colt and Zip.

Most of the Old Ladies had stayed home—it was the middle of the night—and they had children.

I could feel eyes on me, silently asking questions people knew I had answers to.

"I need to walk," Willa murmured.

"I'll go with you," Duke said.

She shook her head. "Evie? You want to walk with me?"

"Yes," I said, desperate to escape the cloying guilt.

The two of us wandered down the hallway, away from the waiting room.

"Cafeteria?" I asked.

"I'm not really hungry, but yeah, that works."

We went to the elevator and waited for it. We didn't

speak again until we got to the cafeteria. We took a seat at one of the tables, facing each other.

It was like neither of us knew what to say to one another. I hadn't seen her since the club barbecue two days ago, when the brothers had learned about my past. Did the Old Ladies know about it too?

Willa shattered the silence when she spoke. "Duke told me Savage used to fight in an illegal ring but that he quit."

"Yes," I concurred.

"Just tell me, Evie. I feel like I know pieces of the story, but I don't have the full picture. And it's driving me crazy."

"Did Duke tell you anything . . . anything about me?"

She paused and then she nodded. "Yes. He told me."

"How much?" I asked.

She bit her lip and met my gaze. "That you grew up in a cult. That you were married to a bad man, and that you . . . *handled* it. And then you came to Waco and met Savage."

Before I could reply, she reached across the table and grabbed my hand. "I only know because you're Savage's Old Lady. The other Old Ladies . . . they only know about the cult. And that you came here to start over after your husband died. They don't know details. But Colt had to tell them some of it, because if there's trouble . . ."

"I see," I murmured. I looked at the table.

"I'll never mention it again, Evie. I just want you to know that I'm happy you're with Savage and I'm so glad you're safe. You and the babies."

"Thank you, Willa." I squeezed her hand. "You don't—you're not completely horrified by what I've done?"

"My husband is a biker. My best friend is too. Do you think life is black and white? I don't. Not even a little bit."

I paused for a moment and then I told her the truth about how I met Savage and why Acid was in the ring tonight instead of him.

Why Acid was in emergency surgery.

"I'm scared for Savage," I said softly. "He lied to Colt. He lied to the club. I hope—they're not going to kick him out, are they?"

"I don't know, Evie. I really don't. That's part of club business that I'm not privy to."

Willa squirmed in her chair and pressed a hand to her lower back.

"You okay?" I asked.

Nodding, she grimaced in pain and closed her eyes.

"Willa," I asked calmly. "Are you having contractions?"

"Yeah." She sighed and opened her eyes. "Since this morning, actually. They're picking up steam. They've been getting stronger this last hour."

"Let's get back upstairs and get you checked in," I said. I remained calm even though I was secretly panicking.

"This is the worst possible time for this," she muttered as she riffled through her purse for her phone. "I need to call Waverly and Sailor."

"They don't know you're at the hospital?"

"They do. They're on their way back from the lake house." She rubbed her third eye. "They went with Dylan—Waverly's boyfriend—and some friends. They should be here in a few hours."

We returned to the waiting room. Savage's eyes found mine.

"Duke," Willa called to her husband. "I need to be admitted."

"Are you okay?" Duke asked, rising from his chair and coming to her.

"Fine," she said. "But I'm definitely going into labor, like right now."

Duke's eyes widened and the anxiety set in. He gathered his wife and ushered her toward the nurse's station.

I took the seat next to Savage and he laced his fingers through mine. "Any word on Acid?"

Savage shook his head.

"Is Colt really mad?"

"Putting it mildly," he said. "Gotta have Church to discuss what's going to be done. That won't happen until after Acid . . . What did you guys talk about?"

"Stuff," I said evasively. I rested my head on his shoulder and before I knew it, I was dozing off.

I only woke up because I heard Waverly and Sailor enter the waiting room. Dylan wasn't far behind them.

"Savage," Waverly said. "Where's Willa?"

I sat up and rubbed my eyes.

"She's in labor," Savage said.

"Why didn't you text me?" she demanded.

"Kind of a lot going on here, Little Punk," he said.

Her eyes softened.

"Any news about Acid?" Sailor asked. Her voice sounded thin and far away. Fear was etched across her face.

"Not yet."

"I need coffee," Dylan said.

"Me too," Waverly added. She grasped Sailor's elbow and steered her out of the waiting room.

"What was that about?" I asked Savage once they were gone. "Sailor, I mean. She seemed really upset about Acid. I didn't even think they knew each other."

Savage ran a thumb across his jaw. "Acid saved Sailor from a really bad situation. Sailor's been sort of in love with him ever since. Hero worship, you know?"

"I see."

"Can we go for a drive?" he asked. "I can't sit here."

"Sure," I said. "You good to drive?"

He nodded. "I'm jacked up on energy drinks."

Heartbeats & Highways

We didn't speak again until we were in the elevator.

"It's my fault," Savage said. "It's my fault he's in surgery."

"No." I shook my head emphatically. "It's not. He went behind your back to get into the ring. You didn't ask him to do this."

"He wouldn't have been there if I hadn't gotten involved in fighting in the first place."

"You want to play the blame game?" I swallowed, my throat tight. "It's *my* fault. He never would've volunteered if you hadn't met me."

He sighed. "I guess we both have a lot of misplaced guilt, huh?"

The guilt would be a million times worse if there was bad news. If Acid didn't recover.

The lobby of the hospital was empty and quiet, the only sound being Savage's heavy motorcycle boots across the pristine floor.

I didn't understand hospitals. Sterile yet frenetic energy, people dying in the same place other people were being born.

My hand went to my belly. I wasn't sure I wanted my babies to come into the world with all of that around them.

But there was plenty of time to talk about it with Savage.

Everything was a mess. Just when I thought we were able to move forward, something dragged us down into the muck.

We walked side by side in the dark parking lot, heading toward the car.

"I think I lied about not being hungry," I said. "But cafeteria food sounds horrible."

"Yeah. Let's get you something to eat. Something good."

"I want a strawberry milkshake."

He hit the clicker, and my car beeped and the lights flashed. "I hope Prez calls soon with news. The waiting is fucking killing me."

I kept walking toward the passenger side, but Savage fell behind me. I turned to look at him. He was reaching into his cut pocket for his phone.

A dark blur moved through the night; I let out a scream.

Savage's head whipped up, but he wasn't fast enough.

The bat crashed against his skull. Savage hit the ground, his body thunking against the pavement. He was still.

Fear caked my tongue as I recognized the man who loomed over him.

I turned and ran, scrambling for the handle of the passenger door as footsteps dashed behind me. Just as I managed to get the door open, he was on me, pressing his large muscular body against mine, effectively slamming the door shut and pinning me against it.

Trapped. Like an animal.

He grabbed my shoulder, turned me to face him and then smiled; a slow, sinister grin revealing the demon within.

"Hello, Evie."

Chapter 43

Sweat dripped down my temples.

My eyes flipped open, and I met the view of an unfamiliar ceiling with a spiderweb of cracks. Daylight poured through the window.

I made a move to sit up—only to find that I was strapped down to a table. My wrists were bound by my sides and my legs were splayed open with my ankles cinched.

Panic bubbled in my throat. A terrified scream wanted to emerge, but I shoved it down. Screaming wouldn't help . . . but it might alert my captors that I was awake.

Savage . . .

Oh God . . .

A bat to the head. His still body. Is he alive?

Tears threatened to spill down my cheeks, but somehow I held them in. I couldn't lose it now.

Morning sickness came with a vengeance. I turned my head and retched, shaking and quivering until not even bile came up.

I looked at my surroundings. I was in a house I didn't

recognize, but I assumed I was back on The Farm. The heat blasting my skin emanated from a wood stove chimney.

Someone had undressed me and put me in a white muslin gown. My body had been naked.

Unprotected.

The Grand Patriarch's second-in-command had stuck a needle in my neck. After that, everything went dark for hours, and I had no recollection of anything.

I tugged my wrists, but the braces had no give.

Shuffling footsteps in the hallway alerted me moments before the door opened, revealing a balding man in a white doctor's coat. He stepped inside the room and closed the door.

He looked at the floor and the mess I'd made.

Without a word, he went over to the window. He fought with the sticky sill but managed to get the window open. A waft of fresh air blew through the room, relieving the heat from the wood stove chimney and the acrid stench of my sick.

Drugs sloshed around in my veins; my sluggish mind slow to form thoughts.

He walked to the door and opened it, murmuring something I couldn't hear to the person on the other side. When the conversation ended, he opened the door wider, stepped out into the hallway, and wheeled in a sonogram machine.

Swallowing, I kept my mouth clamped shut, refusing to ask questions, refusing to give one word to this stranger I didn't know.

"I assume you know where you are?" he asked. His voice was nasally, like he had habitual allergies.

"The Farm," I replied slowly.

He inclined his head. "I'm Dr. Winchester."

"How nice for you."

His brown eyes narrowed. "I've already drawn your blood and had it sent off to the lab." His gaze dropped to my stomach. "I will be giving you a transvaginal ultrasound to determine how far along you are in your pregnancy."

"*Don't touch me,*" I snapped, anger whooshing through me, obliterating my fear.

He gave me a patronizing smile. "I don't think you have much choice in the matter." Dr. Winchester placed his hand on my belly, letting his palm rest there for a moment before he inched the muslin dress up my legs, baring me to him.

I turned my head away and closed my eyes.

"Yes," he purred. "It's much better when you cooperate."

There was no electricity in the house, but The Farm had several generators and one of the machines hummed in the background.

I heard him prepare the ultrasound and then wash his hands using the washing basin and pitcher. The dichotomy was almost laughable. A modern medical machine juxtaposed against historic, handmade furniture in a room where a woman was being held prisoner by a cult.

Dr. Winchester sat down on the wheeled stool and rolled his way to the edge of the exam bed. He took the probe, and I felt it at my entrance.

He slid the wand inside me and a few moments later I heard a *whoosh*, followed by an echo sound.

"Well, isn't that good news," Dr. Winchester said. "The Grand Patriarch will be very happy."

I opened my eyes and looked at the ceiling, praying the invasion of my body would be over quickly.

He spent a few moments moving the wand, no doubt gathering more information about me and my babies.

After he removed the probe, he lowered my dress.

There was a knock on the door.

"Come in," Dr. Winchester called.

The door opened and the Grand Patriarch entered the room.

My father-in-law.

My husband had been the spitting image of him. Tall, muscular. My father-in-law's hair was all gray now, and his face was lined with grief. Yet he was still a formidable adversary.

And he'd put the idea into my husband's head to kill me. A true master of puppets. His followers were his marionettes.

The Grand Patriarch carried a tray with a plate of food as well as a glass of water and a straw. He set it down on the dresser next to the wash basin.

"Good news," Dr. Winchester said. "She's having twins."

"Twins," the Grand Patriarch murmured. "How far along is she?"

"Middle of her first trimester I'd say," Dr. Winchester said. "I'm concerned about her stature."

"Go on."

"She's petite, and I'm worried she won't be able to carry the twins to their full term."

The Grand Patriarch looked at me and smiled. "Then we must do everything in our power to ensure she births two healthy babies. After all, they are the future of the Seed Reapers."

His eyes focused on me, but he addressed the doctor. "Leave us."

The doctor didn't even bother looking at me, instead

doing as the Grand Patriarch commanded without hesitation. The door closed with finality, and I wanted to shrink inside myself.

The Grand Patriarch said nothing, but his gaze dropped to my stomach. He walked toward me and placed his hands on the gentle swell of my lower belly.

His eyes gleamed with fanatic zeal.

"You are the bearer," he whispered. "You carry my son's legacy inside you. You are fruitful. Yes, you will carry *many* legacies."

Many . . .

Terror bathed my spine and my fingers went cold.

"You must eat." He lifted his hands from me and went to the tray of food. "I will feed you. And we will talk."

My throat was parched.

"What did you drug me with?" I rasped.

The Grand Patriarch frowned at the tray of food before looking at me. "A mild sedative. Dr. Winchester assured me it won't harm the baby—*babies*."

"How did you know I was pregnant?"

He lifted the tray and walked over to the stool with wheels. He sat down and rolled toward the side of the exam table. He pressed a button, and the table lifted me so that I was now propped up.

"We didn't," he crooned. "Not until we got you here and saw that you are showing."

He stuck the straw into the glass and before I could reply, he shoved the straw into my mouth. I gulped greedily.

When I'd downed half of it, I released the straw, and he set the glass aside.

"How did you find me?"

He paused for a moment before replying. "We caught your face on camera at the bus station. It wasn't hard to figure out you bought a ticket to Waco." He smiled but it wasn't at all pleasant. "Calvin has always been like a dog with a bone. I knew once I put him on your scent it was over, and if he kept asking around, he'd find you eventually. He finally picked up your trail, and here you are." His gaze slid over me. "You cut your hair."

"It's *my* hair."

"No . . . your hair—like your womb—belongs to the Seed Reapers."

He sliced a piece of sausage and held it out to me. If I wanted the food, I'd have to lift my head and lean toward it. He'd make me meet him halfway. He'd prove his power over me every chance he got.

I didn't want to give in, but I wasn't eating for me. I was eating for the babies.

So, I leaned forward and opened my mouth.

"Where is my son?" he asked. His blue eyes shone with determination.

Would he withhold food from me if I refused to tell him?

No. He wanted me alive. He wanted the babies alive.

They're his own flesh and blood . . .

"That night you came over for dinner and I went to bed early . . . I heard you tell Randall to kill me so he could take a new wife. A *fruitful* wife."

"I make no apologies for doing what's necessary for the good of the Seed Reapers." He clenched his jaw. "And yet his seed finally took root, didn't it? Did your body finally succumb to his power, or was it the sacrifice your parents made?"

The words he spouted were scripture to him.

He was certifiable.

"Sacrifice." I snorted. "*You* convinced them to take their own lives. Next time you want to have a private conversation, make sure there's no one lurking around the corner."

He looked like he was pondering my words and then he touched my stomach again. "Their sacrifice was not in vain. Their blood was spilled, but life now grows within you."

The sausage I'd eaten threatened to come up my throat.

"You know what's supposed to happen now, don't you?" he asked, his brow furrowing in thought. "The heir of the Seed Reapers has died. I know you killed him, or else he'd be here with me now. There is no other explanation. Tradition dictates that the wife of the deceased heir be burned alive on a pyre so that she may accompany him to the afterlife where she can serve him for all eternity. Purity . . . sacrifice by fire. However, you are carrying his heirs—*my* heirs."

My expression flattened. "You're going to burn us—*the babies*—"

He scratched his jaw. "No. Purity by fire would be such a waste. You have finally proven your worth, and you have something within you that's far more valuable to me than your death ever could be . . ."

His smile was cold and clinical, and it caused fear to battle its way up my throat and nearly strangle me.

"You will deliver these babies. And when you are healed and recovered, I will take you as my wife and I will put several more babies inside you. You will continue my family succession and ensure that it is our flesh and blood that rules the Seed Reapers for generations. *That* will be the price for your redemption."

"But you already have a wife," I choked out.

"A wife who can no longer bear children due to the trauma of birthing our son. A wife who believes in duty above all else. A wife who understands her place . . . a wife who will understand when the time is right that making the ultimate sacrifice will be her greatest achievement."

She doesn't know . . .

"You'll murder your own wife just to take another? You're insane," I blurted out. "I'll never agree to this."

He placed his hand on my belly and began to rub circles across my flesh. Tender, gentle circles.

"My incubator, what makes you think I'm giving you a choice?"

Chapter 44

After the Grand Patriarch's terrifying announcement about the fate of my life, he'd calmly set the tray of food aside and left.

His second-in-command—the big man who'd kidnapped me from the parking lot—entered the room. Calvin held up leather and iron shackles attached to chains. He undid the brown strap around one ankle and even though I tried to kick his face, all he did was laugh and catch my small foot in his hand before shackling me. He made short work of the other one.

There were no shackles for my wrists, not that they were needed. I wasn't going anywhere with iron around my ankles.

I nearly collapsed to the floor when I got off the exam table. Calvin caught me and all but dragged me to another room. A room with a cot, a single window, a wood stove chimney, and two old-fashioned chamber pots and a wash basin with some toiletries.

"I'm pregnant," I pointed out. "I need a bathroom and—"

"Take it up with the Grand Patriarch," he quipped.

I snarled at him and ripped my arm from his grasp.

"I like it when women fight," he taunted. "So much more rewarding when they finally break. And you *will* break."

He stared at me for a moment after making that declaration and then he left, locking the door behind him.

I sat down on the cot and gripped the edges of the mattress, wondering how I was going to get out of this mess.

I had no light in the room except for what came through the window. I attempted to lift my legs, but they were heavy because of the chains, so I had to use my arms to raise them. One after the other, I got them onto the bed. I even managed to elevate an ankle to my thigh so I could examine the iron shackles.

If I could find something long and thin, there was a chance I'd be able to pick the locks and free myself.

And then what?

I shut that line of thought down. I didn't need to think that far in advance. The first order of business was finding something to help me remove the shackles.

The room was bare, devoid of anything useful.

I wondered if the Grand Patriarch was going to keep me locked in this room for the entirety of my pregnancy.

Swallowing, I shoved that thought away, too. I'd managed to escape once.

I'd have to do it again.

I *would* do it again.

My legs were heavy as I set them on the floor. My steps were slow, but I combed every inch of the room. I ran my hand along the windowsill, hoping for a loose nail that I could pry up. But there was nothing.

I got down on all fours and peered underneath the cot.

I moved the chamber pots out of the way and grazed my hand along the wooden floorboards that were in desperate need of a refinish.

My palm caught on something.

A raised nail that was sticking slightly out of a plank.

I immediately attempted to grab it and yank it from the floor, but I didn't have enough strength.

Dejected, I pulled my hand back and sat on the floor.

If only I had something to leverage against it . . .

My eyes dropped to the iron chains between my legs.

Was it possible?

I heard the tromp of footsteps on the stairs and hastily scrambled up. I was standing by the time the door opened.

The Grand Matriarch held a tray in her hands, and she paused when she saw me. Her salt and pepper hair was pulled up into a tight bun. Her gaze dipped down my body, resting on the slight swell of my stomach.

"You need to eat," she said in way of greeting. "For the babies."

"For the babies," I said snidely.

"If it were up to me, I'd let you starve," she said, her eyes glazed with pain. "You took my son from me. It seems only fitting that I take your children from you."

Any sympathy I had for the Grand Matriarch withered inside me and died in that moment.

"Do you know what your husband and son were planning?" I didn't give her a chance to reply. "They were plotting to kill me because I wasn't pregnant—"

"*Lies*," she spat. "You never loved my son. You weren't a good wife to him, no matter how much I tried teaching you. But that's what happens when my husband decided to let outsiders join us. If you'd been born here, you would've known your duty from birth. You always had too much . . . spirit."

"And your goal is to beat the spirit out of us, isn't it?" I demanded. "Your son tried that . . . several times."

She slapped me across the face. The sound of her palm hitting my skin echoed in the room. "Clearly he didn't try hard enough. You never should've left us. The world isn't safe for a Reaper."

I laughed through my watering eyes and stinging cheek. "And you think it's safe here? Have you spoken to your husband? Do you know what he plans to do with you?" When she didn't reply, I stated, "Your husband plans on taking *me* as his new wife. You know what that means for you, don't you?"

"I have been the wife of the Grand Patriarch for thirty years," she sneered. "He protects me, he cares for me, I gave him a son. A son *you* took from me!"

"I feel sad for you. Sad that you can't see what's right in front of you."

I turned away from her to stare out the window.

"Don't expect your savage biker to come rescue you. If by some miracle he isn't dead already, he won't come for you. You're not worth the trouble."

She strode from the room and slammed the door shut behind her.

The light was dying. It would be dark soon.

~

After I ate my meal, which was bland yet filling, I curled up onto the bed and waited for night to fall. Though it was dark, there was enough light from the moon shining through the window that I could see inside the room.

At some point, someone returned to fetch the empty tray. I heard the snick of the lock and waited for the footsteps to retreat.

When I was sure no one was loitering outside my door, I got up. I grimaced when the sound of chains hit the wooden floor. I expected to hear footsteps coming to investigate, but it was quiet. I lowered myself to my hands and knees and used the chain between my legs to catch the nail sticking out of the wooden plank. I leveraged the chain and attempted to pry the nail loose. I lost my hold on it and the chain clunked against the floor. My frustration grew with every setback, and I thought about moving the cot to make access to the nail easier, but if someone came to check on me, I wouldn't be able to get the cot back into place quickly enough.

I worked tirelessly even as my fingers went numb, but eventually the nail wiggled far enough out of the wood that I could remove it.

A cry of triumph nearly escaped my lips, but by some miracle, I managed to keep it in. I began to try and pick the lock on my shackles with the nail.

My mind finally slowed down enough to think about Savage. The Grand Matriarch knew what Calvin had done to him and she'd taunted me with it.

Fear spiraled through my stomach.

She didn't know Savage like I knew him.

Even injured, Savage would be relentless. But what if there were no miracles? What if Savage was dead?

That line of thought brought tears to my eyes, but I hastily brushed them away. I couldn't lose my focus. I couldn't tumble into a fog of grief like I'd done after my parents' deaths. I needed to stay alert, determined.

I'd get to safety and then I could fall apart. But not before then.

I worked through the night, my mind turning sluggish as the hours went by. After a while, I wasn't even paying attention to what I was doing, but then I heard a click.

Holding my breath, I pulled at the shackle on my ankle, and it came apart.

It had taken me hours to pick the lock. I didn't have time to pick the other. Dawn's early light painted the sky purple.

Knowing the Grand Patriarch, he'd send someone to check on me before full daylight. I hastily clamped the shackle back around my ankle, but this time it would remain unlocked. I lifted the fitted sheet off the mattress and shoved the nail into the corner of the bed stuffing before securing the sheet over it to conceal it again.

The nausea started and I was retching into one of the chamber pots as a key slid into the lock.

I didn't even bother to look when the door opened.

"You're sick," the Grand Patriarch commented as he came across the threshold.

"It's called morning sickness." I sat up awkwardly and wiped my mouth.

"Glorious," he murmured. "Did you sleep well?"

"Hard to sleep in a prison."

His expression flattened. "I'd hoped a night back with your family would change your attitude."

"You're not my family. None of you are my family."

"We *are* your family," he countered. "When your parents joined the Seed Reapers, we became your family. You married my son. We are bonded. Forever."

"Family loves and cares for each other. You want me to produce offspring. I'm just a broodmare to you."

His gaze narrowed. "And you think those heathens are your family?"

"Yes," I said automatically. "They're my family."

"And where are they? Have they come for you?" His grin was smug. "You're with us now, where you belong. You have nothing to do but rest. Rest and grow ripe."

His eyes slid to my belly. He stepped forward and reached a hand out to touch me.

I batted him away.

He clenched his hands into fists and rage swept across his face.

"Just like your son," I murmured. "You hate being denied."

My words landed. He opened his hand and slapped me hard across the cheek. The pain was instantaneous and my eyes watered.

"You get to choose how you want me to treat you, Evie. You can either cooperate and bite your tongue, or I can make things *very* unpleasant for you."

I pointed to the shackles around my ankles. "More unpleasant than this?"

"If you think this is unpleasant, you're in for a rude awakening."

I began to laugh which only made him angrier. "You're so deluded."

My laughter turned maniacal. He'd already told me my fate—a fate worse than death.

My brain was on the fritz.

"The chamber pot," he stated.

"What about it?"

"I need to see it."

"What? Why? You just saw me throw up in it."

"Not that one. The *other* one," he insisted. "I need to know if you're getting enough fluid."

The Grand Patriarch didn't wait for my reply. He crouched down and reached for the chamber pot that was underneath the cot.

He looked into it and shook his head. "You need more liquids."

"Tell that to your wife. She's in charge of feeding me, isn't she?"

He clenched his jaw. "Breakfast will be up shortly. You will eat every bite."

The Grand Patriarch marched toward the door and when his hand was on the knob, I spoke.

"You told me they weren't my family."

He froze but didn't turn around to look at me.

"You said they wouldn't come for me. I don't believe that, and neither do you." I moved my legs, the chains clinking together, reminding us both of my position. "You better hope he's dead. Because if he's not, you're going to find out why he's named Savage."

I grinned when he slammed the door behind him.

Chapter 45

I napped in between meals. Staying up most of the night had left me exhausted and I knew I'd need to be well-rested so I could work on my shackles throughout the night.

I wasn't sure how I was going to be able to escape because even when I got my shackles off, the door was still locked. Depending on how much time I had before dawn, I might be able to pick that lock, too. But no doubt someone was guarding the house.

Thinking too far in advance caused anxiety to ricochet through my belly, so I forced myself to only think about the first step in front of me.

Despite what I'd told the Grand Patriarch, I was losing hope that Savage was alive.

I have to rescue myself. Rescue my babies.

I couldn't wait. I wouldn't stay here and let my due date draw closer. At some point, it would be too dangerous to try and flee. I'd be too big and there wouldn't be any chance of success.

And after the birth of the babies, he'd begin to use me . . .

The room was stifling. The heat from the wood stove chimney warmed my sick in the chamber pot and the scent of it permeated the air. The Grand Matriarch brought me meals, but she would not empty my refuse bins. Apparently *that* was beneath her.

Breathing through my mouth, I wondered if the window was sealed shut, or if I could open it.

I slogged my way over to the window, the iron chains clanking across the wooden floor. I unlatched the window, grasped the bottom of the frame and heaved. It shot up quickly, not having been stuck at all. Cold air immediately washed over my skin. I took a deep inhale and closed my eyes.

Clunk!

My eyes flipped open. The window had slid shut because the rope holding the cast-iron metal sash weight had snapped.

I picked up the weight that had fallen and held it in my hand. It was heavy and round, and about ten inches long . . . just the right size to be used like a club.

I put the sash back into the window channel and hid the broken rope beneath the mattress. I didn't want to keep it near me in case someone unexpectedly decided to search the room.

After dinner, I washed my face and brushed my teeth. I retrieved the sash from the window and climbed into bed. My fingers closed around it. I tried to stay awake, but when the room went dark, my eyes closed, and I fell asleep.

Hands clamped around my neck and my eyes flipped open.

Moonlight bathed the Grand Matriarch's rage-infested face as she attempted to strangle the life out of me.

"You think I'll let my husband set me aside for a slut like you?" Her fingers pressed deeper into the sides of my throat as she squeezed with all her might. "You took my son from me! I won't let you take my husband!"

Black spots twinkled in front of my eyes.

I tried to fight—I tried to move my legs—but the iron shackles prevented me from kicking.

My hands went to her wrists, but she was bigger than me and she had anger and adrenaline on her side.

Something hard poked me in the back as I struggled to fling her off.

My hands fell from her wrists and felt for the sash weight from the window that I had dropped sometime when I'd been asleep. My fingers clamped around it.

My vision was nearly black, and my energy continued to drain, but I could still see the faint outline of her face and murder was in her eyes. I lifted my hand, and with all the force I had left inside of me, smashed the cast-iron weight against the side of her head.

Her cry of pain met my ears, and her hands loosened from around my neck.

Sweet air fueled my strength.

I hit her again and again until she fell over next to me on the bed. And then I pummeled her skull until the sheets were stained with brain and blood.

My hands shook with adrenaline. I dropped the sash weight and quickly scrambled to the side of the bed, lifted the sheet, and pulled out the hidden nail.

The nail kept slipping between my bloody fingers, so I wiped them on a clean part of the bed sheet.

I worked at a fervent pace, but with only the light from the window, my vision was compromised.

I heard the rush of heavy footsteps trekking up the stairs and it renewed my efforts. I was rewarded with the final ankle shackle falling off, but it was too late—someone was coming, and they were almost to the room.

The glow of an oil lamp appeared in the open doorway, painting the face of the Grand Patriarch in a demonic blaze.

His eyes burned with intensity as he surveyed the room. His gaze strayed to the bed. He lifted the oil lamp higher to get a better view.

"What have you done?" he murmured.

I searched for the sash weight, preparing to fight again.

"You killed her." His attention sought mine and a wicked smile spread across his face. "You saved me the trouble. Now I am free to take you as my wife. In all ways . . ."

He rushed toward me.

My hand found the sash weight and wrapped around it. I chucked it at his head. Unfortunately, he darted out of the way and the weight hit the glass chimney of the brass oil lamp, causing it to shatter. Broken glass littered the floor.

While the Grand Patriarch was tending to the unprotected flame, I hoisted myself off the bed and gripped the iron chain and shackle.

I moved toward the door and stepped on a shard of broken glass. A cry of pain escaped my mouth.

The Grand Patriarch blew out the flame and tossed the oil lamp aside, the brass base clunking against the wooden floor.

He reached out and grabbed my wrist to stop me from using the iron chain against him. He squeezed until I was forced to let go. My makeshift weapon fell to the floor, useless.

"There's no escaping me," he growled as he pulled me to him.

He smelled like sweat and raw onions.

My body recoiled and my stomach gurgled in protest.

He wrapped his arms around me to cage me in.

The scent of him was too much for my pregnancy nose.

I opened my mouth and spewed up my dinner.

He howled and released me, shoving me away from him as I continued to vomit.

Through the sounds of my own retching, I heard the clomp of heavy boots on the stairs.

A silhouette appeared in the doorway.

The Grand Patriarch stripped off his shirt and began using it as a cloth to wipe the vomit off him. He was consumed with rage and wasn't paying attention to the shadow that had entered the room.

Moonlight shone through the window. The shadow raised a hand.

A pistol...

As the crack of gunfire went off, the room suddenly lit up in a flash of light and the Grand Patriarch clutched his chest.

A startled gasp escaped his lips, and he stumbled backward before falling to his knees.

Savage stalked into the room; each step like a predator within sight of his prey.

A carrier of death and judgment.

He's alive.

The Grand Patriarch attempted to speak, but blood

bubbled from his mouth and began to run down his chin and onto his bare chest.

Savage walked right up to the Grand Patriarch, raised his pistol and said, "*Burn in hell, motherfucker.*"

And then Savage put a bullet in the Grand Patriarch's head. This time the back of his skull exploded, and his brains and blood splattered the bed.

His end came at Savage's hands. Just like his wife's came at the end of mine. Both their insides on the outside.

"Evie?" Savage's voice was raspy in the night. He stepped closer. "Babe. It's me, Savage."

My mind took a moment to process that I was safe. "*Savage?*"

He rushed toward me, glass crunching beneath his boots. He tucked his pistol into his jeans. "God, you're covered in blood! Are you hurt?"

He ran his hands up and down my arms, checking for wounds.

"Not mine," I stuttered out. I gestured with my chin to the body lying prostrate across the cot.

With a low curse, he grabbed the edge of the sheet and managed to fling it across the corpse on the bed.

"We need to get out of here," he said. He took out his pistol again and then reached for my hand. "Stay behind me."

Savage led the way, and I shadowed him as we went into the dark hallway.

"Hold onto the railing. I don't want you to fall."

He took the stairs slowly, but when we were only a few steps from the bottom, the front door opened.

Savage raised his pistol.

"It's me," Duke said. "We're all set."

Savage stuck his pistol into his waistband and then grabbed my hand again. We followed Duke outside.

Crow and a man I didn't know appeared from the darkness like smoke in the night; they both held plastic gas cans.

"It's done," the stranger said.

"You want the honors?" Duke asked Savage.

"No." He looked at me. "This is for you, Evie. If you want to."

Savage reached into his inner vest pocket and pulled out a long barbecue lighter and held it out to me.

"If you can't do it, I will," he said so quietly I knew the others couldn't hear.

"No." I swallowed. "I can do it."

I took the lighter from him and marched toward the house. I angled the lighter to the base and watched as fire licked the rotting wooden boards of the farmhouse.

Savage pulled me back and filched the lighter from me. It took a few moments, but then with a *whoosh* the flames drew sustenance and fury from peeling paint and wood.

The five of us stood and watched as the roof finally caught fire, and then I turned from the sight. I started walking away, walking nowhere, but I didn't look behind me. Not even when I heard the glass of the windows shatter and smelled the smoke that filled the air.

I felt Savage's hand slide into mine and squeeze my fingers. I squeezed back and left my past behind me forever.

Chapter 46

After we walked away from the burning house, we drove to the hospital. The nurse looked ready to call security; a barefoot woman covered in blood showing up with bikers inspired a lot of questions. Savage pulled her aside and said something intense, because she immediately backed off and showed us to a room.

The nurse gave me a pair of clean scrubs and removed the shards of glass from my foot. They hooked me up to a fetal monitor and Savage cleaned the blood from my face while she took my blood pressure. The last measure had been a sonogram.

Everything had looked good; the babies were safe, and their heart rates were normal. The doctor told me to see my OBGYN just to ensure there were no potential issues.

"The ER's been quiet tonight," the doctor said. "No one saw you come in, but you guys need to leave. I'll get a nurse to take you out the back."

"Thanks, Doc." Savage shook his hand.

Crow knocked on the door of the hospital room and came in to give me a pair of flip-flops.

Heartbeats & Highways

We left the hospital. The scent of disinfectant lingered in my nose and my throat was sore from the Grand Matriarch's fingers. Duke pulled the car into a parking lot of a highway motel on the other side of town.

"I'll check us in and get the keys," Duke said, cutting the engine.

"Thanks, brother," Savage murmured.

"Sure thing." Duke looked at me over his shoulder. "You hungry? Thirsty?"

I didn't reply.

Duke looked to Savage for direction.

"Don't worry about it. I'll take care of her later."

Duke nodded and then climbed out of the car. He shut the driver's side door and then I watched him walk with Crow to the check-in building.

"Babe?" Savage reached into my lap and took my hand. "Jesus. You're freezing. Why didn't you say anything?"

I hadn't spoken since we'd left the hospital.

Savage took both my hands in his and rubbed them between his own, not caring that mine were stained with blood.

"We'll get you into a room, have a nice hot shower. I'll wash your hair." He stared at my fingers. "And your fingernails."

When I still said nothing, he droned on. "You're in shock. So I'm just gonna keep talking until you come back to me. But you take your time. And when you're ready, you'll tell me everything. Okay?"

I stared at him, wanting the words to come out of my mouth, but they remained steadfastly trapped.

"I woke up about thirty minutes after you were—you were taken. Hell of a headache, blurry vision. Thank Christ I was in a hospital parking lot, yeah?" He shook his head. "Doctors told me I needed a CAT scan while Prez and the others formulated a plan. We knew it was your . . . family that took you."

He kept talking, but his words had no meaning. I was trapped in my body, in the horror of what I'd done.

"Willa had a healthy baby girl. And she told Duke to go with me."

That seemed to shake me out of my stupor.

"Why?" I croaked. "Why did she let him go when she just had a baby?"

"I took a bullet for Duke once," was all he said in explanation. "I'm not cleared to drive for a few days. He offered."

"Acid?"

"Out of surgery. But his brain is badly swollen. So, we don't know if . . ."

I looked at my hands that were held between his palms and tugged them free. I glanced at my fingertips. My nails were stained with blood. I curled my hands into fists, so I didn't have to see them.

Duke and Crow exited the check-in building and trekked back to the car. Savage climbed out and closed the door. He and Duke had a conversation and then Duke nodded before handing over a keycard to Savage.

Savage went around to the back of the car and pressed a button. The hatch released like a spaceship. "I had Crow buy you some clothes while you were in the hospital."

He closed the hatch and then came around to my side of the car with the bag of clothes in hand. He opened the door. When I made no move to get out, he unbuckled the seat belt and then gently took my hand and helped me down.

I shivered in the cold night. The scrubs I'd gotten at

the hospital were warmer than the muslin dress, but not by much.

"We're this way," he said, taking my hand again and leading me to a room. He slid the keycard into the slot. It clicked and then he pushed the door open.

It reminded me of the highway motel I'd stayed in when I first got to Waco.

The room was old and a little run down, but it was clean.

A sob escaped my throat.

Savage dropped the bag on the floor, closed the door, and immediately took me into his arms.

"Cry it out," he urged.

I did just that. I sobbed, feeling the emotion come from the base of my spine. It spilled out of my eyes. I clung to him like a child needing protection.

"You didn't doubt that I'd come for you, did you?" He stroked my back.

"I didn't doubt that you would, but I—I thought you were dead!"

He hugged me even tighter. "I'm so sorry, babe. I'm so sorry you were taken. I'm so fucking sorry you ever doubted."

"You came for me." My throat was tight, strained with emotion.

"I always will." He led me to the small bathroom. I stood by while he adjusted the temperature. "Tell me if it's too hot."

I stuck my hand under the water. "It's fine."

"It's not hot enough, is it?"

"Is it going to be too hot for you?"

He looked at me. "You want me in the shower with you?"

I nodded.

"It'll be fine." He gently caressed my chin. "You get in first. I'll get you some clean clothes."

"Thank you," I whispered.

His hand dropped from my face, and he left the room, closing the door behind him. I looked at my stained hands; the sight of them would be forever imprinted on my memory.

I glanced at my appearance in the mirror and noticed the redness on my neck and the deep blue underneath my skin as bruises were beginning to form.

Savage knocked on the door before coming in. "Evie?"

"I look like a heathen," I remarked, turning my head to the side, as if I didn't believe my own reflection. Even though Savage had cleaned my face, my hair was matted. "A savage and a heathen. We're a perfect match." I swallowed. "Who was he? The one who came with you? I don't know him."

"That's Ghost," he explained. "A friend of Slash's. He has certain . . . clean up skills."

"Oh." I nibbled my lip. "Is he good at finding people?"

"What do you mean?"

"There was another person who . . ."

Savage waited for me to finish.

"Examined me—"

"*Name*," he gritted out.

"Dr. Winchester. I don't know his first name."

"I'll take care of it."

"And what about Calvin, the Grand Patriarch's second-in-command? He's the one who kidnapped me."

He clenched his jaw. "I'll find him, too."

"Savage? I'm worried. You took me to a hospital. What if—what if they report what happened to the police? There will be an investigation, and they'll find out what I—"

"Hey. Stop. There won't be an investigation. Prez has already spoken to the police chief in town. We dealt with it, and you don't have to worry about that place ever again. Okay?"

"Okay," I whispered.

"Shower," he said gently.

Nodding, I turned away from him.

He left me alone again. I stripped out of my clothes and stepped into the steam. It wasn't hot enough, so I cranked the heat.

I watched the water turn pink as the stain on my fingers dissipated and swirled down the drain. I looked at my belly. "Babies," I whispered, my hand covering my stomach.

I was suddenly lightheaded, and I pressed my palm to the wall to steady myself, but my vision winked in and out. I slid down into the tub, curled my legs up, and rested my head on my knees.

The bathroom door opened, and Savage called out, "Evie? Are you doing okay?"

"I'm fine," I lied. I didn't even attempt to stand.

His heavy leather boots hit the floor and then I heard the jangle of his belt buckle. Savage pulled back the shower curtain. "Fuck, Evie. What happened?"

He climbed into the tub, closed the shower curtain, and then sat down behind me. He folded his body around mine.

"Nothing," I murmured. "I just kind of got lightheaded for a minute."

He held me, not saying anything, not expecting me to speak.

But as the water rained down on us, the words poured from my lips. I recounted everything—from the moment I was kidnapped in the parking lot to the horror of waking up on The Farm.

"He was going to turn me into his broodmare," I said softly. "I told his wife, and she tried to choke me to death. She thought she could keep her place by killing me. Killing my babies. I beat her with the sash weight from the window."

I trembled.

"Fucking psychos." His arms tightened around me. "They're dead; you never have to worry about them again."

"What happens now?"

"We're going to find Dr. Winchester and Calvin, and then we end them for hurting you."

His words were meager reassurance. Until they were found . . . they were out there still.

I brushed my wet hair away from my eyes.

"We're going to stand up and I'm going to wash your body. And then I'm gonna wrap you in a towel and dry you off. Then you're going to eat. Then I'm curling myself around you and we're going to sleep."

"What about all the other stuff?"

"What other stuff?"

"I *killed* her. I know it was self-defense, but God, it was so bloody and violent. I bashed in her skull. That image is branded in my mind, Savage. Every time I close my eyes, I'll see her like that and I'll never—"

"Hey, I know. I know exactly what you're going through."

He scooted away from me and hoisted himself up and then he reached down to help me rise. He gently turned me to him. His gaze searched my face and then dropped to my belly.

"The three of you are safe. Nothing else matters. Nothing."

I let Savage wash me—he seemed to need to touch me as much as I needed to be touched. He was gentle, and with each stroke of his hands against my skin, I came back into my body, little by little.

While I was dragging a comb through my wet hair, I heard a knock on the motel door.

"Probably Crow with your food." Savage went to investigate. I didn't shut the bathroom door all the way, so I heard a murmur of conversation but nothing definitive.

"Food's here!" Savage called out.

I set the comb down, tightened the towel around my body, and went into the bedroom. Savage was already pulling to-go containers out of the bags, but I went to get my change of clothes.

"Oh," I said with a soft smile, lifting a pair of fuzzy pajama bottoms.

"I told Crow to buy you something comfortable," he said.

I quickly pulled on my clothes, including a pair of socks, and then I took a seat on the bed. We ate in silence, but every now and again I'd catch Savage watching me.

"I'm okay," I said quietly. "You don't have to look at me like I'm going to fall apart."

"I cleaned the blood from your face. And you were sitting in the tub, letting the water beat down on you," he replied.

"I feel so . . . heavy," I said slowly. I closed the Styrofoam to-go container and placed it in the empty bag.

Savage cleared away the rest of the containers and I got up to brush my teeth. Then I slid beneath the covers of the full-sized bed and rolled onto my side. He hit the light and then crawled in behind me. He took me into his arms and rested his chin in the nook where my neck met my shoulder.

Savage pressed a kiss there as his hand went to my belly, resting protectively over it.

"I'm sorry, Evie."

"For what?"

"For killing him so quickly. I should've made him suffer. I should've tortured him for the things he's done to you."

What did it say about me that I wished he'd suffered more too?

I took a deep breath. "It's over now."

I fell asleep, cradled in the safety of Savage's embrace.

Chapter 47

A soft knock on the motel room door woke me, but I didn't move. Savage stirred and got out of bed. The front door opened, letting in a slash of early morning light.

"Gimme a sec," Savage whispered. "I'll be right out."

He shut the door.

I rolled over. "I'm awake."

"Oh." He went to grab his jeans which were resting on the chair in the corner. "That was Duke. Prez is at the diner and wants to talk. He has news."

"Colt is in town?" Sleep began to clear from my brain and I sat up.

"Yeah. Last night, I mentioned he talked to the police chief, remember?"

"Oh," I murmured. "Sorry. Last night is a blur."

His jaw clenched. "A few others came with us, too. They were handling the authorities while we handled the other shit."

"Do you think the news is about Dr. Winchester? Or about Calvin?"

"Not sure."

Savage came to the bed and knelt down beside it and wrapped his arms around my belly before placing his head against my chest. My hands sank into his hair.

"I didn't think about how this would affect you," I whispered. I bent over and kissed his head.

"You don't need to think about me." His words were muffled against my body. "This is all my fucking fault."

I grasped his hair and forced his head up, so he had to look at me. "No."

His eyes were pained. "Yes. I'm supposed to protect you."

My heart split in two. And tears gathered in my eyes. "You can't protect me from all the evils of the world."

"But that's my job."

I pressed my forehead to his. "I never thought I'd love someone so much that it hurts. I'm sorry, Savage. I'm so sorry you—"

"What do you have to be sorry for?"

"For bringing all this to you. You didn't sign up for any of this."

"Baby, I thought I had a life before you. I thought it had meaning. But this . . ." He gently palmed my belly. "The three of you are everything."

"Just . . . keep telling me that. I'll need to hear it a lot. Okay?"

"Okay." He reluctantly stood up. "We really do need to meet Prez."

"I'll be ready to go in five." I climbed out of bed. "Savage?"

"Yeah, babe."

I shot him a wobbly smile. "You've got the makings of a beard."

"I'll shave."

"Don't even think about it."

Duke met us by the car and drove us to the diner. Several motorcycles took up spaces in the parking lot.

"You said a *few* others came with Colt. It's more than a few," I remarked in surprise.

He cupped my cheek. "You're my Old Lady. And the club protects its own."

Colt and the others were already in the back seating area. It was deserted except for the tables that had been pushed together to accommodate the group of bikers.

They quieted when they saw me enter with Savage. I didn't know them well yet, but all of these men had come to my rescue.

Emotion choked me and I quickly battled it away, not wanting to break down in front of them. But all that went out the window when Colt rose from his chair, placed a hand on my shoulder and asked, "How are you doing, Evie?"

I burst into tears and turned to Savage for comfort. He quickly enveloped me within his arms. The big, silent biker —Torque—pulled out several napkins from the dispenser and offered them to Savage. Savage gave them to me, and I hastily wiped my eyes and blew my nose.

"I'm okay," I mumbled.

"Yeah, you look like it," Crow joked.

A startled laugh escaped my lips, and I gave him a watery smile. "I'm hungry."

"Then let's get you fed," Savage said.

There were three empty chairs near Colt, which Savage, Duke and I took. Colt waited to speak until after the waitress had taken our order. Finally, Colt looked at me when he said, "We caught the man—Calvin—who kidnapped you for the Grand Patriarch. He was headed out of town, but we got him."

"And the doctor?" Savage sneered.

"No leads yet," Colt said. He looked at me. "Don't worry, we'll find him."

"So, what happens now?" I inquired.

Colt's eyes met mine. "Now you go home with Savage, have your babies and live your life, and you never worry about those people ever again."

"They kidnapped me. That means I'll have to testify, doesn't it?" I asked, fear permeating my tongue. "The whole thing. The fire, the bodies—"

"No," Colt stated. "Listen to me. The Grand Patriarch and his wife are dead. The cult has no leader. Whatever they have going on with local law enforcement is too deep for us to get involved in, but it also means there won't be an investigation. So, as far as the world knows, a little old house on the outskirts of town burned down and that's that. No one is coming for you. After what we did, they wouldn't dare. You're free of that place, forever."

I frowned and looked at the table.

"Babe . . ." Savage said. "What is it?"

"Nothing."

"Not nothing," Savage insisted. "What is it?"

"What about Dr. Winchester? What's going to happen to him when you find him?"

Colt clenched his hand that rested on the table. "You're going to let us deal with it, and you're going to do us all a favor and forget he ever existed. You're never going to speak about him again, to anyone—*ever*. Do you understand?"

"Yes, but—"

Savage held my hand and looked me in the eyes and said, "It's over, babe. You've been through enough. You have to trust us, it's really over. You're safe."

The food came out and the bikers dug into their meals.

I pushed the potatoes around my plate, my appetite suddenly nonexistent.

I shoved back from the table. "I'm gonna step outside for a bit."

I didn't wait for anyone to respond, I just got up and left the diner. I was nervous about being alone, without the protective shadow of Savage, but the threat to my life was gone. It would take time to remember that, but hopefully, one day, I'd no longer feel like a trapped rodent, always waiting for someone to jump out and hurt me.

The front door to the diner opened and Savage stepped outside. It was cold and I hunched lower in the coat that Savage had brought for me. Savage didn't appear at all put out by the weather. He wore a flannel with a long-sleeved white undershirt, and his hand was warm when it engulfed mine.

"Talk to me," he said quietly.

"I feel too exposed out here to say what I really think."

He tugged me toward the car, hit the clicker and let me climb in first. Savage quickly followed me into the back seat.

"Okay, it's private now. What's going on?"

"I want them both dead," I seethed. "I *need* to know they're dead."

"What do you think we meant when we said you don't have to worry anymore?" Savage asked softly.

I looked at him. "Really?"

He inclined his head. "I can't tell you the details, but I promise you, I'm going to kill those motherfuckers myself."

I reached over and grasped his hand, squeezing it tightly. I laid my head against his shoulder. "I'm so tired, Savage."

"I know, baby."

"I just want to go home."

"Let's get inside, finish our breakfast, and get home."

I sighed. "Home. Yeah. I'm ready to go home."

◈

"Lay down," Savage said, patting his thigh. "You look like you can barely stay awake."

"I *am* tired," I admitted. I stretched out and placed my head on Savage's lap.

"I can turn off the radio," Duke said.

"It's fine," I said. "I don't mind."

I closed my eyes, and Savage began running his fingers through my hair. With each mile, I relaxed more and more. Savage had disappeared for a couple of hours before we left town and taken care of Calvin, and now I was determined to leave the past behind me. The Grand Patriarch couldn't hurt me anymore. The doctor couldn't hurt me anymore.

No one can hurt me anymore.

Sleep washed over me, and I fell into unconsciousness.

It wasn't until the car slowed to a stop that I came awake.

"When are you going to tell her?" Duke asked.

"Soon."

I yawned. "Tell me what?"

"That we're here," Savage announced.

I sat up and wiped my eyes. We were at the back of the bakery. It was past business hours and closed for the night.

We climbed out of the car.

"Thanks for everything, brother," Savage said.

"No thanks needed," Duke said. His eyes slid to mine. "Glad you're back with us, Evie."

I hugged Duke. "Congratulations. I never got to say—I don't even know her name."

"Christ, I don't know her name either," Savage echoed.

Duke placed a hand on Savage's shoulder and looked at the man he considered a brother. "We named her Cooper."

"Fuck, man," Savage rasped. "I'm honored."

The two of them had a moment and then Duke slapped Savage on the back.

"How are you getting home?" I asked.

"A prospect is coming to get me. See you guys soon, yeah?"

"Yeah," Savage murmured.

Duke walked through the alley toward the street.

I unlocked the bakery and disarmed the alarm. Savage set it again behind me as I trekked up the stairs. Despite the nap in the car, exhaustion weighed me down. I didn't know how much of it was pregnancy and how much of it had been what I'd just lived through.

The apartment looked the same, but I was seeing it through a new lens. It was my haven.

"Good to be home, isn't it?" Savage asked quietly from behind me.

"You read my mind."

He shut the door and locked it. "You hungry? I can whip us up some eggs, or something."

"You can whip up eggs?" I asked with a small smile.

"Eggs are easy, but I wouldn't mind being taught a few things by you."

"Yeah?" I smiled. "I could do that. You've taught me a few things already."

"Oh yeah, like what?"

"How to love with my whole heart," I said softly. "So,

whatever it is you want to tell me, it won't change anything for me."

He looked at me and nodded slowly. "Let's sit."

We sat on the couch. He grabbed my hand and laced his fingers through mine. His gaze was intense when he said, "Acid died last night."

I swallowed.

"His brain swelled too fast. They tried to relieve the pressure in emergency surgery, but . . ."

"I'm so sorry."

"The funeral is tomorrow," Savage explained. "They wanted to wait until we were all back before we . . . before we said goodbye to him."

I was so broken, so traumatized—barely breathing after what I'd just lived through. And now we would have to deal with the truth—the horror—that Acid died so that Savage and I could have a life together.

His sacrifice couldn't be in vain.

But I didn't say anything of it to Savage. Instead, I took him into my arms and didn't let go. Not even as early morning light winked through the blinds like proof that the world would keep turning and you'd find a way to go on despite grief closing in on you.

Chapter 48

"I don't have anything to wear to a funeral," I said to Savage.

He was sitting on the edge of the bed, bare-chested, his arms resting on his thighs. Savage looked up at me, his face gaunt, his expression shuttered.

I wasn't sure he heard me but then he said, "We'll go to Willa and Duke's. Between Willa, Waverly and Sailor, they'll have something you can wear."

Both of us were exhausted down to our marrow, but somehow, we had to rouse ourselves.

Because we had to put one of his brothers into the ground.

"Do they know?" I asked. "The Old Ladies, I mean?"

"The entire club knows," he replied. "They know why Acid died. They know you were kidnapped, and they know that we brought you home. They know it all."

I flinched.

His expression softened. "Sorry, babe. I should've been gentler about it."

I shook my head. "No. Better that I know that *they* know."

"Roman and the guys are coming to the funeral, too."

"Roman," I repeated. "God, I haven't even thought about work."

Savage stared at me and my face fell.

"They know, too, don't they?"

"Yes."

"*Savage.*"

"Couldn't be helped, babe. Roman knew how we met. And when you didn't show up for work, they had to know why."

"So now everyone I know is going to look at me with pity?" I asked, fury heating my cheeks. "I don't get the luxury of any sort of privacy?"

"No," he said, rising, his own expression turning angry. "You don't. Because like it or not, people fucking care about you. And they worry about you."

"Well, great. Now they can worry about me forever. Because I know how they're going to look at me. All of them. They'll say *poor Evie*. Escaped a cult only to get dragged back to them. They'll say—they'll say . . ."

"What will they say?"

"They'll say I'm not good enough for you, Savage. They'll say I'm too messed up and that all I wanted was a father for my babies. That I wanted protection, and that I don't really love you."

He stood up and came to me, cradling my cheeks in his hands. "If anyone is stupid enough to say that, then they don't know you."

Savage kissed me and then pulled back. "And if they do say that I'll punch them into the ground."

I wrapped my fingers around his wrist and gave it a squeeze.

He let me go.

"Come on. Today's going to be a long fucking day."

~

Duke answered the front door, looking somber and tired. He hugged Savage and then me.

"Willa's upstairs feeding the baby. She'll be down in a minute."

"You don't look like you've slept," Savage said.

"I didn't get much sleep last night and it had nothing to do with the baby." Duke rubbed the back of his neck. "You both look like you didn't sleep either." His gaze locked in on my neck and the bruises that I didn't conceal, but he didn't mention them.

Willa came down the stairs, cradling the baby. She handed the infant to Duke and then hugged Savage, and then me.

"Cooper's good for a while," Willa said. "I'm taking Evie and we're going to raid Sailor and Waverly's closets."

The newborn looked even tinier in Duke's arms and my heart went squishy, thinking about how small and pink my own babies would be.

I was immediately flooded with a batch of hormones and tears misted my eyes.

"You okay?" Savage asked me.

I nodded and turned my head away.

Willa took my hand and gave it a squeeze. "She's looking at my baby and she's thinking about her own."

Savage stared at the infant in Duke's arms. His jaw clenched and his expression tightened.

The two men went into the living room while I followed Willa through the kitchen to the back door.

"How's he doing?" Willa asked.

Because it was Willa and she was Savage's family, I felt no compunction about hiding the truth from her. "Not good. Holding it together, but his mind's a mess."

"Did he go for a ride last night?" she asked as we began to trek across the lawn.

I shook my head. "He hasn't left my side. To be honest, I think it'll take more than a long ride on his motorcycle to help."

"How are *you* doing? Your neck . . ."

"I'm . . ." I shrugged. "Alive."

And afraid to sleep.

"You two have been through the wringer," she murmured.

"So have you," I pointed out.

"Yeah, you're right. It's amazing any of us aren't curled up in the corner, holding our knees and rocking back and forth."

We fell silent for a moment, but I wanted to talk about something else, so I turned the conversation.

"Did you always plan on naming the baby after him?"

She smiled softly. "Yeah. That was always the plan. He joked about it a lot. So I'm sure he didn't think it was ever going to happen, but . . ."

"But?"

"But the baby is his, too, in a way. He's family. He's our best friend. The three of us work because it's the *three* of us. It's hard to explain and I'm sure it's weird. But . . . Duke and I never wanted Savage to feel like he was being replaced, even when we got married and had a baby."

I nodded slowly. "Can I ask a question?"

"Always." She smiled.

"Was it ever romantic? Between you and Savage?"

She looked at me and arched a brow. "What do you think?"

"I think based on how you three interact, no. Probably not. But I was curious if I was missing something."

"No, you aren't missing anything. You're astute, Evie." She took a deep breath. "There was always something between me and Duke. Something we had to force down because when we were younger, it could've been the end of us. The end of all three of us. The two of them and their friendship . . . They never would have survived it. And not because Savage wanted me, but because if we'd gotten together too young the dynamic would have changed. A lot was at stake. But the heart wants what the heart wants, and eventually the time was right."

"It worked out in the end, didn't it?"

"It's looking that way. It's weird, right? Acid's death is devastating. And so, while I'm mourning my friend, I'm also ridiculously happy."

"Right there with you," I commiserated. "Maybe that's just the way life is supposed to be, you know? And hopefully there are enough moments of light that dispel the darkness."

As if by tacit agreement, Willa and I had slowed down our walk toward the shop apartment so we could talk candidly. But now we'd arrived at the door.

She didn't bother knocking, but when she opened it, she tread softly.

Waverly and Sailor were facing each other in the kitchen, looking like adversaries instead of best friends. They were too consumed with each other to notice that we'd come in.

"I'm *not* going!" Sailor yelled. "You can't make me."

"You're seriously standing there telling me you're not going to his funeral? That's insane," Waverly replied. "You have to go."

"I can't do it. I can't watch while they bury him." Sailor's voice broke.

"You have to face it."

"Don't tell me what I have to face, Waverly. You don't understand. The man you love is still alive."

Willa cleared her throat.

Sailor's fists were clenched at her sides and when she turned to look at Willa, horror etched across her features. She ran from the apartment.

Waverly tried to go after Sailor, but Willa stepped in front of her sister. "Let her go."

Waverly reluctantly nodded. "I don't know what to say to her. I think I just made it worse."

"Sometimes saying nothing and being there is all someone needs."

Waverly turned blue eyes to Willa, pleading. "It's been awful. She's been crying or yelling. Sometimes both at the same time."

"She's processing," Willa said. "We all are. But it's no secret how Sailor feels about Acid."

"Yeah." Waverly nodded. "I'm afraid this is going to be the thing she never gets over."

"Making her go to his funeral is not going to help that. If anything, it might make it worse, and she'll just be mad at you too. Just let her be in her feelings. This is for her to deal with in her own time. And if she skips his funeral and later regrets it, that's not your fault. We can hold space for people to make their own choices, but we don't have to carry the burden of the consequences of them. Only they can do that."

She looked at me when she made that last statement.

"Subtle," I mumbled.

Waverly rubbed the back of her neck. "I wish I could help her through this."

"You can. Just by letting her be who she needs to be. That's all any of us can ask for, at the end of the day. You know?"

Waverly sighed and looked at me. "Hey, Evie. Sorry you had to hear all that."

"Don't apologize," I said. "We're all just trying to feel our way through an emotional mess."

"Do you have anything Evie can wear to the funeral?" Willa asked. "I don't have anything that will fit her."

"I have some clothes that will probably work. If not, Sailor does." She shook her head. "God, it feels like just yesterday I was giving Sutton something to wear to a funeral. But the last funeral we went to . . . I want to stop going to funerals."

"You and me both," Willa murmured.

Waverly sighed. "Come on, I'll show you my closet."

"I'm going to go check on Sailor," Willa said.

I nodded and then followed Waverly to the shared closet. It was brimming with clothes. They were both teenage girls of a similar age, but they were so different in style. I could tell where Waverly's funky 80s and 90s clothes ended and Sailor's softer, more conservative style began.

"I suggest this dress," She pulled out a turtleneck sweater dress with long sleeves. Her gaze lingered on my bruises, but thankfully she didn't outright mention them.

"Thanks."

"I know . . ." Waverly bit her lip. "I know why we're burying Acid. How you and Savage met. Where he—you —have been the last few days."

"Oh," I said, slowly sinking down on the edge of one of the beds. "I wasn't sure if you knew."

"The club is strange like that," she said slowly. "They try and keep you in the dark. The women and children, I mean. But I'm not an Old Lady and I'm not really a child."

I was silent as I waited for her to go on.

"Savage is basically my older brother," she said. "He's always looked out for me even when I haven't wanted him to. And I *know* him. The guilt must be eating him alive."

"Yeah, I would say that's an accurate assessment."

She plowed on. "He's different with you. Caring. Thoughtful. But he's still Savage. He will always be Savage."

"Yes," I agreed.

Her blue eyes pinned me with a stare. "Duke and Willa . . . they're wrapped up in their own life right now. That's understandable. But I don't think they see what this will do to Savage. But you know, don't you?"

"I know," I whispered.

"Do you think people can change?"

"Yes and no. I think we are who we are at our core. But I think, with enough life experiences, your lens shifts a bit."

"You'll never leave him, will you?" She looked scared, scared for the man she loved as a brother. "Not even if it gets hard? Not even if he tries to self-destruct because of the guilt? And God, I feel like an asshole even asking because you've been through your own shit. I can't even imagine."

"No. I won't leave him. I don't know what the future holds, Waverly. I just know that I'll be by his side for whatever life throws at us. He came for me in a very dark hour. I'll do the same for him."

She smiled and in a show of affection, leaned over and hugged me. "Welcome to the family, Evie."

Chapter 49

Sailor stood next to Waverly at the funeral but refused to look at the grave.

I stared at the bare winter trees. In a couple of months, the flowers would be in full bloom. Leaves would be green. Birds would be flirting and building their nests.

Life would change again with the seasons.

I placed a hand on my stomach.

Tears flowed like rivers, streaming down the cheeks of the Old Ladies. How many losses had this club, this *family*, sustained? Quite a few, judging by the fresh headstones of the plots next to Acid's grave.

The Jackson siblings, along with Cozy and Jazz, had come to pay their respects. Loss brought people together in a way that not even celebrations did. I hadn't had enough merriments. I was only twenty years old, and my short life had been filled with so many deaths, so much darkness.

But I had something now I'd never had before; a family to lean on. A family that had showed up in my hour of need. A family that had been created by bond, not blood.

When the service was over, the Old Ladies gathered

their children and ushered them to cars. Several of the brothers went with them, but Colt and Zip stayed behind to speak to the reverend.

Savage squeezed my hand as Roman approached us.

"Sorry for your loss, brother," Roman said to Savage.

Savage inclined his head but said nothing.

Roman's gaze slid to mine. "Evie, can I—we—talk to you?" He gestured to the crew that had come with him. They were standing by a cluster of trees. A gust of wind blew through the cemetery, and I shivered in my coat.

"Sure." I looked at Savage.

"I'll be here," he assured me.

I followed Roman, my insides quaking.

But it was for nothing, because the moment I was within reach, I was suddenly engulfed in a collective embrace. I hadn't shed any tears during the funeral, but I cried at their touch.

"Okay, let's give her some room," Brielle said, stepping back and wiping her own eyes.

"You know everything," I stated.

"We do," Roman said with a tight nod. "When you didn't show up for work, I called Savage. Duke answered his phone because Savage was in the hospital."

"Oh," I murmured.

"And when he told us what happened to you, I told him I wanted to know the minute they found you," Roman said.

"And then Roman told us the truth about how you and Savage met," Virgil added.

Cozy took my hand. "It must've been terrifying for you."

I squeezed her fingers. "It was. I'm not—Colt said I'm not supposed to talk about it ever again. But I—thank you. For being worried for me."

"Just glad you're back safe and sound," Homer said gruffly.

I looked up at him and said, "Not such a secret teddy bear anymore, are you?"

He grunted, causing us all to chuckle softly.

It felt sacrilegious to laugh in a cemetery, but that was life for you.

"I think it goes without saying but take as much time as you need. Don't worry about your job. It will be here if or when you're ready to come back," Roman said.

My heart filled with love for these people.

"Are you coming to the clubhouse? We're having a—I don't know what you call it. Wake? Anyway, there will be food and drinks," I said.

Jazz shook her head. "No. We're not really invited. We're not part of the club."

"You're part of *my* club," I said softly.

"And that will never change," Brielle said. "But we don't belong there."

"So we'll see you later?" Virgil asked.

"Later," I agreed with a nod.

"Family dinner still needs to happen," Brielle said.

"I can only imagine what your parents will think of me."

"They'll love you. Just like we do," Roman said.

My heart melted.

"Cuddle Bug misses you," Jazz said with a rueful smile. "So if you need to borrow her for some cheer-up time, you let us know."

"Or we can buy you a puppy," Virgil said. "Puppies make everything better. That's what Clementine says anyway."

I chuckled.

"Don't cave," Cozy said to him. "Otherwise, you and Riley will be sharing the bed with a dog."

"Yeah, one dog in the bed is enough. Riley doesn't need another when she sleeps next to you," Brielle said to her brother.

The teasing and joking lightened my spirits. All I wanted to do was stand with them for a while. To forget about the horrors of the world. To forget that we'd just buried a man who'd barely had a chance to live.

To forget the guilt that threatened to consume me.

~

Savage was standing in front of two graves, his back to me as I approached. I came to his side and took his hand. His warm fingers wrapped around mine.

I read the names on the stones.

"Lily and Cam's parents?" I asked.

He nodded. "The night I took a bullet for Duke was the night Gray died." He ran a hand through his hair. "It feels like it happened both yesterday and years ago at the same time."

I squeezed his hand in comfort but said nothing. There wasn't anything to say. He was reliving all his losses, all his mistakes. I saw it on his face.

Reckoning.

Without a word, he turned away from the graves and we walked to the car. We were the only two left; everyone else had already gone to the clubhouse.

My eyes were gritty, and I had a low-grade headache from being awake so long. "I'm really tired."

"I'll drive," he said, opening the passenger side door for me.

Nodding, I climbed in. I sat on my cold hands as he got into the driver's seat.

"We'll stay at the clubhouse tonight," he said. "Everyone else will too. Not just because of the drinking, but Prez is calling Church tomorrow morning."

"Church?"

"He wanted to give it a day. Before we met and talked about shit."

I swallowed. "Any idea how it's going to go?"

"No." He drove us away from the curb. "But I don't expect it to be good. Everyone knows what I was involved in. Why we had a funeral."

"It could've been *your* funeral," I murmured.

He shook his head. "No. It wouldn't have happened if I'd been in the ring, but I couldn't stop him. He already made the deal."

We'd never know the outcome of a hypothetical situation. All I knew was that the guilt we both felt was swallowing everything good.

I put my hand to my belly.

Life grew within me, despite the darkness.

We didn't speak the rest of the drive to the clubhouse. When we got inside, trays of food had been put out and the liquor bottles were already open.

I'd never been to a traditional funeral or wake. Before my parents had joined the Seed Reapers, I hadn't known anyone who died. But the way the cult handled death . . .

I shoved the thoughts away, wishing they hadn't entered my mind.

"Food?" Savage asked.

"Yeah," I said as I grabbed a plate. He went right for a bottle of bourbon.

"You mind if I go talk to Duke?" he asked.

I shook my head. He left the main room and headed down the hallway.

After I got myself a heaping plate, I took a seat next to Mia on the couch. "Where are the kids?"

"Waverly and Sailor took them down to the theater room," Mia said. "To watch a movie. Which is probably all Sailor can handle at the moment."

"Yeah, she looks completely destroyed," I murmured.

Mia looked at me. "You know about her history with Acid, right?"

"A bit," I admitted.

Brooklyn picked at her plate. "I don't know why I got this. I'm not even hungry."

"Is no one going to talk about the elephant in the room?" Joni asked.

Sutton glared and placed a hand on her belly. "I feel called out."

Her remark cut the tension and several of the Old Ladies laughed.

I stared at my plate, so I didn't have to see their prying eyes.

"I mean Evie," Joni said. "Evie is the elephant."

"Yeah, I know you meant Evie," Sutton replied. "We all knew you meant Evie. Even Evie knew you meant Evie."

"Someone save me," I muttered.

"It's awkward to pretend we don't all know," Joni carried on. "You don't ever have to talk about it, but you can if you want to."

"Colt said I wasn't supposed to talk about it."

"Yeah, to outsiders," Mia said. "We're not outsiders."

"I don't want to talk about it. Ever," I said quietly. "I just want to try and put it behind me. So please don't look at me like I'm about to go mental. Or look at me with pity."

"Never pity," Doc said as she held up a scarred hand I'd never asked about.

"I saw my husband's grave today," Rach said quietly. "It hurt a little less than I thought it would. Sometimes you can't breathe. Other times . . ."

"We all have trauma," Logan said.

"Boy, do we fucking ever," Mia muttered. "We're going to have to build a room onto the clubhouse just to store it all."

"I don't have any trauma," Tavy said.

"Your boyfriend and father were about to beat each other up." Logan looked at her best friend. "Because you were sleeping with your father's biker brother behind his back."

"You sure there are no *daddy issues* there," Sutton asked.

"None," Tavy said. "Raze was hot and he has a *big* dick. Of course I fell for him."

There was a chorus of laughter and even I chimed in. It felt good to laugh. It felt good not to wallow every moment.

"When's the ceremony?" Brooklyn asked her. "Raze claimed you and made you his Old Lady. There's got to be a celebration for it."

"When Dad and Raze can be in the same room as each other without wanting to fight," Tavy said dryly. "Maybe if you just told Dad you were pregnant, that would shift his focus away from *me*," Tavy blurted out.

The room fell into silence.

"Pregnant?" Doc looked at Logan. "You're pregnant?"

Logan glared at Tavy. "How the hell did you keep you and Raze a secret for so long? You just run your mouth when it comes to me?"

"We need something to be happy about," Tavy said. "Babies are happy news."

Logan's face softened. "Yeah, they are. But I was hoping I had the chance to tell Smoke before everyone else."

"Congratulations," Joni said with a smile. "There must be something in the water."

"What do you mean?" Logan frowned in confusion.

"I'm pregnant again too," Joni admitted.

"Jesus, Mary and Joseph," Rach said with a laugh. "Everett's not even a year old."

"Yeah. It's a myth that you can't get pregnant while breastfeeding." Joni shook her head and looked at me. "Remember that when the time comes."

"I'll remember," I stated.

Willa had left to change Cooper, but she came back with the baby to her shoulder. She looked around the room. "What did I miss?"

~

Day turned to night.

I stayed with the Old Ladies, taking turns holding their babies. What was it about holding a baby that just made everything better?

Eventually, I couldn't keep my eyes open any longer, so I went into Savage's room. I was stripping out of the dress when Savage came in. He quickly shut the door and leaned against it.

"You're beautiful," he rasped.

His eyes were glassy with exhaustion and booze.

"Will you hold me?" I asked.

Nodding, he took off his leather cut and got down to

his boxers. We crawled into bed, skin to skin, breath for breath, and fell asleep.

The next morning, I woke up before him and used the bathroom.

His eyes were open when I returned to the bedroom.

"You slept," I said.

"So did you. You had a nightmare."

"Me?"

He nodded.

"I don't even remember . . ."

"We both have things that haunt us," he murmured. He swung his legs over the side of the bed and went into the bathroom. "I've got Church."

"Yeah."

I curled my knees up to my chest and watched him get ready. He looked at the leather cut hanging on the hook, like he wondered if he should put it on. Eventually, he did.

"I'll find you after." He leaned over and kissed me quickly, his breath minty.

After he left, I hauled myself up. I threw on one of his hoodies and a pair of my pajama pants that had found their way into Savage's dresser.

I went out into the living room and kitchen to see if anybody else was awake.

Several of the Old Ladies were sitting on the couch, drinking coffee, nibbling on platters of yesterday's food. No one had seemed inclined to cook.

"Hey," I said. "You mind if I join you?"

Joni smiled at me. "You never have to ask." She patted the seat next to her.

Her baby was asleep against her shoulder, and I looked at him.

It was hard to believe I had two babies inside of me, two lives that were entrusted to my care, but I wasn't sure I was at all prepared or capable of protecting them. I couldn't even protect myself.

"I can't believe they're having Church," Brooklyn said. "Slash was drunk as a skunk when he came to bed. He has a wicked hangover this morning."

"Boxer too," Doc said.

"Most of them were drunk last night, I imagine," I said.

"Not Colt. He didn't even come to bed," Mia said, biting her lip.

The group fell silent until I finally asked, "Does it get any easier?"

"Does what get any easier?" Allison asked. Her toddler was using her knees as support, his chubby hands hanging on.

"Being an Old Lady. Being part of the club . . . being part of a family that has no secrets," I said finally.

"It's a blessing and a curse." Mia smiled. "Sometimes it's nice because everybody already knows what happened, so you don't have to rehash it. Other times, you just want a moment of peace to think before you have to know how you feel and wind up talking to people about it."

I still didn't know how I felt about anything. It was a whirlwind of loss. The dominoes kept falling.

Sailor and Waverly came up from the theater room to grab some food before heading back down.

Everyone was awake when the brothers came into the clubhouse from having Church.

I felt the mood in the room shift.

Savage met my eyes, and without a word, I got up and went to him.

He wasn't wearing his leather cut.

Savage grabbed my hand and led me out front. The

chill from the air bathed my cheeks and I crossed my arms over my chest.

He closed the door behind us, to give us some measure of privacy.

"What happened? What did Colt say?" I prodded when he remained quiet.

"He said he was too angry to make a final decision about my status as a brother," Savage replied. "And he said there has to be severe consequences for what I've done. He had the right to make the choice for the entire club on his own without their input, but he was too mad to make the call. So, he put it to a vote."

"A vote," I repeated.

"I've been temporarily suspended," he said quietly. His eyes slid from mine, and he stared out over the land. "For three months, I'm not allowed in club territory, anywhere on club property, or allowed to do anything except clear my shit out of the clubhouse. At the end of the sentence, Prez will decide whether or not I can come back."

In three months, I would be well into my second trimester. At the end of three months, it would be summer. In three months, our whole lives could look completely different.

"You're not included in that," Savage went on. "You're welcome at club events, the clubhouse, anything to do with the Old Ladies."

"Absolutely not," I stated.

Savage blinked at me, and then his brow furrowed. "What do you mean? You're welcome here. You're welcome to spend time with the Old Ladies. Your life doesn't have to change just because I'm—"

"I'm not going to be part of this club while you're not," I said. "I won't build a life without you, Savage. Your life and my life are tied together. I chose *you*. I chose you long before I knew what being an Old Lady meant. Well, now I'm going to prove it to you."

"I'm not allowed to wear my cut for three months either." He looked like he'd swallowed glass.

His hands clenched. He wanted to do something. Hit or fight back somehow. But that's why he was in this position in the first place. Fighting when he shouldn't have been—a brother dying because of him.

"I understand," Savage said. "I understand why it had to be this way . . . but it's going to tear me apart."

"So what do we do?" I asked. "What happens now?"

"Will you go away with me? I can't stay in town. I can't be here while my life hangs in the balance . . ."

"Where will we go?"

"I don't know. I need time away, and so do you. We both need time to heal."

Would three months be enough time for that?

I didn't ask.

How did you ask a question when you weren't sure you wanted to hear the answer?

Chapter 50

"Have you ever been to Yellowstone?" Savage asked as he gripped the steering wheel.

"I haven't been anywhere," I said, pulling my eyes from the window as I watched the flat terrain glide by.

He reached over and took my hand. "I thought we could see some stuff on our way up to Idaho."

"Sounds good." I forced a smile, trying to remain cheerful despite the heaviness on my heart.

Two days after the funeral, we'd left Waco. We'd stopped at Willa and Duke's on the way out of town, and they hadn't tried to talk Savage into staying. His mind was made up. And because they loved him, they let him go.

When Willa hugged me goodbye, she said in my ear, "Check in once in a while."

"I will," I promised.

I would be their lifeline to Savage. No one expected him to remain plugged in.

He'd left his motorcycle at their house because it was still winter in Idaho, and it was dangerous to ride. But it was also too close to the club for Savage's wounded heart, and it would hurt him too much to be reminded of a future he might not have.

"Want to stop for lunch soon?" Savage asked, shattering the silence.

"Yeah, that sounds good."

My phone pinged and I reached into my bag to grab it. It was the Jackson family group text.

> **JAZZ**
> Come back.
>
> **VIRGIL**
> Agreed. Three Kings isn't the same without you demanding I put money in the swear jar.

There was a whole slew of messages, and even though I wanted to reply, I turned my phone on silent and put it back in my purse.

"The Old Ladies?" Savage asked.

I shook my head. "The Jacksons."

"Ah."

He fell silent again.

"Did I tell you that they put Cozy and Riley in the thread?" I asked. "Seems the entire Jackson clan is settling down."

I realized I wouldn't be around to watch their budding relationships. I would miss out on girl talk and people committing to each other and moving in together. And I'd miss seeing Virgil interact with Riley's daughter, Clementine. I wondered if she would be able to nag him into getting her a puppy.

By choosing Savage, I had inadvertently chosen to cut myself off from people I'd just begun to bond with.

"I'm sorry," he said quietly.

"For what?"

"I can see it on your face," he said. "You don't want to leave town."

"No, I don't," I admitted. "I mean, I do. I do think we need some distance. But three months? That's so long."

"It's not *that* long."

I placed a hand on my stomach. "Long enough that I'll be sporting a big belly when we get back."

"I didn't think about that," he murmured. "I didn't think about a lot of things. I guess I didn't realize how much this would affect your life, not just mine. Pretty selfish, huh?"

"We're doing the best we can, Savage," I murmured.

"You didn't answer my question."

"You need what you need." I shrugged. "And you need this more than I need to be in Waco. That's bound to happen over the course of our life together, Savage. There will be times when my needs will be more important than yours and vice versa. And right now, you need this. And I need to be with you. So, let's see some stuff on the way up to Idaho and take a breather. Yeah?"

"Yeah."

He looked relieved.

How could I ask him to turn around? He had demons he was trying to outrun. But demons were relentless, and they always caught up with you and swallowed you whole.

Savage's phone buzzed on the nightstand of the motel room. He reached for it and unlocked the screen.

"Well, that's one bit of good news," he said, setting his phone down and then cuddling me close.

I snuggled into his embrace. "What is?"

"The club found Dr. Winchester. Now they'll take care of him."

I let out a sigh of relief. "That *is* good news."

"But is it enough to help you sleep at night?"

"Eventually . . . probably." I propped up on my elbow so I could look at him. "Are you upset that you weren't there to help the club find him?"

"Yeah. But as I'm learning, I can't do everything myself."

"You're learning that, are you?" I teased.

I traced his chin with my thumb.

"You want to tell me about your nightmares?" he asked.

"I don't remember them," I lied.

"I don't buy that for a second. You've been having them every night for the past several days." He grabbed my finger. "Stop trying to distract me."

"You're already going through it, Savage. I don't want to add to your stress."

"We never talked about it," Savage said quietly. "Not really."

"You walked in just after the worst of it," I said with a sigh. "You saw everything. I didn't think there was really a point of rehashing it."

He waited and I knew he wasn't going to give up. Not until I told him how it was making me feel.

"It's the same nightmare," I said quietly. "I wake up in a room, strapped to a table. My stomach is big. Really big. And it's—you can see my stomach move because the babies are ready to be born. Only I don't get to have them. The Grand Patriarch is standing over me and he's cutting open my stomach and stealing my babies from me. He laughs and laughs, completely unhinged as he pulls them from my body. There's blood everywhere and I try to scream and make him stop . . . and then I wake up."

He stared at me and then his expression darkened. "You've been keeping *that* from me? Jesus Christ, woman!"

"What are you going to do?" My voice cracked. "It's *my* nightmare. It's not real. It didn't happen. Well, I mean, I did wake up strapped to an exam table."

"Evie . . ."

"And I *was* examined against my will . . . but the club found the doctor and it's over."

"It's over," he agreed. "But not forgotten. You don't just move on from that."

"No. That takes time," I agreed.

"I'll hold you, babe. And tell you that you're safe, that the babies are safe. And when we get to Idaho, I'm teaching you how to shoot."

"I know how to shoot."

"What?"

I raised my brows. "I lived on a farm. There were coyotes."

"And you didn't think to shoot your husband and be done with it?" he asked.

"The thought briefly crossed my mind. But if I got caught it would've been premeditated. And if I didn't get caught, then I still would've had to dispose of his body. I still would've had to go on the run." I suddenly started to laugh. And laugh. I laughed so hard my sides began to hurt.

Savage just stared at me.

"Oh God," I wheezed. "I'm so messed up!"

"Why? Because you thought of murdering your husband prior to actually doing it?"

I shook my head. "No. I just never thought I'd be able

to say it out loud without being sick. I'm certifiable, aren't I?"

"No," he said softly. "This is what it's like. I told you it would come at you in weird ways."

I bit my lip pensively.

"What is it?" He asked as he brushed a strand of hair away from my cheek.

"Why haven't we been intimate?"

"We haven't been intimate for several reasons," he murmured. "I cleaned blood from your face. I sat in the bath with you while you shook. You need time to heal, Evie. There's no rush. And you can't rush it, even if you wanted to."

"Are you telling yourself that as much as you're telling me?"

"Yes." He paused. "But this is different. Acid's death . . . that's my fault."

I wouldn't give him empty platitudes. But I didn't want to make it worse by agreeing with him.

"You know what Prez told me?" he asked after a long silence. "I was sitting there, and they were weighing this against all the things I've done . . ."

"What did he say?"

"He said that even though I was loyal and willing to protect the people I love, I live my life selfishly, and that's why Acid is dead. He told me I've spent my life asking for forgiveness, but never permission. Taking a bullet for a brother is one thing but putting them in a dangerous situation is another thing entirely. That's been sticking with me."

He swallowed, like he was trying to swallow his pain.

"I'm the human equivalent of dynamite," he said. "I walk into situations without thinking them through, and I

Heartbeats & Highways

make them worse. He's dead because of me, Evie. I didn't mean to, but I killed him."

I didn't know what to say, so I remained silent.

He sighed. "You can't go back. Can you?"

"No. Only forward. So, let's go forward."

"It'll be slow," he warned me.

"No doubt."

"And now we both have nightmares."

"I'll comfort you, and you comfort me," I said. "Maybe it's supposed to be this way. Maybe we're the lucky ones."

"Lucky? How do you figure?"

"Eight billion people in the world. And somehow we met. We met, and we fell in love, and now we're a family."

"Lucky," he repeated.

I placed my hand on his heart. "So lucky."

Chapter 51

"I'M STARTING to think road trips are overrated," I said from the passenger side of the car. "And exhausting."

He laughed. "Exhausting? I've done all the driving. Thank God I was cleared to drive, huh?"

"We can switch at the next stop," I said.

"Nah, I like you as my passenger princess. And road trips aren't overrated. We just haven't seen anything good yet. Just motels and diners."

"What are we going to do when we get to Idaho? Not live in a motel for three months, right?"

"No." He paused a moment. "I found us a house to rent."

"You did?"

"Yeah." He reached into his pocket and extracted his cell and handed it to me.

It was a new phone. The one he had for the club was off and in the glove compartment.

"I don't know the code," I said.

"Your birthday."

"Savage," I murmured.

He shot me a grin. "Unlock it. Go to my email. It's flagged."

I did as he said.

My breath caught in my throat when I saw the photos. It was a two-bedroom cabin in the middle of the woods perched on the side of a mountain. "Oh my God, it's gorgeous."

"Gorgeous and quiet. And at the moment, completely covered in snow."

"I've never seen snow." I looked at him. "This is perfect. Except for one issue."

"What's that?"

"I don't have winter clothes. Not for an Idaho winter. I barely had Texas winter clothes."

"Don't sweat it. We'll buy you whatever you need. So yeah, anyway, the house is waiting for us."

"It says it's outside of a town called Huckleberry Hill. That's for real?"

He grinned. "Yeah, that's for real."

"Is it as quaint as it sounds?"

"Yeah. I've ridden through the town during summer. It's a hidden gem."

I closed his phone and set it in the console between us. "You took care of it. Without even asking me."

"You mad about that?"

"No." I looked out the window.

"You *are* mad."

"I'm really not. But when it comes time for something more permanent, I want to be involved."

"Without question."

"Savage?"

"Yeah?"

"What happens if they don't let you back into the club?"

He gripped the wheel but didn't look at me. "Then I'll get a normal job. I'll still be able to provide for you, Evie."

"I wasn't worried about you providing for me. I'm worried about you providing for yourself."

"I don't get it."

"The club gives you more than just a paycheck, Savage. How can a normal job replace that?"

"Nothing will replace the club. But if Prez decides the club is better off without me, then I'll have to make peace with it. Nothing lasts forever."

I adjusted the air vent, and I placed my hands in front of it, trying to thaw my cold fingers.

Savage adjusted the temperature to make it warmer.

He looked strange without his leather cut. Like he was missing a part of himself.

"Have you talked to Duke?" I asked.

"Just texts."

"And?"

"And what?" he demanded in exasperation.

"Don't get mad at me," I snapped. "I was just curious."

"I'm telling him where we're stopping. We haven't touched on the subject of me being on probation with the club. He voted in favor of the probation."

"You said the vote was unanimous," I murmured. "But somehow I didn't put that together. You mad at him for it?"

"No. He had to vote that way. He had to vote for what's in the best interest of the club. He's loyal to me, but it was the right call, and I respect him for it."

We fell silent and it was clear neither of us wanted to talk anymore. He turned on some music, and I pulled out a sketchpad and a pencil. I curled my knees up to my chest to make my lap a makeshift desk.

It wasn't comfortable and I soon lost interest.

I leaned my head against the seat rest and closed my eyes. I was jostled awake, and my bladder immediately let me know it was full.

Savage had pulled into a truck stop with a big travel center.

I set my sketchpad aside. "I need to use the bathroom."

He nodded. "I'll get gas and then go in after you."

I went inside the travel center and used the facilities and then I bought us snacks for the rest of our day's drive. I was already sick of being in the car; I wanted to get to our final destination. I wanted the quiet and the solitude, not the endless buzzing sound of rubber tires on the highway.

"You're up," I said when I got back to the car. I opened the candy bar and took a bite.

Savage pulled the car into a parking spot to make room for the next customer in line and then he went inside.

By the time he came back to the car, twenty minutes had passed, along with two candy bars finding their way into my belly.

He held a plastic bag.

"What did you get?" I asked, buckling myself in.

"It's for you."

My heart cartwheeled. "Me?"

I reached into the bag and pulled out a lap desk with a cushioned bottom that rested on my legs.

"So you can draw easier," he said.

"Thank you." I looked at him. "That was thoughtful of you."

He frowned.

"What?" I asked.

"You're being polite."

"Uh yeah, it's called having manners."

He shook his head. "No, I mean you're talking to me like you would talk to a stranger. What's going on?"

"Truth?"

"Truth."

"I hate being in the car. I hate feeling trapped. I hate that everything is so . . ."

"Unsettled."

"Yes."

He sighed. "I'm trying."

"Trying to do what?"

"Trying to move forward, but all I want to do is fight or ride because the guilt is eating me alive. And I can't do either of those things. That's the old Savage. The old Savage who got us into this mess. Who got Acid . . . I'm trapped too, Evie. Trapped between the old version of myself and wanting to be better. But not knowing if I can."

I reached over and cradled his cheek in my hand. He hadn't shaved in a few days, and he had stubble.

He kissed my palm, and I dropped my hand. He then started the car, and we got back on the road.

The endless, unceasing road.

"You didn't tell me you draw."

"I don't really," I said. "I was doodling at Three Kings one day. Not sure if I'm any good."

"You're good," he said. "You're a natural. Do something for me?"

"Anything."

He smiled. "Draw me something. And I'll get it inked on me."

"Really?"

"Yeah. I'd like to have something of you with me, always."

I sighed. "Savage."

"Love you, babe."

"I love you too."

Nodding he said, "Everything else, I can figure out. As long as I have you."

Chapter 52

"We could stay here," Savage murmured against my rounded belly. The babies were currently napping, but earlier they'd been active, kicking me in the ribs and doing cartwheels inside me.

"Stay here. In this bed?" I quipped.

"In this bed, in this cabin."

I traced his lips with my finger.

He was beautiful in the low lamplight. The sheets were tangled around us, and it was one of those perfect moments—but reality intruded.

"If we stayed it would mean we ran away," I said softly. "Ran away from everything we didn't want to face."

"It's been so calm here. *I've* been calm here."

When we first arrived in Idaho two months ago, a three-day snowstorm had dumped over two feet of snow. It had covered everything in white and ice.

Savage had lit a fire in the wood stove while I cooked. We'd made love and reconnected. Our days were slow, our nights filled with passion. He'd taken me to Coeur d'Alene, and I'd found an OB to see. She was nice, but she wasn't

Doc. A stranger had been the one to tell us the sex of our babies.

The little town of Huckleberry Hill was something out of a nostalgic postcard. It was quiet and calm, with cowboys and ranches dotting the mountainsides.

"We could put down roots here. We could raise the girls to be Idaho girls. They'll ride horses and fish."

"We could do that in Waco," I reminded him. "We don't have to live in a place with eight months of winter."

"No, I guess we don't."

"You'd really want to raise the twins away from everyone you know and love?" I asked. When he didn't reply, I went on, "I want to go home, Savage."

"We don't have a home."

"We *do*," I insisted. "I miss our family. And I know you do too. Cooper is almost unrecognizable; she's growing so fast. Jazz and Homer just got engaged. I don't want to miss their wedding. Please, Savage. I can't hide anymore. And I'm wanting to nest. I want to nest so bad, but I can't because this isn't our home, it's just a cabin in the woods. Something's gotta give."

"You've been so good to me," he said. "Giving me time. But I don't think there will ever be enough time."

"I know," I whispered, dragging my fingers through his hair. "That's why we have to go back."

The nightmares had subsided for both of us. But we were living in limbo.

"All right," he said softly. "We'll go home."

The next afternoon, Savage was drinking a cup of cold coffee while I sat on the couch and doodled in a sketchbook. A knock on the front door had us both frowning in confusion.

"Are we finally going to meet a neighbor?" I asked.

"Open up, you bastard! I know you're in there!"

"Is that—"

"Duke," Savage said, a huge grin spreading across his face.

Savage got up from the chair and went to answer the door. Only it wasn't just Duke; Willa and the baby were with him.

I smiled in elation. "What are you guys doing here? Did you drive?"

"Drive?" Willa snorted. "With a baby? No way. We flew and rented a car. We stayed last night in Coeur d'Alene." She removed the diaper bag from her shoulder.

"At the clubhouse?" Savage asked.

"A hotel," Willa said.

Duke looked at me and set the baby in her carrier down. "Hi, Evie." He embraced me and stepped back. "Don't take this the wrong way, but wow."

I laughed and placed a hand on my belly. "Yeah, I know. It kinda just . . . popped."

"I remember that moment. You wake up one morning and all of a sudden, it's just *there*," Willa said.

"Get you guys a cup of coffee?" Savage asked, still looking momentarily stunned that his two best friends were here.

"Please," Willa said.

After the coffee was poured, we all took seats.

"You never answered my question. What are you guys doing here?" Savage asked again.

"It's time for you both to come home," Willa announced. "Enough already. You've had your time and space. But you need to come back."

"Running away isn't going to solve your problems," Duke added.

"Agreed," Savage said, taking my hand and linking his fingers through mine.

"Agreed?" Willa raised her brows and looked at Duke before staring at Savage again.

"We already talked about it," Savage announced. "And we've decided to come back to Waco."

"Oh." Willa frowned.

"Feels anticlimactic, doesn't it?" I asked with a smile.

She nodded. "Kinda, yeah."

"Well . . . good," Duke said awkwardly.

"How's the club?" Savage asked.

"Fine," Duke said. He didn't elaborate.

Savage sighed. "Yeah, thought so."

"We miss you, brother."

"I don't believe that. I'm sure life has been easier without me around. Have you guys decided what's going to happen when I get back?"

Duke rubbed his jaw. "No. We're not allowed to discuss it in Church until the three months have passed."

"I'd ask what's been going on, but I doubt you'll tell me anything," Savage said.

"What do you want me to say?" Duke demanded. "You put me in a shit position, you know. I had to vote *against* you. I had to, brother—"

"I know." Savage sighed. "We're good."

"Whatever happens, you need to know that I'm with you. I have your back."

"I know you do."

Duke looked at Willa and nodded.

"No," Duke continued. "I don't think you understand —if they don't let you back into the club, then I'm out. I'm walking away."

"*No*." Savage's tone was emphatic.

"Yes." Duke's gaze was intense. "We were brothers before the club. If you think for a fucking second that I won't choose you over the club, then you're dead wrong."

"I'd never ask you to do that," Savage said.

"That's exactly why I'm willing to do it."

"Fuck, man. Way to lay it all out there," Savage muttered.

"I named my daughter after you," Duke stated. "You think that was bullshit?"

The two of them looked at each other, having an understanding without words.

I cleared my throat. "Speaking of daughters . . . We're having two girls."

"No shit," Duke said with a laugh. "That's a reason to celebrate. Where's the nearest bar?"

"I'll show you. You're driving though," Savage said.

"And I guess that means Evie and I will stay here and catch up." Willa looked at me and I nodded.

Duke and Savage needed time together. They could say things to each other in private that they couldn't say in front of us.

Savage grabbed his coat, kissed me goodbye and then the two of them headed out the door. Once it was shut, Willa asked, "What time do you think it will be when they call us for a ride?"

"I don't even think the sun will be set yet," I said with a chuckle. "Coffee refill?"

"No, I'm good."

We sat in silence for a moment and then I asked, "How's Sailor doing?"

"Getting through it. Waverly won't leave her side." She looked at the coffee table at my open sketchbook. "You've gotten good."

"Not much else to do," I said with a laugh. "You can look at them, if you want."

Willa picked up the sketch book and perused it. "You

ever thought of apprenticing as a tattoo artist? I'm sure Roman would be happy to teach you."

"Maybe," I murmured. "I've kind of got a lot on my plate at the moment."

Cooper began to cry, and Willa turned her focus to her infant. "She's hungry. You mind if I feed her?"

I shook my head.

She reached into the diaper bag and pulled out a nursing blanket and set it across her lap before getting Cooper out of her car carrier. Willa put the baby to her breast and covered her with the blanket.

"I don't know how you did it, Evie," she said, returning her attention to me.

"Did what? Convince him to go back to Waco?"

"Yeah."

"If it were up to Savage, he would stay here. But I told him what I needed and that was to move home. Waco is home."

"He's not going to be happy for a while."

"He hasn't been happy here," I said. "And as much as he doesn't want to go back and face it all, he needs to. Besides, you and Duke are there. He needs to go home as much as I do. Even if he doesn't know it yet."

∽

"I think you're going to be mad at me," Savage whispered.

"I'm not mad at you for drinking with your best friend and then calling for a ride. I expected it," I said, helping him take off his boots.

He plopped down onto the bed. "That's not what I meant."

"What did you mean?" I asked with a raise of my brows.

Savage scratched his chest. "I think I bought us some land."

"You *think* you bought us some land?" I repeated. "In Idaho? You promised me we were going back, you—"

He shook his head. "In *Texas*. Waco."

"You were only at the bar for a few hours, how the heck did you do that?"

"Shhh. You don't want to wake up Cooper."

Willa, Duke and the baby were staying in the second room of the cabin instead of driving back to Coeur d'Alene.

I lowered my voice. "You bought land in Waco? How?"

"I know I was supposed to talk to you before I did anything permanent about our lives, but I think you'll be okay with what I did. I mean, I hope so."

He fell silent and I prodded him to continue.

"Duke and Willa bought the land behind their house when it came up for sale. Duke sold it to me. Well, he said he'd sell it to me. If I wanted it. If you wanted it. I was thinking we could build a house. Get some lambs. You like lambs, right?"

I smiled gently. "Yes, I like lambs."

"And bees. You said you kept bees. And chickens. Fresh eggs might be nice." He yawned. "And I thought it would be nice to live near Willa and Duke and Cooper and Waverly and Sailor and we can all be one giant family."

He looked up at me, his eyes glassy.

I cradled his cheek with my hand and leaned down to kiss him softly.

"Let's go home, Savage."

"Home," he repeated. "You're my home. And I'll go wherever you want. I promised to make you happy."

"When did you promise me that?" I asked with a gentle laugh.

"When I fell in love with you." His brow furrowed. "Didn't I promise you that?"

"No, baby. You promised me you'd always protect me."

"Protection is good." He nodded. "But so is happiness. I want you to be happy."

"I'm happy," I assured him.

"Evie?"

"Yeah?"

"I'm gonna fall over."

I smiled. "That's okay. I'll catch you."

Chapter 53

It was spring and everything was in bloom—including me. I seemed to grow bigger every day.

We'd been welcomed back to Waco with open arms and a club barbecue. Colt and the brothers had decided to take the vote early. It was unanimous; they'd wanted Savage back as a brother. Colt told Savage that the club had already lost too many brothers, and they weren't going to lose him too.

Still, restitution had to be made.

Savage would take a pay cut for a year. We wouldn't be uncomfortable financially, but we wouldn't be able to buy the land from Duke and Willa and build a house. That would have to wait.

I wasn't upset about it, though. Whatever had to be done for Savage to be in good standing with the club needed to be done. We'd stay in the apartment over the bakery and even though it would be crowded, we'd make do. We'd turn the bedroom into the nursery and move our furniture into the living room.

Heartbeats & Highways

"We'll be able to watch TV in bed," Savage said with a smile. "It'll change your life."

"I don't watch TV," I reminded him.

"You will."

Cozy took over my receptionist job at Three Kings, but Roman insisted on continuing to pay me. When I tried to fight him, he said I deserved it—a customer had seen one of my doodles I'd left at the parlor and wanted it tattooed on them. He then demanded I continue to send him my artwork so his clients could have custom designs.

I wasn't going to look a gift horse in the mouth and gave in to Roman's offer.

Not working at the tattoo parlor allowed me more time to nest and soon the apartment was filled with crafts and my attempts at new hobbies.

I went back to making sourdough loaves for the bakery, which gave me plenty of time to hang out with Jazz and Brielle.

Jazz gabbed non-stop about her wedding. For all her talk about making Homer work for it, when he'd proposed, they'd set the date for late spring, wanting to beat the heat of summer. They'd have the ceremony and reception at the Jackson property and had decided that it was going to be an intimate affair. Just family and the club.

Brielle was happy for her best friend, but every now and again, I'd catch her unguarded expression. She was keeping a secret, but she hadn't shared it with me. And even though I was dying of curiosity, I didn't push.

Life was sailing along. I was blissful and content.

With raging hormones.

Still, I was happy, and I was back where I belonged.

"Babe?" Savage called out, closing the door to the apartment.

"In here!" I replied.

He walked into the bedroom doorway and stopped. "What are you doing? You said it was an emergency."

I slid my hand down my naked body between my thighs. "It is an emergency."

"You and I have different definitions of that word." He shook his head. "I was in the middle of something with the club. It was important."

"Mhmm . . ."

I kept my eyes trained on him. He was watching me like he was under a spell.

"I bought you a toy for these second trimester hormones. To help you when I'm not around."

"I used it already. Twice. And it didn't even take the edge off. Please, Savage. I need you."

With a groan, he shucked off his leather cut—the cut that had been returned to him after the club reinstated him.

He got his shirt off and went for his belt buckle when I let out a moan. With a curse, he climbed onto the bed and batted my hand away from the apex of my thighs, only to replace it with his tongue.

"God, you're fucking sweet," he murmured against my flesh.

I cried out in pleasure as he sucked me into his mouth. "So sensitive."

My free hands went to my breasts. They were heavy and fuller, my nipples darkening with my pregnancy.

Savage slid his hands underneath me and lifted, angling me just the way he needed to. He devoured me and didn't stop until I was convulsing with my release.

While I was still quivering, he finally shucked the remainder of his clothes before coming back to the bed.

"Roll over, babe."

I got up on my hands and knees and presented myself to him like an offering. He teased his crown at my wet entrance and then slid into me.

We both groaned as he filled me.

I spread my legs and pressed my chest to the bed while lifting my butt into the air. He slid in deeper. He grasped my hips and drilled into me. My hand went back between my legs to play with myself.

"Fuck, babe."

I gasped as shivers danced along my spine and ripped through my nerves.

"I'm close, Savage," I whimpered, greedy for him and everything he could give me.

"Me too."

His grip on my hips was possessive, bruising.

I clenched around him and came with a cry.

Savage thrust once, twice, and then he spilled his warmth into me.

He held me for a moment and then gently eased out. I felt his release on my thighs and shivered with desire again.

"Greedy, greedy, greedy." He kissed my shoulder. "When I've recovered, I'll get you a washcloth."

"Hmm." My eyes were languid as I looked at him. "And when you've recovered, I want to have my way with you again."

"You'll be the death of me, woman," he said with a tired chuckle. "Keeping you satisfied is a full-time job."

"Any complaints?"

"Not one."

First Epilogue

1 month later

EVIE

"A toast," Brooklyn raised her flute, "to Jazz finally locking Homer's ass down."

"Here, here," Brielle added. She knocked back her champagne. "Barkeep, hit me."

Willa snorted. "Pace yourself. We're supposed to be helping the bride get ready. Not getting smashed."

"Barkeep, *hit me*," Brielle repeated.

"Oh, I'll hit you all right," Jazz joked.

We were currently in Brielle's parents' home in a guest room with a bathroom. It was the staging area for the bridal party to get ready.

Brooklyn and Willa had left their babies with their

Heartbeats & Highways

fathers so they could be free to enjoy this time before the wedding.

"You're okay that I didn't ask you to be a bridesmaid, right?" Jazz looked at me, concern in her eyes.

"You didn't ask Willa either," I said with a laugh. "Homer's only got two brothers, so you only needed two bridesmaids. But thank you for including me in this."

Jazz hugged me tight.

"You talk to your mom?" Brooklyn asked Jazz.

Jazz nodded. "I video chatted with her this morning. I promised to send the nurse a picture of me in my wedding dress."

Her gaze was wistful, and she hastily brushed her fingers under her eyes to prevent the tears from smearing her makeup. "I wish she were here."

Jazz's mother had been diagnosed with early onset Alzheimer's and was in a care facility. Her spurts of clarity came and went; and stress brought them on. As much as Jazz wanted her mother at her wedding, her mother insisted that Jazz focus on her perfect day, instead of having to worry that she would have an episode and ruin everything.

"We'll take lots of pictures and videos," Brooklyn said, squeezing Jazz's hand.

Brielle tried to hand Jazz a champagne flute. "Absolutely."

"I'm good," Jazz said, not taking the drink.

"Come on, you're marrying Homer. For life. You need a little bit of liquid courage."

"No, I'm really okay," Jazz insisted, her cheeks flaming with heat.

"Oh my God," Brooklyn said with a smile. "You're totally pregnant!"

"Pregnant?" Brielle squeaked.

Jazz didn't say anything.

"Well, are you?" Willa demanded.

"Kind of, yeah," Jazz muttered.

"On purpose?" Brielle asked.

Jazz glared at her.

"I meant, was this planned? Did you guys get busy as soon as you were engaged?"

"I, ah, don't really want to talk about it," Jazz said, blushing furiously.

Brooklyn covered her mouth but couldn't stop the laughter.

"You *have* to talk about it," Willa demanded.

"I'll tell you when Brielle isn't around," Jazz stated. "Because she doesn't need to know certain things about her sibling."

"You're right about that," Brielle agreed. "Does Homer know you're pregnant?"

Jazz nodded. "I told him last night."

"Are you telling other people?" Willa asked.

"Well, I won't be drinking today, so I think it's going to come out eventually." Jazz shrugged and then she looked at Brielle. "You're okay with this, right?"

She frowned. "Why wouldn't I be okay with this? But also, kinda late to be asking that question, isn't it?"

"I just mean, a lot has changed for us in the last couple of months. And now this . . ."

"This? You mean my niece or nephew? My godchild?" Brielle flashed a grin. "I'm so happy for you, Jazz. I really mean it."

"I think I went overboard with the champagne," Brooklyn said, gesturing to the two unopened bottles. "Only Brielle can really throw it back."

"Don't worry, I'm up to the challenge," she quipped.

Heartbeats & Highways

There was a knock on the door and then Cozy and Riley joined the bridal party.

"Ah, just in time," Brielle said. "I need help drinking the champagne."

"Just one for me," Riley said. "I can't hold my liquor."

"It's hardly liquor," Cozy quipped.

"Fine, champagne makes me horny. And I don't think Brielle wants to hear that I'm going to be jumping her brother's bones later." Riley took the flute from Brooklyn.

"Yes, please don't tell me that." Brielle wrinkled her nose.

"Are you going to tell them?" Willa asked Jazz.

"Tell us what?" Cozy asked.

Brooklyn opened another bottle of champagne.

"Guess I better tell you," Jazz said with a shy smile. "I'm pregnant."

There was another round of squealing and hugs.

The door opened again, and Riley's daughter Clementine burst through the door, her hair curled into ringlets.

"What's going on?" she asked, putting her hands on her hips and pouting. She clearly didn't like being out of the loop.

"Er—nothing," Jazz said.

"I can keep a secret," Clementine said. "I keep lots of secrets."

"Like what?" Riley asked her daughter.

"Like the ring Virgil has in his pocket." She blinked. "Whoops. I wasn't supposed to say that."

"A ring?" Riley asked.

"Give me your glass," Brooklyn said. "You look like you need another drink."

～

I settled my bulk into the chair next to Savage. He took my hand. "Missed you."

"I had to help the bride," I said with a smile.

"How is Jazz? Shaking like a leaf? Cold feet?"

"Nah, nothing but warm toes," I said, laying my head on his shoulder.

Horace and Angie Jackson lived on property and had more than enough room for a ceremony and party. A white event tent had been set up the day before and the caterers were ensuring everything was ready.

Homer stood in front of the wooden pergola. Pink and white flowers twined around the wooden beams. Roman and Virgil were with him, and they were conversing quietly while they waited for the ceremony to start.

Cozy and Riley sat in the front row next to the Jacksons, their heads bent as they exchanged some words. They saw me. Cozy gave me a finger wave. Riley looked flushed but happy at the news that Virgil had bought a ring.

I wondered when Cozy would come around to the idea of marriage. But like me, she'd been running scared. Roman was patient with her though, and that's what she needed.

The string quartet struck a chord, signaling the start of the wedding. Everyone took their seats, and our attention turned to the back of the aisle.

Clementine was dressed in a pink dress, and she carried a basket of rose petals. She dropped them on the ground and when she got to the front, she went and sat on Horace's lap.

Brooklyn and Brielle came down the aisle, one after the other. They looked gorgeous in their sage green bridesmaid dresses that complimented both of them. They went to stand under the pergola and waited for the bride.

Jazz hadn't opted for a traditional white gown. Instead,

it was satin cream with a spring flower motif. No veil covered her face.

She walked down the aisle as though a magnet were drawing her to Homer.

I looked at the groom, expecting to see a stoic expression crossing his face. But he surprised me. He wore a picture of awe, his jaw dropping a bit when he saw his bride-to-be.

"Well, look at that," Savage whispered.

"I'm looking."

The couple recited traditional vows, and I couldn't stop the tears that gathered in my eyes. Savage reached into his pants pocket and handed me a handkerchief.

Smiling in surprise, I took it and dabbed my cheeks.

When the minister announced they were man and wife, Homer gathered Jazz in his arms and kissed her.

Hoots and cheers went up from the audience.

"Now for my favorite part of the wedding," Savage said with a grin. "We get to eat."

"Such a romantic," I teased.

"I'll show you romance," he quipped.

Savage rose and then helped me from my chair. We ambled our way to the tent. Cater waiters swarmed us and offered us finger food and napkins.

"We should get married just so we can have goat cheese stuffed figs wrapped in bacon," Savage said after he swallowed.

"We could just have that whenever we want," I pointed out. "They're not hard to make."

"But they taste better at weddings."

"What's gotten into you?"

He took my elbow and led me to the bar. He asked for a bourbon and a mocktail for me.

"I just think you'd look gorgeous in a wedding gown." He shrugged.

"Uh-huh." I arched a brow. "Before or after I give birth? Because as it stands, I'd have to waddle down the aisle."

"Is that a yes?"

"Yes? To what?"

"My marriage proposal."

"Your marriage—" I huffed. "If you're trying to convince me to marry you, maybe you should put some thought into it."

"Hmm. Maybe you're right."

"What's she right about?" Willa asked as she pushed a pram toward us. Duke was next to her, holding a beer.

"That if he actually wants me to marry him, his proposal has to be more than just *hey you'd look good in a wedding gown.*"

Willa glared at Savage. "Seriously?"

"Oh, you think a big declaration is necessary," Savage murmured. "Don't you?"

"Well, kinda. It would be nice not for you to think I was a foregone conclusion," I snapped.

"Hmm. For someone who said they never wanted to get married again, you're getting kinda bent out of shape about a marriage proposal."

Duke let out a laugh and Willa elbowed him in his side.

"I'm going to find the bathroom," I stated. I pointed at Savage. "Don't follow me. I'm mad at you."

"Oh, more fig things," Savage said, flagging down a waiter.

"Jerk," I huffed.

I toddled toward the house. The kitchen was busy with catering staff restocking trays of food and drinks. I darted up the stairs toward the guest bedroom where the bridal party had gotten ready.

And came to a complete stop.

Brielle was pushed against a wall, a dark-haired man leaning over her. His hand was on her hip, and he stared at her like he wanted to consume her.

Something about him looked familiar, but I couldn't place him.

Not until he turned to look at me and I knew who he was.

Recognition flashed through his eyes, but then he tamped it down.

Without a word, he pushed away from the wall and sauntered past me, heading down the stairs to disappear.

He hadn't been wearing formal wear, so I knew he wasn't an invited guest.

"Sorry to interrupt," I said softly. "I had to use the bathroom."

Brielle came to me, grabbed my hand, and dragged me into the guest room. She closed the door and leaned against it, her chest heaving.

"Uh, I know it's none of my business, but who was *that?*" I asked.

"The man I'm sleeping with in secret."

My eyes widened.

"You can't tell anyone," she begged. "Please."

"I won't tell anyone. Does Jazz know?"

"No. No one knows." She bit her lip. "He wasn't—I didn't ask him to be my date. But he showed up and . . . and . . ."

"What's his name?"

She paused. "Gage."

I wondered if she knew that the brothers from the club knew him as simply—Ghost. Then again, I couldn't very well ask questions without coming clean about how I knew him.

"How'd you two meet?"

She blushed. "I, ah, one night I went out to a bar. We met. We spent the night together. And then we've been . . . in secret."

"You don't think your brothers would approve? Because you met someone in a bar?" I asked in confusion.

"Every man I've introduced to my brothers, they've scared off."

"No offense, but he looked like he could've held his own against them."

"Yeah." She bit her lip.

"What aren't you telling me?"

She sighed. "The entire story."

"Keep your secrets, Brielle. God knows, I've got plenty of my own."

"That's just it, though. I'm dying to talk about it with someone, and now that you know I can tell you."

"I want to hear it all. But now's not the best time," I said.

"Right, because of the wedding."

"That, and I have to pee." I grinned. "But the minute we have a free day, it's you and me."

"Thanks, Evie." She beamed. "Do your thing. I'll see you down there."

I took a few moments to myself. After I used the bathroom, I looked out the window. I could see the tent and the party and the wedding spot.

A lone figure stood underneath the pergola. A blond man wearing a leather cut. I knew by the stance that it was Savage.

With a sigh, I felt my annoyance at him dissipate.

I went to him, wondering if I could convince him to

dance with me. I walked down the aisle toward him. He waited for me.

"What are you doing over here? Why aren't you at the party?" I asked when I got to him.

His grin was lopsided. "Do you really think I'd propose to you in the middle of a party while I was eating a fig stuffed with goat cheese?"

"I don't know what to think," I admitted. "Since we've been back, you've been really busy with the club, which makes sense. But I—I miss you. Going to sleep without you. Waking up and you having to leave almost immediately."

Savage didn't say a word. Instead, he took off his leather cut and handed it to me to hold and then he began to undo the buttons of his white dress shirt. Savage was not a suit guy, not even for a wedding. But he had dressed up in his own biker way.

"You can't get naked," I snapped. "This is a wedding!"

He smirked. "I'm not getting naked. I wanted to show you something."

Savage opened his shirt enough so that I could see the bandage concealing the spot over his chest. He then gently peeled back the covering to show me what he'd gotten tattooed on him.

Two peas in a pod.

"When did you have that done?" I whispered. "I sent that sketch to Roman only a few days ago."

"This morning. I had Roman do it for me."

"It's beautiful."

I started to cry.

"There's another handkerchief in the inner pocket of my leather cut."

I reached into the pocket, but there was no handkerchief.

Instead, there was a square velvet box.

I pulled it out and stared at it.

Savage took it from me and opened it, presenting it to me.

"I love you, Evie." His eyes burned into me. "You're my Old Lady. You're the mother of my children. Be my wife."

I swallowed, emotion pouring through every part of my heart, blasting away every worry, every concern.

Savage was Savage. And I hadn't known it at the time, but I was his from the moment we'd met.

"Yes, Savage. I'll marry you."

Second Epilogue

17 years later

E̶vie

"I got my license!" Iris yelled as she blew through the front door.

"I'm proud of you, sugar," I said with a wide smile, hugging my oldest daughter to me. "Open the oven, will you?"

"Sure."

I set the timer and turned to give Iris my full attention. "What about Fern?"

She looked over her shoulder toward the front door. "She—ah—didn't pass."

"I see," I said, my brow furrowing.

"Dad's talking to her now, but I think she could use some cheering up. Or at least a brownie sundae."

"Ooh, that sounds delicious," I murmured.

Rapid footsteps pounded on the stairs and my youngest appeared. Twelve years old and not only the spitting image of Savage, but had his father's *ask-for-forgiveness-not permission* motto stamped into his DNA.

"Hey, Iris," Wylder greeted. "Did you get it?"

"Yep!"

"Awesome. You think Duke would let you take his Mustang for a drive?" Wylder queried.

"I don't know," Iris said. "Should we go ask?"

Wylder looked at me. "Mom, can we?"

I smiled, tamping down my worry. "Sure thing. Head across the property and ask him. You've got an hour before dinner. And no music while you drive. I want your eyes on the road. Promise me, Iris."

"Promise. Let's roll." Iris looped her arm around her brother's shoulders and the two of them headed for the front door.

Nerves blasted through my belly. You couldn't stop children from growing up, but God, where did the time go?

Iris exchanged a few quick words with Savage and then I heard the heavy trudge of his motorcycle boots before he appeared, Fern trailing behind him. Her face was despondent.

"Hey," I said.

"Hey." Savage kissed me on the lips before wrapping his arm around me and hugging me into his side before letting go.

"Hey, kiddo," I said to Fern.

Without a word, she flung herself at me and buried her face into my shoulder. I kissed her red hair and held her.

"I'm a loser," she muttered.

"You're not," I said, shooting Savage a look. "I'm sure your father told you he's proud of you."

"But I failed."

"Failing is okay." I gently maneuvered her away from burrowing into my body, so she was forced to look at me. "You just need more practice."

"I got nervous," she admitted.

"And you accidentally went too fast?"

She bit her lip. "I accidentally went too *slow*."

I let out a laugh and Savage started laughing too.

Fern glared at me. "It's not funny!"

"I'm sorry." I hastily covered my mouth. "I'm not laughing at you. I swear. It just reminded me of the time when your father was teaching *me* how to drive."

"Dad taught you how to drive?" Fern asked in surprise. "I didn't know that."

There were a lot of things our children didn't know. Like the truth about how I grew up, and what we'd done to protect me from those people and get me out of that situation.

"When I moved to Waco, I didn't have a license," I said. "And when your father met me, he taught me how to drive. You know what he called me whenever I was behind the wheel?"

"What?"

I smiled. "Grannie. Because at the time I was afraid of the gas pedal."

"You were?"

"Yes." I nodded and shot Savage another smile before looking at my daughter. "You'll practice some more and then you'll take your test again. You'll pass. I know you will."

She grinned. "Thanks, Mom."

I tucked a strand of hair behind her ear. "Why don't you run over to Willa's and see if you can catch Iris.

They're gonna get ice cream sundaes and I know you want to spoil your dinner."

"You're the best." She hugged me quickly and then ran off to join her siblings, the front door slamming shut behind her.

"Hey, babe," he said.

I looked at the man I'd married. After all these years, he still made my breath catch in my throat.

"Hey yourself."

"We've got the house to ourselves," he said, resting his hands on my hips and pulling me toward him. "I know what we can do before the kids get back."

I looped my arms around his neck.

"Oh yeah?"

The front door opened. "Helllllloooooo!"

"*God damn it*," Savage muttered.

I cleared my throat and gestured with my chin to the swear jar on the counter.

"Thanks, Willa. You just cost me a buck." Savage glared at his friend.

Willa was carrying a pie, and she set it down on the counter. "I thought Duke was going to be violently ill when he handed over his car keys to Iris for a joyride. He popped a beer to calm his nerves."

"He could've told her no." Savage laughed.

"When has he ever been able to tell any of the kids no?" Willa demanded.

"I guess I better go over there and drink with him in solidarity."

"Guess you better," she agreed.

Savage winked at me and then left.

When we were alone, she asked, "Did you tell him?"

"Tell him? I didn't have time to tell him." I rubbed my third eye. "It's been kind of nuts today."

"Welcome to my life. Cooper is already a menace on the road. I'm just glad I have another two years before Ava gets her license."

Our conversation turned from children to the trip Duke and Willa had booked. "I can't remember the last time we took an adults-only vacation. You're good to check in on the kids?"

"Of course," I said with a laugh. "You only live across the lawn."

She chuckled. "It's been convenient, hasn't it?"

I nodded, my eyes misty with memories. Savage had bought the land from Duke and Willa behind their property and built us a beautiful two-story home. I'd gotten over my aversion to stairs and the house had been filled with laughter, joy and home cooked food for years.

Both our phones pinged at the same time.

I didn't bother looking at mine because Willa already had hers open. "Old Lady group text. Poker night next week at Sutton's."

"Why do we continue to play? I lose every time," I said.

"Because we can drink and gab and gossip." She cocked her head to the side. "No drinking for you, I guess."

I groaned.

"Screw it." Willa reached for the pie and uncovered it before getting two forks from the drawer. "The kids are having ice cream before dinner. We can have pie."

We'd eaten a quarter of it by the time Savage and Duke walked through the door. Without a word, they grabbed forks and dug in too.

"It's missing something," Savage said.

"It is not. It's perfect," Willa said, reaching up and flicking Savage's forehead.

"I meant, we have ice cream," Savage drawled,

rubbing his skin. He went to the freezer and pulled out a carton of strawberry ice cream. He frowned when he saw it. "This won't be good with apple pie. Where's the vanilla?"

"I didn't buy vanilla," I said.

"You never want strawberry," Savage said slowly. He looked from the strawberry ice cream to me. "The last time you wanted strawberry was—wait, you aren't . . . are you?"

I swallowed. "Yeah."

"Unless you're what?" Duke asked, completely oblivious.

Willa set her fork down. "Duke, let's go."

"Go? We're in the middle of—"

She yanked his arm and all but dragged him toward the front door.

"I'm taking their fork," Duke said. "Let me give it back to them."

"Later," Willa commanded.

The front door shut, and Savage stood at the open freezer holding the pint of strawberry ice cream.

"You're pregnant?" he asked finally.

"Yeah."

"But *how?*"

I raised my brows. "Seriously?"

He shoved the ice cream into the freezer and closed it. "I know how it happens. But we're so careful."

"Not always," I said.

Emotion played across Savage's face and his expression cleared. "It was the night we—"

"Yep."

His gaze heated. "It was a good night."

My hand went to my belly.

Without another word, he strode toward me and

Heartbeats & Highways

enveloped me in his arms. "We always said we wanted a big family."

"I know, but I thought our family was complete." I burrowed my head against his chest.

"Me too. But we did okay with the first three. Now we can make sure this one is perfect."

I laughed. "The other three were just practice, huh?"

"Exactly.

"Two."

"Two what?"

I leaned back to look up at him. "Two, Savage. We're having another set of twins."

"You're shitting me."

"Nope. It seems I'm the most fertile woman in existence."

He chuckled and then cradled my cheeks in his hands and stared into my eyes. "I love you, Evie."

"I love you, too, Savage."

He glanced at the timer and then back at me, grinning wickedly. "We've got fifteen minutes. I know the perfect way to celebrate."

The front door opened.

"We're home!" Iris called out.

"And we made it before dinner!" Wylder added.

The kids crowded into the kitchen.

Fern made a face. "Gross. We interrupted them. *Again.*"

"I just threw up in my mouth a little," Iris joked.

Savage leaned forward and kissed my lips, not caring that we had an audience. He pulled back just enough to murmur in my ear. "Celebrate later?"

I peered up at him, my heart beating for this man, my husband, the father of my children, my universe.

I sighed. "Isn't that how we got into this position?"

Savage whispered in my ear, "I can think of several positions I'd like to get you in."

Laughing, I stepped away from him. I looked at my three beautiful children, thinking about how we were about to add two more to the bunch.

Our home was filled with laughter.

Love.

Family.

It was filled with joy and tears, and everything in between.

It was filled with life.

Thank you for falling in love with the men of the Tarnished Angels Motorcycle Club! It's been a wild ride, but I've got a whole new world for you…

Take a ride with Declan Brewer to the small town of Huckleberry Hill, Idaho and fall in love with a cowboy biker in a surprise pregnancy romance!

Read on for a sneak peek at the first chapter of Huckleberry Hill (Saddles & Spurs Book 1), and check my website at **www.emmaslate.com** for details!

Huckleberry Hill

Chapter 1

The Ranch

"*Oh, shit!*"

I fumbled with my keys as the grizzly bear ambled from the tree line twenty yards from the cabin's porch.

The waxing moon bathed the four-hundred-pound predator in a bright glow, yet there wasn't enough light to help me get the key into the lock.

"*Come on,*" I muttered when the key refused to go in.

The grizzly stood on its hind legs for a moment and sniffed the air, and then charged.

"Shit, shit, shit!"

Just as the key slid into the lock, lights flicked on inside the cabin. The door opened, and before I could react, someone grabbed me by the shirt collar and yanked me inside. The door slammed behind me but the force of being pulled inside propelled me into a warm, bare chest,

Huckleberry Hill

and we both tumbled to the ground in a blaze of tangled limbs and curses.

A grunt of pain, followed by a breath of air in my face told me I'd knocked the wind from his lungs as I lay atop him.

The scrape of claws on the wooden porch made terror churn in my stomach. There was a huff and a loud sniff.

I looked over my shoulder to make sure the door was really closed.

Bear paws thudded across the porch steps and all sound disappeared. No doubt the grizzly went back to the woods, in search of an easier midnight snack.

"I usually buy a woman a drink before winding up in this position," wheezed the man.

"Sorry," I cried, scrambling to get off him. But in my haste, I accidentally kneed him in the ribs. At least it wasn't his—

He grunted again.

"Woman, are you trying to kill me?" he rasped.

I leaned my back against the door and raised my knees to my chest.

"No," I replied. "Wait, is that a rhetorical question?"

He arched a dark brow at me.

Awareness flooded my stomach when I finally realized the man I'd fallen on wasn't wearing a shirt. And his gray sweatpants were riding ridiculously low. Low enough that I could see the V of his stomach . . . and the smattering of dark hair the same color that was on his head trailing down even farther out of sight.

He sat up and ran a hand across scruff covering his angular jaw.

"Who are you?" I demanded. "And what are you doing in my family's guest cabin?"

"Your family?" He cocked his head to the side and peered at me with blue eyes the color of a North Idaho sky before a storm. "Ah, you must be one of Connor's daughters."

"Hadley Powell," I confirmed. "And you are?"

"Declan Brewer." He flashed a pleasant grin. "The new wrangler."

"New? How new?"

I had talked to my father and grandmother recently. They hadn't mentioned a new wrangler.

"Got to Elk Ridge about a month ago." He bent his legs and stood. Declan held out a hand to me.

I took it, hating the betrayal of warmth that curled through my belly at his touch.

"Connor didn't say anything about his daughter coming home for a visit," he said.

"My trip was unexpected. I texted Dad and Muddy, but they must've already been asleep."

"Muddy?"

"Grandmother," I clarified absently. "When I was a baby and I tried to say grandmother, it came out Muddy."

"Cute."

I looked at the door. "My suitcase is outside. And my keys are still in the lock."

"Both will be there tomorrow morning," Declan remarked. "I might like a bit of danger in my life, but I'm not opening that door so a grizzly can make a spring snack out of both of us."

"Fair point," I drawled. I twisted my long, chestnut-colored hair into a messy top bun and secured it.

"Why didn't you head to the main house?"

"I didn't want to wake them up."

If I'd woken them up, then I would've had to explain

why I'd come home in the middle of the night without warning. And I wasn't ready to explain it.

"Ah. And since you didn't know about me, you figured you'd crash in the cabin and head to the main house in the morning."

I nodded, my gaze dropping to his naked, sculpted chest. He had a tattoo wrapped around his upper arm like a cuff and another on his left pectoral.

"Do you have a shirt?" I asked pointedly.

"Several." He grinned. "I can lend you one to sleep in."

"Oh, that's not what I—"

"You can have the bed."

"I'm not taking the bed."

"The sheets are clean," he promised.

I sighed in exasperation. "I meant, I'm not kicking you out of your bed. I intruded on your space. I'll take the couch."

"And then I'll have to tell Connor that I let his daughter sleep on the couch? No way. Take the bed. I don't mind. Really."

I nibbled my lip and inclined my head. "That's very . . . chivalrous of you."

"Aww shucks, ma'am," he drawled with a teasing grin.

Before I knew it, I was grinning back.

No. Bad girl. No.

"Follow me. I'll get you something to sleep in," he offered.

The cabin wasn't large. It had a single small bedroom, a separate bath, and a kitchen and living room area with a wood stove.

My sister and I had spent many nights in this cabin with friends, having sleepovers and movie nights.

"You took down the twinkle lights," I stated as I stood in the doorway of the bedroom.

Declan went to the dresser and opened a drawer. "Hmm?"

"The twinkle lights. From the porch."

"Oh. Yeah, well I plugged them in and a few of the bulbs went out and the whole strand went dark." He pulled out a faded gray T-shirt and a pair of flannel boxers. "This okay?"

"I usually know a man's middle name before I wear his boxers," I joked.

"Ah, sorry. You couldn't waterboard my middle name out of me."

"It must be really embarrassing."

"It puts embarrassing to shame," he replied.

I took the clothes from him, our fingers brushing against one another. A tingle of awareness flashed through my belly. "Thanks for this."

"Sure. Bathroom's there." He pointed and then looked sheepish. "Of course you already know where the bathroom is, don't you?"

"Yep. You didn't ask why I showed up in the middle of the night."

"Figured you have your reasons." He shrugged. "Not my business."

Nodding again, I took his clothes to the small bathroom. There was a clawfoot tub and shower, and you could barely turn around. I hit my elbows as I shucked my jeans off. My cell phone clattered to the floor.

It was only 2 a.m., but my body thought it was nearly dawn due to the time change from New York. I was exhausted.

Before I left the bathroom, I sent a quick text to the

group chat I shared with my twin sister and two best friends, who were also our roommates back in the city.

> ME
> Made it home safe. Almost got eaten by a bear. Will explain later.

I opened the bathroom door and saw Declan's sleeping arrangements on the couch.

"You hungry? Thirsty?" he asked.

"Thirsty," I said.

"I've got water and beer. And half and half."

"Water's good," I said, smiling faintly. He made a move to get me a glass, but I held up my hand. "I've got it. You've already done enough."

"Done enough? By lending you my clothes?" His gaze dipped down my body and shivers prickled up my back.

Prickles I shouldn't have felt. But Declan had three things in his favor: chest hair, a sense of humor, and the fact that he was a cowboy. He was checking off the list of my ultimate weaknesses.

"By saving me from a bear . . . and for giving me your bed. To name a few."

He pretended to doff a nonexistent hat.

Bet he looks good in a cowboy hat and chaps.
Assless chaps.
Shit.

"I am curious about one thing, though," he said.

"What's that?"

"How did you get here? It's an hour and a half drive from the Spokane airport."

"Cab."

He raised his brows. "You got a cab to drive you all the way out here in the middle of the night?"

"I have the power of persuasion," I joked.

More like power of the pathetic.

I'd spilled the truth to a complete stranger. Luckily there still were understanding and empathetic people in this world because not only did the cabbie say he would drive me, but he'd also turned the meter off and given me a flat rate like a car service would've done.

"Huh," he stated. "Okay then."

I went into the kitchen and got myself a glass of water. I drank half of it and then put the glass into the sink.

"You good?" Declan asked.

"I'm good."

"Get into bed," he said. "I'll hit the lights."

"Thanks."

I climbed into the bed of a near total stranger, wondering why I felt more comfortable around him than the man I'd been dating for the last two years.

Not wanting to examine that feeling too closely, I shut my eyes and willed myself to relax.

The cabin went dark, and I exhaled a long, deep breath.

After a few minutes of silence, Declan called out, "Whenever I can't sleep, I count sheep."

"You do not," I said with a laugh.

"I do," he insisted. "I count blacknose sheep."

I closed my eyes and tried as he'd suggested. But every now and again, a picture of a shirtless Declan hauling a bale of hay or riding a horse entered my brain.

Soon, it was just a never-ending stream of Declan doing manly cowboy things and glistening in the sun.

I rolled over and pressed my face into his pillow. The sheets were clean, but Declan had been sleeping in them long enough that his scent was on them. Sandalwood and something else. Something that was uniquely him. Something I couldn't place.

"I'm doomed," I whispered.

There was a hot cowboy who was completely my type sleeping one room over.

It was going to be a long night.

Additional Works

Saddles & Spurs Series:

Huckleberry Hill (Book 1 - preorder)

The Tarnished Angels Motorcycle Club Series:

Wreck & Ruin (Tarnished Angels Book 1)
Crash & Carnage (Tarnished Angels Book 2)
Madness & Mayhem (Tarnished Angels Book 3)
Thrust & Throttle (Tarnished Angels Book 4)
Venom & Vengeance (Tarnished Angels Book 5)
Fire & Frenzy (Tarnished Angels Book 6)
Leather & Lies (Tarnished Angels Book 7)
Heartbeats & Highways (Tarnished Angels Book 8)

SINS Series:

Sins of a King (Book 1)
Birth of a Queen (Book 2)
Rise of a Dynasty (Book 3)

Additional Works

Dawn of an Empire (Book 4)
Ember (Book 5)
Burn (Book 6)
Ashes (Book 7)
Fall of a Kingdom (Book 8)

Others:

Peasants and Kings

About the Author

Wall Street Journal & *USA Today* bestselling author Emma Slate writes romance with heart and heat.

Called "the dialogue queen" by her college playwriting professor, Emma writes love stories that range from romance-for-your-pants to action-flicks-for-chicks.

When she isn't writing, she's usually curled up under a heating blanket with a steamy romance novel and her two beagles—unless her outdoorsy husband can convince her to go on a hike.

Made in the USA
Columbia, SC
07 July 2025